Robert Hugh Goldsmith was born and educated in Belfast. After a short sojourn in a newspaper office he moved into printing. On gaining his honours degree from Queen's University, he went on to spend twenty years teaching at St Louise's Comprehensive College. While there, he also obtained his Master's degree from the University of Ulster at Coleraine. A published poet, he has written for RTE radio and has recently contributed to the political and arts magazine, *Fortnight*.

Though the Night is Gone

Though the Night is Gone

Robert Hugh Goldsmith

THE BREHON PRESS
BELFAST

First published 2005 by
The Brehon Press Ltd
1A Bryson Street,
Belfast BT5 4ES
Northern Ireland

ISBN 0 9544867 5 7

Cover image courtesy of Getty Images
Cover design: Jake Campbell, December Publications

Printed by Cox & Wyman Ltd

ACKNOWLEDGEMENTS

Above all others my thanks is due to my wife Sally for her constant reading and re-reading of the manuscript, encouraging me on the one hand, while at the same time, making sure there were no skipping of issues.

I must also thank my children Eugene (Rudie), Terry, Olive and Brenda for their involvement in my work. Other relatives who read the manuscript were my sister Ann and my brother Brendan along with his wife Anne. Ann Tanney, my cousin, and my granddaughter Bronagh also gave opinions and suggestions as did my friends: Jim Turner, Jim Feeney, Emma Wallace, Ena Smyth, Paddy Barry, Eddie McArdle and Bronagh McVeigh.

Others did some research for me—Michael and Rosaleen Rice in Australia, my son Eugene and my friends Vin and Sheila Hannon. Thankfully, my son-in-law, Paul Brady, kept my computer and me up to the mark throughout.

I am not allowed to forget or ignore my other grandchildren. They made it clear that they deserved a mention so here it is—Corina, Conn, Aisling, Lee, Shane and Tara: many thanks for the happiness you brought me, without being aware of the pleasure you gave.

Finally I must take responsibility for the final product while appreciating the work of those others behind the scene for their efforts on my behalf throughout the final run-in to publication.

This book is dedicated to the memory of
Doris Goldsmith and Patrick Oliver Goldsmith,
who unintentionally gave me the basic idea for the novel.

CONTENTS

Who without reproaches shewed us what out vanity has chosen,
Who pursued understanding with patience like a sex, had unlearnt
   Our hatred, and towards the really better
   World had turned their face?

W. H. Auden, Poem XXXVII

PROLOGUE
(1924-1938)

THE 12-YEAR-OLD girl ran into the middle of the road to intercept the boy on the bicycle. She had gathered that the signs he made were rude and she was determined to stop them by one act of violence. The boy gleefully stuck out his tongue and swung the bicycle round her but she was much too agile for such a manoeuvre as that. She merely arched round on the ball of her right foot and planted a size 6 shoe in the spokes of the front wheel. The boy shot over the handlebars and banged his head on the road.

The cobblestones had not long been removed, probably to act as a disincentive to people who used them to attack members of the opposite persuasion. As Mr McGovern put it, "Just because it's the widest street in the area, doesn't stop it having the narrowest of minds dwelling there." But those intent on throwing stones soon found other means of getting them and the usual number of stone throwers were produced over the years. "It's not much comfort but it beats the hell out of dodging bullets!" Whether McGovern was referring to the late war or the recent pogrom was anyone's guess as he had learnt, like everyone else from that place and time, not to be too explicit.

The incident involving the girl and boy had occurred many years ago, now there was a sense of an acceptance of the past that didn't fit with the need for change. The little girl's house had been condemned since 1907, like so many in the working-class area of East Belfast. However, the kitchen still had lines of shelves where stood reference books and a collection of fiction that recognised the Englishness of the owner. In addition, this 'library' had been germane and catholic to the point that local clergy visited outside their allotted times to take advantage of the tenant's kindness.

Years had passed without the area ever being rooted in the notion of peace, as each of the inhabitants followed their predilections in the politics of Belfast and its narrow surrounding countryside. The Hegels were relatively newcomers to the street having been forced to move after an attempt on Mr Hegel's life. His library never adequately fitted into their 'new' house and he constantly had to add shelves but in the end the lack of space defeated him and he resorted to opening the roof space and depositing them there. His mark remained in the sparse little kitchen for many years afterwards. Meantime Xerophyte Street had gradually become a mixed street and was heading towards being part of the Catholic ghetto that lay adjacent to it but some of the Protestant families were reluctant to up roots from homes which had been in their tenancy for at least two generations.

With all that was going on in the street the peaceful probity of the home, in all probability, lay somewhere between the ineffable Englishness of the father and the contemplative spiritual approach an Irish mother gave to a relationship. The two sons and two daughters characters were regarded as an amalgam of the two parents and whatever genes they had brought to the marriage.

Mr Hegel had been unaware of the nascent rebellion within his own household when the children were young, but the signs were there to be seen with those with eyes to see. In his defence, it must be said that his weakness in this regard was due to his intrinsic belief in proper parental rearing of his children. No father worked harder, nor more diligently, in assuring that his offspring's morality was that imbued in him by his Victorian parents. He was never privy to the idea that any type of morality was a piece of elastic, which expanded or retarded according to some unknown force in society. An added hazard was the cumulative knowledge of history given to and accumulated by each of his children in a rendition far from Macauley's historical account, which had enlightened his early years.

Halle had been Mr Hegel's youngest child and was the most rebellious child either Mr or Mrs Hegel had ever come across. There was a constant battle to subdue her during her pre-pubescence and in her teens, little had changed. Yet as a child, her grandfather had told her, that she had a strong character but at the same time she had concern for others. Her granny had given her five pennies for her new purse and when her grandfather asked for them she refused. But when he reduced his request to one penny she immediately gave it to him.

She associated with Republicans, according to Mrs Hegel's friends, and was constantly at war with her siblings because of their alleged Britishness. Her mother was anxious enough about the situation but she didn't wish to be the so-called inspiration for Halle's pronounced Irishness, so she kept this information to herself and away from her husband. The incident with the boy further up the street had almost started a holy war in the family. What it came down to was whether the provocation was of such an order that it required violence to resolve it. The fact that young Ian was badly cut about the face tended to earn him sympathy from the Protestant faction of the street, particularly as the Pattersons were seen to be, like so many of them, anxious to stop the flow of their co-religionists out of the district. Halle, on the other hand, was a heroine to her section of Republicans and, more secretly, to many of the Nationalists who had suffered the jibes of young Ian for longer than they anticipated when the Patterson family arrived in Xerophyte Street. Consequently the Hegels and Pattersons kept their distance through the years and Halle and Ian barely looked in the other's direction despite the fact that they were ordinary in every sense except in their hatred for all the other stood for.

Mrs Hegel hoped that her husband's near murder had been sufficiently hushed, within the family, that there would no concomitant violence from any of her children when they reached adulthood. Apart from her sense of being a good Christian and forgiveness an essential part of that belief, her own grandmother (on her mother's side) had been Presbyterian until being 'converted' on her marriage but on her deathbed sought the comfort of her previous religion.

For his part Mr Hegel pursued his own interests with a dignity that only someone unaware just how ugly the situation might become could muster. Books were at the top of all his interests. Whether fiction, bibliography or reference they all came to him to be reverenced. Henry Hall's bookstore in Smithfield was the main supplier but his net was spread wide and handsome. His brothers, stretched across the globe, were capable of finding histories on the Boer War in South Africa, biographies of Smuts, Kruger and Cecil Rhodes. Military histories looking at the work of Roberts, Kitchener and Haig were there in force and had come mainly from his brother in London, while Edgar Wallace was the author to whom he turned for light entertainment. Irish affairs took a back seat because he considered himself an expert on the country from close-up experience.

In addition his relatives and friends sent him postcards from the corners of the earth, particularly those areas of British 'concern'. Cities, ports and landscapes adorned the front of these cards that were carefully preserved in large scrapbooks and Halle as a child loved to peruse them. By the age of eleven or twelve the comments on the cards baffled her: "Heavy going! See you in Sept."; "Missed you last trip"; "Bloody awful place. Ignore photo on front." The succinct nature of the messages made them unintelligible to Halle and left her less than impressed with her uncles' descriptive powers. At one point she started to write what she thought they meant in her jotter; her teacher was unimpressed in turn. Nothing of her father's sensitivities sat well on her with the exception that she loved books almost as much as he did.

Later, when her brothers told her of their father's close brush with death, she was sufficiently aware that it had happened and sufficiently Republican to see the incident as being brought about by her father's ardent Empire Loyalism. His unwillingness to think badly of anyone who supported Britain and its overseas dominions obviously had led him to be over-confident and the result was he walked into an attempt on his life by those who did not appreciate his marriage to a Southern Irish Catholic.

By the age of twelve Halle had a set view of the "north of Ireland", she had adopted the familiar Republican stance of refusing to call the partitioned part of Ulster "Northern Ireland", preferring to call it the Six Counties. She felt revolted by all the changes she heard her friends' parents discuss—the RIC was now the RUC, there was a new parliament, whatever that was, here in Belfast and none of the adults in her immediate circle seemed to like it. As a consequence, she felt overwhelmed with revulsion when she saw her father dressing for the Armistice's Day Remembrance parade to the Cenotaph at the City Hall in Belfast. All those medals for campaigns he never fought in; his stick for being the best turned out on parade, presented in Cape Town, were anathema. Yet, in spite of all the chinks she saw in his English personality, she loved him dearly and his love for her was everything one should expect from a father.

July 1924 was no different than any previous Julys in living memory. While none of the other children were affected by the Halle—Ian incident other forces came into play. Union Jacks emerged from Protestant homes and from the first of the month the children from them were not permitted to play football, handball or to take part in any other activity that included 'Roman Catholics'. Among the children it was regarded as the dismal month because it killed so much normal activity. Fortunately the Hegels visited their relatives in England during the Twelfth fortnight; while there they were tired of explaining that the 'Twelfth fortnight' didn't mean there were twenty-four weeks in July! The Pattersons went to Portrush once the annual march was over, as tradition and custom required.

The year 1939 arrived without the parents' awareness of the division that would soon wreak havoc, not only on the world they knew, but also on their own household. Hitler's antics in Germany left no doubt, in the minds of thoughtful people, other than Mr. Chamberlain, that Britain was within an ace of going to war. But for others there was another war that had been going on unabated for 800 years.

Besides all this Halle thought, hadn't her father fought in two wars without a scratch? Why would she be different? But then again her father had been a clerk in the Army Service Corp and not too many of them paid the supreme sacrifice. Being stationed in the south of Ireland before 1914 and then transferred to Victoria Barracks in Belfast after the war he had remarkably little experience of the fighting going on in any part of Europe. Being married to an Irish Catholic, however, made him less British than an Ulster Protestant who hadn't been too bothered about buying guns from the Germans. Consequently when an assassin attempted to murder him in

1922 it was no surprise. Nor was it strange that the side, which attempted the killing, claimed it was the republicans that did it, claiming that they were anxious to murder a former British Army soldier.

While Halle's dad took up the whole of the front room with his library of books. Reproductions of Millais' "Between Two Fires" and Hals' "Laughing Cavalier" held dominant places on the one wall not adorned with bookcases. What Halle failed to see was the humour and the 19th century liberal attributes of her father, in spite of his Englishness, in having not only an English painting—by a man who had married Ruskin's former wife—but having a Dutch portrait as well. Why her mother let him, with space at a premium, was beyond her. Of course she blamed it on his selfish English ways. Evidently he was not concerned with the practicalities of everyday living putting a store on education well in excess of everyone else. Her maternal grandmother, on her few visits north, would castigate her father for his eminently foolish ways. She would use Halle's formal education as an example of his folly, saying to the girl in front of her father, "You should be out earning your keep young lady, not wasting your time with lessons at this time of your life." Halle, in turn, would rattle off Miss Kelly's dictum—"You just don't educate a girl, you're educating a family and all who come after her!"

It was clear that Halle had been more affected by the attempted murder of her father than her siblings, yet, as she grew older, this tall, dark, willowy girl with green eyes never gave anyone the sense that under such a pleasant exterior lay a violent streak. A streak, which would find its way into police files and change her life forever. As a child she had been wiry and tough as old boots. She didn't tolerate fools gladly; even members of the family got the sharp edge of her tongue from time to time. Yet she regarded herself as a caring and concerned person and she was known to visit the elderly and the sick asking if they needed any help. It wasn't merely the Protestant neighbours who failed to see this side of her nature; those who had felt the rasp of her tongue didn't see these other characteristics as outweighing what they considered her obvious faults.

Ian had been described as a roly-poly young boy with his tongue always at the ready, either to stick out or to vociferate. His fatness was criticised by the 'other side' who saw it as a symbol of the differences between the two communities at a time when most of the working class children were emaciated. He had gone to the Tech where he had done well, especially at Art and having the right connections soon began an apprenticeship in printing—although the opportunities for advancement were few. His earlier quick temper had given way to the point where he considered himself to be a calm and self-assured person. There was a certain respectability about printing that he wasn't allowed to forget; "You are entitled, even yet, to carry a sword as a gentleman because you are a printer; never forget that!" Old McArt, his teacher at night classes, constantly reminded them of this, as they were the few who constituted the newly selected printers of the future.

Ian was obsessed with honours and privileges, indeed he took great pride in the photographs hanging in the kitchen of his father and grandfather in their Orange regalia as Honourable Masters of their local lodge. He was aware that copies of these photographs hung in the Orange Hall. The probability was that the combination of printing, as an occupation, and the involvement of his family in local matters had changed him to the more respectable young man he now was. As early as he could remember, he couldn't wait to be old enough to join the juveniles, now he was within an ace of being the next Grand Master, one of the youngest ever known. But, far and away, the greatest honour, he believed, for his family was his father's serving with the UVF at the Somme in the Great War. However, the fact that his grandfather fought in the Boer War didn't have the same sense of honour and duty to it when he related the Britishness of his family's history.

A staunch Presbyterian all his life there was a Calvinistic streak that he thought of as a gold standard as to his aspirations and ambitions. Irishness never entered into his consciousness—it was outside his normal day-to-day experience of life. On questions of politics and religion in Northern Ireland he radiated a certainty that some people admire, while others despise it. Sure there were Roman Catholics who regarded themselves as Irish but they were so wrong about everything why should he bring himself to consider being like them? The rhetorical question on Irishness was as far as he got. His mother's hatred of blacks wasn't dissimilar to his father's rabid hatred of Roman Catholics. Both of them appeared to believe that hatred was a necessary balance to love. They may never put it in the way he did, but clearly their scriptural approach was ninety percent Old Testament and five percent the New. The remainder was such a mixture of superstition and paganism that at times he felt that the percentages he had given to their respective positions were constantly in flux.

As a boy his father had been moved from Ballymartin Street by his parents because Roman Catholics had just built a chapel around the corner and they knew it wouldn't be long before there would be many more of them. Ian's father considered it a mistake and now he wouldn't move for any thing or any body.

Ian had once asked his mother why she hated the blacks. She began by saying she wasn't alone in hating them, the Boers and the Roman Catholics also hated them. When he pressed her as to what exactly it was that she took exception, she gave a graphic description of them when she first went to South Africa. The blacks, regardless of gender, used the river to relieve themselves. As the river was only a few yards away from her home she was angry that they squatted on a plank across the river for this purpose. The fact that she had nothing but Boer friends had nothing to do with her racialism, according to her. Jews didn't rate very highly on her scale of what was commendable either but in his youth Ian noted that this was an area where Protestants and Roman Catholics shared a similar opinion.

He was tall for that period of time being five foot ten inches tall when he reached full growth. As a boy he had been fair-haired but as he got older he became darker and his serious demeanour wasn't unattractive to the young women in his locality, particularly those who attended his church. Yet he was uncertain in his dealing with women, mainly because of the church's teaching on sex left him uncertain as to how to engage a young woman in conversation without being conscious of her body.

He looked forward to the onset of war as an opportunity for him to add to the glory of the family's record of devotion and to aid the cause of the British Imperial family throughout the world. Chamberlain's return from Munich he regarded as an act of treachery, leaving the British with the slur of cowardice being thrown by Nationalists who were actively engaged in accusing anyone of British extraction of an inability to face up to bullies and anyone of a right-wing persuasion. Although he had no time for socialists, the Government's determination not to become embroiled in the Spanish Civil War on the side of democracy had left him with a bitter taste in his mouth. Everything had, by extension, to be compared with the Northern Ireland situation. Clearly, in his opinion, the Unionist position was inviolate—they were in the majority and democratically entitled to control the country. If Chamberlain could ignore the position of a democratically elected country what was to stop him handing Ulster to the terrorists in the South? On the other hand, Chamberlain's cabinet and party was unionist to a man—so what he was thinking was impossible. Why then did the thought bother him?

Ian was haunted by 'ifs'; was it the nature of his religion or was it the situation he found himself in? Would he be justified in taking up arms in such a case? By extension, is there a genuine case for fighting the Germans this time round? In the past there was an acceptance that the elected politicians knew what was best for the country. Uncertainty crowded his mind, too many had died the last time and to what purpose? He put it aside until another day, there were too many conundrums to unravel as it was and to consider all the possibilities would leave him looking as unsure as Chamberlain and that would never do.

CHAPTER 1
(June 1939-August 1939)

HALLE SAT SMOKING her last Gallagher's Blue, a leftover from her last visit home to Belfast. The smoking compartment of the train might just as well have been a non-smoker for the sense of guilt that she felt yet was able to retain the poker face that the family card-players envied. Everything was going to pieces, despite what others said she knew she was only an errand girl, but the mistakes, genuine or otherwise, made by others were now jeopardising her very life. She felt uneasy about going to their first stop, which was in Leeds. Somehow her superstitious observances became advanced to the point of it being paranoia. Not that the word or its application meant anything to her. Psychology belonged to foreigners and as she didn't fit that terminology there was no need to pulverise her brain with thoughts that could easily betray her anxiety to be courageous. Still, when that porter insisted on carrying her case, it took all her time to avoid smiling at Molly. If he had only known he was carrying the next load of explosives to be used to attack targets in London he would have had a heart attack!

Molly Lynch was a different proposition. There was calmness in her manner that would surely get her picked up. Indeed there was such a thing as being too good at the job. Yet this hadn't always been the case when they first met at the Sean McDermott's camogie club. Her volubility and irascible behaviour annoyed Halle to the point where she considered leaving the club but gradually Molly began to change and Halle realised that something else was going on in Molly's life. Initially she convinced herself that it was a growing up process but later she was convinced there was difficulty in Molly's romantic life. She had met Vincent, Molly's beau, and was impressed with his seriousness. Not many young men were as mature as Vincent was and when she got to know Molly better she realised how much he influenced her political opinions. "I'll have to stop looking back all the time," thought Halle, clearly nostalgia was regarded as a weakness in her view of character making.

She knew what she was about to do was anathema to her parents but she had long ago dismissed their views on Irish affairs as regressive and British, which were, in turn, anathema to her. The intelligence services in Britain were on to her by now because Brian, at work in the pub, told her that the house had been "taken apart" when she rang him from Heysham.

The fact that there were few telephones in people's homes meant it was difficult to communicate. Even if they used them, trunk lines needed to be booked and sometimes this meant hanging around for ages depending on how busy the line was to Belfast. Then there was the danger of being overheard in an office containing a large majority of Unionists.

The RUC learning about her so quickly convinced Halle there was an informer at work. She had been convinced that the small cell to which she was attached was air tight and impenetrable but clearly that wasn't the case. Molly was thoroughly put out when she had told her to ring her sister Sally at work to find if her family had also been put through the mangle. Sally's non-committal response frightened her more than she would admit to Halle. Could they be listening in on their conversation? At any rate, it was evident that the Lynches had been through the mill and Halle saw that as additional evidence for her view that her group had been penetrated. Her mind ran across a range of possibilities from Sean Long to Maura McConville both of whom she had reservations about and now she was having doubts about almost everyone—that is with the exception of Molly and Vincent.

When the campaign started at the end of 1938 Halle hadn't been long in the Cumann na mBan. Whatever hopes she entertained about being used only rose when she learnt that much of the staff of the IRA, active in Britain, had been replaced over some scandal involving members of the Cumann na mBan. Whatever it was she was grateful when Vincent and Molly approached her to go on active service. She knew there had been set backs in some of the operations and now the awareness that the group was known to the authorities made it likely that some of the active service battalions would be stood down. Halle being put in charge at Killiney Castle must have hurt Molly's pride but she quickly realised her silliness when she was young probably caused them to discount her.

Their arrival in Leeds had been arranged so that they could find out what precisely was going on in the North of England. When the campaign began Manchester had three bombs explode and it was there that the first death took place but the clampdown, which followed, was of such an order as to make it next to impossible for anyone to successfully move explosives anywhere in the north. The men sent at the beginning of the year found it almost impossible to find places to create dumps because of the huge amounts of potassium chloride, sulphuric acid and iron oxide required. The couriers, like Halle and Molly, were to be sent piecemeal as the situation demanded.

They found lodgings in Burley Street more by fortune than good planning. No one showed up at the station to meet them and consequently they took it upon themselves to get rooms. Halle considered it a bit much for Molly to include her in 'they took it upon themselves'; Molly always went for a snobbish place. "The landladies are that busy keeping the standard high for their reputation's sake that they accept anyone with a nice voice and who looks well. Besides they always provide the better beds," was Molly's dictum. There was only one problem, the area was populated with fishermen at the weekends and some of them stayed in the boarding house. Halle felt that it wasn't wise to fraternise with the English, it would be all too easy for them to point the finger after an explosion had occurred nearby. Despite her fears she didn't want to draw attention to herself or Molly by appearing unsociable. So that evening they sat on at the end of the meal while the fishermen discussed the size of hoped for catches. Molly wasn't pleased at the decision and when they got back to their room demanded that in future Halle should consult her about issues of that kind. She felt that everyone there was aware of her Irishness. Halle assured her that she was a better actress than that, yet there was a strain between them the next morning when they prepared to find out what had gone wrong the previous afternoon.

Molly wanted to prepare incendiary devices because she felt they needed to do something to show they were more than couriers. Halle agreed but was anxious about the mess up the previous day. It was at this point that Halle talked about a meeting place in the event of anything going wrong; they always had an emergency plan but on this occasion they both felt that it was more likely to be used. Ever on the optimistic side of things, Molly felt that there had been a mix-up over the day and she suggested that they go to the station at about the time they reached there the previous day. Halle in an attempt to make up for their differences the night before was quick to agree to all Molly's suggestions. However, when they reached the station their hopes were dashed, once more, when no one showed up and, worst of all, they knew that they had been closely observed by the railway police who appeared to be present in large numbers. Nevertheless Halle wanted two letter incendiary devices to be left in the railway station for two reasons, first, to let the people know they had been there and secondly to show the authorities that the campaign was proceeding in spite of the enormous sentences being handed out by the courts. Molly was anxious to do the deliveries so Halle agreed provided that they left immediately afterwards for London. At the station Halle acted as lookout while Molly planted one in a post office letterbox and the other in a W. H. Smith's newsagent's shop. Carefully they walked out of different exits and met around the corner when they considered they were in the clear.

Once back at their lodgings Halle urged Molly to pack quickly as she sensed more than knew something was not right. The more she thought of it the more she realised that the landlady had looked at her oddly when they came in. Molly assured her that her imagination was playing on her nerves but Halle wasn't to be put off. "Look she's probably heard about the incendiaries going off and having two Irish girls arriving at the same time has made her suspicious. Why don't you go out, as if to the shop, and test to see if she acts any differently." Molly's suggestion wasn't what Halle wanted to hear but for the sake of peace she went along with it. Once down the stairs she was uncomfortable, as she was now certain that the woman watched her every movement. "She probably keeps an eye on all her lodgers," thought Halle trying to convince herself that Molly had weighed the probabilities better than she had.

Across the street she saw a man watch her come out of the house, immediately she turned to go the other way but he caught up with her with relative ease. "It is Molly, isn't it?" She couldn't decide what to do; is this a detective or someone from the special branch? Halle was determined to have a go if he grabbed her so she kept walking, "Look, I missed you yesterday because I imagined I was followed or maybe I was; whatever I'm here now; have you the stuff?" Halle thought he could easily be all that he claimed but she didn't recognise one hair of his head. Quickly she told him that they were about to leave for the station and that if he didn't mind they would hand the material to him there. He was more than reluctant after his experience of the previous day but could think of no other place that would be familiar to the girls and him. By this time they had travelled a good distance from the lodging house and it took Halle a few minutes to get back. When she reached the room Molly was missing but her clothes and the material were still intact. Halle concluded that Molly had spotted her talking to the man and by the time she reached the door they were gone. "She'll think I'm round in the shop and go there," concluded Halle.

Molly wasn't in the shop, but was standing in a doorway waiting to see if Halle and the man returned. Her mind was working overtime trying to imagine what was going on. "He could be someone sent to show us round or it might be he is the guy we should have met yesterday..." The possibilities were many and she hadn't excluded the likelihood of it being the police or she wouldn't be standing where she was. She was quite relieved when she saw Halle hurry back into the house and stopped herself rushing back in so that she could watch the reaction of the landlady to all the coming and going. All too soon the lady came out and Molly followed at a short distance; she headed directly to the police station. There was nothing left to do. Molly sprinted back to the lodging house and rushed up the stairs but there was no sign of Halle instead there was a note on top of the bed saying, "Meet as arranged". Lightning didn't move quicker than Molly but she felt as if she was taking an age to get her things together. Thankfully the explosives were gone so Halle must have taken them. Once outside she pondered about the message but at the same time walked purposefully towards the city centre where she was due to meet Halle at the bus station.

Halle, in the meantime, had arrived at the bus depot and was already determining in what direction they should head. If the man was from the security people he would be aware that they must have been heading to or towards London, of course if he wasn't it was no issue. There was a bus leaving for Norwich in half an hour and she concluded that it was sufficiently away from London not to constitute a suspicion in police minds. "That's where we'll go, off the beaten track. But not so far as to draw even more attention to ourselves. Molly will just have to lump it, I'm not hanging around to be spotted." A quarter of an hour elapsed before Molly turned up to exchange her information on the landlady for Halle's news of the man. For once Molly agreed with Halle's assessment of the situation and they made for the Norwich bus.

Nothing untoward occurred on the journey yet their imaginations caused them to eye each and every new passenger as a possible police informant. On arriving in Norwich they were struck by the number of steep hilly streets, probably because of the weight of their cases and the number of lodging houses which either were full or, in their view more likely, didn't want anyone Irish. Eventually they found a room in a somewhat dingy house closer to the city centre than they had wanted. They would make a few phone calls and see if it was all clear for their journey to London. Molly was anxious to contact home as well and see how everyone there was making out but the telephone was now out of the question, except as a last resort. Halle felt the same way but was reluctant to admit what she regarded as her weakness. There was a significant difference to both girls' approach to the duty they had been allocated and it was only now that Halle began to see that they would be in difficulty if they didn't get their act together.

Halle agreed to toss a coin to see who should go out first. They had been warned before leaving Ireland that many landladies were nosy and not to have explosives in the room they were staying in. However explosives could be kept in the lodging house if they were in pairs, so that if one went out the other remained to ensure the security of the supplies. They had broken the rule once already and Molly was conscious that she was the culprit yet she looked disappointed when Halle won but smiled, "Give my love to your family". Halle should have known of Molly's ability to see right through her but she, grudgingly, smiled back and left. It was getting dark when she reached the telephone box around the corner from their lodging. She began by ringing her London contact but got no reply, not unexpectedly when she considered how everything else was going. She tried a few times without success and was about to ring Belfast when she realised she could be putting somebody there in jeopardy; Molly could ring later and, with some luck, get through.

On returning Halle thought Molly looked disconcerted by something, even before she spoke. "What is it?" Molly explained that soon after Halle left she heard a key in the lock and rather than let the intruder in she made a noise to deter them. She heard footsteps going in the direction of the attic, so she didn't know whether it was an inquisitive owner or a lodger with an eye to the main chance. Curiously she didn't consider it was the police. Halle wanted to know did she do any checking, and Molly set her mind at rest for the moment by saying she watched through the keyhole to see if anyone came back but it turned out to be the landlady who was snooping. "I saw her as she returned from the attic," explained Molly. "OK, you go on but try that London number, I failed to get through. By the way after getting no reply from Tom I thought of ringing Belfast. Maybe you should ring, OK?" Halle was conscious of her overuse of 'OK' in her attempt to avoid sounding like she was giving an order but she knew Molly would get the message. If Molly was unsuccessful in getting in touch they would postpone going to London but if the landlady proved to be too inquisitive they would move to some other house or to another town.

On her return Molly's cheery demeanour brightened Halle, "Well, how did you get on?" The smile deepened on Molly's face, "Tom was there and he said he couldn't meet us but Joe would be there…"

"Where abouts?"

"Kilburn, in a pub called 'The Three Bells', but hold your whist who else was there?"

"Don't let's start playing a guessing game, please, just tell me."

"Vincent!"

"What a surprise, if I had enough wit your face would have given the game away. How is he?"

"A bit depressed at the number of men caught already. He is to get back to Dublin to help with the investigation of what's going wrong. We're to get to London tomorrow and help keep things moving until he returns from Ireland."

"So, you didn't need to ring Sally?"

"No, but I did. The police are searching for both of us but Sally says they have the descriptions mixed up. According to her you're the blonde and I the brunette. Both our homes have been searched again; the usual, everyone turned on to the street while they pulled the place apart. Apparently your da was the least pleased and gave them a lecture on civility and democracy, it must have sounded strange coming from an Englishman and an old soldier at that."

"Now that convinces me that 'the man from Leeds', as I keep calling him, must be from the cops. He called me 'Molly' and as you say they have us mixed up so who else could he be?"

"You're right—I'd take a bet on it."

"Oh, God what about my da? As if I'm not in deep enough with him, he'll never forgive me for this! Particularly when the British press are making it out that we are deliberately out to murder people, which we aren't!"

"You don't need to convince me, I know."

"Well we'd better start packing and attempt to get some sleep because I'm sure we'll be exhausted tomorrow. Oh, by the way, I hope you know this Joe, do you?" Molly didn't know him but assured Halle that she knew everyone by sight from their training days.

Halle slept fitfully that night. Her concern to do the job well was what kept her awake. It was only when she heard a distant clock strike three that the moral efficacy made a dent in her armour. Fine, she was in the right in terms of what was just for the Irish people but could she accept the responsibility for the deaths of innocent members of the public who had no opportunity to rectify a situation they didn't understand? "Ignorance of what is wrong does not enable one to stand with lily white hands on the last day before God and say, 'I didn't approve of what my government did but I was unaware!' God will ask what exactly you did do to find the truth." Halle woke with a start, conscious that she hadn't resolved the issues but drifted back into that half-sleep that never seems to bring elucidation but, in its place, nightmares.

Martin appeared and she felt a tingling at the thought of his being in London but she soon realised it was her mind playing tricks. That didn't stop her assessing where she stood with him. She fancied that she could make a go of it if she changed her stance on the militancy policy, which she endorsed. Tall, well built, handsome, he was all these she concluded but the state of drowsiness enhanced these attributes so that by the time she drifted back to sleep he was in every aspect a Greek god—except in the logic of his arguments. There he fell off his white horse. What did he know about a Workers' Republic? She warned him of the dangers of reading Connolly's works, but he knew better. The priest had already warned them that

Communism was anti-God, anti-Christ and anti-working class. Surely Martin should be able to see that for himself. "Country before all else," didn't Pearse make that clear? Wasn't he a martyr for the cause of Irish freedom? There was no equality in this world—you only had to walk the Newtownards Road, the Shankill or the Falls to see that. "Neither in them or on them," as her mother so profoundly put it.

But Martin said, "The dice is loaded against us." Halle could just see the gleam in his eye once he was on his high horse. "These capitalists are corrupt from morning till night, shuffling their profits to make more."

"Of course," Halle thought, "he couldn't explain the hows and whys so he repeated some garbage that some idiot had said or written for a mug like him." Almost instantly she saw there was a correlation between Martin and the bible thumpers at the Customs Steps—they couldn't explain why they believed their version of the bible either. Eventually the final doze came.

The train from Norwich to Liverpool Street left at 9 a.m. and it took them all their time to make it. They collapsed into a compartment, once again conveniently empty. Halle thought that now was the time to think things through. Recently it had been all action but no considered plan nor orderly thought had taken place; now at least it looked as if matters were in hand at last. Her father had always warned that it was wrong to suppose that everything was fine; until you had weighed the cons and pros you couldn't be sure and she agreed with this, although she had been taught in primary school to say "pros and cons". The difference probably said more about her father than she had previously realised.

Her mind came back to the job on hand, Molly and her were to go by taxi to Kilburn and deliver the goods to a man known to them only by the fact that he had been trained in Killiney Castle at the same time as they were. Halle knew that she wouldn't recognise him in a thousand years but Molly said she knew "the look of him". Why had it to be Kilburn? The very Irishness of the place meant that Scotland Yard would be keeping a particular eye on the movements of everyone turning up in that area.

"Do you think it very clever meeting your man in Kilburn?" Molly thought for a moment, "Surely they must have thought about it before arranging it?"

"You're making an assumption that things are now what they were when they first decided this. But the newspapers are now full of court reports on IRA men and suspects, by the way, not one of them got less than ten years. Yet they're always on about British justice and how balanced it is."

"You're right! That's true but I still think that if there is a particular danger we'll be warned well in advance."

"It can't be that well in advance when we're less than an hour from the terminus. Let's think this out; what happens if this guy doesn't turn up?"

"We'll ring Tom and get his advice."

"How are you off for cash? I'm getting close to broke."

"Vincent has some cash stashed for me, I'll be able to get it."

"But you said he was on the road to Dublin."

"I never thought about that. Don't be looking for the dark clouds, give us a break, everything will be fine."

"Let's hope so."

Halle and Molly arrived in London on Saturday 14 June not long before a series of bombs exploded at three of the main banks in Piccadilly Circus. Clearly all those involved were on the move elsewhere. Halle recognised that the IRA was telling the government that ten- and fifteen-year sentences wouldn't break their resolve to carry the war into England. As far as she was concerned the S-Plan was working but when she made her way down through England a series of doubts began creeping into her thoughts. Communication wasn't easy and undoubtedly contributed to many of the meetings failing to take place but she sensed rather than knew that some of the people selected weren't fit for the job. Consequently the spread of attacks which were meant to make the British public fearful never materialised.

Both of them had followed the events in England while they were still in training. In discussing the situation Molly and Halle were in total unanimity. Right from 16 January 1939 and the major attacks on power stations in London (twice), Manchester (three times) and once in Birmingham and Alnwick they felt that the IRA was following the right course of action. And although there was a drop-off in activity in March they believed that it was part of the over-all direction from headquarters and when they were prepared for active service naturally they saw this as part of the plan to increase the bombing of England.

Molly wanted to remain in London but Halle argued that she was letting her heart over-rule her head, wanting to see Vincent at a time when she would be endangering both of them. The problem was that they still had the remains of the bombing supplies and if they didn't meet someone pretty soon they would be caught in possession. The quicker they got out of London, Halle protested, the better. Eventually Molly went along with her thinking, probably anxious to avoid putting Vincent in jeopardy. After some discussion as to directions to take they agreed to make for Oxford, their thinking being that it was least likely to be swarming with police and Special Branch detectives.

The girls left London for Oxford on the Sunday, taking an afternoon train. Somehow the sense of failure prevailed. Halle had been anxious to unload their cache of explosives where it could do the most damage to British installations in order to push the British government into making a unilateral statement of intent to leave Ireland. The train was practically empty which suited them fine.

Halle woke with a start. She wondered where the hell she was... it didn't last long; they were on their way to Oxford with a parcel each. She looked at Molly and began to blame her for being in this situation. "If only she had kept all this to herself I would be happy at home just keeping house." Once the adrenaline started all the misgivings flowed out of her system.

"Do you ever feel that we're the female version of Don Quixote?" asked Halle to an intense looking Molly. "Is that what you were dreaming about? The moans of you were not ordinary." Halle persisted, "Do you?" Molly smiled, "Is that the Spanish guy who tilted at windmills? No." Halle retreated into her diplomatic guise; "Well every now and again I have a feeling that all this effort is a waste of time—not that I'd say it to anyone else. We're like sisters so I can speak my mind."

"Please don't speak it again. We all have self-doubts, whether it's to do with Vincent or having the nerve or fearing the consequences of being caught. But because I know I'm doing this for a good cause, I'm proud of my part in it."

"But do you see Don Quixote thought he was doing it for everyone's benefit but the reader knows that it is all illusory; my mind tells me that in a hundred years readers of this historical period will wonder what the hell this was all about. Just think, there are men still alive who took part in the American Civil War, do you think that they think it worthwhile now?"

"What did I just say? Give it a rest ... but I'm saying this and that's all, nothing would be done if everyone stood back and tried to judge history's verdict."

Halle knew when to call it a day, Molly was right you have to act on the evidence you have at hand not what might be discovered in years to come. Still she felt it was wrong not to consider all that the mind brought to the forefront. "What will we do now we're in Oxford?" she thought as the train drew into the station. They made their way into the street carefully noting anything suspicious, they had previously agreed that if anything struck the wrong note they would make off in different directions and meet at the nearest bus depot. The fact that they had never been in the city previously did not deter them.

A local bus outside the station seemed the natural move. When the bus moved outside the immediate area of the colleges they watched to see if there were any likely looking boarding houses which filled Molly's dictum. As the bus travelled along St. Bernard's Avenue Molly nudged Halle and they both got up on the conductor ringing the bell. Getting off Halle spotted what she thought was Molly's likely place for their sojourn in Oxford.

St. Bernard's Avenue suggested all that Halle despised in the English. The landlady's 'snootiness'—she supposed it was a Belfast colloquialism suggesting the nose in the air of one who feels a long way superior to those about to give them business—was part of that view. The overly fussy, conservative with a small 'c' whose viewpoint on all things began and ended on how it profited them. Still, she thought, a good soldier knows how to knuckle down to a situation regardless of how irritating it is.

"Halle have you any money?"

"Why are you out?"

"I don't know how we're going to manage here without a job—unless you have some stacked away."

"No," said Halle and then went quiet, she—unlike Molly—had spent most of her time at home helping her mother, although occasionally she helped her aunt run her newsagent's shop. "Do you think I could get work without having any experience?"

"Of course, everyone starts somewhere. I'll ask the landlady if she has a local paper advertising jobs." Molly left intending to be as good as her word. "Oh God, this is a new show altogether! The last thing I thought of was finding work. I must close my mind when I hear something unpleasant. They did warn us at Killiney to be prepared for this as a possibility," thought Halle dreading Molly's return.

Eventually Molly entered the room looking as pleased as nine pence. "Your woman enjoys being buttered up to, and better than that, likes to think she is St. Vincent de Paul. I got the local OK."

Halle noticed that the headlines were more national than local and seemed to indicate that the IRA "is expected to attack more rural areas after their success in the cities." However, it went on to enlarge on the Government's "success in apprehending the terrorists involved". Halle wondered how the editor could have passed the censorship that operated in all British newspapers to make such a statement. It never dawned on her that there were mavericks everywhere.

On Monday morning Molly went to call on a firm of estate agents who had advertised for a secretary. She was away for most of two hours and just when Halle was getting anxious she returned flushed with success. Halle had to bite her tongue to stop herself saying something bitchy like; "we're here to make war not money." Instead she indulged the hypocritical side of her nature by congratulating her friend adding that she trusted she would be equally successful. Molly thanked her and said she had spotted a 'barmaid wanted' sign in a pub not a hundred yards away. Although it wasn't what she wanted she felt obligated to call and see what way the land leant.

Halle wasn't quite sure of the dress needed for such an interview and Molly's responses to her questions were more hums and haws than helpful suggestions. She was too full of her own needs to give Halle any attention in spite of the fact that she knew Halle had no experience of interviewing nor the technique required.

After lunch Halle sallied forth thinking once again of Don Quixote but this time regarding herself as Sancho Panza. The pub was about to close when she arrived. "Why do these pubs have such odd hours of opening?" was one of the questions she would address to the owner once she had the job sewn up. Immediately she was at a loss whether to ask for the owner or the manager. Metaphorically she tossed a coin and went with asking for the manager. "At least I've got this right," when the barman departed looking for his boss. A man came through from the back and merely said, "Yes?" and momentarily Halle was nonplussed. "I wondered had you got anyone for the vacancy advertised in the window?"

"As a matter of fact we've had none so far, it only went up this morning." The man looked older than she had first thought, probably about fifty. But then she was a bad judge of people's ages. She remembered her grandfather asking her to guess the age of the man to whom he had just been speaking. She had said 'seventy' thinking granda's that age and the likelihood was that this was one of his mates. In fact he looked about sixty but she wouldn't please him to flatter the man that much. "Well Mr. Hutchinson is 113. It was his birthday last week." The fact that the man died a fortnight later didn't detract from her uncertainty about age ever since.

At least this man, a Mr. Murchison, although elderly was pleasant and anxious to please. She felt she only had to show willing and the job was hers. After a few hypothetical questions related to the kind of orders customers were likely to ask for it was clear that she could deal with them. "When can you start?" asked Murchison, "As soon as you need me," was Halle cautious reply. "Tomorrow then, say 10 o'clock, OK?"

"Thanks," this in a much lower tone of voice than she had used previously, but by this time the manager had disappeared into the back.

Halle was almost back in her digs when she realised that she had failed to ask her wages. "What am I going to tell Molly?" Later, when thinking this over, she remembered that Molly hadn't been too forthcoming when she tried to get details from her about her job. When Molly arrived from work she wanted to know every detail of the interview and how much she would earn. Halle put her off on the question of money by saying that tips would be taken into account when working out her weekly wages.

In the next few weeks Halle found herself less and less the active revolutionary that she had wished to be and became even less suspicious of the English that she met on a daily basis. Indeed she found herself on first name terms with many of the customers in the pub and without attempting to familiarise their faces she discovered that she knew them pretty much as she did anyone at home, outside of her friends. Of course she had offers to take her out, which she politely declined. But there were others, who by their looks and gestures, put her on her guard and reminded her that she was not there to fraternise.

One Friday evening, when she was in the best of spirits, she spotted a man taking more than a passing interest in her. At first she felt that it was just the usual kind of experience she dealt with daily but the following night when he didn't speak she became suspicious. On her way back to the boarding house she kept stopping to ensure she wasn't followed. At one point she deliberately passed the house and went some thirty yards further on before checking and turning back. There was no sign of him.

CHAPTER 2
(August 1939-July 1940)

MOLLY GREETED HALLE with the usual, "What kind of a day had you?" but Halle was reluctant to cause concern so she spoke in her up-beat fashion of how she had enjoyed the banter and the English moaning about everything from lack of work to the taste of ale. Yet in the last few days there had been a decided swing in the mood at the pub. "What is going on?" asked Molly. "I think it's the possibility of war that's getting to them but English propaganda about the Nazis has them up in arms," said Halle, "but mind you there's still some joviality there." When they got down to comparing their jobs Molly was reluctant to go into details, she always made the same excuse, "It's not like a pub, it's mostly dealing with customers who wish to look at some property and I suspect that it's more nosiness than real interest in buying." Halle accepted that but when Molly directly asked her about how much she earned she discreetly repeated that it varied greatly because of her reliance on tips. Of course Molly didn't offer any information on her earnings.

Molly, in an attempt to move the conversation away from an area, which she felt unpleasant, asked, "Did you get a chance to play darts yet?" Halle laughed, "They're as bad here as they are in Belfast. The men hang on to those darts as if their lives depend on it."

"At home you'd complain bitterly about it. Why are you taking it so well here?" It hadn't dawned on Halle that she was acting differently; "Maybe I'm putting on a front to deceive them. I don't know. I must admit I wasn't conscious of it but that's the only reason I can think of."

Later that evening Molly asked her to go out for a drink. Halle, more to get out of the house, agreed. However, there was one condition, they would give her bar a miss. As they walked to the bus stop Halle, by way of something to say, reminded Molly that if anything untoward happened she should make her way to the bus station and return to London if she didn't turn up within an hour. If they got separated for any reason they should return to the boarding house taking every precaution to ensure they were not followed, in the case of any doubt they wouldn't enter.

Molly eyed Halle suspiciously, "Is there anything I should know?" Halle tried to look her brightest, "No, it's just that I want both of us to be ultra precautious with so many of our people being deported or sent down for long terms of imprisonment."

"OK, I've got the message, I've been too taken up with this job and you see danger in it."

"You could put it that way."

They proceeded down the avenue and caught a bus into town. Without drawing Molly's attention to her suspicions Halle determined to keep her eyes on anything odd or anyone paying them too much attention.

On reaching the 'Pig and Whistle' they stepped down from the bus. "The English are really original with their names, aren't they?" remarked Halle as they entered the pub. "Not like us Irish eh?" said Molly, "Kelly's, Dempsey's, Mooney's etc. We don't even bother to think of names!"

The evening went well with plenty of chat and laughter. More and more both of them were seeing another side to the English way of life. To their minds, undoubtedly the people across the water were more open and candid than these people here. They had more than their fair share of withdrawn types whose faces would crack if they smiled but the inhabitants of public houses were, in the main, pretty forthcoming personalities with little time for the IRA, Hitler, Mussolini and Stalin.

Just before closing Halle saw the man from Leeds entering. He stopped to light a cigarette but it was clear to Halle that it was a device to enable him to look around the room. Instinctively Halle ducked pretending to adjust her stocking and clearly he missed her but his eye caught the blonde hair of Molly while she was standing at the bar getting a last drink for the both of them. Halle watched as he pushed his way in Molly's direction. There was no way Halle could warn her but she sat on to see the outcome.

At the bar Halle could see the man mouth the name 'Halle' and she immediately left realising the chances were stronger that he was with the police; after all they had been told that the police had confused their identities and he had done precisely that for the second time. Seeing that he was going to be busy with Molly, Halle thought she could safely go back to the boarding house and collect her things, including the explosives. Nevertheless, she was extra careful because she knew that the police often had the suspect's accommodation under scrutiny. She saw nothing to cause her concern so she took her suitcase and bag and departed.

Later, at the bus station, she waited the hour agreed but when Molly didn't appear she boarded the first bus that was beginning to move. She told the conductor her mother was ill and she was in a hurry to get to London; he was very helpful, explaining that the bus was only going as far as Luton but in the terminus a London bus would be leaving shortly after they arrived.

Halle's mind was in turmoil—how did the police find them in the wilds of Oxfordshire? Why was she exaggerating so much? Why did they not come directly to the boarding house if they knew so much? Why am I saying 'so much'? Clearly it was someone in London who was providing the information—but that wasn't the most important consideration just now. Was it sensible to go to Kilburn? There were too many arrests and too many deported as it was. If she was not going to London where should she go? Her mind was bombarded with questions and doubts. Perhaps she was making too much of the circumstances—worse, she felt guilty at not telling Molly of her suspicions.

She would chance 'The Three Bells', Joe or Tom would be there—what if they weren't? She had to get rid of the explosives, somehow! This would never do, she felt that she was losing control and that was unlike her. She changed the focus, now was the time to alter her looks or her clothing, fortunately she had spent very little of her pay and should be able to afford lodgings, maybe not luxurious but adequate.

Halle had never worn a hat, conscious that her naturally curly hair held its shape better without its help. Circumstances alter cases and the issue of disguise required her to literally hide her hair—which was a give-away even if it didn't fit Molly's description. At one point when she heard from Belfast that the police had confused Molly's and her descriptions she had thought of getting Molly to cut her hair to a reasonable shape but that wasn't a starter now.

At 5ft. 6ins. Halle was regarded as tall; her father who wasn't that much taller often said that he had been regarded as tall as a young man. Molly, on this basis, qualified as a giantess being almost an inch taller than Halle. Back home and in England they were above average height and this was difficult to hide. Of course she could use flat shoes but she felt that she needed practice in walking in them and there just wasn't time. Halle was desperate for a way out and for a moment considered developing a limp but discarded the idea when she realised she would be more readily remembered. She was back with the flat shoes regardless of how well she walked in them.

The change over in Luton was completed within ten minutes of arrival. Halle had never felt so alone; the need to make decisions without Molly's contribution to the discussion made the pressure all the greater. She almost decided to get the new shoes in Luton and have her hair cut as well but at the last minute decided to stick with her original plan.

When she saw the 'Centre of London' appear on a signpost she decided to change buses. Still conscious of the need to take care she was equally anxious not to draw attention by constantly looking around her. Having left the bus she instantly changed her mind thinking that anyone seeing her get off one bus and take another in the same direction would be suspicious.

Instead she asked a passer-by the directions to the nearest Underground Station. Fortunately it was a short distance away and once on foot Halle went into a shoe shop and later a hairdresser's. By the time she reached Kilburn she was completely altered, physically and psychologically.

'The Three Bells' looked anything but busy. Alarm bells rang in Halle's head whether from the pub's name or the settled quiet about the place. This was where they were to have been on the 24th June but here she was, almost five weeks later, still trying to make contact and still as unsure of the circumstances prevailing in London as she had been then. The newspapers were giving mixed signals—"the campaign was being brought to a halt by police intelligence"; the attacks were continuing in a "more bitter and brutal way"; cries that the "Irish be thrown out of the country" and consequently Halle was uncertain about the exact position she was in. Indeed, on their first Monday in Oxford they read about a Republican march in the centre of London! The English must be mad, no where in the world would they let a parade, attacking their government's policies, take place, yet here was this parade the day following a bomb attack on the centre of London! That week and the following week had reports of firebomb explosions on what Halle gauged to be major targets. Evidently the huge prison sentences and deportations weren't working and the report of the intervention of Ellen Wilkinson, the Labour MP, during the first week of July, in the House of Commons asking for Irish grievances to be addressed was a sign that the operation in its entirety was working. Yet the drift of the main newspapers was that the government would be bringing in an Act that would make it difficult for her and her fellow conspirators to avoid being detained.

The determination to get rid of the explosives was uppermost in her mind and she meant to get to Tom or Joe at all costs but her feelings of guilt clouded out the need for purposeful thinking. "What must Molly be thinking of me? I should have made known my fears about being followed." A last look round before entering 'The Three Bells' convinced her she was all right but after her recent experience she was less than wholeheartedly convinced. The half-light of the interior suited her, as she knew that she would be out-of-place in such a pub at this hour of the day. No sight of the barman; nothing was in her favour! "Excuse me!" in a loud voice produced nothing. Once again she shouted but this time heard a whisper of a reply from somewhere in the back. She waited and eventually a grey-haired Irishman gasping for breath arrived. "I'm punctured!" was all he could manage for a minute. "I'm looking for Tom or Joe," began Halle… "You'll not find them here… they've been missing for a fortnight." Halle sensed the man was testing her genuineness but she had no way of hinting that she was

41

reliable. "There was a John O'Driscoll in here last week looking for them but I told him the same story." Halle knew the name; he was mentioned more than once as an IRA agent working for the Germans. "He didn't mention where he could be contacted, did he?" The man gave her a long purposeful look, "No, he didn't but in the conversation he mentioned he was going on holiday to Guernsey, you know… the Channel Islands?"

Halle felt gutted and decided enough was enough. "Do you know of any decent accommodation near here?" The man was quick to offer bed and breakfast there but no sooner did he make it than he withdrew it with, "On the other hand this isn't the safest place at this time. Get out of Kilburn there's been a lot of raiding round here." Halle took him at his word and made her way back to the City Centre.

When she was young her father took her to London for the funeral of her grandfather. She didn't know why she had been brought but she remembered the area around Paddington where her grandmother lived. Her aunt and uncle lived there now; not that she wanted to go there but if push came to shove with her finances it may be the place to head, especially if things got hotter. Thankfully it hadn't come to that yet. She wandered the streets around Paddington Station haunted by the London accent of her grandmother as she described her own childhood around St. Pancras Station. At the time, for some obscure reason, she thought her granny needed to live beside railway stations.

Eventually she found a B&B, not of a standard that would have satisfied Molly but would have to do as she strove to keep within the budget she had set herself. The room was no different from all those others she had used from time to time when on holiday back home. A large delph jug sat in a basin of similar design, all of it resonant of that Victoriana which she so heartily despised. In the evening what little light there was came from a gas mantle that had a little hole in it and gave a guttering sound when it was lit. If she hadn't been so anxious to avoid drawing attention to herself she would have complained.

She followed a set rota daily. In the morning she rose early washed and left the house before 9 a.m., this to give the impression that she was employed and that she was reliable. Halle walked in the same general direction once outside but once sure that she wasn't being followed she bought the local newspaper and searched the 'Situations Vacant' column. If anything caught her eye she would go to it but she would vary the timing—one day it would be in the morning the next in the afternoon. These things had to alternate with the hunt for Tom and Joe.

The days dragged by without relief, still no one approached her. She rang the London number that both of them had used without success. Clearly the boys were long gone but whether out of London or out of the country she had yet to discover. She felt reasonably certain that they were still planting bombs as the newspapers continued to report explosions in various parts of the country. Halle made up her mind to rid herself of the explosives. Reconnoitring the immediate area she concluded that the railway station was as good a spot as any other was.

The following evening 'after work' she made-up the device in the bathroom and ensured the fuse would give sufficient time for her to ring the police with a warning. It was only when she completed the work that it dawned on her about how she would carry it. She needed a bag but what type of one. After some consideration she thought a music-bag would be ideal, it was commonplace among young women. Now it was only a matter of buying the bag but Halle was afraid that if anything went awry the bag would be easily identified and traced to her. Nevertheless, it had to be done; the explosives had to go! The next day in Kilburn she bought a bag from the first leather goods shop she came across.

Halle knew it was all a matter of timing to ensure that no one was hurt. Her intention was to leave it in the left-luggage office and she brought a change of clothes with her to enable her to alter her appearance. Everything worked well until the point of handing the music-bag over the counter—however the place was closed because of "the present situation". A surge of panic enveloped Halle—she had to get rid of the bomb somehow. Maybe leave it in the toilets but as she had already ruled this out because of the danger of deaths she wasn't prepared to chance it.

There must be an earmarked target if she could only bring her mind to concentrate—electric pylons, water systems, factories of all kinds, public service areas… "That's the one!" The post-office just across the road was ideal, as good a target as she was likely to find at short notice! Time wasn't on her side, if it was going to be done "now was the acceptable hour"—why does scripture rear its head at this juncture?

As soon as she approached the place she noticed the long hall up to the front door and decided that her judgement was sound now that all the office workers were gone. She left the music-bag by the door and walked briskly to the nearest telephone box. The call was answered immediately and she told them precisely the details. Knowing she had time she deliberately walked past the hallway and there was a man standing looking into the office, seemingly anxious to get in. He looked familiar and Halle thought it may be Joe so she deliberately spoke aloud as she passed, "I wouldn't stand there if I was you!" His sure-footed reaction and speed off the mark confirmed in her mind that it was indeed Joe. He passed her in a twinkling and Halle decided on the spot to follow him and make contact once they were out of the immediate vicinity of the bomb.

Joe boarded a bus for Piccadilly with Halle hot on his trail. If she missed the bus her chances of finding him in the horde of people that always congested the pavements around Eros was next to impossible. It took a flying leap and the help of the conductor to get her on board. "For Christ's sake missus! There's one passes here every minute!" Turning he said to Joe, "Twenty-four hours a day ain't enough for some people." Halle handed him the correct fare, more to shut him up than to be a prompt payer. She edged past him off the platform and squeezed into what little space was left beside Joe. "It is Joe, isn't it?" queried Halle. "Should I know you?" came the quizzical answer. "Suspicious to the bitter end," thought Halle. "You were in Killiney with Molly and me."

"Easy on, there's a lot of big ears around here," darting a glance to either side of him. "I'm getting off at the next stop, you hang on to the one past it and I'll catch up on you. OK?" Halle gave the merest nod of agreement.

When they met Joe wanted to know who authorised her planting a bomb in that area. Halle, not to be put down by anyone's authority, explained the situation as quickly as she could and how little alternative she had short of delivering it to Scotland Yard. Joe angrily raised his voice, "What do you think I was doing there? Buying stamps?" Halle laughed hysterically, "You mean you still have the bomb on you?"

"Of course I have; where the hell did I get a chance to dispose of it? Luckily I never set the fuse too early."

"Well then, where are we heading."

"Back to a place Tom arranged before he got offside."

"Surely a place like that would be the first place the police would raid?"

"Tommy let it out to anyone but the Irish knowing he would need it some day."

"He's got a real head on his shoulders has that guy."

"I'm certain he'd have done well at university—if he ever got the chance."

They arrived at a large terrace house with plenty of movement taking place inside. "You're my sister over to get work and staying with me. OK? There's a party on, I told them I'd call in later—you know, an alibi—but I can't go until I get rid of this encumbrance, which you caused."

Halle couldn't get a word in as Joe proceeded to greet everyone within hailing distance. "This is my sister. She's only arrived so I've got to settle her in before I can get down. I'll be back shortly," and with a wave he ran up the stairs two at a time but the chorus of shouts halted him. "What is it?" The partygoers wanted Halle to stay but Joe was adamant, "She's exhausted, she needs the rest." Meantime Halle, in a more dignified way than she had behaved in rushing to the bus, proceeded in a lady-like way up the stairs.

Joe took himself to the bathroom and Halle hazarded that it was to deal with the explosives. When he issued through the bathroom door Halle demanded to know what had happened to Molly. "She's in Holloway, on remand, waiting trial." Tears coursed down Halle's face, "I could have saved her, you know…?" and she looked directly into Joe's face but it was unresponsive. "Look, we all walk this tightrope, so please don't start telling me where you imagined you failed. Too many of my friends are in prison because I sent them to do jobs that were next to impossible to do without being caught. It's the nature of the business…"

"But you don't know what I did…" Joe turned on his heel and somehow threw his answer over his shoulder, "For God's sake leave it alone, I'm carrying enough of my own…" all this as he walked away, "My advice is give it a miss. You'll have enough to do before this is through." There was a long pause as Halle gathered her wits to enable her to come to terms with all that had happened, "Are things terribly bad here? That's the impression we were gaining from the papers—which we know is probably untrue."

"Things are tight and are getting tighter but the operation is still going on successfully. More places are being bombed or set on fire than ever, so we're expecting the British to bring in more laws to apprehend anyone Irish and of course that's what we want because sympathy will sweep the game our way."

"Look, I was originally sent over to make contact with your group in London. Nothing's worked out but have you any contact that could direct me what to do?" Halle's face was a picture of tension. "I've about had it wandering about trying to find something to do instead I'm working for a living in order to stay here to do nothing."

"Don't worry; there's a guy here from Dublin who's involved with something else… I can't say so don't ask me or him!"

"You only have to say once and I get the message. I only hope it's not the man that the barman in 'The Three Bells' was telling me about."

"Now what precisely are you talking about?" asked Joe somewhat stiltedly. Halle knew she had touched a nerve. "Well, the barman did say there was a guy looking for you and in the conversation that followed he mentioned he was going on holiday to the Channel Islands."

"As sure as God made little onions… I can't believe it but then he's the type to jump to conclusions… like assuming you were to be trusted, just take it as a compliment but you're right that's the man I'm talking about."

"I suppose the Islands have no significance?"

"I've no way of knowing it, probably just a piece of conversation to keep the barman chatting. Look, give me that address you're at and I'll be in touch or more likely this merchant will do the business. Good luck, I'll have to get back to this party, as I don't want people remembering that I was very late. It would be desperate if I got knocked off for something you'd done…" and he laughed as he showed Halle the backway out to avoid her being seen by the partygoers.

Halle was relieved to find she was smiling again—Molly's arrest and likely confinement, although expected, went to her heart. She regretted bitterly not warning her about the guy from Leeds—as she had started to think of him—why was she so slow to react? Looking back it was too obvious that the man had been trailing them all the way from Leeds. She should have heeded her own feelings, and if she had both of them would have been long gone. "But Joe's right," she concluded, "Life's too short to be constantly going on about the 'might have beens'."

Two days later Sean Hartington called. A confident tall dark man— "handsome is as handsome does" her grandmother often said but which Halle never quite figured out, two too many metaphors. Clearly this was someone from the top echelon of the IRA. He introduced himself; with a handshake for good measure. "Joe sent me to put you in the picture and to allocate you some work. For the life of me I can't understand why he didn't tell you, there and then, what was needed. My hands are full and I'm due to leave England in a few days." Halle took a deep breath, "I hope you meant it when you said 'you'd put me in the picture'. Hartington appeared to be taken aback, "I can give you information directly related to your circumstances, but with the best will in the world I can't do more than that."

"At least tell me about Molly's arrest. I assume you have been told about it?"

"Molly and Seamus were arrested in Oxford. They were on their way to find you when they were picked up by Special Branch detectives."

"Who the hell is Seamus and what was he doing with Molly?"

"Apparently he had been trying to make contact with both of you at Leeds but he missed the meeting because he was being followed and he didn't want to draw attention to you pair. He reported that he did meet one of you but you were suspicious and disappeared."

"How the hell did he trace us to Oxford, I was convinced he was with the police…?"

"He lives there! It was a coincidence!"

"How were they caught?"

"He approached Molly in a pub without realising he was being followed… and the rest is history now."

"What a mess! How did he mix up our descriptions? That was the factor that convinced me he was a cop."

"Our intelligence have an inside man working with the police and anything he gets he passes it on to Seamus, so he thought the police descriptions were bound to be OK."

"My God, what a circus!"

"No, if Seamus hadn't gone back to that station in Leeds to find you and Molly the police would never have twigged he was one of ours. As it happened the railway police were on the watch for a thief who was working the railway stations in the north. They were suspicious of him but he didn't fit the description they had so they contacted the local police who recognised him."

"But I was the first he approached and if I had had sufficient wit none of this would have happened!"

"Joe told me you were blaming yourself on Molly's arrest, now you're cleared you're away again. What can one do with you?"

"What the hell good would I be to anyone?"

"Not much if you go on like this! Put a sock in it! This yearn of yours to be a martyr isn't worth a damn at the moment, later on when I need one I'll send for you, OK?" The barbed comments of Hartington brought Halle to her senses, "I'm sorry I'm acting the fool, forget I ever said any of this—my nerves need some active employment."

"As it happens I have a job for you. John O'Driscoll is at present in Guernsey. By the way, he is 'John' here but 'Sean' at home. You should be able to put two and two together and figure out who he is!"

"Wait a minute… is this the guy the barman told me was looking for Joe?"

"No! That was me. I was due to meet O'Driscoll there but I've other fish to fry. I need a courier to get information to him and you're ideal."

"What kind of information and how am I to carry it?"

"Well I was told to go through Poole and you had better go that way. The papers you'll be carrying are about strategic centres, such as airfields. All I know is that O'Driscoll asked for details and I assume it must be the Germans who asked for them. I'll have to go; I have arranged for Joe to deliver the package directly to you. As soon as you get it leave for Poole. A few of us sense that things will be too hot round here in the next few days or weeks, that's why I want you to go as soon as possible. Whatever you do don't repeat any of my guesses to O'Driscoll. Good luck! I'm away, I've been too long."

After he left Halle was assailed with all kinds of doubt: should I go to Guernsey; it's so far away from Ireland and home; should I take on such a menial job—a child could do it; what did I join the Cumann na mBan for; surely not this; I'm a soldier and I have to obey orders; is this really an order or are they trying to find something I can manage? Finally she determined to put all these negatives aside and start preparing for the journey.

The following day, just as Halle was going through the pretence of returning from work, Joe arrived carrying a briefcase. He didn't tarry, merely handing her the case and telling her that the railway ticket to Poole and the steamer ticket were in the lining. "What about that parcel I delivered the other night?" the inference was straightforward, "I think they got the contents out without anyone being the wiser," said Joe by way of a cheerio.

Halle was disappointed; she'd hoped that at last she would have some confirmation of a successful outcome to her military operation. Not that many would have agreed with her interpretation of 'military operation' but the word 'terrorist' revolted her. She noted that the British newspapers tended to see people, she considered liberators, as terrorists. On the other hand they saw any British involvement in killing 'foreigners' in their own country as heroic. They 'according to their lights' had the best justice system, the best footballers, and the best people in the world. Halle comforted herself by agreeing with her interior voice, "They are the most hated people in the world!" Then she remembered her father—ah! But he was the exception that proved the rule! The voice in her head refused to stop there, "Didn't the Irish think they were better than any other country?" Halle assured herself it was natural to love one's country. The voice grew haughty; "You allow that of the Irish but deny the English the same right." The voice for all its haughtiness retained a remarkable calmness, never stressing particular points, that Halle acknowledged to another inwardness, were winners. She persisted, "No, indeed I don't, it's the British imperialist I hate and detest—their sole purpose is to profit from every other country they can possess."

"Don't they bring civilisation and education to the mass of these people? The white man's burden is what I have in mind?"

"The British said the same kind of things about America when they colonised it, so don't get me annoyed, they fashion their political theories to their own economic ends. When they can't sell the goods, which the natives produce, they simply let them starve. What kind of white man's burden is that?" The voice was quiet then, "You don't want me to assert

48

Martin's theories borrowed from Marx and Lenin?" Halle smiled, "No, I had my fill. And I don't dispute that many of the people in England and Ireland were on the bread line for most of this decade; it's the persistent putting out of propaganda, to suit the motives of the few at the top, about how wonderful they are to others, that appals me."

Halle shook her head to halt this eternal interior debate she had in order to justify her actions. She knew her interminable arguing would continue to crucify her so, for the present, enough was enough—she had to get out of the house and set out on this journey that she had so many reservations about.

The train seemed more pedestrian than what she had become accustomed; still she enjoyed the lassitude of sitting back on a fine sunny day reminiscing about train journeys to Portrush and Portstewart when young. Once she boarded the steamer, which only plied between Poole and Guernsey on Tuesday, Thursday and Saturday, she realised why O'Driscoll was so precise in his instructions for her to leave when she got the briefcase. Seated on the wooden benches on the deck she felt anything but comfortable but she was relieved that the weather still held because she had been perturbed about the steamer's 9 p.m. start. Yet she saw the similarity between it and the Heysham boat which plied between its homeport and Belfast.

It was afternoon before the boat docked, whether this was usual or not she had no way of knowing. On the quayside she spotted O'Driscoll immediately from the description given to her by Joe. A tall—some would say handsome, others would say swarthy—man suggesting something of the gypsy, stood with his back against the wind and every so often he turned his head in the direction of the boat, clearly assessing how long it would take to dock. Halle sensed rather than understood an antipathy springing from a source she imagined was in her stomach—the less genteel would call it a gut reaction. Over the years the sensation proved occasionally to be accurate, but only occasionally. Consequently she had learnt not to make rash judgements and at this stage in her life she constantly reminded herself of the 'man from Leeds' when tempted to jump to hasty conclusions.

O'Driscoll proved to be a charming man and Halle felt even more uneasy. "I've arranged for you to stay in a boarding house for a week and hopefully we might arrange to rent a cottage outside the town." This statement compounded Halle's uncertainties and unease. "I'm going to need work to survive, unless you've the means to pay my keep." O'Driscoll smiled, "I can't manage to meet my expenses without help, so I'm unlikely to be able to keep you! As I said you are OK for the first week and you should be able to get a job here. The hotels are always looking for staff during the summer season—what with girls leaving to get married or have babies, there's always something."

On leaving the dock Halle was amazed on two counts: the fact that O'Driscoll carried her case and that he had a car where he placed the case. "Is this yours?" asked Halle trying to keep the amazement out of her voice. "Yeah, I need it to get around," this in a matter-of-fact voice that suggests it was no more than having the bus fare. "Do you travel much then?" Halle had the words out before she realised she was being too inquisitive. O'Driscoll looked her full in the face and after a pause, "I'm rarely here. If it hadn't been for needing these documents which you brought I'd have been in England doing the rounds. By the way, that's the other reason I asked them for someone. I get radio messages and I need you to take them down when I'm away. I'll train you in Morse but not in the code; they'll make no sense to you. There's no point in putting you in any more jeopardy than you're in already."

"Does that mean I have to stay in your digs when you're away?"

"No, you'll have to be there between 8 and 11 at night, that's all."

"What if something urgent arrives how will I know and how will I contact you?"

"There'll be nothing urgent but just in case I'm not there it will save a lot of double checking on the telephone, which I feel is a danger."

O'Driscoll parked the car a little way from the cottage he lived in and Halle thought he was being ultra careful but after a few days she knew that nothing was done by him without a great deal of thought. For herself, she was grateful that she wasn't to be travelling between England and Guernsey on a regular basis. Perhaps now she could build a more settled life without being constantly on the run.

Thankfully the issue of the cottage never arose and Halle spent the next six months working in the Hotel Ritz in St. Peter Port. She started as a barmaid—nothing short of a skivvy—and eventually was put on reception when the management realised she was more than a pretty face. She enjoyed the work as it allayed the boredom of waiting for O'Driscoll's radio set starting up and her jotting down the messages—not that they meant anything to her.

Learning had been difficult but O'Driscoll was a good teacher and in a reasonably short time she felt confident enough to handle the coded information. The only annoyance was her inability to know what precisely was going on—although she was aware from the call signal they knew whether it was O'Driscoll or herself receiving. She often wondered did that change the nature of the message—did the strong language get played down when she was receiving. O'Driscoll was unforthcoming and she got to the point where she gave up asking.

Halle occasionally rang Brian at work but kept the conversation to matters relating to the family. She was still fearful that all calls to her family were being intercepted so she used an old pet name, Dinah, known only to members of the immediate family. When she gave it more thought she realised that if the police knew anything they would be knocking on O'Driscoll's door. Later she considered writing to some of her friends in Ranelagh in Dublin. Surely they would be in a position to answer some of her questions on her family... but without doubt the same thing applied, if it wasn't the British checking up on the post it was Dublin Castle doing its age old job of snooping on the Irish.

The seasonal nature of the work she was doing suited her well but the increased workload was just sufficient to keep her busy a few hours a day. In her spare time Halle used the library in St. Peter Port and although the majority of books were in English there was a large proportion of French novels and poetry. In her reading she was surprised to find that the name Hallé or Halle occurred in a few books, so she asked the librarian what was the significance. She herself had come across the name, Adam de la Halle, a French poet and composer who had been born in Arras in the 13th century. Here she found he was known as 'le bossu d'Arras' (the hunchback) even though he was not deformed but it was to him that the intellectuals looked as the originator of French comic opera. Of course she wondered if her father had been responsible for the choice of name. "I can't believe that I never once asked about this. If I ever get back I'll make sure to hear how I got Mary Barbara Halle as Christian names."

Looking back to her schooldays she remembered her music teacher at secondary school thought she was named after Sir Charles Hallé, the founder of the famous orchestra in Manchester. Consequently she added the acute accent to Halle's name when marking her homework, in spite of Halle's complaints. Of course that had been the proper time to take the matter up with her father but she was going through a bad time in school and was least anxious to draw attention to herself. Her sister, Sofia, had excelled in the same institution and the constant comparisons set her at a disadvantage with the result that Halle failed to do herself justice. It was probably at that point that Sofia and Halle drifted apart. Their differences weren't just at the periphery, politically they were as far removed from one another, as it was possible to be and be on the same planet. Halle professed a belief in a united Ireland, which was regarded as the height of nonsense by Sofia. Indeed she had her father's imperialist attitudes and, in addition, was a well-rounded Conservative politically and in every other sense.

In the back of her mind Halle recalled something about her parents agreeing to name the children in a certain order, but it had gone astray when the boys turned up first. She listed that along with the series of questions she needed answering at the end of her sojourn abroad.

The Hotel Ritz was an upmarket hotel but, in Halle's view, lacked some of the amenities that she suspected those on the mainland possessed. She acknowledged that she was no expert in these matters and based her opinion on what she had seen in British films back home. However, the word 'mainland' got up her nose and her mind went off at a tangent, as usual. Republicans in Ireland found the word repugnant, as it implied that Ireland was inferior to Great Britain. As a result the Unionists of the North used it ad nauseum and, she had to admit, in her case, they succeeded in making her violently opposed to its use. But here it seemed somewhat appropriate. Then there was the "Great in… enough was enough," thought Halle.

Initially time passed pleasantly enough, O'Driscoll was rarely about and the job had just enough arduousness to be mind consuming without causing any kind of real pressure—yet listening to others in the hotel they would have you believe that the stress was beyond endurance. The early months passed unspectacularly, except that she succeeded in giving up cigarette smoking, and just when the season was coming to an end war was declared. Halle listened stoically, along with the rest of the staff, to Chamberlain on the radio as he reported on Herr Hitler's reply, or lack of one, to his ultimatum. For a moment she felt sorry for the people who would endure the brunt of this war but was confident that the Germans would bring the whole European edifice down and with it Britain's mastery in Ireland.

However, the shock of war being declared was quickly replaced with euphoria as she believed England's tragedy was Ireland's opportunity… "That's not quite the Republican cry but it's close enough. It will end the need for us to bomb England," she thought. "Modern aircraft with huge bombs will blast cities to smithereens. We'll stand back and wait for them to re-negotiate that damned treaty."

The disappointment was acute when September passed and the 'combatants' were reported as having no more than peashooters in action. As that was about the height of hostilities Halle's certainty about the outcome was reduced one hundred per cent. Later, when it dragged on, month after month, she realised the hotel was going to be as busy as usual come spring and summer. Indeed Halle saw adverts appearing for Jersey in the British press.

Once she accepted the situation she settled down to her double rôle. She still was as wise as ever about O'Driscoll and the part he was playing with the Germans but if it led to the success that she hoped for, so much the better. Still she hoped the British would surrender before the country was in ruins and the Irish question settled permanently—politics in the real world weren't her main suit!

Spring merged into summer and the hotel trade was exceptionally good—a combination of the glorious weather and the playacting of the countries at war. The advertisements were still being printed for the two main Channel Islands and the tourists were still braving the chance of a hot war breaking out at any time. On Guernsey, and Halle suspected it must have been true of Jersey, the English inhabitants were uneasy and the atmosphere continued to build as uncertainty was created by the British government's lack of information about the situation. Queues began to form outside railway booking offices and suddenly the English began leaving in haste. The locals wondered what they knew which they didn't. Halle sensed rather than knew the banks would be in trouble with people withdrawing all their accumulated savings, so she drew out what little she had managed to put past.

Halle knew that the phoney war was affecting more people on the island than she had originally thought. Typical of the British, thought Halle, after Guernsey voted £180,000 to the cost of defence, thus doubling its income tax, to see the wave of English residents leaving. Jersey, which had the larger tourist industry of the two, in 1939 had started an airline, "Jersey Airways" and between it and the ships, tourists were still arriving that spring and early summer. On the 3 June 1940 Guernsey imposed a curfew, from 10 p.m. to 6 a.m. for all inhabitants other than British or French. (Halle was delighted that her Britishness was never questioned and she had the freedom to get about.)

However the only time she panicked was when she heard rumours that a battalion from Britain would be landed on each of the two islands. The British were having a bad time according to the locals who had relatives in France and it wasn't long before the stories were confirmed. Apparently the French and British were being over-run by the German blitzkrieg tactics. On the 19th June the British demilitarised the islands to the astonishment of everyone and, of course the 'wild rumours' were found to be true. Halle didn't want to be seen as less worried than the rest but she insisted on staying behind, which was a surprise to the locals who had nowhere to go in Britain and didn't fancy the camps which were being set up.

O'Driscoll had been away for the best part of a fortnight and the radio was hot every night with messages, which Halle struggled to get down accurately. She didn't fear discovery now because the British authorities were, in the main, gone. It dawned on her the following day that O'Driscoll needed to be back soon or the people in the area would be very suspicious at his returning when all the other outsiders had left. It was then Halle, purporting to be an optimist, told all and sundry there was no danger of German invasion—"What would be the benefit from the German point of view?" People grasping at straws were incredulously foolish in accepting her opinion because they made no preparations at all for the impending invasion.

O'Driscoll must have sensed the situation was getting away from him and returned two days later, on the 21st June, the same day the two Lieutenant-Governors of the islands were re-called after all those who wished to be evacuated had gone. The British kept it a secret and consequently the Luftwaffe bombed both islands on the 28th June and Halle who was down at the harbour to see if there were any arrivals for the hotel was fortunate not to be killed. As it was 29 people were killed in Guernsey and 9 in Jersey. Quite a few changed their minds after this and Halle guessed that Guernsey's population was about half what it had been and hotel staff travelling back and forward from Jersey said it was even worse there. O'Driscoll soon piled into the workload set aside for him by Halle. Nothing was to disturb him and Halle knew he was busy sending reports from his visit to England as well as replying to the coded messages she received.

O'Driscoll made a point of telling her that she wasn't to indicate who or what she was doing there. As far as the local inhabitants were concerned she was an Irish girl who had obtained work at the hotel. He didn't want her to show support, either for or against the Germans, even if they occupied the place. Halle assured O'Driscoll that she was neither stupid nor unaware of what was going on—indeed she had played dumb about his rôle as an agent for the Nazis but she was well aware of his activities. The look on O'Driscoll's face told her that she had deceived him about her qualities. "It wasn't too difficult because you were rarely there and even though you told me nothing I could see through the coded messages that your journeys back and forward to England didn't make you a commercial traveller." Halle held back on telling him about her natural loathing for the Nazis and within a few days O'Driscoll was hinting that the Germans might have a job for her on the Continent. Clearly he knew that the Germans would occupy the Islands and on Sunday, the 30th June a German Navy Group arrived and the occupation began.

From the onset Lanz, the German commander treated the islanders as if a foreign country had occupied them and they, the Germans, had lifted the siege. It took him a little while to realise these people where indeed British. Yet Halle couldn't understand their letting the States to meet with the British royal coat-of-arms and the portrait of the King remaining. Worse was the prayers said for the royal family and the British Empire.

By the end of July the Germans had introduced new laws: driving had to be on the right, road signs were in German and lessons in the German language, which originally had been voluntary, later became compulsory. Of course the press was censored from the start and after British reconnaissance raids, radios on Guernsey were confiscated. Now all money was in Reichmarks and the standard time on the Islands was the same as in Germany. It was then that Halle saw another side to occupation that was frightening. The early occupation of Ireland must have been horrendous, even more so than what was going on in the Islands, as the Irish people were deprived of their culture, language and laws permanently. "I wonder where the Germans got their ideas from?" she facetiously asked herself. Pondering on this Halle saw that she had a legitimate excuse for her adoption of violence in pursuit of a return of the country to the Irish people. As always her mind found a tangent and targeted the word 'excuse' and she recalled a poem her father recited on Armistice Day:

… this uncomely man with a smoking gun …
What the devil will he gain by it?

And wondered had her father saw the futility of war.

A fortnight had passed before the Germans did an assessment of all those living in Guernsey. O'Driscoll used the opportunity to advise the naval detachment, which called, that he had an urgent need to see the commander. The following day a vehicle arrived to take both of them to the City Hall where Lanz had taken up residence. O'Driscoll spoke privately to the commander and came out smiling saying that Halle was wanted. Clearly something had been agreed between the pair and Halle knew that the matter concerned her.

CHAPTER 3
(July-August 1940)

HE REALISED AFTERWARDS that he must have been half-awake when they left headquarters an hour or two before him. Perhaps it was the calmness of it all which left him unperturbed; but Lord Gort and his staff leaving at the same time should have been enough to have caused him some serious doubts on how the war was going. He knew that this was the town where Edward Thomas, the poet, had fallen in the Great War but he consoled himself that he knew this war was a phoney, right from the start. He knew he had to control his thoughts; before long he would be thinking of Vera and that's the last thought he wanted. Or was it because John had convinced him that the only way out of his financial predicament was to join the Territorials saying the prospects for war were small. Ian later regretted joining the Territorials because of his financial difficulties, the spirit of his ancestors was precious to him and he wanted to have the faith and certainty they had in facing the horrendousness of war. He should have joined the Army before Chamberlain got back from Munich. There was so much phoney-baloney about John—his new Müllard radio, his financial nostrums taken from the national newspapers and his women, powder-puff beauties with the brainpower of chickens. Now was the time to quit his reliance on others and take responsibility for his own mistakes. No sooner had the thought occurred, than he realised he couldn't find anyone to blame for the break-up of his marriage. His mother had warned him that he was too taken in by good looks; but he couldn't admit to her that he fancied every young woman, near his age, that he had ever met… Yet it hadn't been that which caused the break-up…perhaps his over seriousness… and certainty about how to live…

"Why the hell do I let my thoughts intrude when I'm in a crisis?" he darted a look sideways and behind, at least nobody was close enough to hear. When he joined the TA he had been selected for the signals section, despite being a compositor. Later, he logically concluded, that the officer responsible assumed that being in printing meant that he was concerned with communications. And clearly as this lay within these parameters his proper rôle lay with the Signal Corp; but with the passing of time he realised that logic had nothing to do with it and they just filled a vacancy with the first face that fitted.

Being assigned to Arras, the Headquarters, he regarded as a stroke of luck. It meant that he was far enough away from any danger of military action, at that time there wasn't any real likelihood of any occurring, the place was as phoney as the war, with officers who spoke as if they were peeling grapes with their teeth. He realised the Germans had attacked to the north of their position, probably working over the Dutch and the Belgians but the British and French armies were no powder puffs. He had better make some attempt to get his orders. He moved back to the lorry in search of the three who were in his company. The heat of the mid-day sun was overpowering, indeed many of those familiar with France thought it was seasonally unfashionable. He wondered what was the date, thought about it for a moment and remembered he had left Belfast on his nephew's birthday, the 16 April. That was more than four weeks ago and by deduction he reckoned that the date was the 24 May 1940, John's birthday. What a horrible thought and his mind went off at a tangent wondering where John had got to in this crazy world.

Just then his comrades in arms arrived with rifles slung at the most peculiar angles, "Why the hell do we have to carry these to every point in the compass?" Rob was an Englishman who moaned persistently and made everyone within listening range want to be anywhere but near him. Ian knew his luck was out the moment he saw him arriving. The other Mancunian in the group raised his eyes to heaven after he told Rob "to button his lip". Thank God for Ned's presence and also George's shrinking violet impersonations of the officers in their company. Ned had the stripes and they all looked to him for the orders of the day. "There are a number of lines down between Arras and Douai, so we have to find them and repair them. OK?" Rob wanted to know what was the purpose, "That should be a job for civilians, shouldn't it?" Ned wasn't up for discussions, "It's an order and that's that! Understood?" The heat was making everyone exasperated, "For Christ's sake let's go!" yelled someone and Ian agreed with all his heart even though he would have preferred to have Christ's name left out.

There was hardly a soul on the road and the young men sang to their hearts' content, until Ian's unmelodic voice became the topic of conversation rather than the songs of the day. "For God's sake Paddy hum will be sufficient!" Ian knew sooner or later he would get it over his voice but the additional knockdown "Paddy" was too much. "I'm an Ulsterman, not a Paddy; I hope you've got it once and for all, OK?" They were already laughing before he completed the sentence, "You're too thin skinned to be real; anyway if you were born in Ireland you're Irish, OK?" the final few words of George mimicked him and Ian was more incensed than ever. "Halt!" cried Ned, "with all of your arguing we nearly missed that broken wire over there." He pointed to a pole in the middle of a field and they soon found the gate and drove to the offending wire.

By now the sun's rays were making most of them red but Ian was already as brown as a berry. They divested themselves of their shirts and tin hats. "Not much of a break this," shouted Rob once he ascended the telegraph pole. "Just get on with it and less of the chat", shouted Ned, "we've quite a few to do before the day's out." Ian took the opportunity to lie on the ground and enjoy the heat, which reminded him of his early childhood in South Africa. Soon he would be up there dangling from the end of the cross bar, which reminded him of the crucifix he once saw in a Roman Catholic chapel. He felt, rather than heard, the thud of large guns firing in the distance. Ned commented that the only practice the gunners and tank crews got were in these fields. Someone grunted agreement and Rob shouted down, "They are over there," pointing at some distant objects. Ian climbed the ladder to have a look but Ned and George went on with preparing the wire. The vantage point was sufficiently high to enable both Rob and Ian to see. Suddenly there was an explosion too close to them for comfort, Rob almost hurtled past Ian in his anxiety to get down but Ian managed to get him to stay still while he took another look. Another explosion near them soon had him galloping down the pole with Rob in hot pursuit. "They're definitely German tanks," yelled the both of them as they rushed to don helmets and shirts. George and Ned responded much slower convinced that there was some carry on occurring that they weren't privy to.

"For Christ's sake get a move on you two," yelled Ian. "That's the real McCoy they're firing!" Urgency was the new creed and soon the lorry was on the road racing in the direction of Arras. "How in the name of all that's holy did the Hun get there?" George's normal pretence of finding something funny in everything was suddenly dropped and an anxious looking young man took his place. Silence engulfed the cab; no one had an inkling as to what was going on. Five kilometres from the town they came upon a mass of people running as if engaged in the Olympic Games but not running fast enough for the signallers. The lorry was proving to be useless and when the first German dive-bombers arrived to machine-gun the road all four of them abandoned their vehicle for the safety of the ditch. There seemed to be a mass of bodies writhing or lying completely still on the road. But there wasn't time to deal with them. So it was back to running flat out then diving into the ditch. The living bodies of women and children, in the main, and the elderly supplemented what little cover that was available if and when they reached the ditch. Their army boots soon were proving to be a bigger handicap than they expected but when they saw the handicaps the civilian population was coming to terms with they decided that they weren't too bad. Nevertheless Rob and George took their boots and socks off at the very next opportunity. Men as old as their grandfathers pushed long unused prams on which were set anything from grandfather clocks to chamber pots, of course these were left on the road each time a Stuka dive bomber attacked.

It was late afternoon when they reached the outskirts of Arras and were greeted with the chaos of a beaten army. At headquarters there was absolute bedlam and no sooner had they reported than they were ordered to the outskirts to defend the town. "Are there no regular infantry here?" Ian asked an officer who looked like a lost sheep. "They have all been withdrawn and are in full retreat and so will we when we destroy whatever may be useful to the enemy." Ned raised his eyes to heaven or its nearest equivalent, the ceiling. "So what is this rearguard made up of?" Everyone nearby was listening, "I suppose it's no secret by now; any company or group of men who chance on this place are to make up the rear guard but it shouldn't take long to clear these documents and destroy everything else." The horror of the situation was only hitting home with Ian when Rob added to the overall misery, "Surely you don't mean we are to defend this town with these pea shooters?" was his querulous cry. "We have nothing else, unless someone comes in with bigger weapons. I suggest you get out there quickly or they'll be on top of you before you can get a shot in."

Ian knew a final order when he heard one, "Just whereabouts are we to go?" The officer pointed to a sergeant standing outside mustering a group of men, "He is positioning the men at the north end of the town, follow him and take your instructions from him, all right?" The whole group of them nodded dismally, "Do you think they'd time to put up any fortifications?" asked Rob and Ned in a less than kind voice, "Of course! Something akin to the Great Wall of China!" No one smiled let alone laughed but trudged dolefully out to follow the herd going to their final resting, at least that was Ian's view.

Once there they realised the position was worse than they had imagined; a dozen men were told to spread out and to stop the first tank to appear and thus hold up the advance of the main German group which was a mile or two in the rear. Ned shook his head, "We have only a kerbstone as protection; the first time those guns of theirs let loose we're done for." Ian thought that Ned's summing of the situation exactly matched his own assessment. "How long do we stay here, then?" George's question mirrored everyone's thought on their plight. "We stay until we are told to move back," answered Ned. "There's no one of sufficient rank to tell us when that will be," shouted George from his position across the street, "you'd better be prepared to tell us to go or I'm suiting myself."

Ian saw that the whole show was disintegrating but there was no time to debate the issue as the rumble of a German tank made everyone lie flat and take aim. The fusillade of shots were answered with the bang of the tank's gun and Ian was conscious of George's head disintegrating, he fired as often as the rifle would allow but it was as futile as Ned had indicated back at headquarters. It was only after that thought that he was conscious of George's blood covering the top half of his uniform. The next attack took out at least half of the men Ian was with and he determined to retreat if another of his group was killed. He didn't have to wait long because Ned was blown to bits and Ian, once he checked if there was any chance of saving Ned, decided to go and almost simultaneously the others departed to greener pastures.

Unknown to Ian and the others the German flank had swung behind the town to cut it off from any British or French reinforcements. Consequently when Ian ran in the direction of the opposite end of the town it wasn't long before he found German infantry emanating from every street. Somehow in the confusion his uniform didn't attract the attention he thought it would. At the Rue de Michel he saw a group of children entering a church and followed them regardless of his feelings for Roman Catholicism and its dogmas. Inside he was hit by the tremendous contrast with what was occurring outside where his friends and comrades were dying. He was sufficiently aware of the Church of Ireland's act of confirmation to recognise this was something of the same. The pew at the back seemed to give sufficient light for him to see and at the same time cloak his movements. He sat for a few moments before an elderly woman approached and clearly was attempting to tell him to go before the Boche arrived but she kept pointing to his rifle and he gradually realised she wanted him to get rid of it. He shrugged sufficiently like a Frenchman for her to realise he didn't know where to put it. She reached down and placed it under her shawl and disappeared down the aisle. Ian settled down to wrestle with the problem of what to do next. Probably because of the fighting outside the bishop called a halt after the last child was confirmed and parents and sponsors rushed to get their children home to some kind of safety. Ian's response surprised him: 'What was he doing sitting at a ceremony which celebrated life? His Protestant certainty deserted him and left him wondering where religion fitted in all of this.

Ian stayed as close to the children and the adults as he could but just as he reached the porch the old lady reappeared and led him back along the aisle to the sacristy. The bishop and the priests had obviously withdrawn in a hurry so Ian quickly left by the side door, without drawing attention to himself. He hurried along the back streets but their eerie silence in the middle of the day did nothing for his peace of mind. In the next street he saw a bicycle at the windowsill of a house and there and then decided that it was his best means of escape. Once he left the immediate vicinity of the church the lack of German infantry convinced him that he must be close to the British and French line of battle. It was only as he approached a crossroads that he realised the men on points-duty were German military policemen. At first they appeared to pay no attention to him but there was no long-term future in persisting along this road. He thought of finding somewhere to spend the night and from there attempt to reappraise what he should do. He decided to return to the church thinking that the Germans would have searched the place and he would be free to spend the night. He entered but the German soldiers were waiting and Ian went down to a series of blows from the butts of their rifles. Someone must have caught him a glancing blow on the head and he passed out.

Ian came round wondering how the Lambeg drum got into his head. He appeared to be in a single iron-framed bed in a single room with a massive door. He tried to retrace his steps to this obvious fall from grace but could do nothing to stir his memory into some kind of recall. Minute by minute as he worked hard at it he realised he was suffering from amnesia. "How the hell did I remember the word yet can't put two memories of my own to rub together." Instinctively he withdrew the phrase—it didn't make sense yet some part of it sounded familiar when he spoke it aloud, "Couldn't put somethings to rub together." No; something else was odd. Maybe like the other phrase he had used a word in the wrong context? Something smelt of gibberish in this as well. Better rest and see what was on the other side of the door that is when he felt reasonably able.

"Why then am I unreasonably able?" he thought but this was clearly the wrong variable to be adding to the 'un-' prefix. He tried again, "Why then am I reasonably unable?"

Now he felt he could analyse this statement and possibly find an answer; however the drum had not diminished and in essence suggested pain—he had a headache! This was a momentous moment, there was a pain in his head and if he thought about it he, more than likely, would discover the cause. "I wonder if I am a teacher or a scientist? My words sound strange in my mouth." No, go back to the pain. "From where is it coming?" Something strange about that formulation as well. No, concentrate on the head. He withdrew his hands from under the single blanket, which covered him to feel the contours of his head. Immediately the pain increased immeasurably. "Ah, a large bump. I've either fallen or been hit." Yet that wasn't the centre of the pain; it appeared to be close to the middle of his back. He tried to touch it but found he would have to move in order to get at it. He sat up with a great deal of difficulty enduring more pain in order to discover what was the matter with his back. There was a massive bandage right around him. He couldn't think of a likely possibility for it.

"What age am I? Twenty-eight," was the quick response. "I don't know who I am yet I know my age! I give up. It's easier to ask whoever has put me here."

Ian fell into a deep sleep and was eventually wakened by a nurse who indicated she wished to take his temperature. How he knew he couldn't say and why she didn't speak was a mystery. "Could you tell me my name?" The girl hunched her shoulders, which he took to mean she didn't know; it was only after she left that it dawned on him, "Maybe she didn't understand me."

He thought about this double uncertainty, "She didn't know my name," seemed the likely answer initially but when he thought about it he realised that she was far too quiet to be a normal nurse. "What do you know about a normal nurse?" he wondered. For the first time, as far as he knew, he thought life was too complicated. If the nurse didn't understand how was he to communicate? This had far-reaching consequences—How and why did he ever get there? Who were his relations? Where is 'here'? The questions were too numerous to go on. "I give in too readily," he pronounced to the walls of his room, which he now saw as a symbol of his mind—a closed trap.

Just as he reached a stage of complete despair the massive door swung open and a young man in a white coat came in, "How do you feel?" Ian noted the heavy German accent. The series of questions flooded back but the young man was impatient, "How do you feel?"

"Woozy," after having given it sufficient thought; then away was his mind up the avenues of lexicography searching for an explanation for 'woozy'. "Could you explain that please?"

"Yes, uncertain about many things and my mind seems to be in a constant haze."

"Very good; no … no that is not what I meant … just that I understand how you feel."

"I doubt that very much. You see I don't know who I am and I have no memory of my past. Yet I seem to know words and I have ideas which come readily."

"Ah, amnesia ... it sometimes occurs ... just for a few hours, often less."

"So I'll recall what happened?"

"Oh yes. Your name is Ian Patterson and you are a prisoner of war here in France. Sorry, you are in a *German* prison hospital in France."

"I don't fully understand... but I'm grateful for the information. What was I suffering from?" asked Ian in a more upbeat tone of voice. "You had damage to your back. It's repaired now and soon you will be sent to a prisoner-of-war camp." The model prisoner started to nod off and the doctor left him to sleep.

Early the next day Ian woke and was immediately reassured when he started to recall all the vicissitudes he had encountered since his arrival in France and, indeed, well beyond that, his memories of his childhood and youth in Belfast. Then his memories took another turn and his wife came to mind with all her beauty. "Lord," he thought, "I was the luckiest man on earth when she agreed, even if it was somewhat reluctantly, to marry me".

His mind took off in another direction: overly religious people should not marry; they worried unduly about sex. If they were women they either did or did not want babies. The thought had run its course and he found he was challenging his own positions on a variety of subjects. "Intelligent people move on—they accept that their views are altered by situations over time. It's only when you experience dread that you recognise situations alter cases." His youthful belief in the glory and honour in war was radically changed. Perhaps it was the headless bodies at Arras or maybe the loss of so many of his comrades, but whatever it was it had completely undermined his whole approach to war.

Putting the analysis out of his head wasn't as easy as he had thought. Now he wondered if one such upset could do so much how would he respond to the undoubted troubles that lay in store for the months, maybe years ahead. Could he be certain that the values and heritage he cherished so much would persist in the face of the enormity of change that he visualised was coming his way ... "You need to rest because you can't be sure this sinecure will last much longer." But his mind wouldn't rest ... "was sinecure the right word..." and so it went on until sleep took over once again.

He woke with a start thinking that the world had gone Nazi overnight and he had no hope of ever being freed. Despite the memories flooding back and providing provender for his weakened ego he still couldn't deal with his short-term memory loss. Of particular concern was how issues of such importance to him, some which he regarded as being priceless, indeed more to him than life itself, could so easily have been erased. How could this loss of identity occur? Out of the blue he recalled old Mrs Cunningham calling for him to go out to play when he was a boy about six years old. His parents said she was in her second childhood and later in life he never used the term, preferring 'senility' or 'senile'. Whatever the reason she had lost all those beliefs she had held and in addition had lost her identity. "Why do I make such an issue of something so fragile?" But then again his Protestant identity started to reassert itself, "Roman Catholics would impose a series of dictatorial commands which would lead to the eradication of all that was Protestant and reformed. Freedom of thought was too important to be jeopardised by giving the same rights to those opposed tooth and nail to all my beliefs. The same applies to the Nazis, no wonder I woke in such a sweat."

Later that afternoon, after the initial examination by the doctor and the nurse, Ian started wondering about his blood transfusion. Undoubtedly the blood must have come from some German, probably a Hitler supporter, who felt he was helping the war effort by providing blood for young soldiers who had been wounded. "What would he have thought had he known it was going to a British soldier? Probably aggrieved… Come to think of it, imagine getting Republican blood back home if you needed an operation! The mind boggles! I shan't forget this thought for a long time!"

Just before the doctor left he made it clear that he was fit enough to be sent to a prisoner-of-war camp. All too soon, from his point of view, an officer and two soldiers arrived to escort him to the train for the first part of his journey into captivity. Outside the hospital was a large lorry and already some POWs were aboard, whether they were destined for the same camp was another matter. Ian wondered was he strong enough to make an attempt to escape, after all in France he had a better chance of getting help than in Germany—he thought Germany was the more likely destination even if the doctor had said Poland. As the lorry filled the impossibility of an escape bid dawned on him. Far too many prisoners were still in a bad way with injuries from all types of weapons, not counting those badly beaten when captured. He would be endangering them as he would have to clamber over every injured man in front of him to get into a position to leap from the back of the lorry.

At the railway station there was a great deal of mayhem, unlike everything he had been taught about German efficiency, and it was an ideal time to make the attempt but he became mesmerised by the huge group of civilians on the platform being herded into all kinds of trains. He asked if anyone knew who these people were and where were they going. No one had a clue—all kinds of possibilities were suggested but there wasn't sufficient evidence to sustain any of it. They waited for hours on end for the train supposedly allocated to them and like their civilian counterparts they suffered without complaint, knowing their lot as the vanquished compared to their enemies' position as the conquerors. Consequently, when the train arrived, he was past being able to do anything but lie on the floor of the cattle wagon to which he was assigned.

Ian was taken to Posen to join many of the men captured on the Channel coast. He didn't realise just how many men were on board until he arrived in the railyard. He knew that the vast majority of prisoners had been transported well in advance of his leaving hospital, yet here were hundreds of men, many of them suffering from dysentery and hunger. The cattle wagon, which he had been in, contained those like himself just released from hospital and, in comparison with the rest of the prisoners, they looked much the healthier. Many of the non-hospital men had no footwear and were forced to march through the town of Posen to show the Polish people just how abject were their hopes of an Allied victory.

Not unexpectedly many of these men collapsed long before they reached the camp; in the main they suffered from malnutrition yet guards forced them to their feet and they slowly made their way to a fort which undoubtedly had been there for countless years. The gates were opened in a rather sluggish manner and Ian saw the first of the guards, which he suspected would become familiar faces to him in the months and, if German propaganda was to be believed, years to come.

As a new arrival Ian had to line-up while he was assigned a category. The Germans were keen to keep as many differences as existed between the various British contingents and the Empire soldiers from South Africa, India, Canada and Australia. In some camps they were completely segregated but inevitably the Irish, Northern or Southern was often regarded as colonials. The final result for Ian was that he was regarded as a South African colonial with Irish connections, a conclusion he regarded as the worst possible one.

A German soldier searched new arrivals. If they spoke while this was happening they often received the butt of a rifle in their stomach or the small of their back. On the train Ian had been warned by a friendly guard to make sure he kept quiet while this was going on because he assured him it did not end there. Consequently Ian watched helplessly as those who didn't hear the warning asked what seemed to be sensible questions and were hurt because of their query. Anything of value was literally stolen, watches, rings, jewellery; no pretence made or excuse given—confiscated in the name of the Reich.

The idea of a long-term stay was anathema to Ian long before he reached his final stop. He was under no illusions about what might face him if he should attempt an escape. Even before he left hospital the officers warned all of them of the consequences of making an attempt. Yet he watched every move, every aspect of the landscape, where guards were billeted and the farms along the way that employed POWs, all this with the intention of using these details in the not too distant future.

German soldiers were the first on the parade ground every morning for drilling and afterwards the prisoners lined up to be counted and to hear the commandant's lecture on the state of the camp and what would happen to those found to be the cause of disruption. Ian found the lack of food the most difficult adjustment to make, but make it he must and he determined to use it as a means of preparing for his leaving. After Appal, on his second day, Ian was shocked to hear his name called by a Belfast voice, turning he was amazed to see John—the guy who got him into this mess! "Good God, John! I couldn't believe my ears. I must tell you that retribution is a wonderful thing—not revenge because I wouldn't wish that on anyone but retribution is good!"

"You always were one to get round the words of the Bible, 'Vengeance is mine sayth the Lord, I shall repay!' Of course you won't say it, you toss in 'retribution' to absolve yourself of your sin—but you're the one who laughs at the Roman Catholics and their confession! You haven't changed Ian, have you?" Ian gave a forced laugh, "Funny you should say that but I was thinking of that girl in our street, years ago, who kicked the back wheel of my bike from under me—she had the same impression of me that you have. Maybe you're right, who knows?"

"I suspect that wee girl knew then and it hasn't changed."

"Let's get back to the real questions. How long have you been here and where were you captured?"

"I arrived yesterday but I know I'm due to be moved on, or so they tell me. Somehow I've been wrongly designated—my da was Scottish and my ma Ulster, not that my ma's birthplace had any bearing, they only go by your father."

"So you're as ignorant as myself about this place?"

"Not quite, a day is a long time here, for example, the Red Cross hasn't heard of this place yet, so forget about any parcels. From what I hear even if they hear about it the Germans will confiscate anything worthwhile."

"I'm truly disappointed John, when I saw you I felt that at last things were turning for the better." The two friends continued with their conversation about home, friends and relatives until forced to return to their huts for lights out. Sadly, but still optimistic, Ian wished John all the best of "British luck" on his departure to his new abode and hoped it would not be long before they met again.

John was gone before Ian had a last chance to wish him well. He asked if any of the others had seen his departure but no one had. "That's about the best chance I had to see someone from home, and it only lasted a matter of hours. God alone knows when the next one will be." Yet it wasn't long before he was lured into playing cards with his hut mates in order to while away the hours. The fact that it wasn't genuine gambling, since no money changed hands, made it acceptable.

Ian soon learned that the Red Cross parcels, or the lack of them, was a standing joke. No one blamed the Germans, not at the outset; rather they saw the shortage of workers back home as being the main reason for the delay. If it wasn't that they claimed that only the lame, the blind and the naturally slow did the work. As the situation worsened there was a gradual realisation that the Germans were the cause of all their hardship, as a result the prisoners lived on rumours. "Soon those very ill would be exchanged for German casualties in British hands," was the latest story doing the rounds and the queues for the doctor's examination increased enormously, and so it went on—humour being the antidote to depression and lack of hope. As the weeks passed the situation approached despair and consequently when the Germans forced men to accept employment on nearby farms Ian was glad of the opportunity to get away from the dreariness of the camp. He, along with most of the others, felt that this was an opportunity to get an increase in their food ration but, more importantly in Ian's mind, was the chance to survey the lie of the land, both metaphorically and literally, in his pursuit of escape.

On the first day they had to work the farmer brought along a number of horses and carts, probably to keep the men fresh for the work they had to do. But within the week they were marched to the fields and Ian's hopes rose as he felt there were many more opportunities to get away—to where and in what direction didn't play a part in his preparations. The need to hoard food likewise didn't come into the reckoning; nor did he consult others about the odds of getting away—just to be out on one's own would be "sufficient unto the day".He waited almost a week for an opportunity and when the cart which collected the produce which they had harvested broke down he watched until he saw the guards become involved in helping to lift it and then crawled into the wheat field. Ian enjoyed every second of his freedom but it didn't last very long as the Germans soon unearthed him from his hideout.

CHAPTER 4
(August 1940-March 1942)

CORNFLOWER BLUE EYES were those that Halle had grown to fear, whether at home or in England. Here, in Berlin, they had seemed to proliferate and, consciously or unconsciously, she felt they were anything but benign and she grew to attribute all that was evil to them.

Her interviewer's eyes didn't suggest it was the foregone conclusion that O'Driscoll had claimed. And when he began, what she thought would be a set drill, she feared her chance was gone.

"I assume you're of German extraction with such a surname?" His accent was a mixed one, clearly he had been educated in Britain, possibly Oxford or Cambridge, but his stresses were Germanic and Halle committed the mistake of making assumptions about him on the basis of just one question. She concluded he had the Nazi type mind, which required him to determine race as the first priority. She wondered if she let Irish names dominate her approach to nationalism—how could she though with an English father and a name, which suggested a Teutonic origin? "No; I'm of a mixed breed like 98% of the world's population."

Why she said it so instinctively was beyond her but it was out and she had to accept the consequences. Clearly the answer wasn't what he wanted. "We Germans don't see it like that. We are anxious to rid ourselves of any racial impurities and so we constantly search out and separate those with racial features that are inferior to those of the pure race."

Halle was too familiar with this position—it was fine and noble to proclaim an Ireland where Orange and Green could co-exist with those of no persuasion but would it have been possible if there had been a number of land boundaries? The noble ideal would be just another part of fascism in Europe where gypsies and Jews of every European country could be mocked in the name of "racial purity." The need for land to resource the increase in population needed to create an empire would never apply to Ireland but if there was a natural increase they wouldn't be sent to the far reaches of the earth in future, why not take over Britain? Halle knew fantasy was a dangerous element in all of us but since arriving in Germany she was aware that it appeared to be the main ingredient in the psyche of those she met, and now she was applying the fantasy to Ireland and the mix that she considered Irish.

Halle recognised that her hopes for a job were now entirely reliant on

O'Driscoll's recommendation to Lanz. "Herr Menske we in Ireland are not in a position to find which of us is of purely Celtic origin so we accept those who acknowledge that the island of Ireland is one indivisible land, separate from Britain and proud to be independent." At last Halle felt that she was contributing something of herself but Menske took it that she was lecturing him.

"I know my Irish history Miss Hegel but I want someone who can appreciate the German point of view and relay it to the Irish people." Halle saw that she could still save the situation and quickly assured Herr Menske that she was ready to do just that. "Miss Hegel we are interested in two types of people, personalities for the radio and people capable of writing scripts. Outside the door will be a young woman who will take you to another room where you will find a desk and writing materials. Take as long as you like but write something on Ireland or a topic concerning Germany and this war that is proceeding at the moment. This is to help us determine which would suit you best from our point of view."

"Does that mean I am in the running for one or other of the two positions?" asked Halle. "No. Clearly you would have to satisfy us that you were capable of either one or the other of the two jobs. The position would have been somewhat different if you could have given a talk in the Irish language but the person who recommended you said that your knowledge of Gaelic was limited. Is that the case?"

"Yes, I'm afraid it is the case."

"Well we will see how you get on with the written test. In any event you will be notified of the result in a few days time."

Halle left the room dispirited, feeling that the pressure to write something to impress this man was coming too soon after her arrival from the Channel Islands. Nevertheless, it had to be done and in all probability she was only getting one attempt to prove herself. In the end she did as well as she could, given the circumstances and she hoped that allowances would be made for doing it in examination conditions which were not conducive to writing well. Still she comforted herself that she had handled Lanz, the Channel Islands commandant, sufficiently well as to have him recommend her to the radio authorities in Berlin. Indeed, she had been flown out in a matter of days after the interview, so she consoled herself that they must have wanted her urgently.

The days dragged by and she could foresee that she was going to be resorting to the soup kitchen if she didn't get this job. She determined that the beginning of the following week was sufficient time and if she didn't hear from them she would apply for jobs in the local press. Fortunately she heard she was successful, after a three-week delay, and that she would be employed, initially, for one year as a scriptwriter on programmes to be beamed to Ireland.

She had heard nothing directly from O'Driscoll since she left Guernsey, almost six weeks previously, but his reputation was high with the people with whom she had contact but the reaction generally suggested that there had been some kind of dispute in which he had been involved. On reflection she wondered if this had been the reason for the delay in appointing her.

The day to day work was enthralling and she relished each morning rising and washing in preparation for the day ahead. But the first inkling she had that all was not well was when she was summoned to Herr Menske's office. "Well Fraulein Hegel, how have you been getting along?"

"Fine," Halle couldn't think of anything else to say. "What particular work have you been doing?" Halle instinctively knew there was a purpose to this kind of questioning, he wasn't interested in her health or happiness in the post. He already knew what she was writing—he had a day to day report and she knew, from what the others had told her, he listened to all the programmes broadcast. "I have been writing about British injustices in Ireland and around the world," Halle was uneasy now because she nearly said 'empire' and she was uncertain just how this would be taken. "Are you working alone or as part of a larger team?" Again Halle knew he knew the answer but she was forced to play this game, which he insisted on doing. "There are five others involved." Menske hesitated before continuing, "How many of those involved are Irish?" Halle felt her frustration about to boil over; "I'm the only one. Could you tell me what is this about? I know you have all the answers in front of you, so why are you testing me, have I done something wrong?" Menske blue eyes unblinkingly stared at her, "No, I am anxious to see that you have settled in." Halle, for all her earlier attempts to debunk psychology and avoid awareness of it, now knew she was involved in some kind of psychological warfare where she would be the pawn in some end game that defied her understanding.

Suddenly he smiled what undoubtedly he regarded as a reassuring action; "Do you often discuss your work with colleagues in the office, or outside of it?" Halle felt herself being wrongfooted so she was particularly cagey in her reply, "Not outside the office, simply because I was warned of the dangers in speaking on topics which are not already in the public domain. But in the office I regular consult with colleagues and debate various ways about putting over ideas on the radio."

"Do you discuss countries outside of the British Empire?" Halle couldn't remember talking on anything but Ireland, "Ah, I do recall asking a colleague about the Jews and their history, is this what you are anxious about?" His demeanour told her it wasn't and he said so, "No, I often get comments from various departments, it could well have been England Redaktion, on issues talked of during programme making. This one was about Russia and Napoleon, it was not you, was it?" Halle thought for a moment, "It could well have been. I was talking about the British over-reaching themselves, across the world and I happened to refer to what had happened to Napoleon when he attempted to occupy Russia, that's all."

"Ah, that explains it. No, the way it was reported to me suggested you were talking about the present conflict in Europe and drawing conclusions from the past and I wanted to know if you were suggesting that Germany had similar aims as Napoleon and the British."

"No, of course not."

"Thank you for being so patient but I just wanted this matter cleared up in my mind. Don't let me put you off coming forward with ideas by my asking questions."

"I am glad you did, I wouldn't want to suggest that anything I say is an attack on German military policy."

"Thank you once again. If ever there is a problem my door is always open."

Outside Menske's office Halle took a huge breath and calmed herself, "He has carefully gathered every cliché he can for occasions like this," she muttered before returning to her work. Now she was reluctant to ask anyone about anything other than about Ireland and events in Germany.

There was one girl in particular that Halle was concerned about. She was as tall as herself, perhaps slightly taller, which Halle admitted only to herself. Fair bobbed hair and blue eyes with an athletic build. She was the only genuine speaker of English in the whole department, outside of Menske and herself, and if there was anyone who could follow Halle's arguments she was that person but she was also the one capable of deliberately misconstruing the context and the issue. Her name was Sheila and from the gossip in the office she was originally English and married to a Frenchman who had been an out and out National Socialist but the irony was the Germans had killed him when they overran France. "Obviously they gave her a job to make up for their error in executing him," thought Halle and initially gave her the cold shoulder treatment—a person of such a mixture suggested an archconservative Unionist of the type Halle hated.

After the Menske' summons Halle watched, at the various meetings within the department, as each critical comment was being assessed. Sheila rarely spoke and appeared to keep her thoughts to herself. Halle realised that the girl was a conundrum inside a riddle, and smiled as she repeated an expression of her father's that he often said about her. Still she avoided the normal day-to-day contact with her.

Sheila had been quick to catch on and every now and again tried to start a conversation but Halle wouldn't bite and now the circumstances indicated that she had been right all along. "The bitch set me up. Luckily I was able to make a case that got me off the hook. I'll bloody watch what I say in front of her in future," thought Halle.

"What happened in Menske's office?" asked Sheila a few days after the event. Halle was reluctant to open her mouth but she lied instead, "He just wanted to know was I happy with what I had been given." Sheila looked around before speaking, "Each time I have ended up there, there's always been a sting in the tail. Just watch yourself," and with that Sheila departed for her desk.

Later that evening Halle had a visitor and she regretted ever having mentioned her new apartment in work; it was Sheila anxious to talk of the events earlier in the day. At first Halle was determined to listen and say nothing but as Sheila spoke about her experiences with Menske, Halle felt confident that Sheila was innocent of passing on information. "Look whatever you do, avoid certain subjects—issues of politics which are pushed down your throat every day are taboo, never mention the treatment of the Jews nor the people sent to concentration camps because of their political affiliations, especially if they are communists."

Halle couldn't help herself, "But I thought there was a treaty between the Soviet Union and Germany?"

"Yes, there is. Neither the Nazis nor the average citizen like it, both groups suspect it won't be long before the whole thing collapses. But this is an absolute no no in the office or outside it, OK?"

"Who the hell is carrying the news back to Menske?"

"There are that many paid up members of the National Socialist Party, it's hard to say. But let me put it to you like this, two of the men who worked in your office before you arrived disappeared a few months back and the rumours suggest that they are in concentration camps on account of their views. Whatever the hell they were!"

"Apparently I spoke about Napoleon's defeat at Moscow. I didn't think it was a big deal but apparently it is. They seem to see it as defeatist talk around here. Am I missing something in all this?"

"You probably hit on something accidentally that's hush-hush and they are wondering where you're getting the information. Do you know someone in the Foreign Ministry or someone in the Abwehr?"

"I don't think so, I know O'Driscoll, who worked here for a time, but what his activities were I haven't a notion."

"Now we *know*, how did you get involved with O'Driscoll? Do you realise that Goebbels, Menske and him had a huge row about the direction the radio broadcasts were to take and shortly afterwards he disappeared. God knows where he is, I know he isn't in Berlin. Some of the old-timers here are convinced he has more than a passing say in what is broadcast and what isn't."

"You're kidding? O'Driscoll? I don't believe it. Look I worked with him in England and the man just doesn't fit the picture you're painting. He's hardly what you'd call educated..."

"Oh, it's strange that you should say so because the German directors here wouldn't accept his suggestions because of that very fact. They relied on two other Irish men who had been lecturers in the University here but the general belief was that he had the ear of the Foreign Minister, von Ribbentrop, and it was that which counted in the final analysis. God this night has flew in, I enjoyed all the gossip but you know just keep it between us, OK?"

Halle was sorry she had spoken at all, once she weighted the information Sheila gave her but was glad she hadn't tied O'Driscoll and herself to the Channel Islands. It was clear that the girl was knowledgeable and must be friendly with someone close to the top brass. She convinced herself that Sheila was bound to be watched and sooner or later would be in trouble and Halle didn't want to be named as one of the conspirators if it came to it.

Halle attempted to clear her mind of the petty office politics that were going on; it had taken the penny a while to drop but now Halle realised that she was less politicised than she had thought. It was one thing to be concerned about Ireland and to fight for the cause of Irish unity but quite another to seek answers to the enormous economic problems that confronted the whole of Europe. Now, to find herself in Berlin addressing problems more to do with German fascism and totally outside her Irish interests seemed incredibly stupid.

She knew that she had more than mocked Martin's arguments and what she considered his quasi-dialectic materialism when she hadn't understood a word of his argument. Now, when she looked back, and thought about the scripts she had written for Joyce and a couple of others, whom she had failed to recognise, her lack of knowledge had made the job difficult and the information she had provided was probably unreliable. Still the sum of her knowledge, especially about the Jews, left her feeling embarrassed. On one occasion she realised her up-to-date history of the Jews amounted to Christ's statement that they would be forced to wander the face of the earth—this being a paraphrase of what a priest had voiced from the pulpit. In addition her lack of information about the Middle East put her at a distinct disadvantage. Indeed one team member had to tell her that 'Semitic' referred not only to Jews but also to a group of Hebrew and Arabic languages and, in some instances to both sets of people. Now she was aware that this had suited the German propaganda department as they were in a position to influence her thinking.

If she knew little about the Jews she knew even less about Soviet communism. While she had been writing she had thought, "If only I had paid more attention to Martin these scripts would be a lot easier to write." Things were no easier when the Foreign Ministry asked her to write detailing Britain's atrocities through various wars. At least she had the use of an extensive library plus the accumulated learning of the entire group, who appeared to have some gripe with the English or British depending which segment of that society at whom they were having a dig. Knowing how sensitive the Nazis were about concentration camps she didn't know whether they would appreciate her reminding the listening audience that the British government, during the South African War, were the first to use these camps and by so doing caused the deaths of thousands. The advice among her colleagues was to insert it and let the 'censors' decide; when the script was returned the first thing she noted was that the reference to the British and concentration camps had been deleted.

Halle lived near the Nordbahnhof railway station on Chausseestrasse. It was an old building, which had once been the town house of a wealthy aristocrat but now was divided into apartments occupied, in the main, by government employees and local government politicos attached to the Nazi party. A few tram-stops away was the Ackerhalle, a covered market, where she did most of her shopping. By and large she was content with the circumstances in which she found herself but loneliness could be a problem from time to time and from her earliest days in Berlin she went walking and gradually found herself fascinated with the city's history and heritage. It wasn't long before she began visiting museums and art galleries, which existed in large numbers.

Occasionally Sheila would accompany her and as she had been living a little longer in the city was able to explain some of the changes that had taken place since the advent of Hitler. Things like the empty homes of the Scheunenviertel, once occupied by poor emigrant Jews who had been removed from the city, the broadening of the main avenue through the

Tiergarten and the removal of many trees on Unter den Linden to enable the large military parades of which Hitler was fond.

Sheila, in passing, also explained why the Nazis in work regarded Berliners with suspicion. Apparently, in the early '30s Berlin rejected the Nazis at the polls, consequently Hitler suspected them of every crime in the Nazi catalogue: helping Jews, being communist and being anti-Nazi. Left-wing writers and a variety of intellectuals, long associated with the city, departed for the west—particularly America.

Halle was occasionally asked by Sheila to accompany her to some of the beauty spots around the city. The number of lakes and their serenity captivated her in a time when war dominated every thought and when she was lonely started to go on 'safaris' on her own. One small town proved irresistible—Potsdam. She thought, at first that her fascination for the place owed much to the bay in the Havel River reminding her of so many places that she had visited in Ireland. However the Am Neue Palais built by Frederick the Great in the 18th century and its grounds where a source of wonder for her and on another visit she found the San Scouci gardens in all its magnificence. "Once this war is over I will return here and spend a proper holiday," as she boarded the train back to Berlin.

Slowly it began to dawn on Halle that Sheila didn't fit the story she had heard when she first joined the department. At the first opportunity she asked her how she came to be working in Berlin. Apparently she had been working between Berlin and Paris for a number of years when she met a man whom she married. She hadn't known him long when she agreed to marry him so she was somewhat surprised to discover his association with the Nazis in Germany and the French right wing. She herself came from, what her husband regarded as a mixed race, her father was English and her mother Irish but the attitude of her husband, Edmund, was anathema to her and when he died she passed herself off as someone with a similar view to his.

Halle was taken aback by the similarity of both of their backgrounds, yet here was this girl entirely English working for the Nazis, while she, a committed Irish Republican, was doing the same. When Sheila quizzed her as to her involvement Halle told her about working in Guernsey, breaking a vow she had taken not to relate the episode to anyone. Then, to repair the damage, she said that the German occupation force sent her to Germany to be a slave worker but because she had known O'Driscoll was an admirer of all things German she used him to get the job and as she was Irish they readily appointed her. "This is a damn sight better than being a slave worker in some factory!" this being said with the assertiveness now known by all who worked with her. Halle was never going to reveal her past background with the Cumann na mBan to anyone English or of English extraction.

As the months passed Halle found she needed something more exciting to do and when she was approached to read the news she jumped at the opportunity. No sooner had she agreed to do the test than she had second thoughts, "My father would never forgive me. As it is he doesn't know of my involvement with the propaganda industry but this would bring my name to the attention of the authorities and they would start checking the mail to their house and any callers they got." Her new found friend, Sheila, advised her to take the job and change her name. "I can see all the advantages for my family in doing that, but what way does it affect my standing here? Won't they think that I have no faith in the Third Reich?" Sheila smiled grimly, "You're not under the illusion that these people haven't made provision for themselves in the possibility of a German defeat? You really are naïve. Believe me they would expect nothing less from a rational thinking person."

That was enough for Halle, she accepted and told them she wished to broadcast under the pseudonym 'Sally O'Riordan'. It meant that she had less script writing yet more responsibility for the final product. Everything looked to be on the up and for a time she found herself being quizzed, as to her views on a variety of subjects, by the chiefs of Irland-Redaktion, which left her uneasy and fearful of saying the wrong thing. However, the constant reference to Ireland's future after the war warmed her emotionally. And with the sweep of German advances right across Europe she felt that it couldn't be long before Britain sued for peace. And at last Ireland would have her place in Europe confirmed by right and she would be able to get home, away from the madness of 'right answers' that was fascism.

As time wore on Halle sensed that Sheila was a genuine person and although she was reluctant to pass on any tib-bits of office news herself she realised that Sheila kept her ears open as well as her eyes. It was about this point that Halle dismissed her earlier thought that Sheila had contact with a superior in the department but she still had suspicions that someone fed her information that wasn't generally known to the staff. The usual office jealousies took pride of place in their daily conversations. Halle's 'promotion' was regarded by some as an indication that O'Driscoll had a hand in it but the general consensus, according to Sheila, was that it was only a matter of time before the position was reversed. "Why's that?" asked a somewhat incredulous Halle. "Well, just how much is supposition, I don't know but the story goes that he was the Foreign Ministry's man and that he has been spying abroad for some months now and he is under suspicion for handing secrets to the Allies."

"Look Sheila, you know I worked with him in Britain and the one thing I know about him is that there's no way he would have any dealings with the British. He's too like myself in that regard."

"I've told you all I know but if there is a sweet way to have a dagger stuck in your back these guys here know how to do it!"

"I suspect they have underestimated this man. I'd be amazed if some of the people here don't end up in a concentration camp in Poland over this!"

"I hope you're right, Halle. Because if you're wrong the chances are you'll be right there with him! If I were you I'd try and contact him and let him know the tales that are flying around here. There's too much at stake for both of you."

"I'll leave it for the moment Sheila and see how things pan out."

"I wouldn't leave it too long. We'd better stop, we're drawing too much attention," and with that Sheila went out off the office.

Halle had been reluctant to tell Sheila or, for that matter, anyone that she had no knowledge of O'Driscoll's whereabouts. Denials made people suspect the reverse was the truth, so what had she to gain by indulging in that kind of argument? No, if the opportunity arose she would take it and let O'Driscoll make of it as he will.

If days were made to wander and wonder in, Halle had her fill by the following week. She knew Sheila was avoiding her for obvious reasons and of course the rest of the office, suspecting the worst, gave her what she called the smallpox treatment—a type of quarantine. Even if she approached some of the senior people for information on some of the stories she was working on they scrutinised every word to ensure, in Halle's opinion that they were in no way compromised. Indeed attitudes weren't reserved to the work place; the old habit of going out directly after work to a coffee shop or a restaurant ceased. Each evening the stress of the day and the lack of communication during it left its mark on Halle, if it hadn't been for the presence of Sheila she knew she would have had a breakdown. She couldn't ask Sheila to put herself in jeopardy by constantly asking her to meet her after work and yet what was she to do?

"Weeks have a way of turning into months," thought Halle as she walked away from the studio one day, "and if I don't get out of this soon there'll be only one end product—a concentration camp! Or my contract will have expired and I'll be the slave worker I claimed I was to be!" She could hardly believe her eyes—O'Driscoll, the shock all but caused Halle to stare at him incredulously. When he came over he was all smiles and greeted her with a kiss on both cheeks, a continental style she had never got used to but obviously it suited him. Back on Guernsey she regarded him as another Irishman doing his bit for the country and its re-unification but here he was a legend in his own lifetime. He was the first Irish man or woman to have been recruited to broadcast to Ireland and that was some achievement!

"Where are you heading?" remarked O'Driscoll. "Home," was all Halle could manage. "It's a pity I would have liked to have bought you a drink for old times sake but I have some business in here," nodding in the general direction of the Rundfunkhaus which Halle had just left. Halle didn't know whether to warn him about the state of the game at Irland Redaktion but in the end merely said, "Things are none too cordial in there," and gave him a look which she knew he would understand as 'watch out'. "Thanks," was all he said and he marched quickly into the building.

Heading towards the tram Halle turned her thoughts to O'Driscoll, from the little she knew of him and his beliefs Halle had assumed he was an ardent Irish Republican but with the passing of time she was uncertain of where his loyalties lay. From the attention he got from the Nazi overlords it was clear that they saw him as one of themselves. She wondered if he was like so many people she had met in the Movement, and for that matter outside it, who had more faces than the Albert Clock in Belfast. She determined that at the first opportunity she would quiz him about his position, particularly on the issues on which he had spoken while broadcasting to Ireland.

Back in her apartment Halle settled down to write the script for the next day's work but found that she needed more research than she had anticipated. The Germans were fond of bringing out the treachery of the British and they liked to hear stories of the tyranny the English had introduced in the countries they had subjugated and they seemed to be particularly partial to tales of old wrongs concerning Ireland. It never seemed to dawn on the average German member of staff that a corollary could be drawn between the two countries.

Africa had been the promised theme for her broadcast and she had wanted to use the example of the work of Roger Casement in the Congo. She had intended to show how he had concluded that the British were denying rights to his fellow Irishmen, and as a consequence had been executed in the Great War for attempting to recruit Irishmen captured in France to fight for Germany. His involvement with Germany was the difficulty; she hadn't sufficient information on that aspect. She decided to do what she could and fill in the German details in the story by going into work early. She didn't want any trouble as some people had been dismissed for not sticking rigidly to the topic they had been given and she was aware that Menske had deliberately created the situation where she could expect no help unless it came from him directly.

Halle was well into her work when she was interrupted by a knock at the door. It was no surprise to her to find it was O'Driscoll—not the terribly confident and popular Irish broadcaster but a man with the problems of the world on his shoulders. "Come in, come in," Halle no sooner had the words out than she realised that she was too welcoming. "Thanks," in a somewhat laconic tone told her that O'Driscoll hadn't missed the subtleties of language and was wondering what rôle she was playing. "Well, I didn't get an opportunity to chat earlier and I hoped you'd call. Have you been back home at all?" She knew she should never have started to engage him on an equal footing, he was in the stratosphere in terms of knowledge and she was a microbe shuffling on the earth in comparison. The silence was stifling and Halle's mind told her that she hadn't diffused the situation by her opening welcome and 'chat' was decidedly the wrong word—which was something they had never done. 'Chat' idle or otherwise wasn't in O'Driscoll's scheme of things. Everything was to the point and Halle feared he would clam up and she would be left in the dark. She decided to take the bull by the horns, "You look worried, is anything the matter?"

O'Driscoll, on the point of being seated, stood erect again and began prowling about the small room. He spoke no word beyond the 'thanks' he said when he entered. Halle was determined to play down his behaviour; "Won't you sit down?"

"Thanks." Clearly he was weighting just how much to tell her. The minutes passed and Halle offered him coffee, which he accepted yet he apparently didn't miss her out of the room when she left to make it. Halle started again once she sat down to sip the beverage, "I was surprised... no, shocked to see you this evening. Apart from the fact that you never let me know what a legend you are in these parts." She paused to see if he would react but he didn't speak, "Rumours ran wild about you working for the Abwehr or the SS; indeed in some instances you were alleged to be a double agent."

"Oh, you are up to date with the latest. Is there anything else I should know?" The suddenness of hearing his voice respond caused Halle to stutter her answer, "A... A girl called Eileen has disappeared and the belief is she has been deposited in a concentration camp because she was a double agent. Again the rumours had it that she was passing information on to you."

"Sweet God; is it any wonder that everyone has been looking quizzically at me today. In fact I came over to see you to find out what the hell is going on. Now I know!"

"Then, what's the truth? Or better still, what part of it is?"

"Halle, the last thing I want is to get you involved. In fact I wouldn't be here now if I had known just what was in the air. With all this going on it's a certainty that I've been followed."

"They already know we're old working companions and they're aware that you recommended me to get the job at Irland-Redaktion. So, inevitably, they'll be watching me in any event; I suspect that they've been keeping an eye on me for a few weeks. The stories in work have been helpful from my point of view; in as much as they suggested a reason for what was going on. That place is a hotbed of suspicion—the Irish, in particular, are regarded with doubt as they show deep scepticism about the Nazi philosophy—as indeed are local Berliners."

"I think your last remark points to why I'm under a cloud." O'Driscoll took a packet of cigarettes from his pocket and quite deliberately took his time to remove one, place it between his lips, and lit it. "Now what I say next must be in total confidence—if I hadn't worked with you in Guernsey I wouldn't whisper a word of it." Again he paused for dramatic effect, a characteristic in him that Halle loathed, "I am due to go to Ireland in a few days time—don't ask me how—but with all this rubbish flying around it's put the whole thing in jeopardy. If you are approached tell them anything but that, admit we met tonight, talked over old times and were glad to see each other. Let them make fire from that smoke!"

When O'Driscoll left Halle sat down to consider the next steps she should take. Should she attempt to remain and make a full-time career for herself? The more she considered it the less she liked herself and anyway there was no guarantee they would renew her contract. Too many of the stories she heard, it must be said, away from work, indicated that the Nazis allowed no deviation from the party's philosophy. The morality of imprisoning all opposed to them seemed bad enough but when one considered where would they find the space or the manpower to control that number of prisoners the mind boggled.

Regarding her own position, she felt that she had to remain as long as O'Driscoll was in danger; if she left at this point there would be a suspicion that the pressure on O'Driscoll was based on assumptions which were correct. "No, I'll hang on until a decision is clearly taken."

Two days later Sheila told her that she had seen Ryan, a former leading member of the IRA in the early '30s, and that he looked ill. "But the word was that he and Russell had returned to Ireland to organise a new campaign." Sheila looked askance at Halle, "You know I never believed that story. As it is there are too many spymasters in Berlin and their propaganda ploys are such that they each claim they're responsible for each and every success, imagined or real. You know that the Foreign Department thinks it has control of propaganda here but we know that Goebbels has his finger in most pies. But, then again, the Abwehr and the SS are too involved in politics to see the full picture on any front. There is a genuine maze in this city and it has nothing to do with hedges."

"Then who do you think O'Driscoll's with?"

"Personally I've always thought of him as being with the Abwehr but the stories about him are legend and on that basis I wouldn't venture a halfpenny. You know him best—the best guess in here is that you and him are lovers—*what* do you think?"

"Let me make one thing clear first; you and whoever couldn't be farther from the mark regarding O'Driscoll and me, OK?" Sheila's smiling eyes and shrug of the shoulders could have meant anything but Halle decided to let it go. "Apart from that you'd get more speech out of a dead duck than you'd ever get out of O'Driscoll."

"Halle, I was genuinely surprised by your question. Personally I didn't think you were lovers because you're so religious but I thought you were close. I'm sorry but all I have are rumours and you know the score there!"

"Indeed I do! Half the stories put about are from people interested in feathering their own nests."

"Exactly. And there are others like myself, if they are asked a question will swear to whatever you want, provided that you make it out that they are one of the few totally loyal supporters of Hitler in this organisation. I'm easily bought!" and she gave a staccato burst of laughter that merely added to Halle's discomfiture about the situation.

"Why am I so tied in knots over this issue?" thought Halle once Sheila had departed. "I've said to others it's because I worked with him but is there more to it than that? Do I fancy him or what?" However, the longer she contemplated Sean O'Driscoll as a partner for life the less she liked it. His mannerisms and attitudes had a way of antagonising her, and his superior air didn't help the situation.

The day passed unproductively as she was unable to come to terms with all that Sheila and O'Driscoll had told her. Her mind turned back to Ireland and the continuing story of Ryan and Russell. In spite of what Sheila had said she believed that the original story was correct—they were bound for Ireland—but each one she spoke to had a different version of why they were going. The longer she speculated on them the more it dawned on her that she was deliberately changing her thought patterns to stop herself thinking about O'Driscoll.

She had never met Ryan, although she had heard of his daring do in the Civil War at home and that he had left the IRA because they weren't sufficiently left wing for him. He then went to fight in Spain for the Republicans against the Nationalists but was captured by either the Italians or the Germans who were fighting on Franco's side. Clearly someone saved him for a purpose; no Nazi would want to help a supporter of the left wing Government in Spain. "I wonder did Russell put in the good word?" thought Halle, "After all they fought side by side at one time and while Ryan was an internationalist and Russell was solely concerned about Ireland, nevertheless old ties don't break that easily. Or do they? What was the Civil War but a breaking of ties? In any event where did Russell spring from, the last I heard he was collecting money in the USA, so how did he get here?" She concluded there were no answers just many mysteries.

During the next few days each time Halle attempted to catch Sheila's eye it seemed that her friend looked right through her. Even when it came to actual work their conversations were limited to the details of the job on hand. "Something's going on," thought Halle as her world of propaganda and espionage was breaking up and she hadn't a notion as to the cause. At the first opportunity she would stay behind and catch Sheila before she left the premises to see what was going on.

In the interim Halle's article on Britain and its activities on the African continent pleased Menske and he asked her to concentrate in the coming weeks on Kenya and Uganda. However, the evidence wasn't easy to obtain as the Germany library in the building had little or nothing on these two countries. Halle thought seriously of writing to her friends in Dublin to get them to send on information—but she realised the time it would take would be much too long for Menske to wait patiently. She reported the dilemma she was in to Menske and he said he would try to find the material but in the meantime she could undertake researching India and the British presence there—there certainly was enough reading on this topic for her to begin her work.

One evening while reading over an account of Gandhi's constant imprisonment because of his persistent support for the campaign of civil disobedience she recalled Roger Casement's trial for betraying 'his country'. She thought of his attempt to recruit captured Irish soldiers to fight for the German Army in the Great War and she came to a halt: "Now there is a great idea! Not that the prospects are great of recruiting men for the eastern front but it would give her an opportunity to travel to a variety of POW camps in Germany, and more importantly, from her point of view, Poland. Closeness to any of the ports on the Baltic would give her a way out via

Sweden!" Suddenly full of enthusiasm she rapidly finished the first part of her story on Gandhi and proceeded to put together her suggestion for recruiting troops.

The following day Menske was not impressed with her idea and she could see that he was struggling to recollect where he had heard this idea before. She wasn't there to enlighten him but she merely wanted to be able to say that she kept her superior informed. From the objections raised by Menske she rewrote a large section of the proposal which took her two evenings to finish and she finally posted it to the Army Command Headquarters, not far from their office in Berlin.

A week passed before Halle saw O'Driscoll again and this time she paid even more attention to his looks and mannerisms in an attempt to see what lay behind her concern. As soon as he started to talk she knew he had no interest in her other than as a shoulder to cry on. "This is moving much too slowly; I'll never get to Ireland at this rate."

"Surely they wouldn't have put in so much time on you and then be uncertain about your allegiance?"

"It seems that to be diligent and concerned to do well is not a good sign. Double agents, seemingly, are much more anxious to pick up every detail and just because I'm the conscientious kind I've drawn attention to myself. But change is in the air."

"Sean, I'm more concerned about how you really feel about all these philosophies that seem to be pedalled on a daily basis. Are the Army and the SS playing with the same deck of cards; for example is the German Foreign Department trying to do a deal with the Allies so that they can control mainland Europe, in other words letting the Brits off the hook? Where do the SS stand in regard to all this? Are they there just to chase the Jews out of Germany and all the other odds and sods to work as slave labour..."

"Give us a chance to answer," answered O'Driscoll reverting to the vernacular, "or at least say I don't know. Oh, by the way when did I become Sean after months of being O'Driscoll?" Halle felt her face burning and tried to hide her embarrassment with another attempt at getting information because she was sure this was O'Driscoll's way of avoiding the question. "What rôle is the Abwehr playing in all of this?"

"Look Halle I am no information centre, all I can say is, ignore all the rumours. The sooner they die down the sooner I'm away. Everything has been sorted out to both their satisfaction and mine."

"Whose satisfaction?" enquired Halle in a quiet voice.

"Both Admiral Carnaris and von Ribbontrop, the Foreign Minister, will that do?" Halle nodded silently, this man was powerful and if everyone in the Rundfunkhaus spoke to her tomorrow she would simply stick out her tongue and shout, "Ra! Ra!"

"You still haven't answered the main question Sean, about your politics."

"Look, I'm not a political animal at all. Back home when O'Donnell and the others tried pushing a left wing agenda I went with the others who wanted country first, politics second and that's where I stand."

Halle tried to hide the look of disappointment from her face. "She must have travelled a long way," said one of her voices to the other. "Close to being a traitor, I think," responded the second. "She's still prepared to fight for Ireland, isn't she?" queried her first voice. "I don't know, I think she's putting conditions on it."

"But why?"

"I think Sean touched a nerve there. Wasn't it Aquinas who said there was no such animal as an apolitical one? Who ever it was, was right!"

Halle shook the troublemakers from her mind, knowing all too well they'd be back. "Any word Sean on when you're leaving?" Reluctantly O'Driscoll told her he would be gone by the end of the following week. He emphasised, once again, on no account was she to divulge this to anyone, as he was afraid the Allies had people planted in every government organisation in Berlin. Halle accepted the kiss on each cheek when he left, feeling particularly hypocritical on this occasion but refused to acknowledge hers voices telling her it was a Judas kiss.

Knowing O'Driscoll's miserliness with words she knew that when he said something it had significance. The deliberate warning about Allied spies was not merely to cover his own back but to warn her to be careful not to be making comments of the kind she had made to him. Yet he knew from their casual conversations that the only person she had any dealings with was Sheila—was he saying that Sheila was the plant? "My God, what next?"

She needed to analyse his statement further, what precisely did he say: 'he was afraid the Allies had people planted in Berlin', it was something like that anyway. Halle considered this remnant of O'Driscoll's statement and decided that it was too flimsy to start drawing conclusions about Sheila. She would say nothing whatever about O'Driscoll to her and see what happened next.

The next morning after less than four hours sleep, Halle realised she had to go soon. Too much was happening and if she weren't careful she would be in the front line of suspicion. All night she considered the recent change in attitude of Sheila: "What was going on? Did she have an inkling that she was suspected of being a double agent? If so, is she trying to avoid me in order that she doesn't drag me down with her? Perhaps she thinks I can help her but unless she says outright what she wants I'm washing my hands off her. No, I won't help her, she's a British agent... At least if my interpretation of O'Driscoll's words is correct... it's all supposition, I'll have to stop thinking like this! More importantly I need an idea that will give me the chance to escape and at the same time look as if I'm still involved with them."

As the day progressed she became more despondent. Sheila had not appeared; apparently she had reported sick first thing in the morning and had gone home. "I'll have to go and see her but I haven't her address and I daren't ask for it in here." Her mind went berserk at her suggestion and a second voice claimed that she was seeking the coward's way out by 'luckily' not having a notion where Sheila lived. Back at work again Halle couldn't concentrate on the item she had been given nor could she find an answer to the most pressing problem—how can she get out of Germany in one piece? Apart from the obvious need to get away she was also conscious that her contract was close to its end and that was putting more pressure on her to deal with the situation in a hurry. The more she thought on it the more difficult it became—maybe one idea wouldn't be enough; what she needed where two ideas which could be combined into a reasonable proposal to put to Menske or his immediate supervisors.

Sheila was missing for a week and on the following Monday Halle determined to find out what was the matter if she didn't turn up, even if it meant asking for her address from Menske. There had been quite a number of people leaving because of the arduous nature of the work but others left for a variety of reasons; from marriage to babies, to promotion in Luxembourg or of movement to England Redakation. Halle didn't think any of these situations applied to Sheila but she could be wrong—the nagging doubt created by O'Driscoll still bothered her. By the late afternoon Halle had lost her nerve and postponed asking for Sheila's address. And about an hour before finishing she received a memo, as did the rest of the staff, asking employees to contact their immediate supervisor if they knew of anyone Irish who would be suitable for employment. Almost instantly Halle had an idea which she decided needed some polishing before going to management.

Halle thought that there were enough Irishmen for the purpose in the POW camps and someone, like herself, should be sent out to recruit a few for the Propaganda Ministry. After submitting the idea she was sent for within a few days and a group of five officials interviewed her. The idea was well received but from the questioning it was clear they wanted people from the officer classes. An unhappy choice as far as Halle was concerned as she knew their POW camps were, in the main, in Germany, a less than useful place from which to attempt to escape. At the conclusion they thanked her for the suggestion and said they would give the matter thought and if she had any further ideas, which would be of use to the Third Reich, they would give them consideration.

That afternoon she went to see Menske about Sheila and he appeared pleased that she was concerned for her colleague and willingly gave her Sheila's address. She lived not too far away from work on Friedrichstrasse one of the luxury parts of the old city. Halle wasn't at all certain she was doing the right thing but at least she was covering her trail. At least she thought by doing it this way—in the open, going to Menske—she will have shown them that she didn't know Sheila all that well or she would have known her address. But as O'Driscoll had said: 'to be diligent and concerned to do well is not a good sign. Double agents are much more anxious to pick up on every detail'. "Could I have unintentionally drawn attention to myself by doing it this way? O'Driscoll knew what way they thought, no doubt they'll jump to conclusions similar to the way I did when O'Driscoll gave me the impression that it was Sheila who is spying for the British. I still think I'm right about that but just in case she is ill I'll call."

Knocking produced no response but when she finally found a doorbell, Sheila came to ask who it was and she was delighted to see Halle but her anxiety was too obvious to be overlooked. "What did they say in the office?" began Sheila. "Oh, they are concerned that you are still ill and are wondering are you receiving the right kind of attention." Halle repeated Menske's words as best she could remember them. Sheila brightened with the news but Halle couldn't control her fears. "Look Sheila, I am about to make a fool of myself and if what I say makes no sense I want you to promise me that you'll forget everything I say. OK?"

"Whatever you are going to say, don't say it here. I'll get dressed and we can go for a walk. Is that fine with you?" Halle was slightly taken aback but agreed to go along with it. Once out of doors Sheila walked briskly and when she saw a tram a few metres away encouraged Halle to run and they caught it. Whether Sheila knew the direction it was going was beyond Halle but it soon turned and she found it passing her own apartment. "Can we go in?" asked Sheila and when Halle nodded added, "It will be safer talking there."

Sheila walked into the building with an air of someone glad to get home.

No looking up and down the street, nor sense of anxiety exuded from her. Halle rushed to be in front of her to open the door and to avoid standing in the corridor. Once they were inside and seated Sheila asked Halle to speak frankly. For a moment Halle could feel herself lose the plot, what should she say? So much of what concerned her was speculation that it would be insulting to even contemplate telling anyone not alone Sheila. She could see that the delay was leaving Sheila upset. "Look, don't be upset at what I am about to say it's just that I want to warn you that if I suspect some things on the basis of putting two and two together and making twenty-two there are others in the Rundfunkhaus who will get it to make four."

"For God's sake don't keep me in suspense—just give me what you think and I'll be as honest as I can." Halle detailed her suspicions without involving O'Driscoll, claiming that she overheard a head of department saying that there was a spy network working in Berlin which involved foreigners and asking German members of staff to be particularly careful not to let everyone see papers marked 'Confidential'. "But why are you selecting me—there are a number of French, Czech, Poles and Irish there?"

"You and me have been friendly for some months and naturally I was worried about you more than the others. Neither of us are Nazis, that I'm sure of and when I started thinking about this it suddenly struck me that you have been avoiding me recently and when I weighted the probabilities I was convinced you were trying to keep me from being arrested. So all told it seemed to me that the more likely explanation is that you're the one they are looking for. Are you?"

"Halle, I was determined to admit to nothing but your logic is so penetrating that I couldn't convince you, so in essence you're right. From your expression, when you arrived at my apartment this afternoon, I thought this is it, they have had Halle in and hauled her over the coals."

Sheila's openness confused Halle causing her to reconsider her feelings, "Surely I can't be glad to have warned off a British agent," thought Halle, and worse, she wasn't going to be parsimonious with the information she had. But on reflection she realised she had better be careful about O'Driscoll's part in all of this. "Why, oh why do I think of telling things to people who are a danger to me? What do I want, praise or admiration?"

Sheila, almost by way of recompense, told Halle that she had been warned to avoid the Irish girl because she was an active terrorist. Halle was more interested in hearing Sheila admit to being a British agent but got the shock of her life when Sheila said the Canadians had infiltrated her into France. On the Canadians hearing how the French resistance had disposed, or more accurately, executed a man attached to the National Socialists they had put

Sheila in as the grieving 'widow' with a cover story that Halle already knew. "The clever part was making the Germans think they had accidentally killed the man and therefore owed me a debt which is how I got the job in Berlin, on my 'husband's' credentials."

"What have you to do with Canada, you're English, aren't you?"

"Yes, my real name is Sheila Gray and I'm English by birth but my people emigrated to Toronto when I was ten. Back there I speak like a native, French and English, sorry I mean like a Canadian, but I can turn on my English accent at the drop of a hat."

"What is your married name then?"

"It's Gourmont; but I'm surprised you didn't know it."

"I meant to ask you because I never heard you called by it… but… what do you think you did that drew their attention?"

"I was warned that they were on to me. Apparently some of my so-called husband's relatives turned up. This is where the Canadian boys slipped up they were convinced he had none. They became suspicious when the Germans talked of his wife and eventually they told the authorities in Paris that he was a homosexual and there was no way he could ever have married. Of course when I heard this I decided to distance myself from you."

"Thanks for that. Myself, I'm desperate to get out but *you* need to get out of Berlin now!"

"I have set the wheels in motion. The less you know the better for your sake. Don't worry I'll be gone in a day or two. But what have you in mind?" Halle told her about waiting for a decision regarding her idea for Irish recruits to help her get out of the country. "How much chance is there of them going for it?" asked Sheila. "I think they'd go for it if it was their last hope of getting anyone and besides they are looking for officer types only and that wouldn't suit me."

"How do you mean? Surely you're not biased against officers, are you?"

"No, of course I'm not! Nearly all their camps are in Germany and that's no good to me."

"Good luck anyway, I hope your idea comes off and you can find some way out. Oh, by the way, I have a 'flu if they're asking, OK? I'm off, I have a hell of a lot to do still, that's why I had to take time off to get everything organised."

"I hope you get away without any difficulty—and for God's sake be careful. The best of luck—I nearly said, 'The best of British'—which would never have done!" Sheila laughed in acknowledgement of Halle's joke at such a time. Halle left her to the door and peered out to see if the coast was clear before signalling to Sheila to make her move.

It took ten days before they informed her that they had been able to fill the vacancies from the names submitted by members of the staff, so they would not be going ahead with her suggestion. On the same day it was announced that Sheila had been found dead in her apartment from some form of cancer. The shock nearly destroyed Halle—according to the report she had been dead for some time, the best estimate they could give was a fortnight at the earliest. Clearly none of the circumstances added up and Halle concluded that they had found Sheila and simply eliminated her, as they had been known to do to others.

Menske came to pass his condolences to Halle and the rest of the staff, and to announce that the funeral would be on the following Friday. Halle wondered at the supposed length of time taken to bury Sheila but apparently in the circumstances the time was not considered long.

The funeral was in the cemetery near where Sheila lived and was in the manner befitting an official of the National Socialist movement. A deputy from Goebbels' office, representing him and another representing von Ribbentrop were also present as were all those staff not on duty. A eulogy was given by Menske who referred to her work in the department and the regard with which she was held. Halle was thoroughly upset by the whole proceedings knowing the falseness of all those allegedly speaking from the heart. How she put up with the condolences being offered she didn't know but it took some deep gulps of air into her lungs to survive the actual lowering of the coffin into the grave. That evening, on returning to her apartment, she found a letter from the Army awaiting her. It was an invitation to come to their offices to talk over the matter in some detail. She prepared herself with a great deal of care, even asking Menske what he thought were the weaknesses of the scheme. It appeared he was more concerned about losing her than about obtaining volunteers for the army. "You would be very difficult to replace; indeed almost impossible as there are so few 'real' Irish people in Berlin. But why are you so desperate to get out?"

"I'm certainly not trying to get out," replied Halle attempting to retain her equanimity while telling a lie, "Indeed I'm anxious for promotion and the cash… As I see it this is a way to revitalise the Army on the Eastern Front. European history echoes with Irish regiments which fought on many battle fronts, particularly if the English were the enemy."

"That's the second time you have mentioned something from Irish history when talking to me. It sounds as if you are telling these 'new' facts which are unknown to me and you know as well as anyone in this department that I taught history in Ireland before I returned. So why do you do it? Do you think that Irish history belongs solely to the Irish?"

89

"In effect I think everyone, of whatever country, believes their country's history *is* their private property—particularly if they are naturally patriotic… Why, don't you feel that way?"

"Of course I do but did you think I was a dry stick of an academic—nothing affects me? Do you imagine all those years studying and teaching Irish history, sometimes through the medium of Irish language, would leave me cold? Fraulein Hegel you really don't know the German people!"

Halle couldn't think of a suitable answer having always associated him with the description given of Berlin by Goebbels in 1926 when he was sent there by Hitler, "A monster city of stone and asphalt." She was relieved when he suddenly turned back to his work and left her to see herself out of his office. In spite of his many years in Ireland she wondered at his use of 'Fraulein' in addressing her. Some weeks back Sheila had assured her it never happened to other foreigners. So what was his point—was she an accepted member of the world-wide German Family in spite of her sallow skin and brunette hair? Whatever was going on in Menske's mind she wanted to be detached from it immediately.

The interview went particularly well and a confident Halle left the room fairly sure that they would be in touch in the near future. During the following week a number of people remarked on her ability to recover after the death of her friend. Halle, in an attempt to keep her cover secure, said that while she was fond of Sheila she didn't regard her other than as a fellow-worker having little contact with her outside of the office. She knew there was some puzzlement at her reply but it was the best she could think of in the circumstances. What concerned her more was the sudden death of Sheila—she knew in her heart that the story was a figment of someone's imagination, they either killed her or they failed to stop her getting away. If she was a betting person she would have favoured the latter given the time they said she died was well in advance of the last time she had been with her. Or was that a concoction to cover Sheila's murder?

Two days after the interview she received word in a letter to return to the Army's office for a final confirmation on the details of her appointment. The letter went on to state that she would be regarded as acting Colonel, Oberst in German, for the purposes of pay and any future promotion. The actual details of visits to camps would be agreed on her suggestions, which they hoped would be settled to both sides satisfaction. Halle knew this would be the first step on her road to freedom and provided that she had the good sense not to rush to the first port she would be echoing the title of Christopher Isherwood's recent novel, *Goodbye to Berlin*, very shortly.

CHAPTER 5
(March 1941-April 1942)

THE POSEN GUARDS were not particularly pleasant when they were escorting Ian back to the camp and he was thrown into solitary confinement immediately. Next morning he was dragged before the Commandant and given an opportunity to explain himself and his behaviour. He had nothing to say and he was given seven days solitary by way of a warning. No one felt as foolish as he did, even the guy waiting to go in for his punishment looked serene as if his offence was well worth while. Still, "you must be out to be in with a shout" was a cry of many of the escapees who were dragged back. "Out" was a relative term in his case, fifty yards at most; there was something disgusting about having this on his record as an escape.

The cell he was allocated was decidedly less than 'solitary'. "I suppose on the ordinary run of things it would be pretty deserted but they appear to be doing plenty of business." Ian was thankful that so many men were trying to get back to the ranks of the Allies. Getting away from Posen was important, not in the mere notion of escape but in as much as the Germans would have to organise a wholesale search. German troops would be tied up, who otherwise would have been fighting elsewhere—not that he knew where 'elsewhere' was, or indeed if there were any forces still opposing that pulverising machine called the German army.

There was plenty going on in this part of the prison, whistling, singing, cheering, booing anything that would put the guards' nerves on edge—"I wonder do these guys ever think of the other inmates' nerves? It must be pleasant here when there's peace and quiet." Of course he was wrong because as it grew dark and the troublemakers retired for the night he found he couldn't clear his head sufficiently to enable him to sleep.

The seven days were a new form of eternity, something for which his faith in God had made no allowance. His prayers became more erratic and unsure. For the first time in his life he had doubts about the existence of God—surely He wouldn't deliberately let people die at the whim of an arch dictator; yet he had seen bodies of dead troops and in some instances of civilians.

His earlier certainty about the reasons for men escaping now started to desert him, "They are out to get away because they can't stand the idea of being captive for years and years. Yet yesterday I was putting forward the

91

idea that the men were keeping the Germans busy trying to recapture them and so helping the war effort. Imagine being taken in by propaganda of such a dismal kind. The Germans would have troops allocated to all these areas so what the hell was all this about 'tying up troops'?"

Significantly he accepted that he was on his own and if he used the brains that God had given him that should be his greatest asset; that plus his wish to be free to get home. His doubt wasn't long lasting but he was aware that this wasn't going to be the only time he would be visited by the devil tempting him to doubt "the Lord his God" and he prayed that the Lord would look after him in the coming battle.

On his release into the main camp Ian thanked God for the light of day; that had been the one item he missed most of all. Once he had adjusted to the eerie silence at night he regarded it as a luxury, which lulled him to sleep. How the others persisted with their noises all day long was beyond him and aggravated him the whole time. He made his way to John's hut on his release and he appreciated John's obvious pleasure at seeing him whole and as strong as he had been when going in. "Not too many come out of there unscathed," and as he spoke there was the sound of a fight right outside his window. "Come away Ian, it's that mad Irishman at it again." In spite of the warning Ian opened the window to survey the scene, "What do you mean 'again'?"

"Well he's no sooner out of solitary than he goes to the nearest guard and thumps him and back he goes again. What he is about I've no idea, but there are rumours that he is determined to get out of here by passing himself as mentally defective."

"What do you think?"

"Those southern bastards are mental anyway, we always claimed they were and here's the proof."

"What if he is fighting the battle here in his way? Could you accept that?"

"No, I'd always be suspicious that they were up to no good."

"I'd be the same except that I once met a man, the worse for drink, who told me he had enlisted in the UVF at the start of the Great War when he was fourteen, passing himself off as being sixteen. At the Somme his division were crucified and a big man from the Connacht Rangers saved him, and even though he was as full as a lord he said he would never let anyone run down southerners again."

"So you're taking 'southerners' to mean Mickeys or Fenians or more precisely Roman Catholics?"

"Of course I am but it doesn't mean I believe the likes of those who lived in our street when we were young."

"For example?"

"I'll give you one, Halle Hegel!"

"You'll never get over the mess she made of your face, will you?"

"There's more to it than that, she was a vile bitch even as a child."

"Can't you be honest for once, she changed your looks dramatically and you owe it all to her! I wonder whatever became of her?"

"I'll ignore your slagging about looks. I wonder at times where she is. The odds are that she will be married by now with a brood of children—as is commonplace among the Roman Catholics determined to outbreed us."

"Yet there was something about her determination and lack of fear that spoke volumes about her as a person."

"Do you think so? You're sending me up aren't you? Probably she's as fat as a pig with a mouth on her that could swallow whales."

"I can see that you've not been affected by her—not much!"

"Can we leave this subject alone now? You know I've been tortured about her since the day she kicked the wheel of my bicycle from under me and that face of mine, you're always referring to it, got damaged irreparably."

"OK you've been through enough, I'll give it a rest. Tell me has the solitary confinement cooled your ardour any?"

"You mean about escaping? No I'm more determined than ever; what about you, have you given it any thought?"

"The more I think about it the more I'm convinced I'll stay here and survive the war—them's my religious beliefs. How do you like those apples?" replied John with a malevolent grin on his face.

"You do whatever you feel you can live with, personally I think at the rate of deprivation of food we'll be lucky to survive another year. I suppose if the Red Cross could pull up their socks life here would improve immeasurably but the Germans would hardly allow us to have better rations than their own people, would they?"

"Do you think that the Germans are short of grub? They don't look it compared to the men in here."

"But they can supplement their diet with things like apples and beer as well as pears, grapes and wines. I wouldn't say no to any of those."

"Well you're hardly likely to get any of those in here, are you?"

"No, but I'll be alive when the armies on both sides toss their hands in."

"Don't hold your breath, I'm going again at the first opportunity—I'm not waiting to join the escape committee's list. I've heard all the arguments about making it easier on the ones that go because they'll receive all the specialist help; and if there is only a few go each year the Germans won't be on their toes, giving our fellows a better break in getting all the way home. How long must I wait to get a chance? Too long for me."

"Be realistic, once the first signs of winter arrives you know it's damn near impossible to travel anywhere on the continent. Why not put your name down and prepare to go all the way."

"I intended to be out of here by the end of '42. I couldn't see that happening at the rate of one every few months. If I was a gambling man I'd take odds that someone will get away before the officially approved candidate gets over the wire."

"By the time your man's back here you'll have changed your mind and joined the queue, even if it means sometime towards the end of '43. You've too much sense to do what you did again in that field last week. Stupid you aren't but woefully pig-headed you are. Make a promise here and now that you'll think this over for a few months before making a move."

"OK, you've convinced me that this needs time and thought, so that's what I'll do."

In the next few weeks Ian made a friend, an unexpected one at that. The guard was a Pole who had been claimed by the Germans as he lived in the German occupation zone. Occasionally Ian had come across him while he was working on a nearby farm. Apparently being a local he was often the one selected to accompany the prisoners to work. After a few days the prisoners were used to him coming round to complain that they were not producing enough and that they had to keep up with the cart that collected the produce otherwise other sections were getting very long rests. Ian and John, who were in the same group, soon twigged that the best method of achieving long rests was to work flat out so that the cart would be able to leave them earlier than the others. Consequently, when they reached the next section the cart was held up while they waited for the prisoners to fill it. Of course Ian plus the others used to throw their hands in the air, shouting, "Oh Lord have mercy on our backs!" an irony that didn't escape the others. When the cart returned, after delivering each load to the barn, they cried out, "Here it comes again! Is there no rest for the wicked?"

The Polish guard spoke English poorly but he managed to convey to Ian how frightened he was to be wearing a German uniform. "What I do when Ruskies come?" Ian and John taught him a series of sentences in English and when he asked them why English they explained that the British would be there first, this with a great deal of tongue in cheek. But they cruelly had him repeating expressions like, "Me in SS, me good soldier." At the time it never dawned on them that there could come a day when the guard would see either Russian troops or any Allied ones. The man was convinced that if he knew sufficient English he would be able to surrender to whatever army came on the scene.

Ian didn't forget his promise to John to apply to be considered as a possible candidate for escape; it was the onset of winter before he reconciled himself to await the committee's say-so and help. He asked them to help him get away no later than April '43. But the best possible date to allow them time to finish a tunnel, they were presently working on, and to prepare clothes, passports, travel documents and enough money to buy the sundry items that would keep him alive was July. The look on his face when he was informed of the situation should have been enough to indicate that he would go at his first opportunity.

The committee expected that each person, having their names listed, should be working alongside the others who were involved in the various projects, which were required for each prisoner. Ian volunteered to work on the tunnel and spent up to four hours a day on two shifts but by winter fatigue became a familiar problem for all the tunnel workers as the food shortages started to affect their condition and fitness for the work. Consequently, the work slowed almost to a halt and when the weather was at its worst, in the depths of winter, they had to stop altogether.

The slowness of the whole operation left Ian feeling irritable most of the time. John was constantly being berated for failing to put his name forward, "If there were two going together I'm sure that we would be close to the top of the list by now," complained Ian. "Anyway you should be volunteering to help the committee regardless of whether you're interested in going or not." John had reached the point where he simply shrugged his shoulders each time Ian made an issue out of it. By early spring John kept out of Ian's way and spent most of his spare time playing cards for the money they had earned during the summer working for the local farmers.

At the first sign of the weather changing for the better Ian was constantly attacking the committee to get someone away as soon as possible. But they wouldn't budge from their set formula: "As soon as everything's ready will be soon enough." Ian wasn't prepared to wait and knew the first chance he got would be his opportunity. In early spring he felt the first stirring of a toothache and the camp medical attendant got permission from the Commandant to send him into the nearest dentist for attention. The first trip on the lorry was used by Ian to look at the lay of the land. A railway line passed behind the dentist's surgery and he noticed a level crossing some one hundred metres to the right of the premises. The only train he saw during two visits was a goods train, which slowed appreciably at the level crossing and took some time to pick up speed after it. There was a two-week interval between visits, which Ian used to obtain information from the committee about the directions and the likelihood of destinations that the trains would take. The third visit presented the best prospects of an escape as the guard who travelled with him relied on the dentist to keep a watch on Ian. On the previous occasions Ian had to wait outside the surgery door while a local was attended and on average they took about half an hour. The rear door was often used by the dentist's assistant and Ian thought he could make it to the level crossing without being spotted and if a train passed within fifteen minutes of his leaving the surgery he could make good his escape.

At the surgery everything worked in his favour, he was happy enough to be on his own and once he felt the fresh air on his face he heaved a sigh of contentment. However, the hoped for train didn't materialise and he knew he would be back in the camp before he became accustomed to freedom. Rather than be caught red-handed he decided to return to the dentist's house. But half way along the line he heard the sound of a train braking as it slowed to cross the roadway, immediately he lay face down in the field and watched it slowly gain momentum before coming abreast of him. He jumped to his feet and propelled himself forward with as much force as he could muster and hurled himself into a wagon, which had its door open.

As the train passed from slow to medium fast back to slow and then very slow Ian wondered just what advantage it was to travel on this mode of transport. "Well I'm getting my rest, I suppose and no one saw me get on board and I'm going east towards Warsaw. Wouldn't it be nice if this went all the way to there! I suppose one can dream. On the other hand it's likely that they'll think of this train and arrange to have it stopped and searched at the nearest big town—I think once I get a night's sleep on it I'll make a move to leave."

Next morning the emptiness of the wagon and the lack of human companionship made him determine to check if there was any likelihood of food—a chicken, eggs or the like on board. Before starting his search he gazed out of the doorway wondering if the train was still heading east. His sense of direction had been impaired by the persistent changing down of the train as it slowed going over the points. "Was it simply going over one set of lines to another or was it crossing from one track to another which was going in a different direction?" Ian considered the options and ruled out a change of direction. Now he was convinced that this was a runaway train. The thought really got to him and it took him a long time to deduce that he was crazy. "Sure the train slowed each time it changed track or whatever it was doing, so someone must be at the controls. Yet it never stops, why?" Ian was perplexed and he proceeded to add to his difficulties: "And how empty is empty? How hungry do you get before you die?" Curiously the issue of 'emptiness' caused the last point to become the prime mover and consequently fired his determination to find something to eat.

A large man came hurtling into the wagon and Ian jumped to one side fearful that he would be hurt. Instantly Ian knew he had nothing to fear from the man himself, as he was black, "Where in the name of God did you come from?" The man rolled over; "Give's a chance to catch my breath." He lay still for a moment obviously as much aware of how little danger Ian offered him, as Ian had been conscious of how little threat emanated from him.

"I only got aboard this wagon in a search for food—you got any?"

"Strangely I was about to do the rounds looking to see if there are any chickens, eggs—anything."

"Let's go, we can become acquainted later."

They clambered round the sides of the wagons taking a look in each one they passed; eventually they found a lone pig of massive proportions. "That's the beast I have been searching for," yelled the black man above the roar of the engine. He had all the strength one would imagine of an immensely strong man and he grabbed the pig and throttled it while it roared and pulled and rolled around the floor. Ian watched all this in astonishment and when the animal was eventually dispatched he felt there was no way he could possibly eat any of it. But when the American wrenched one of its legs off and handed it to him he felt a violent nausea yet within a few minutes he was eating the meat with a similar appetite as his black companion.

At the conclusion of their eating they pushed the remains of the pig into a corner and talked, "You were asking?" Ian looked up, "Yes, where did you come from?" The American said, "I'd better start at the beginning. My name is Jonah Wayne and I come from South Carolina. I've been a regular soldier for six years. I was captured in North Africa by Vichy French troops. Don't ask me how the hell I got to Poland, I can't really tell you. All I know is they handed me to the Germans, who were so anxious to separate me from the whites that they bungled my orders with so much gobbledegook I have been to places that I didn't know where on the face of the earth. I used to think the American Army were hell for segregation but they're not in the same class as these Nazis."

"Gobbledegook?—that's a new one on me."

"Means a hell of a lot of jargon!"

"How did you get away—a black man's easy to spot on this continent!"

"I just didn't give a damn, I'd had enough and I took it on the lam. You know what I mean? I escaped through the wire."

"I've seen probably too many pictures about jail breaks for my own good; Oh sorry, movies."

"We'll be at this all day, we'll say what we have to and if there's a query we can clear it up afterwards. As I was saying, I got through the wire simply because someone cut it in order to escape that night but I took advantage of the opening and did a runner."

The shock of meeting an American POW was one thing but a Negro was mind-blowing, especially one who was determined to escape despite all the disadvantages which stood in his way. It dawned on him that he hadn't seen a black man since he was a small boy in South Africa. "Where have you been in this war—and I don't mean your tour of Europe? Excuse me for being so blunt but I've been a prisoner for so long that I don't know what way the war is going."

Jonah told him of his experience in the North African campaign, which he constantly referred to as the 'Mid-East' and how Eisenhower's troops had been badly mangled by Darlan's Vichy French and he had been captured. The last he heard was from a recently arrived American soldier who said the allies had won a whole series of battles in North Africa.

Ian was overjoyed at the news because even if this escape was a vain attempt it meant that the duration of the war was likely to be a great deal less than John and his estimate. Nevertheless, he put the thought of defeat to one side and he convinced himself that the prospects of getting completely away were greater because the German civilians and those people in occupied countries would be less worried about harbouring an escaped prisoner of war.

Although Jonah's height and weight were a decisive factor in butchering the pig, Ian knew his lack of agility would prove a handicap once they had to leave the train and proceed on foot. Just how long it would be before the train touched on a 'large urban conurbation' as Jonah called a major town or city was beyond their ability to hazard at. Ian prayed that they would have a sufficient sight of what was ahead to enable them to get off before they were inside the city boundaries. His biggest fear was that they may be dozing and wake up in the arms of the Gestapo instead of the arms of Morpheus. When Ian explained his concern Jonah agreed that they should do a rota during the night hours.

However, the precautions weren't necessary because they saw the city long before the train reached the city's suburbs and as soon as it slowed they decided to jump off but only after they disposed of the pig's carcass. Jonah's effort to dismount was awkward and he twisted his ankle and Ian, with the best will in the world, knew there was no way he could help him make any worthwhile distance. They discussed what they should do and they agreed that if Ian could help Jonah as far as the roadway that would be sufficient. The local peasants or the Germans would find him and he would be helped beyond anything that Ian could manage.

Once this was agreed they concocted a story, which excluded killing the pig, but insisted that they had been alone the entire time. Jonah was the author of this as he claimed that his experience, having tried on three occasions, told him that the Germans would try to suggest that there was some connivance going on between them and they would be questioned for days on end. Inevitably the sense of this was that they part and Ian should put some distance between himself and his friend in case they were captured near by. For all of his common sense Ian felt that it was less than Christian to leave a man lying on the road and trust that a Good Samaritan would turn up.

Once Ian had changed his mind it was difficult to make him re-change it. Jonah tried and although he did not go blue in the face he soon gave up. "You know they're going to put the both of us through hell, so why not go on?" Ian said that the only way he would make an effort to get away was if he saw a German patrol coming and was sure that they were picking Jonah up.

They sat by the side of the road for the better part of half an hour chatting about what would be the outcome of whatever happened in the next few hours. It ranged from imprisonment for life to a fortnight's solitary confinement depending on how pessimistic a view they took of the Germans' conspiracy theory, as applied to them meeting yet coming from different POW camps. It never dawned on them that any other possibility was on the cards, so that on seeing a haycart approaching from some distance away they were at a loss as to what action to take. Should Ian pull Jonah off the road and both of them hide until the cart had passed? Should he ask the driver for some help for Jonah? Was it possible that the man could find them someone from the resistance? The questions appeared to be endless but they had to quickly determine what they were going to do. Finally Jonah felt they should put the driver to the test by asking him for help. "What if he won't?" questioned Ian. "I'll kill him with my bare hands." Ian threw his hands up in despair, "That makes real sense!"

"Look, I'm only kidding. Say he won't have anything to do with us, the only one in danger is you because if he goes to the Nazis it looks like a real conspiracy to them and we'll both face the high jump. No, the best way is for you to hide in those bushes while I deal with him—no, I'm not going to kill him if he gives the wrong answers—I'll draw it out of him one way or another. God but you're jumpy; it's just an expression. You better get going I don't want him to suspect that there's two of us."

Ian slid on his stomach, propelling himself with his elbows and feet until he was out of sight. "We never took into consideration if the man can't understand English," he mouthed to Jonah. Jonah didn't turn but said, as if speaking to himself, "He'll understand me."

The cart came alongside the American and an elderly looking man said something to Jonah in Polish which Jonah clearly didn't understand and in turn Jonah, using a mixture of an odd word of German, Yiddish, Harlem gospel lyrics and an odd word of English completely confused the old man. Ian lay in despair and finally he decided to show himself and take a hand with some kind of sign language. Finally the man appeared to figure out that they were escaped prisoners, later Ian realised that the look of Jonah should have been sufficient to indicate that these men didn't belong to the indigenous people of Poland or Europe for that matter. With some help from Ian and the carter Jonah managed to bury himself in the hay while Ian conducted a conversation with him about where they were likely to end up. "Look why not accept the providence of God and see where it takes us? This is better than sitting on the road wondering what to do next once the Germans re-captured us."

"True, true but I don't want to be butchered by some of these gun happy resistance guys who suspect everyone is an enemy."

"Where, in the name of God, did you get that notion?"

"They, the escape committee, warned us to be careful who we got tied up with. They claimed that some of these guys were mad men, crazy with blood lust and revenge for whatever the Nazis had done to their families."

"It makes a kind of sense, but then beggars can't be choosers, can they? We're not in a position to do much else but ride along and see what comes up."

"Talking about what's coming up, why were you heading east on that train and just where were you coming from?"

"I was in a POW camp in Posen, the Poles call it Poznan, and I thought that I should try to get to Warsaw."

"Why? It seems like a long way from a seaport. Why didn't you go north, if I had been able to make a decision that's what I would have done."

"To be honest I was just going from place to place hoping to meet some resistance fighters who would point me in the right direction."

"We'd better give it a rest, the old man's becoming jittery."

The horse had been slowly walking on the country road prior to the addition of the two men, now it was literally dragging its heels and Ian knew if there was a large distance involved any passing German convoy or group of soldiers would realise they had something to hide. He yelled from his hiding place to the driver to stop. The horse and the driver seemed to be relieved as Ian got down. He tried to get some idea of the distance the man was going and with some more gesticulation on both their parts Ian concluded that it was only a matter of a couple more corners and they would be at his cottage or whatever it was he lived in.

Back in the hay Ian explained to Jonah that there wasn't far to go and got a mutter of either agreement or a soft snore from the giant. The horse waddled onwards taking its own good time and a seemingly unconcerned driver with time on his hands whistled continuously. Ian was in a state of apoplexy conscious that it was taking a lot longer than he had expected. Eventually he realised the cart had ceased to move but just how long it had come to a halt was hard to estimate. Ian called to Jonah, aware that the big man was probably still asleep and after a few loud words the American responded, "Yeah, what is it?" Ian was anxious that he didn't move too soon, "Don't move, the old fellow must be telling others about us and they are probably working out a method of dealing with the problem we have created for them."

"I hope they make up their minds soon, I need a lavatory quickly."

"Oh Lord, you'd better get down, can you manage?"

"Yeah, just about. You'd better tell them I've crawled to the field."

"OK, I'll do my best but how I'll do the actions... Wait a minute I'm getting out of this hay, its tickling places where I've never been tickled." Ian jumped from the rear of the cart just in time to see the Pole emerging from a wreck of a house with an elderly woman in his wake. The woman asked him in halting English where his black friend had gone. He explained how his friend needed to relieve himself and she explained this with much tittering to the man. "Where are you heading?" Ian considered lying because if the Nazis found them in the company of these elderly people the couple would probably be tortured. "I would prefer not to say because if the Germans traced you to us it could cost you your lives."

"But we can't help you unless we know where you want to go," explained the woman. "I can't speak for my friend, we are not together we happened to meet. I would like to get to Warsaw because I have an idea how to get out of the country if I get that far."

"Let me warn you, there are some terrible things going on there. People

101

here who have relatives there are frightened that they may have died in the fighting going on inside the city. Apart from that the British have bombed it a number of times because some of the refugees near here came because they were frightened for the life of their children and themselves."

"What do you suggest?"

"I don't know how you'd do it but go to Gdansk, or Danzig as the Germans call it, avoid Warsaw if you can."

Ian told Jonah that night what he had been told and he thought the suggestion made sense. "Jonah, I know you want to avoid towns and cities for obvious reasons but my gut feeling is for me to go into the areas of big population because I can lose myself in the crowds and also it is easier to find locals tied into the resistance movement."

"That's fine, there's no way I want to hold you up until I recover sufficiently and if these people can't hide me I'll just let the Germans catch me in such a place as to ensure nobody suffers because of their kindness."

"Tomorrow then I'm heading off to Warsaw, hopefully the old man will give me directions to the railway or knows someone going into the city who would be prepared to take me some of the way. I'll see you in the morning before I leave, that is if the good folk here don't give me the shove. Do you think they'll keep us in the house?"

"They would be mad if they did. Personally I would prefer to sleep in a barn, it's safer."

"There's no two ways about it, you're right but if they demand that we stay I'll go along with it."

"OK, as long as we both agree to stick with this."

Dinner that night was a type of thin potato stew, low on meat, high on water. Clearly the elderly couple, whose name was Kasprowicz, were depriving themselves in order to give sustenance to their two visitors. They wanted Ian and Jonah to spend the night sleeping in the cottage but Jonah insisted that he preferred a barn and, somewhat reluctantly, Ian followed suit.

Some time in the early hours Ian wakened to the sound of heavy vehicles drawing up and he immediately suspected that the Germans were raiding the place. He crept to Jonah's makeshift bed in the hay and gently woke him, whispering that they would have to make an effort to get out of the barn before the Germans searched it. Jonah was in no condition to get any distance but he was determined to avoid putting the couple in jeopardy, so he dragged himself out the back door and with Ian's help managed to get to the nearest ditch. They must have lay there the best part of an hour simply because the Germans' suspicions were aroused by the state of the hay and its disposition on the floor of the barn. Finally they left probably assuming that if there had been anyone there it was without the Poles' consent.

It was obvious, as the first light of dawn shone, that Jonah was in no fit state to continue. Ian asked Kasprowicz, through his wife's interpretation, to bring Jonah to a point that was constantly passed by German traffic, and they could safely assume that they would readily see the big man lying at the side of the road. The woman told them that undoubtedly the occupation forces would be back because they had been mighty suspicious the previous night. The anxiety of the Kasprowiczs for them to be gone grew by the minute as Ian and Jonah were fed before leaving. Poverty in the general area was obvious as they passed through the countryside and Ian concluded that the war wasn't the main contributor to their state of hunger. They sat openly on the cart, except that Jonah covered his head as if he was hurt, knowing that no one would put themselves out to report the matter to the Nazis.

When they reached the point that the Kasprowiczs had agreed was the best position for Jonah to be picked up by the Germans, they stopped the cart and Ian helped Jonah down from the back. They adopted the plan they had attempted to instigate the previous day. This time the cart was barely out of sight when a German convoy approached. Ian quickly departed for the nearby bushes and hid with relative ease, while the Germans brusquely arrested Jonah and heaved him aboard a large lorry carrying a few soldiers. Ian could hear the questioning and it went on until the convoy was out of earshot.

The next order of business for Ian was to find the railway track where the Kasprowiczs had earmarked a point where the train slowed sufficiently to enable Ian to mount without undue danger. They told him that it was about an hour's journey on one of the slow goods train but they were much safer than the passenger trains or the huge transport carriers, which were particularly well guarded.

Ian had to let two trains pass because he couldn't be certain that they were the trains to which the Kasprowiczs referred. The first goods train that he was completely certain about passed around mid-day as far as he could ascertain from the almost directly overhead sun. It appeared to take an eternity to get to what he assumed was Warsaw and as previously he dismounted prior to the train reaching the centre of the railhead.

Aleksander Kosciuszko was a name given to him by the escape committee to contact in Warsaw. He lived in 42 Franciszkanska near the Old Town Square but Ian was unable to ask directions and he had been warned that the Germans were in the process of renaming the streets, apparently reverting to the German street names of the 19th century. All Ian could do was pray that St. Francis would be kind and lead him to the correct door—"What tomfoolery am I indulging in now; Oh! What a pun! Is this getting too much for me or am I overcome with all the Roman Catholic symbols about the place?" Ian's obsession with the outward form was becoming a burden and he intended… no he was determined to put these things to the back of his mind. Still the number of churches, monasteries, convents and sacred statuary were well in excess of anything he had seen in Ireland, North or South.

Whether it was through intercession or a 'naturally' occurring miracle he didn't know, nor did he wish to speculate when he found the street and the door. He used the knocker to get attention and was taken aback by the suddenness of the door opening; a young woman said something in Polish but it meant nothing to him, "Aleksander Kosciuszko?" The girl was surprised and answered again in Polish, clearly it was a negative. His look of bewilderment must have solicited her sympathy because she beckoned him in. In strangled English she explained that her father was away and she didn't know when he would get back. Ian sensed that this was the end of the road for him but he put a brave face on it and thanked the girl and shook her hand by way of farewell. She asked him to call late the following evening when the light was "low" and he promised to return.

What to do in the meantime? He returned to the house and asked the girl for something to eat not that he intended to eat there and then but knew that if he could postpone eating until later he could manage another twelve hours of starvation. The girl apologised for her bad manners at not giving him something to eat but insisted that he left upon receipt of a sandwich. It was the sorriest sandwich Ian had yet seen but he knew that everything was in short supply and without a ration book he plainly would not survive.

He had passed a park on his way to Krakowskie Przedniscie, the centre of the Old Town, and he decided to make his way there and spend the night on a park bench, if it looked reasonably safe. Back at the entrance he saw that the park was called Krasinski Park and he made his way to the back of it to ensure that he would not be spotted from the outside by someone looking through the rails. It didn't take long before he was sound asleep and he was wakened by a clapper used by the warden to warn people that the park was about to close. He hid behind a large fern which fronted some trees and when the gates slammed shut he returned to his temporary bed for the night. Luckily the temperature was very mild and he slept every bit as well as he had done earlier.

Ian woke a number of times through the night disturbed by dreams of home. Each time he woke in a sweat after seemingly playing the largest

Lambeg drum ever made. Somehow he was in Templemore Avenue waiting for his father to finish the evening's proceedings with a speech when he was suddenly roped into playing the drum. It was huge to start with but each time he banged it with the large sticks or hit it with his knuckles the drum grew and grew. The nightmare was beyond him, he remembered the initial incident but the growth of the drum was incredible even in his imagination. He was not given to such occurrences but Daniel's interpretation of the dreams of Nebuchadnezzar came to mind as he tried repeatedly to interpret his own nightmare. Even the prophet's name with its associations with infallibility crossed his mind but what it suggested was beyond him.

The next morning he made his way back to Aleksander Kosciuszko's house to see if he could find it again that evening in the dark. His next preoccupation was to find food and after a day of searching had almost given up when he spotted a number of men, seemingly in the same position as himself, going to a house at the back of the Church of the Virgin Mary. Curiosity and hunger got the better of him and he followed.

Inside there were rows of tables and chairs with a longish table at the front where some men were ladling out what he suspected was soup with what looked like black bread. "If they are handing out poison to rid the world of Prods I'll take it," thought Ian. "I'm going to have to be a dumb person for the whole of my time here or I'm in even deeper trouble." He was served without difficulty and during the meal he had to endure a priest praying some kind of litany to which the men replied between mouthfuls of soup and bread. His mind went back to playing in the street as a boy and that hateful girl Halle calling him names. "Ah! That's one of the names she called me, 'a souper'. I often meant to find out just what she was on about. Maybe she was clairvoyant and could see that this was in store for me or, more likely, wishing it on me. There was something of the witch about her and, in spite of John's mocking me, I still think she was a special torment sent to torture the likes of me."

Ian's return to Aleksander Kosciuszko's house went without any incident of note but the rain began to fall and immediately, looking at the wet set-squares of the road, had a sense of home and family. It wasn't merely the looks, which brought those thoughts, it gave a sense of time placed—it was appropriate to the circumstances he was in—lost, wet and anxious. "Any little boy has known these feelings," his mind suggested, "Stop looking down, look up, can't you see the magnificence of the buildings, even those damaged have a look of something that has been achieved against the odds." His other voice was more declamatory—a plain, no nonsense Puritanism which found no appeal in the little rows of decorative bricks, and the naked woman in one of the designs was a disgrace! "Now Belfast, that's a beautiful place. None of your pseudo intellectualism about those buildings, none of that chit-chat about baroque, Byzantine, romantic or gothic, just practical brickwork done by competent hard working men."

"Wait a minute," began the opposition, "What about the City Hall, the Customs House, those lines of buildings on either side of Donegall Place—and what about that place in Howard Street with the sculptured heads of the famous? None of them are in balance with your claims of strait laced practicality, do they?"

"Sure you have to make allowances for all kinds of tastes—that's us, tolerant of all things democratic."

"Please! Don't give me your definition of democratic!"

"All right but you know what I'm fighting for here!" Almost simultaneously he reached the door in 42 Franciszkanska and he paused to look around to ensure there was no German police or soldiers lurking in some military lorry or car. "To be this close to help yet feel so uncertain about the outcome must be the most anxious moment of my life." He would have liked to analyse his feelings but the door opened and a middle-aged man, a little shorter than himself stood in the hallway. There were no conventional greetings; he merely beckoned Ian in. Inside the two women, including the young woman he had seen earlier that day, moved out to accommodate them.

Aleksander asked Ian to call him by his Christian name and bade him sit down. Ian was thankful that he had reached a haven of rest and told Aleksander just how glad he was to find him at home. The Pole encouraged Ian to relax and told him he would arrange transportation for him all the way to Gdansk. Once there he would meet Tadeusz Polonsky, a fisherman, who would see him across to Sweden. "How sweet it is when there is a place for food and shelter for a stranger," remarked Ian by way of thanks to this Pole who had barely enquired about his credentials. "But how did you know I was an escaped prisoner?" Aleksander gave a knowing smile, "Your thinness told me a lot and then that greyness in the face told the rest."

Ian smiled, "Your people are not exactly an advertisement for healthy living. Sorry, I shouldn't be so nasty. You've suffered enough and the recent bombing of the city by the RAF hasn't helped, I'm sure."

"The RAF didn't do that damage. The Germans retaliated—according to them—because of the Jewish Ghetto uprising."

"My God—how have so many of you survived?"

After he was fed and rested Ian was taken to a house a little distance from Aleksander's home where he was given a bed for the night. It was hoped that he would be on his way north within forty-eight hours and that he could remain there and be sure of his safety. Once he was shown to his bed Ian hoped that there would be no return of the nightmare from the previous night. Sleep was a merciful release and Ian wallowed in a freshly made-up bed for the first time since he was captured at Arras all that time ago.

"Life is a thing of many parts," thought Ian. "Here I am luxuriating in the comforts that a few short years ago I would have considered beneath me, eating food that I wouldn't let into my mouth and glad to be alive and kicking. Like yesterday's taste of soup and black bread supplied by Fenians. God isn't it a bloody world that can turn matters on their head. It's not so long ago that I, and my friends, berated Roman Catholics for being scroungers and living on the work and opportunities provided by Protestant professional people. Complained about their lack of gratitude and here I am throwing myself on the mercy of these Roman Catholic people in a foreign country. At least I'm grateful! Would you believe it, I'm still at it even though I'm struggling to keep body and soul together."

The next day dragged interminably to its conclusion and Ian dreaded the thought of going to bed because he was convinced that the nightmare was waiting in the wings ready to make its entrance once he was too well rested. Of course the thought was father to the nightmare and each time he woke in a cold sweat ensured that the nightmare was ready to pounce once he closed his eyes. Eventually he sat up and determined that what ever was in store for him in the morning he was getting out of this house for some exercise.

The widow woman, as Ian thought of her, who owned the house, was very upset when he indicated by sign language that he was going out. Nothing she could utter however would detain Ian and his need to walk to relieve his anxieties. He was barely out of the street when he spotted a car travelling slowly on the other side. Ian still had not come to terms with transport travelling on the right but he had the sense to slow down sufficiently to allow it to turn the corner and he then turned and went back to the house. The widow, who he only knew as Helena, was delighted to see him.

Someone must have told Aleksander about his sojourn the previous day because he spent the entire day in Ian's company. To pass the time from the somewhat desultory everyday conversation Aleksander raised issues on the war and post-war possibilities. Most of the topics were on areas unthought-of by Ian and gave an indication of the breadth of his friend's knowledge. At one point Ian asked directly if he had been to university and Aleksander replied in the affirmative. "I don't know anyone back home who went to Queen's University, in fact I know very few who even got to secondary level."

"You are not suggesting that at least some of these people you knew were incapable of getting there through ability?"

"I've no way of judging these things, the whole matter is a complete mystery to the average person. Only the rich got to darken its doors."

"Darken its doors?"

"Yes, it's a facetious remark, I was trying to be funny. What I meant was I was turning the remark on its head. For example, the rich would be appalled if someone poor arrived and got equal treatment with them. So they would say, 'Don't let them darken the doors', do you see what I mean?"

"Yes, I do now. I suppose there are financial as well as academic obstacles?"

"Indeed there are, someone once told me that my father's earnings would not cover the cost of a term's teaching."

"It is not that different here but people are into making sacrifices for their children, well the plural would be wrong, they sacrifice so that one son will get on in the hope that he will look after them in their old age."

"I'm sure that goes on back home but certainly not among the people I know. By the way, what is your occupation?"

"I teach at the University but because the Germans closed it I am unemployed. The story goes that the Germans were annoyed with the authorities in the university because of the 'large' number of Jewish students attending it."

"Oh! I was under the impression that anti-Semitism was very strong in Poland, so how come there was a large number of Jews at it?"

"The Jewish ghetto here in Warsaw was large until the Germans started using it as a transit camp for all the Jews in the surrounding areas. There must have been half a million people in there until they started to send some of them to concentration camps. Just how many there were originally I do not know, but of course they were small in number compared to the native Poles but if you want to make an issue of anything you exaggerate the problems being caused, I suppose that is true world-wide?"

"I just haven't given it enough thought. As I said about the other issues we tend to accept what our leaders say on any given subject—unless it so offends so we stand on our hind legs and complain. We talk a lot about our constitution but don't ask me what's in it, I assume it assures us a continued union with Great Britain."

"Since we have become similar to a minority under German rule I suppose it has brought it home just what the Jews have suffered—not that

108

I am claiming the same suffering, although it's impossible to know precisely how many Poles died under the Soviets and the Nazis. Apart from the deaths there have been many deported to Siberia and other parts of the USSR—but I'm off on another tangent."

"You have started me thinking that it's important to understand the other fellow's point of view. That's fine until I get home and someone is pressurising me about how they want a united Ireland!"

"Anyway the problems of minorities, world-wide, apply here. For example, they have to be twice as good as the other person to get employment, that is why poor Jews put all their hopes in educating their young. The Poles, on the other hand, with a certain job security, for the most part, neglect the education of their young beyond primary level."

"Why is Poland a Roman Catholic country?"

"I couldn't go into all the details, it is enough to say that the Reformation had a great impact on Poland. It brought religious tolerance unparalleled elsewhere in Europe, probably because a great number of refugee sects settled in this country. By the way it was at this time, about 1596, that Warsaw became the capital. Anyhow, with the Counter-Reformation came the change and Kings were created by a Republic of Nobles..."

"Surely that's a contradiction in terms?"

"They are everywhere, we have the National Socialists—the Nazis here, how can you be nationalist and socialist? Anyway, as I was saying, all candidates for the monarchy had to subscribe to Catholicism, yet only some twenty years previously there had been a guarantee of equality between all religions. There were only a few Protestant strongholds left as many had re-converted to Catholicism, I suppose it was much like England's conversion to Protestantism, it depended on who was King or Queen, the same applied here.

"When you think that the likes of Gdansk—the Germans call it Danzig—was once a stronghold of Lutheranism at the beginning of the 16th century, yet at the end of that century the whole country became fervently Catholic under Henri Valois, a Frenchman who was the first elected King."

"So you see religion as emanating from the rulers not through belief?"

"In the main that is the case because few people are convinced by reason but by their opportunities to advance themselves in the world."

"At home I would say the reverse is true. People are convinced by faith."

"I do not doubt for some that's true, yet if the conditions that prevailed in the 16th century were in operation now I think you would be surprised at the change given what you said. Indeed I would go farther, if Hitler and the

Nazis look like they will conquer all of Europe you will be surprised how many will join them."

"Aleksander you have given me much to think about. The unionists of Northern Ireland feel under threat constantly but as long as Great Britain is a strong nation that would never happen."

"But that seems to be saying, more or less, what I am arguing."

"No. There is a big difference between Irish Roman Catholics and us—we are British and they are not."

"Is this word 'British' refer to a nationality?"

"It's difficult to say exactly, it's made up of three nationalities: English, Scottish and Welsh."

"But that excludes you then, doesn't it?"

"I suppose if you're speaking strictly about those living in those three countries, yes. But there's 'British' in the sense that we are loyal to the British throne."

"Again it is a bit like it is here at the moment. In 1940 the Russians had a part of Poland and the Germans the other and both of them insisted that we were either German or Russian. The Germans still keep it going even though they are now fighting the Russians. They conscript men in 'their' sector to fight in German uniforms."

"No, not really—it is too difficult to explain accurately."

"Then we will leave it. You feel comfortable fighting for Britain then?"

"Yes I am. The Roman Catholics back home claim there is a strong similarity between your two histories."

"I am no expert on Ireland, you could tell me if it is accurate on the basis of the little Polish history I have told you."

"No, we never learnt Irish history, just British."

"Oh! I am surprised."

"We'll leave it then."

The day went on with episodic accounts of the other's involvement in the war and by evening Ian felt he knew Aleksander well and was glad he and his men were looking after his escape. Occasionally there was a visit from members of the AK, the Armii Krojowej, as Aleksander explained after the first visit. Ian assumed that they were discussing getting him out of Warsaw. As each subsequent visit Aleksander became more and more withdrawn and Ian became more and more frustrated. By late afternoon he couldn't contain himself and eventually tackled the issue head on. "Aleksander what's the arrangements for tomorrow?"

"I am sorry I am still waiting for confirmation on the procedure they are going to use. Late this afternoon there was a bit of an upheaval but discussions are still going on, so it may be tonight, at the earliest, before we hear if you are to go tomorrow."

"If your people are tied up in other business I'll go alone—provided you give me the details on how to get to Danzig, I mean Gdansk. At home we're very touchy about the names of places."

"We are not 'touchy'—whatever that means—we as Poles call it by its Polish name, that's all. If there is a problem about going tomorrow I will give you the information you need."

"Thanks—I just couldn't stay another day indoors."

Someone knocking on the front door awakened Ian in the middle of the night. He heard a muffled conversation in Polish and assumed it was about his prospects of getting away. Shortly afterwards a tap on his bedroom door indicated Aleksander's wish to talk. "I am sorry Ian but there is a full alert called for tomorrow and we can not spare anyone, so the army command want you out of Warsaw at first light."

"Who's taking me and to where?"

"There will be a car at the end of this street that will take you to the railway station. You will be given a ticket for Gdansk—you have the name of a contact there, I believe? Yes?" Ian nodded and smiled; his relief to be on his way was patently obvious to Aleksander.

"We are sorry about the problems but we have obtained some papers for you in case you are stopped. They will be fine provided there is no careful inspection. Forget all that you have heard and seen these past few days, all right?"

"Of course but I wish to thank you and the men of the AK for their help—but you most of all. Good luck in whatever endeavours you're involved in."

"I am sorry I have to leave but you will be fine, I am sure," and with that Aleksander left and Ian instantly left for bed.

The car was waiting when Ian got to the bottom of the street and he was surprised and delighted when he discovered that it was a young woman driving it. No sooner had his posterior touched the seat than they were away. "Where are you leaving me?" The woman merely said, "Halina," which Ian took to be the name of the railway station. It was only after a few attempts at questioning her that he realised that she didn't speak English. "That's quelled my ardour, hasn't it?" addressed to no one in particular. The driver drove at a steady pace away from the city, "Halina, then?" repeated Ian hoping for some kind of response. The girl turned her head and it dawned on Ian that he was calling the girl's name. "I am Ian," he managed to get out in a manner that conveyed it was his name. "Yes, railway?" from her suggested that she had been tutored the previous night. A brisk nod of the head carried all the meaning that Ian could summon.

Once clear of the early morning movement of pedestrians and traffic the girl pulled over to the side of the road. From her pocket she produced a set of papers and when Ian checked to see what they were he was pleasantly surprised to find not only tickets for Gdansk and identity papers but also a wad of money. The amount would insure that he didn't starve nor would he be without a bed for the night.

Ian left the car outside the station and pondered whether he should make a show of waving farewell or should he pretend it was some kind of taxi, official or otherwise, leaving him to the terminus. He nearly decided to blow a kiss but his natural instincts prevailed and instead he gave a brisk nod of the head and walked to the ticket office just inside the door. He showed his ticket and was waved in the direction of the platform where there were a large number of people waiting. At first he wondered at the size of the crowds but he realised that someone as provincial as himself would naturally be taken aback at such numbers. Another aspect, which had surprised him, was the lack of security. He had expected to be asked for his papers but the German guards, which he normally associated with the railways, were among the missing. It dawned on him that this probably meant there would be a thorough check on the train, consequently he had to nerve himself for the searches and the checking of papers still to come.

The lack of companionship bore in on him very early, the last few days of constantly having people around him that he could trust was having an effect. His anxiety to avoid drawing attention to himself was adding to his difficulties and his mind was in a constant state of flux—should he move compartments; should he avoid looking at others; was it too obvious that he rarely looked anywhere but out the window? Suddenly he was distracted from his own internal conflicts; people were looking a lot happier than he had noticed previously but why? There must have been a reason but how could he discover it? Clearly the Poles felt that the Germans had lost out on *something*, hardly the battle for Russia, no they were much too cheerful. Why had there been no guards in the station? Had that some connection with the innumerable grins on the train? On the other hand if something has happened back in Warsaw you could bet your life that the checks would be worse than anything he had encountered on his journeying, so far.

The train stopped at Plonsk and it took some time to start up again. Ian soon discovered the reason for the delay was the number of German soldiers put on board to do a thorough check on the passengers. Suddenly the joyful looks of a few minutes earlier disappeared as everyone began reaching into

112

coats, bags and a variety of hand luggage to find their identity papers. Soon the train echoed with, "Papieren, bitte?" which Ian knew, from the sound of it, "Papers, please?" Up to this moment he had confidence in the documents provided by the AK but any kind of questioning and he was as good as caught! The soldiers were taking their time and Ian had a sinking feeling that he had got as far as he was going. The final certainty that hit him was to hear a soldier say, "Verdammte!" when an elderly man couldn't find his papers but an officer brushed the old man aside, clearly *he* didn't fit the picture of what they were looking for but didn't that put Ian in the frame?

He hadn't long to wait and almost immediately, without looking at his papers, they led him away for questioning—clearly his age and the fact that he wasn't working alerted them to look at him more closely. The game was up, what could he do but go quietly? Whoever had stirred the Germans to this state did him no favours. A carriage had been set aside for the purpose by simply pushing the occupants out into the corridor and thrusting them as far away from those questioning as possible. It was while he was being hustled down the corridor that it dawned on Ian that he better not be caught with either the papers or the money and on the instant determined to push both into the first pocket he encountered in the corridor. A young woman was being roughly pushed to one side and as Ian brushed past her he got rid of the danger.

Inside the makeshift office a young German officer, speaking in Polish, asked him for his papers, Ian simply explained in English that he had none. For a moment the officer was nonplussed but soon put him under guard and told him that he would be taken off at the next station. Ian was surprised but relieved that the Germans were so tied up in other matters that they failed to enquire how he got on the train in the first instance. Clearly there were bigger fish to fry. "Could I ask what all the searches are about?" asked Ian innocently. "No, you can't!" was the not unexpected but somewhat abrupt answer.

As soon as the train stopped the German guards pushed Ian to the nearest door and bundled him out of the station into the arms of a waiting group of soldiers. "Is there a prisoner of war camp here?" enquired Ian in a manner he was learning to adopt when under strict arrest. "Yes," came the monosyllabic answer and Ian assumed that the guard had jumped to conclusions as to what he had been asked and knew little or no English, or he understood perfectly and was in no mood to talk. Ian tried to prise the door open, to a knowledge of the man, by asking what was all the fuss. "Fuss?" Ian thought for a moment, clearly this guy had some awareness of

English if he asked such a question. "What is all the commotion…" which he quickly changed to "What is all the action going on?" The soldier eyed him, "Much money stolen by a group of men. We are searching for them."

"Oh! So that is what it is? Any success then?"

"Not yet. Now no more talk!"

Ian smiled as soon as he turned his back but instantly realised that Aleksander and his mates in the AK must have had a hand in the skulduggery that had most of the German army stationed in Poland hunting them.

The camp seemed to be no distance from the station and Ian knew, almost instantly, that his stay would be of short duration. Perhaps it was the speed with which the commandant saw him initially, or the shilly-shallying which followed on about which hut would he be accommodated in but he was confident that tomorrow would see him on his way once more.

The biggest surprise for Ian was the number of Polish young men being held there and that evening he was housed along with a group of them. He was amazed at their spirits, in spite of the situation they were in. They seemed so jovial and united in the face of what would be, almost certainly, a long term of imprisonment after an uncomfortable questioning. He asked a young man, who appeared to be their leader, why they were so merry. "It was today's robbery. The AK intercepted a convoy loaded with 100 million zloty heading for the banks and I am sure it is being redistributed at the moment."

"But what is the joke at this stage?" asked Ian.

"We are composing begging letters to be sent to the Germans by our friends and one of the boys here came up with a great idea. The robbery took place right in front of King Sigismund III's statue and so he is writing pretending to be the King saying, 'I saw it all, but as I have no need for money, I shall not say anything!' I can not wait for the Germans to offer a reward for information so I am busy preparing a sticker to be added to theirs saying we will double their offer if anyone can tell us the whereabouts of the next parcel of money!" Ian laughed uproariously and the others joined in, glad to have someone with whom they could share the joke.

CHAPTER 6
(September 1942-April 1943)

HALLE WAS DETERMINED to ensure that she would not only look the part but that her enthusiasm would carry the members of the panel along with her. Her first interview had been particularly good, making her sufficiently confident that the job was hers but now she had to convince them on the logistics of possible recruitment. With the German attack on Russia she could use the situation to influence their thinking in regards to increasing the size of the army. She was aware that at this stage they would be more knowledge-able as to where the Irish prisoners were being held but she hoped to have enough details to enable her to pick out the more likely POW camps from which to obtain the numbers they required.

"What happens if I'm unable to get these men?" wondered Halle, "How long will they give me before recalling me? But the details of German losses in manpower are being kept from the public so it's hardly likely that these prisoners will be aware of the situation. Can I go along with that? Say nothing and let these men sign their own possible death warrants?" The retributive voice began, "But they're Brits! ..." The voice of compassion intervened, "They're Irish!" The rational Irish in Halle agreed, "You're right, I'll just have to be a failure from the outset, there's no other way." The constant changing of her position on the prisoners did not enhance her chances of convincing the commission that she was capable of doing the job. Besides could she tell them that she knew they were bound to be suffering some losses, which would result in the sapping of the army's overall strength? Besides there were stories that the Russians were starting to out produce the Germans in tanks and aeroplanes. Perhaps if she deliberately asked them directly what was required they would have to be more forthcoming about their requirements.

At the meeting she felt confident that she had all the areas covered and it was with some certainty that she went straight in and asked what kind of numbers they wanted from her. The response of, "All that you can get" from General Eckhard, who was leading the commission, more than hinted that Halle's perception of the situation was accurate. "Can you be more specific?" asked Halle. There was a long silence and there were glances among the members that indicated that none of these individuals wanted to be responsible for giving the actual details. "Our troops are taking part in a massive offensive," answered Eckhard in a voice that projected strength.

"We need a large increase in our numbers to hold what we at present hold—before I go any further I require each and every one in this room to give a solemn undertaking that they will not speak a word of this outside these walls! Is that clear?" The heads appeared to nod in unison, with the exception of Halle's, yet no one appeared to notice.

"Young woman, what are the numbers of Irish held in our POW camps?" asked Horst Hengist, a young Oberst who had recently been added to the Commission. Halle didn't know why but she felt this man's knowledge of the Eastern front was minimal and showed, at the most, that he had fought his war in France.

"I'm sorry, I've no idea and I had hoped that you would make the figures available to me today so that I could determine which camps to visit."

"The figures must exist somewhere, does anyone know?" asked the Oberst. The dubious looks around the room didn't suggest that there was much hope. Halle got to her feet, "Well, let me give a 'guesstimate' of the number of Irish recruited by the British at the outset of the war. From north and south it appears that in the region of sixty- to a hundred-thousand men enlisted. Making another assumption, I think that about thirty thousand men were in France at the start of hostilities and allowing for casualties and those that escaped at Dunkirk it is possible there are about ten thousand men liable to be imprisoned here and in Poland." Halle paused to let the interpreter catch up. She felt that she was exaggerating the figures because she had no actual knowledge but she wanted the commission to feel there was something worthwhile in using Halle's approach. In her heart Halle knew that, whatever the possibility of recruiting Irishmen was, at the beginning of the war, the numbers would be decimated if there was a single battle lost on the Eastern front. But Halle also knew that the confirmed Nazis on the Commission thought only of their credo and assumed anyone with their convictions wouldn't hesitate to take up arms against Communist Russia. And it was this clinching piece that Halle was relying on in obtaining support when it came to which POW camps they would permit her to visit.

In regards to herself, Halle knew that her best chance to escape without too much difficulty lay in Poland, which had its own ports in the Baltic. What she hoped from the Army Board setting up this initiative was that they would accept her suggestions as to which camps were more likely to prove successful. It would suit her if they chose the camps in Germany as her starting point and to use her likely failure there as a sufficient reason to tackle the Polish camps. As a tentative backup she intended to offer to speak to the other groups of prisoners, knowing that large numbers of them were willing to fight the Russians, if it got them out of the POW camps and particularly if they felt they were on the winning team.

From the first meeting it was obvious that Halle had them eating out of her hand with the exceptions of Horst Hengist and General Eckhard. Each of her suggestions was barely discussed before being accepted but she felt that Hengist was holding his fire until he found the right target. It was becoming all too apparent that the army commanders would clutch at any straw that would enable them to report to the Fuhrer they had increased the size of the army—but just what was Hengist's position?

Her first outing was to a camp only fifty kilometres from Berlin and it left her totally flummoxed—zero! The worst of all possible results, seemingly not only did the Irish not care about the Eastern front but, more importantly; they had an intense hatred of Germans. Without questioning each individual thoroughly she couldn't be totally certain as to their reasons but from those with whom she had conversations they told her they abhorred their captors simply because of the treatment meted out to them. The fact that she hadn't been unprepared for such an outcome didn't leave her any the happier. "What if Eckhard recalls me because of my lack of success?" asked one of her voices. "You'll be back on the radio—a bigger success than ever!" was the sarcastic reply. "Hardly, with this disaster hanging over my head!" Halle could feel her heart sinking—"Another Titanic from Belfast!"

General Eckhard sent the list of POW camps within ten days but to Halle's horror it only listed the camps in Germany. Nevertheless it showed the immensity of the task which confronted her—71 Stammlager (Stalags for enlisted men), 55 Offizerlager (Oflags for non-air force officers), 14 Straflager (punishment camps), 4 Luft Lager (for air force prisoners) and a number of transit camps. It also pointed to the difficulty imposed on the German army in providing men to ensure that the prisoners were safely under lock and key. Halle set about drawing up a schedule of visits based, in the main, on their geographical position to her accommodation in Berlin. Still it didn't take long for her to conclude that it would take the best part of a year and a half to travel across Germany on her visits, provided she excluded the 55 Offizerlager and the air force prisoners. She was thoroughly despondent as she saw her prospects of escape being irreparably damaged by this initial examination of the situation. Perhaps there was a way out of this but at this moment in time it didn't seem possible. General Eckhard wanted an immediate assessment of the amount of time and travel involved and also some notion of the approximate numbers she hoped to recruit but he laid down an order as to which camps were to be visited initially. Clearly he had had someone compose the list which seemed to be from one end of the country to the other which entailed travelling backwards and forwards passing other camps to reach those nominated. There was something odd going on behind the scenes.

Towards the end of 1942 Halle realised that unless she pushed the issue of Polish POWs she wouldn't get an opportunity to make an escape attempt. While dwelling on possible solutions her mind drifted and she became aware that Herr Oberst Hengist seemed to be more and more interested in her activities—or was it in her? Did he have some kind of crush on her? Perhaps he had been deputed to keep an eye on her and in particular how she was progressing with the recruiting... It was only then that the penny of opportunity dropped—she would ask for figures on the number of Irish prisoners held in Germany and compare them with those held in Poland. If they hadn't got them she would insist that they send a document to each camp asking for the numbers of Irish held in them. If she was lucky she would be able to go to Poland in a few months time. 'Guesstimates' were all that was possible and she tried to base them on the original figures she had given to the Commission. Eckhard seemed to accept these with a complacency that surprised Halle but he appeared to have difficulty in supplying her with figures of Irish prisoners held in Poland, or for that matter, those held in Germany... Hengist insisted that she call him by his first name, Horst, as they were of equal rank; again was this an initial foray before asking her for a date? No matter how attractive he appeared his wholehearted Nazi approach was anathema... "Would you call yourself a moderate then?" Halle ignored the voice... Was there something being held back deliberately and what could possibly be the reason. Whatever the reason in seemed that General Eckhard was approachable and now that she felt that she had served an apprenticeship he would be prepared to let her attempt to recruit in Poland. She had set her mind on January 1943, as she was conscious of the build-up in Russia for the Allies to open a second front in order to divide the German armies. The situation could rapidly get out of control and the thought of ending as a prisoner of the Russians, just because she was in Poland later than she planned was something she couldn't contemplate with equanimity. In the interim she was forced to visit camps unaware of the number of Irish prisoners held in them.

Halle's daily reports barely dealt with the problems with which she had to contend. At one and the same time she was afraid that her failure to secure men for the scheme would bring about its ending and that very failure would push the Commission to be more extreme in their dealings with prisoners. It wouldn't be the first officer of the Wehrmacht who suggested to her that the need to use men to corral prisoners was a use of manpower that Germany couldn't afford. Yet, in spite of her fears, within a month she was relieved to be told that she was authorised to start immediately on the POW camps in Poland. In her mind General Eckhard was either too gullible, or worse, was deliberately giving in to her. But what could be the reason?

Once she set foot in Poland Halle set about getting details of the Baltic ports. Because of her rank she was entitled to maps of the various areas and she soon made good use of her position. It was apparent that Gdansk was probably her best bet, it continued to have sea routes open to Sweden and there lay her hopes of avoiding both the British and the German police. Her continued failure to make any impression on the Irish prisoners had long since been forgotten. The more she saw on her forays into Poland the more she was aware just how the Nazis were getting rid of the Jews. Once near Wroclaw she was stupefied by the number of corpses lying near the edge of a barbed wire encampment. At first she thought it had been Russian troops whose bodies had been brought there for burial but on reflection she realised that it was too far from the front and besides some of the bodies were clothed in prison uniform.

After her first few visits to Poland she received a list of camps which were designated to have more Irish prisoners than the rest. All told there were almost twenty but the top two were situated in Posen and Thorn. Halle was made aware that these were the 19th century German names and that the Poles working on the railways often feigned ignorance of these towns but on being shown her German Army papers were quick to show her the correct platform from which to depart. "Here we are again," said the voice in her head, "Derry or Londonderry? Is this a world-wide phenomena?" The balancing voice, for once, agreed, "Only when you have two countries at each other's throat as to ownership." The first voice cleared its throat; "You didn't like it when you were on the receiving end, did you?"

"What do you mean, 'the receiving end'?"

"Well, you were none too pleased when those Poles gave you the cold shoulder, were you?"

"Even when you agree with their point of view it's difficult when people ignore you over issues which you had no part in."

"Oh, you sound more and more like your father; 'You can't blame this generation of Englishmen for the sins of the past'. Who else can they blame? After all you're one of the other sort now!"

"Enough is enough! Let it ride."

"No, I won't. To all intents and purposes you're German. It says it on

119

that bloody bit of paper, doesn't it?"

"I'm not answering. You can go on blathering away as long as you like."

"Oh you're hiding behind your skirts of womanhood now. Whatever became of that proud Irish woman prepared to die for her country? She's been among the missing a long while." Silence became the order of the day and Halle on board the train from Wroclaw to Poznan (Posen) regretted the Commission's refusal to supply her with a staff car. There was nothing she could do about the situation and she determined to put the issue out of her mind.

The journey required a number of train changes, mostly because of the damage inflicted by the Polish AK and the Allied bombing of the line. On two occasions she had to leave the train to board a bus which brought her a few miles further to the next point where a train met them. However, on the second occasion she was caught in an inevitable delay, as another train had to be dispatched to pick up her and her fellow travellers. Apparently this delay was due to the AK attacking an earlier train and consequently blocking the line. Then, to her consternation, just as it seemed the train had picked up speed, an armed group suddenly separated itself from the other passengers and brought the train to a standstill.

Their audacity astounded Halle and she was unprepared for their subsequent action. The men beckoned to her and the other six in the compartment to go into the corridor. When they complied they were questioned as to their destination and asked for their identity papers. Halle realised quite quickly that she would be unable to rid herself of the incriminating documents in her possession and when it came her turn to be quizzed she knew she was doomed. It didn't take long for the men to find her German identity and her papers showing she was working for the German High Command. She was forcibly removed from the train and pushed on to a bus where she was required to hide under the rear seat.

Some time elapsed before the bus began moving. Halle's mind was thinking at overtime rates. "I can't afford to be the person on my papers—I'm as good as dead! These men don't go in for POWs—you're either dead or alive." Her other voice reminded her that the IRA hadn't a great record in the field of humanity, at least regarding British soldiers. "At least this gives me time to exercise my brain and come up with a way out." But the brain must have been out shopping because it produced no reply when asked. The minutes were lengthening and shortening; lengthening when she could get no response and shortening when she thought the bus was coming to a halt.

It was during one of the latter periods that she suddenly recalled Sheila

Gray, how or why she wasn't prepared to speculate on at this moment. "I'm going to be Sheila Gray. Right, how much do I know of her and the Canadian end of this? I'll need to supplement what I have with an imaginative scheme of my own."

She heard a loud bang and she assumed it was the Poles blowing up the line or the train. If they were half as organised at this part of the business as they had been in taking over the train undoubtedly they had destroyed all or as much of the train that they wished. Once again she compared her Republican training with what she had seen and concluded that they weren't in the same league as these men. Clearly they had been in the regular army up to its defeat. Everything about them was professional and their weapons were modern German ones. Yet twenty minutes later they were pulverised by what appeared to be, at least, a division of crack German troops.

The AK had the wit to abandon her and the vehicle she was in. Whether they made good their escape she didn't know but somehow she thought it highly unlikely. German troops gathered around her to protect her and she found herself being placed in an armoured car in the company of Herr Oberst Horst Heingist. "That was the closest call in my life," shouted Halle in order to make herself heard above the roar of the huge engine. "You were indeed fortunate," replied the Oberst. "To whom do I owe thanks?" queried Halle. "Quite a number of people, including myself. You see our intelligence had warned us of an AK attempt to capture a German officer, so anyone of that rank travelling in this area was under surveillance."

"Thanks be to God for that, Herr Oberst!"

Hengist invited Halle to a meal in the local Army HQ that evening; as he put it, "they had many things to discuss". Halle determined to proceed to her destination as planned, thinking that in doing it this way she would be able to calm herself and stop her worrying about the near call she had had. Hengist contrived to find her transport that was heading in the general direction of Posen and he impressed on the Army driver to make sure she was left inside the camp—not on the perimeter. He told Halle that he would pick her up around six o'clock so that they could be able to eat reasonably early.

The driver was Kraftsfahrer Boehme, a huge Saxon who had little to say and as Halle's German was equivalent in quantity to his clumsy attempts at conversation they soon lapsed into total silence—the last thing Halle wanted. The voices didn't wait; "Did you believe Horst's statement about how they saved you so quickly?" asked Halle's interrogative voice. "Of course," answered the voice of acceptance and complacency. "Explain then how the guy on surveillance was able to contact the colonel so quickly?" The silence almost caused Halle to choke. "Well? I'm waiting…" ranted the inquisitor. "You can wait forever; I don't know!" The opposition voice continued to rant, "But you're prepared to accept his word on each and every occasion…" He was interrupted, "You're paranoid!"

"Stop it now!" yelled Halle and Boehme crashed his size twelve boot down on the brake. Halle almost sailed through the windscreen but the soldier grabbed her arm and yanked her back into her seat, "Was ist das?" he bellowed. "Sorry, sorry … I didn't mean…" The driver raised his hands above his head and gradually brought them down to cover his eyes—only he had been ordered to drive this woman to Posen he would have dumped her at the side of the road. "Please drive on," said Halle in an apologetic voice and wavered her arms to indicate movement.

They were no sooner underway than the voices were back torturing Halle but this time they were more muted: "Did I make a case or did I not?" started the interrogator. "Well… there is something there to be explained…" Exasperation crept into the first voice, "Well you had better start because I want off this crazy expedition into oblivion." The calmer voice asked for time, "Let's try to make sense of this… it's your turn to answer here: 'What if you're right and that guy was spying on you and had some backup who was able to contact those German forces which turned up?' But 'What was Hengist doing there?' 'What was the point of the spying?' 'What did you do to attract attention?' and 'What are you going to do about it?' Five great questions but have you any answers?"

Halle stopped the voices because she just wasn't in a position to draw any conclusions, at least any that stood up to a full analysis. "This needs time and a great deal of thought," she decided and attempted to ignore her voices' urgency. "Vier kilometers," said Boehme in an attempt to patch up what he thought had been a breakdown in their former cordiality. Halle merely grunted and the huge Saxon retired into his speechless concentration on his driving. "I'll have to make a break for it in the next few days—for whatever reason they are on to me. It's no good going over and over possible reasons; the truth is they don't trust me. I could go on posing questions— for example, 'Why give me this job?… No I'm not going up that cul-de-sac. It's a pity I didn't plan this more thoroughly but I had better get started. Now when I think of it, it's a pity that this guy was ordered to drive me inside this camp, otherwise I could have gone a lot further with him to (Gdansk)."

When Boehme stopped his lorry outside the Commandant's office Halle summoned sufficient courtesy to thank him in German. On reflection she realised she was indirectly telling him that it was his accent that had caused her difficulty. But what she hadn't reflected on was her lack of vocabulary and just how foreign was her accent.

The Commandant treated her with great respect—a courtesy she accepted as a right reserved for a colonel. Immediately she recognised he was surprised to see a woman and, in addition, he was struggling with the form of address, which would be appropriate, "Herr… Oberst," he began with a pronounced pause between the two words. "Sorry, it's so unusual to address a lady with such a rank." The rest of their conversation was about her accommodation and the lists of Irish prisoners that he had prepared for her. She was allocated a room with the Commandant and his wife in their home nearby and Halle repaired there as soon as politeness allowed and she explained that she was in a hurry to dress as Herr Oberst Hengist was taking her to dinner.

Horst was as punctual as Halle expected. "He's as Germanic in his day to day dealing with people as I would expect from an ardent admirer of Hitler," she concluded as she left the Commandant's house with him but she failed to recognise her own predilection for punctuality. As her mother often said, "You'll be at your grave before your coffin!" Considering the meagre variety of food available at Army Headquarters Halle enjoyed the meal and the company of a man, even though she found him reprehensible in many ways he was attractive and pleasant company. Consequently the evening flew by and it was only as they left for her to be driven back to Posen that she felt a sense of relief that Hengist hadn't mentioned the incident earlier in the day.

Once she was in the bedroom, Halle had time to spend time looking back at the events of the day. She realised her voices had neatly summed up her situation and now that Hengist was gone she was certain that she was in trouble. He should have raised the subject of her capture by the AK but he didn't and her suspicions were heightened that she was the person under surveillance. She surveyed the questions that she had listed earlier and found her answers were not the ones she wanted to hear. Hengist shouldn't have been there! It was obvious that she was in danger and the word 'danger' recalled her warning to Sheila Gray, which evidently was too late. That wasn't going to be the case with herself, she was getting the hell out of it. The first opportunity and she would be away. This was going to be a true test of her ingenuity… "Sheila Gray! I'll bet that they were watching her and they saw us together that last night! It's got to be that and that helps explain why they didn't go back on the job promise. They were afraid of tipping me that I was a suspect. Thank God I eventually got my thinking cap on because I would have walked right into it! They had no hesitation in ridding themselves of her, so I'm sure I'm on their list to be executed. I won't be around to please them—I'm no Sheila Gray!"

It was with some trepidation that Halle entered the Commandant's office to start work. At first she thought it had been the events of the previous day that were causing her concern but this was something different, "Maybe it's the usual butterflies." Nevertheless, she was perturbed about something but just what, evaded her, "It's just that I haven't given sufficient thought to escaping that's upsetting me… No, it's the fact that I went to dinner last night without preparing for this morning's work!" She had cast her eye over the list of names the previous night but that was it; normally she would have made a separate list of 'possibles' and 'probables' but not this time. She decided that before she arranged for the men to be called she would take a few minutes to look at their names and regiments—basically that was all that they had to give once captured.

The Commandant asked her was there anything that she required before she began interviewing the individuals. "No, the room you have set aside is grand for the purpose. Perhaps you would explain to the guards I prefer them to remain outside the door but I would expect them to rush in at the first sign of me being in difficulty."

"I've already explained this to the soldiers on duty and also I warned the Irishmen that I wouldn't tolerate any kind of insulting behaviour to our visitor nor would threats of violence be allowed."

"Thank you but I don't anticipate any thing of that sort. In each of the camps I have visited so far, many of the men may have hated all that I said but they didn't resort to violence to my person—a few naughty words and some finger exercises but that was all."

"I am glad to hear it and nothing less will be tolerated today."

Halle adjourned to the room to set about the preparation. Firstly she laid her papers on the desk and put a chair opposite hers, sufficiently distant to ensure that she could react quickly if there was a threat. Finally she was ready to examine the lists in detail, pencilling in what she thought would be appropriate questions. Suddenly it dawned on her, she had been kept from the prisoners' lists because of the suspicion she had aroused in visiting Sheila. She hadn't time to think it through and returned to her list where she was abhorred to see so many names of Irish origin. Normally she put them to the end of her 'possibles' list but she would just have to take them as they appeared seeing that she hadn't given the guards sufficient notice. Then, just near the end, a name that she had merely bypassed the night before suddenly struck her and instantly she decided that here was a person who might be willing to escape with her or, there again, he might not!

CHAPTER 7

(April 1943)

HALLE COULDN'T WAIT to get down to the bottom of the list. He would be surprised, no, shocked to see her. She wondered if she would recognise him, after all the last time she had any recollection of seeing him he was a boy of about thirteen or fourteen. The guard announced that they had got to the surnames beginning with the letter P. Halle perked up after having a conspicuously poor response during the morning; she recognised Ian the instant she saw him, such was not the case for Ian. Although he hadn't seen her since their adolescent years somehow this willowy dark lady with the intense eyes, although attractive, was not the person he would associate with that perverse girl who had no tolerance for other people's viewpoints.

The Commandant's speech that morning indicated that those men of Irish birth or were living in Ireland prior to the war would be interviewed by a lady from German Radio. What the purpose was, was left to their imaginations. Of course this led to massive speculation among the Irish and indeed among the rest of the prisoners, but to a lesser extent. Ian's natural inquisitiveness meant that even without the order he suspected he would have volunteered just to be near someone feminine—but an order must be obeyed.

By lunchtime, a somewhat ironic description of the period around 1 p.m., there were eight men waiting expectantly for the interview. They probably felt that whatever the woman wanted that anything was better than the sheer hell of nothing to do. In any event when Ian's turn came he was just in the office in time to overhear one man tell another that they were recruiting for the German Army. "I wonder whether the man overheard something or is he merely speculating? Maybe the last man out said something," thought Ian. Initially he was amused as he remembered that his father had a similar experience when that Protestant republican, Sir Roger Casement, tried to get him to forsake the British in the Great War of 1914 to 1918. Ian was quite prepared for a set-to and the very thought of it caused him to feel elated.

The waiting time was a drag but he speculated on the approach this woman would take. Clearly the amount of time taken showed that she must be having difficulty or perhaps she wasn't allowing a "yes" or "no" reply. He knew most of the men there and he couldn't conceive of any circumstances that would tempt them to be traitors.

Ian finally went in, deliberately grim-faced yet he noticed the guard on each side of the door. Behind a desk was a pretty girl, dark and attractive looking. "I hope that fellow outside was wrong, I think I could go for this girl in a big way," thought Ian. "Keep your head clear," said another voice, "you don't know what you're walking into." The desk was no more than 15 yards away; the girl's demeanour appeared to reflect Ian's own quixotic mood and he realised none of this would be easy. As he approached she stood up and simply greeted him with, "Hello Ian" in a quiet tone. He was startled at the familiarity of this stranger. "I'm sorry but you have me at a disadvantage," he began, "Do I know you? Perhaps you will introduce yourself," he asked somewhat stiltedly.

"I'm Halle, Ian," she answered in a quietly determined voice. Ian came to an immediate standstill. "Halle? Halle who?" he stood staring at the rather tall young woman dressed in the fashion of some pre-war European city; certainly not the condition of those rare women he had seen when marching to the Polish farm where he worked. "Halle Hegel!"

"Lord above… You recognised me?" Halle nodded.

"Is it true that you're recruiting for the Nazis?" Halle nodded again.

"And you still sent for me?" Halle nodded once more.

"Well that beats Boniker, whoever he was! You have the nerve of the devil himself." He went on to relate the coincidence of his father being approached in the Great War. "But coincidence piled upon coincidence I've never accepted as God's will and you're the living proof that it's all the connivance of the devil!"

"Don't go ranting at me—do you think you're back on the Custom's Steps? Those two guards will put a bullet in you if you persist."

"Am I to take it that you intend this farce to continue?" Halle smiled for the benefit of the guards and pointed to the chair in front of the desk, "Please be seated."

Ian restrained himself with some difficulty and sat quietly while Halle went back to her seat. "Ian I want to speak openly to you, so if you can control yourself until I'm finished… Firstly the guards don't understand English, so when I finish you may speak. Normally they stay outside and only appear if there is some disagreement but I've asked them to come in on this one occasion because I have things to say which you'll find difficult to accept. Again hold your breath until I finish but if you need some comment explained ask there and then, OK?"

"No, it's not OK. I want to ask some pertinent questions, you may think they're impertinent but you'll have to make do." Ian's angry reply made the guards start up as if to intervene but Halle beckoned them to go back to their positions. "OK we'll do it your way, go ahead," and Halle sat down again.

"We used to call your da a Hun, are you German? And how the hell did you get into Germany to do their dirty work?" Halle answered immediately, "Firstly, my father is English, and secondly the Germans found me in Guernsey, you know in the Channel Islands?" Ian was equally quick in responding, "You're patronising me again; I suppose you offered your services?" this with a grin indicating how unlikely he thought it in both interpretations and Halle, forever slow in noting sexual innuendo, hesitantly said "Yes" which completely caught him by surprise. He bounced up and gave every appearance of leaving the room, then, as if a sudden thought had occurred asked what she was doing in Guernsey. "I was on the run. The police in England and the RUC back home had me on their wanted list."

"Don't tell me—you were involved in that bombing campaign in England?"

Halle saw that her approach wasn't working but decided to be as truthful as she could, "I was a courier but I did set fire to a few places." Ian's dander was up, "Oh, you just burned down a few places eh? Is this the kind of morality that you espouse—I suppose you always were of that frame of mind? Well I tell you no matter what your ploy is here, at the end of all this I'll be a witness to the confession you made to me. You make me sick but I'll see you strung up—what do you say now?"

Halle tried to maintain a dignified silence but he persisted in ending his statements with a question. Somehow she let him continue with his attacks on her lack of Christian morality. When he paused for breath she asked, "Are you finished?"

"I am for now; so I won't be wishing you well nor goodbye because I'll make damn sure you get your comeuppance when this is over."

"I hate to point out how far you've fallen from Christian virtue but I notice that swearing is now part of your attacking vocabulary. So you're not prepared to hear my side of the story; I'm not surprised, it was always this way when it came to a tricky or, for that matter, any problem." Halle stood up as she finished but Ian remained seated not prepared to give her any of the high moral ground, which he had gained by his dignified and, in his view, commendable approach.

Halle was uncertain how to proceed; if she was too obviously republican she knew she would get nowhere, on the other hand, if she made out that she was on the run from the Germans God only knew how he would react by way of revenge. There was going to have to be a great deal of trust required of both of them and she was aware that all depended on how well she put the case and how diplomatically she handled herself.

"Well I should begin by telling you to forget all the stories you heard about my visit. As far as the officials here are concerned I am trying to recruit Irishmen for their army. The truth is that I am using this job to get me into a position where I can escape to Sweden." Halle looked as unobtrusively at Ian as she could to see how he was reacting to her story. Clearly he was fascinated by the tale so far.

"I was for a time working for Rundfunkpropaganda nach Irland which was known as Irland-Redaktion in Berlin but I was soon disillusioned. They insisted on editing our scripts and constantly drew the Jewish question into our reports to Ireland. No matter how often we informed them that these issues weren't relevant to the problems facing Ireland the more they insisted on attacking the Jewish 'Question' and Soviet communism, as if they were one and the same thing.

"An English girl who came to Germany because of her belief in Nazism simply lost all faith in them and when she attempted to reach Goebbels was dispatched to some concentration camp. It made me realise I had to be careful so I stopped criticising and started to find things of which they approved. I remembered Casement's ill-fated attempt to recruit in the Great War and so I suggested that I try. At one point I thought of putting forward the idea that I should tour the POW camps seeking men who could broadcast to Ireland but I realised that there were too many problems."

"What kind of problems? Not that I give a damn."

"Well everyone at home would be able to hear you and know you. For people from your background it would be impossible. Also I had worked with these Nazis and the backbiting and the backstabbing are terrible—not that it was my intention to go back but I would have to have made a case for going ahead with this. As it turned out they only wanted men of the officer class and that would have kept me in Germany."

"Why are you telling me all this? Don't you twig on that I care less and if anything, I hope that the Gestapo gets you? What have you done that would give me any confidence in your story?"

"I suppose in your limited way you can't see where this is leading?"

"It's wonderful to be regarded as an idiot by people like you, it makes me realise that I have the right perspective."

"Do you not want to see?"

"Oh I know exactly what's on offer. You need some mug to help you escape and you thought, 'Ah, here he is, that Orangeman from down the street.' Do you remember when we were young you used to call me a 'souper' and when I asked what it was, you made out that all Protestants in Ireland were people who took the soup served out to those who changed their religion during the Famine. I never believed it and even if my kin changed their religion in the past it was because of conviction. I know because I'm like them and there's no way I'd change my coat."

Halle eyed the skeleton of a man sitting before her. The dark handsome youth was transformed into a mere skin full of bones and that was all that remained to tell her about 'reality'.

"Can I assume that you look at yourself in the mirror when you shave?" Ian's nod caused her to resume, "You must realise there is only so long before your body feels the lack of food; how long have you been a prisoner?"

"I was captured at Arras in 1940."

"Two years already and I suppose you have made some attempt to escape?"

"Yes, twice."

"You know that as each day passes your chances of being strong enough to try again are considerably reduced. I could have offered the chance to any one of a hundred men I have interviewed but I didn't. Does that suggest someone needing help to escape? Let me finish this intensely distasteful conversation by saying something I would have died rather than admit. When we were adolescents, in spite of all the hateful things I said, I now think I was attracted to you. Sex must be a powerful magnet if I can endure the hypocritical stance which you…"

"God, you'll go to any lengths to get what you want! The thought that you had ever been human enough to be attracted to any man is hard to believe but to drag me into your fantasy is so incredible that I can't take it in. Of course Jesuits and papists are well known for their lying, so I suppose republicans of your ilk are of the same breed, so what can a good Protestant Ulsterman expect?"

"Interruptions again and again. The problem with you Ian was you never heeded the truth when you heard it, so why should I imagine you'd be different this time? Ian all I ask is that you take one long look at yourself in your mirror tomorrow and ask, 'Can I survive much longer?' Will you do that?"

Ian's concern to win the battle of words dimmed when he grasped just how much Halle had confessed. "I don't need a mirror, I know the score, but then I always did."

Halle ignored the implied dig at her, "What exactly are you getting by way of food?"

"You mean right now?"

"Yes."

"You see at the start we did quite well, what with the Red Cross parcels coming regularly every two, maybe three, months supplemented a fairly basic diet. Now we get small pieces of bread—often full of small black insects, barley soup for breakfast. For dinner watery soup often full of white cabbage worms, occasionally small amounts of horsemeat. Still that's a hundred percent better than the Russians who are dying in droves. Things are that bad over there in their compound that the Germans are frightened to go into it. Indeed one row was so bad they sent in their fiercest Alsatian, a few minutes later the hide of the dog landed on the barbed-wire fence."

"My God, I knew things were bad but I didn't appreciate just how bad."

"But all this is getting away from the point I'm trying to make; I was a genuine volunteer—a word beloved of your IRA—never a conscript. I was prepared to die and I still am."

"Well, so be it. Are you telling me that you never once had a doubt? I don't believe it! Then again your attitude has been drilled into you, yet I hope you survive Ian but I've more than strong doubts. Goodbye." Ian kept his word as he walked to the door.

Halle knew she would have to recast her ideas if she wanted Ian to come with her, "Strange how I didn't anticipate his refusing. It should have been obvious from the outset. The more I think of it the more I wonder if there is something wrong with my head... Herr Oberst Horst Hengist is watching every move that I make and if I were completely honest I would admit to Ian why I needed him. From the outset I must have given Hengist cause to distrust me; I'm sure it wasn't just my association with Sheila Gray."

Halle had difficulty sleeping that night. She knew that arguments often left her in that condition, she felt that she didn't say enough. The dream was a re-run of their meeting earlier in the day but this time her voices spoke out of turn, "You heard him accuse you of being 'sarcastic' and you didn't respond." Halle had no recollection of it but then her voices were not beyond lying. "He said, 'You're as sarcastic as usual; how anyone selected you to recruit for the Nazis is beyond me. But then again people haters of that breed wouldn't see that, would they?'"

"Did I say anything to that?"

"Well you took his demolition of you like a man."

"Is that all?"

"No, you said, 'Have it your own way then. You're as pig headed an Orangeman as I ever met and that's saying something!'"

"I suppose that shut him up?"

"Not on your life, the words he used really touched a nerve, 'That old touch of sweetness will bring thousands of Irishmen flocking to join the Germans. You've a hell of an imagination; but then that's what seems to keep your people going. Reality doesn't play a great part in your lives.'"

"Is that it? Can I get some sleep now?" But the voices droned on and on the whole night long.

It was late the following afternoon when Halle heard that Ian had escaped with two others. She felt that she was bound to be quizzed by Hengist seeing that, not only had she seen Ian but she had listed him in her report as being sufficiently interested as to repay a visit. As she had left the report with the Commandant she immediately went to him and asked for it. She implied that she had left something of consequence out of it and wanted to ensure that the report was accurate. The second, and from her point of view the most important issue, was to get out of Posen before Hengist heard of the breakout and associated it with her visit. The Commandant kindly arranged transport for her to get to the railway station in Posen and she felt all the better the instant she sat down in the railway carriage on a train heading for Berlin.

The journey back was long but uneventful and she changed the report to exclude Ian's name. Although it was late into the evening when she arrived she deliberately visited her office to stamp the report for General Eckhard's attention but primarily her intention was to leave herself free from going back in case she should meet Oberst Hengist.

When she eventually returned to her apartment she was shocked to find a letter in O'Driscoll's handwriting. She hurriedly opened it and was delighted to find that he had contacted her family and was able to reassure her that they were receiving her mail. Unfortunately the German authorities heavily censored it, even though it was being processed through a friend in Dublin who regularly brought her letters north. O'Driscoll went on to say that the early letters had been blacked out but Halle's dad took them to a chemist he knew and was able to restore about seventy-five percent of the original correspondence. But recent letters were being, in O'Driscoll's words, 'circumcised'—in other words offending paragraphs were cut out in their entirety.

O'Driscoll attempted to reassure her about her 'friends' in England, which Halle interpreted as referring to Molly and Vincent. However, nothing he might say could alleviate Halle's sense of guilt about Molly's capture. In spite of her apprehensions she had to concentrate on her own uncertain future. Each passing hour made her realise that working so closely with the

German High Command left her totally compromised if she was to be captured by any Allied army group—her near kidnapping by the AK helped to keep this notion to the forefront of her mind.

The next morning Halle decided at the last moment to abandon her plans to return to Poland, at least for a few days. Later in the day she would contact Eckhard's office and let them know she was ill after her experience near Posen. At any rate she was certain that Hengist would have kept him informed of the situation. She needed time to think out a definite plan for her escape instead of this half-baked, spur of the notion approach she had been taking up to now. "Just look at your approach to Ian Patterson, if you'd had a second's thought in your head you'd have known he wouldn't touch you with a forty foot pole—sorry about the pun!" started Mr Criticism in her head. "Don't you know that I know it was stupid? So why do you bring it up?" Mr Criticism was quickly back, "We're very sensitive today, aren't we?"

"Just shut up and leave me in peace!"

Halle settled down to think of the issues that she needed to sort out. "It's easy for these POWs in countries which support their aims, they have plenty of people out there willing to help. Who's going to help me?"

"Ian Patterson?" queried Mr Comedian.

"I'm sick to death of these voices, I'm going out. It's bound to be better in the park than sitting here arguing with them," and Halle departed for greener pastures.

The park had plenty of life about it. Young mothers with their children were in the majority with a sprinkling of elderly people taking advantage of the nice weather. On the park bench Halle composed herself and produced a notebook and a copying-ink pencil to do the whole thing properly. "The more I think about it the more I realise that POWs have a lot of advantages I don't have. So that said, let's move on. What advantages do *I* have? Well I have German authorisation to travel by road or rail—that's very good. So is there a flaw in this I don't see?"

"The Germans are keeping an eye on you, they might even be doing it right now!" Mr Pessimism was in the ascendant, "Don't forget the near thing you had the other day." Halle did a full 180 degrees but saw no one nearby who was watching her. "How do I skirt round these problems then?"

"Another set of papers would be useful and a few clothes that differ from your normal appearance would help," Mrs Optimistic was always helpful. "How do I get them?" The response was slow in coming, "Well the clothes are easy, you go to the market near you and get them second hand."

"And what about the papers?" kindly enquired Halle.

"Now you're hurting, I don't know." Mr Crafty rarely appeared in these conversations but he put in his four pence worth, "When you came here—what was to happen to you if you hadn't got the radio job?"

"I would be what the British call 'a slave-worker' assigned to some factory producing war materials."

"That's your answer then. Apply to the authorities in a different name to be allocated to a factory. After a few days, when you have everything fixed up, just leave without a word to anyone."

"What about this different name—they won't wear that, will they?"

"Tell them you're reverting to your maiden name as your husband deserted you, they'll accept that."

"How do I explain where I've been in the past two years?"

"Didn't you get paid off by Irland Radaktion? You have the papers, so tell them you have survived on your and your husband's savings since, OK?" Halle wrote busily the whole time this conversation was going on and just as she was coming to an end Mr Crafty shouted, "Make sure you destroy those notes of yours before you leave the park." Immediately Halle sat down again to ensure that she remembered the 'answers' the voices gave.

Halle spent the next two days getting new papers in the name of 'Halle Hale' and going to the factory in Potsdam where she was sent. Fortunately the weekend intervened and she was able to visit a camp not far from her new place of employment. She determined to bolster her reports by merely adding a series of camps she had visited but had judiciously held back the reports so that she could send them when they were needed.

By doing shift work at the factory, 7am to 3pm, she was able to return to Berlin at night and pay visits to camps close to Potsdam and Berlin from time to time. The first few weeks she relied on written reports and the occasional telephone calls to keep her abreast of the news. Inevitably she had to go into the office to keep the pretence going. It took courage, something that Halle did not lack, but a different type than that required to plant bombs; particularly if you were half convinced that there was someone on your trail.

Crossing the threshold she half believed she would be arrested before she sat down at her desk. No one showed the slightest inclination to apprehend her and evidently everyone took it that everything was as before. There was one message that had not been passed on to her on the telephone and it was from Hengist. It merely asked her to visit the Prisoner-of-War Camp at Thorn in the coming week. She greeted the message with joy, "This is it! I'll not be back, I've had enough. I'm determined to make this the jumping-off point for my eventual escape!"

CHAPTER 8
(April 1943)

IAN HAD BEEN anxious to get away from Halle and the office that she occupied. She may or may not have been on the level. All that belonged to the realms of speculation, more importantly he was due to escape that very evening with two others. Although his modesty forbade him saying openly that he was the major figure who had planned their leaving the camp, still he had no doubt that his was the biggest part, even if one included the whole of the escape committee. His one niggling doubt was his choice of companions. On the face of it he chose them but the committee had made the point that they were in front of him on the list of men anxious to be gone and if he wanted to go at this time they would not be leapfrogged.

Three men travelling together would be easily spotted and picked up, particularly if the German authorities were on the watch for that number on the run. Ian came up with the idea of the other two being 'husband and wife' and as he was the ideas man they would travel together on the first leg of the journey to Warsaw. The committee commended him for his idea and, being aware that he had been to Warsaw on a previous escape attempt, wished him well this time and hoped their success would enable them to use the manner and the route again.

On reflection he concluded that it wasn't a matter of genius that concocted such a plan rather the reverse. All good ideas were simple. This one had emanated from the farm work for which he had volunteered. His sunburnt arms and face in particular had many of the men commenting on his French Gallic looks, especially as they were supplemented by his overall appearance. It was then that the idea started to crystallise in his mind; Poland was full of what the prisoners called 'slave workers', they were from every country that the Germans had over-run. He hoped rather than put great faith in his school French but "sufficient unto the day" would have to be the motto. No matter how much he wanted to shape matters he realised that there was a limit to what he could do with the other two. Both of them looked like peasant farmers and their Boer origins and language would be a good cover for them as Dutch workers; indeed the escape committee had a great deal of difficulty getting the correct documents for them. Peasant farmers would have been fine but to turn one into a 'wife' was beyond Ian's ability, particularly when both were concerned about their manliness.

This was the only weakness in the plan and if he had been able he would have got two others more suited to the part. Intellectually they also left a lot to be desired and he hoped that once he had made arrangements for them in Warsaw he could wave them good-bye with a happy heart. For the rest, the documents looked genuine to him—which didn't mean much when he thought about how little he knew about such items. He was convinced that the travel passes were the real McCoy but the clothes only about passed muster. At a distance they looked grand but close up their imperfections appeared to be magnified to the point that he felt they wouldn't fool anyone. The 'tailors' and 'dressmakers' ingenuity was undoubted but the materials were a hotchpotch of every type of uniform being worn in the camp. Still at a reasonable distance no one would notice.

Getting out was a matter of practice for everyone in the camp. Scraps of meat were used to distract the dogs, which constantly roamed the grounds at night. Each hut had its deputed dispenser of 'dog food' and once the signals were given the three men left to ensure they had sufficient time to catch the train. Boarding the train with the 'right' papers and with sufficient money for the tickets was a new experience for Ian. In the past it was always hit or miss but this was perfect, that is if one disregarded the unlikely pair sitting down the aisle from him. How their disguises weren't penetrated mystified him.

Thankfully Warsaw was the terminus; no need to ask where they were. Ian kept his distance from the others going through the turnstiles, "Thankfully I kept the details of where we are going to myself," thought Ian. "If it had been up to them they would have insisted on writing it down and nothing could be more dangerous for everyone concerned than that." The more he dwelt on his companions the more uneasy he became. George, Harry's 'wife', looked more and more in need of a shave each time Ian caught sight of him.

In the station it was clear that Harry was trying to distance himself from George, which intrigued Ian. What were they up to? Maybe Harry was aware of George's beard getting larger by the minute. Once on the street Ian passed them and overheard them arguing in Afrikaans. "After all the talks and the warnings from the escape committee one would hardly credit it." Ian's anger was now another danger to the whole project; he decided to confront them. He pretended to be looking for a light for his cigarette, "What the hell are you two playing at?" inquired Ian in as much of an undertone as he could muster. Harry was in a foul temper, "That one wants to go to the toilet!"

"So what's the problem? Just go to the ladies and that's that!"

"He wouldn't go there; I warned him on the train that he should go because he's so manly about using the gents, but he wouldn't. Now he's in desperation and he's still intending to go to the gents!"

"I'm away to see the American lady. Get yourselves sorted out now and meet me in the park as we agreed. Use your map if you get lost."

The 'husband' and 'wife' departed arguing in loud voices and Ian thought maybe this is no bad thing—there's something realistic about a couple being angry with one another. He watched them disappear round the side of the park and he assumed they were heading for the toilets he knew would be there. In the meantime Ian was conscious of portraying a French slave-worker and he made a point of looking in shop windows to which, normally, he had a natural antipathy.

He hadn't been long in the main street when he noted the amount of damage clearly done by a recent air raid. "There must have been one last night or perhaps the previous night," he thought as he picked his way through the rubble.

Rynek Starego Miasto according to his map was nearby and it was accurate—however the whole street was obliterated and he despaired when he found the American lady's home was gone. He was too afraid to ask what had happened to her and his anxiety to get out of the neighbourhood increased when he heard snatches of conversation mentioning the Warsaw uprising which didn't appear to be over.

Returning to the city centre Ian had some time to put in before the arranged meeting with the others. He wandered about trying not to draw attention to himself. At the same time his mind was working overtime. These were the people who drew Great Britain into the war—it would have been better, from his standpoint, if it had never happened. Worse than that, what was the British government thinking about defending a Roman Catholic nation? On the other hand, these people went to war against the Germans so they can't all be bad. "What a mess this world is in, we're fighting the Nazis for some reason which, at this point in time, escapes me! There seems to be as many Fenians as Prods in Germany yet they're all in this together, it's no wonder I can't make sense of any of it.

Then there is Halle—how did she get into this debate? She's backing the Germans because she thinks she'll get her own way in Ulster, some chance! Where does the religion come into this? Surely morality requires a staunch unmoving viewpoint on all of these issues? No wonder the world is in such a mess… I think this is where I came in." Having paraded the contestants in their many shades of greed he concluded that getting out alive was the most important objective in his life and the first step, in this direction, was to go and wait in the park for the two hambones who considered themselves worthy of being saved.

Once there it took some time to find an empty bench sufficiently near the gates for him to keep an eye on the comings and goings. Almost an hour passed and he was silently cursing the arrangement he had made. "So much for the wonderful plan which I wanted to be seen as my gift to the POW camp. I'm still an amateur at this and if I had any sense I would have gone alone when those two idiots started arguing." Ian sensed rather than knew George and Harry had come a cropper so he determined to find the only other contact he knew. As time passed the odds were that they had been recaptured and the Gestapo would have search parties out looking for the other escapee—himself! Although he didn't think the Gestapo would make much sense out of what those two boys would say, nonetheless they would have sufficient details from the camp to enable them to find him with relative easy. So it was important to get to the people who had helped him the previous time.

Aleksander Kosciuszko's house at 42 Franciszkanska no longer existed. Whatever had happened wasn't easily ascertained but the place looked like a bomb had blown the place apart and all that remained was a shell. "Well he was in the AK and the chances are that they were making a bomb and it blew up," thought Ian recollecting instances reported back in Belfast and how happy he had been that republicans had scored an own goal, particularly if those involved had been killed. "But this is different, these people are fighting their conqueror and naturally they will do whatever is necessary to get rid of them," conjectured Ian, not prepared to give a similar excuse to the republicans at home, "particularly Halle Hegel," he concluded. Later, when he realised what he had been thinking, he assented to another voice that he was bigoted and partial in his views but he still did not relent on Halle, "She was the most vicious Fenian of the lot, regardless of what John says about my face. And if she thinks I'll be asking her help at any point in time, she has another thought coming to her."

Yet another thought took over; maybe he could still contact the American lady. The chances were that she would have left the house when she saw the danger from the uprising but just where to start looking? *All* he had to do was find her; for a moment his mind locked on the word *all* as it dawned on him that the clichéd word 'needle' would be a devil of a sight easier to find. "Where could I start? Well Warsaw is the only place I can explore—I had better get started—the odds are already stacked against me... Now if I was at home and was looking for someone I would walk into the nearest barracks and ask an RUC constable for help and they would point me in the right direction. Why wouldn't it work here? If I kept my nerve and trusted the papers I have, why wouldn't it?" He was becoming sick of the 'whys', "Just do it, you have nothing to lose, have you? Besides if the Gestapo patrols have my description and are out hunting me the last place they'll expect me to be is a police station."

Ian wandered the streets looking for a police station and after something like half an hour he eventually came to one. "Nothing like the barracks at home, are they?" he asked himself. He went in and approached the counter just inside the door. A policeman spoke to him in Polish and he assumed that he was asking him his business. Rather than start a whole palaver where one couldn't understand the other Ian handed the man his papers. The policeman immediately departed for an office in the rear and after a few minutes returned with his superior—at least that was Ian's interpretation. He didn't speak French but said he had a little English, "Excusez-moi, parler vous Anglais?" Ian's "Oui," sounded like a sigh of relief. "What is it you want?" asked the officer. Ian had already prepared a story in his anxiety to find the lady. "I am here to work as you can see from my papers but I have an uncle living here with his American wife. But when I went to their address it was blown up. You understand?" The officer nodded and Ian went on to ask was it possible to find them. "Wait, I will see." The clock appeared to have stopped and yet there must have been some movement because the hands had moved on two minutes. Each person coming into the office looked at him and when two German soldiers arrived Ian thought the game was up but they gave him a mere glance before they dealt with their business and departed. "I think we have found the lady you described but the name is different." Ian knew this would be a stumbling block but he claimed that his 'aunt' kept her maiden name for business reasons. "I have some bad news, your uncle died last year but the lady is now in a large dormitory in a school we have acquired for those left homeless. You wish I give you her address?" Ian hastily uttered "Please" and waited to be directed to the school.

Alice Strephon turned out to be an elderly woman who was still mentally agile in spite of her weight of years. The fact that she spoke English to Ian drew no attention to them, apparently she constantly used her native language at every opportunity. Ian's solicitude for her situation was waved away as being of no consequence, she was more concerned as to how Ian managed to find her and what he wanted her to do. A sense of guilt pervaded each and every utterance emanating from Ian's mouth. Here he was seeking help from an elderly woman who he should, in ordinary circumstances, be helping. "I'm sorry to be approaching you at this time when you are in such dire and straitened difficulties. Firstly, is there anything I can do for you?"

"Don't be ridiculous man! What could you do, eh?" Ian now added a feeling of foolishness to his sense of guilt. "I suppose you're right but is there anything, I have some money, not much but if you need it…"

"Sense doesn't seem to be a quality you're blessed with, does it?"

"Normally I would say it was but horses for courses and I certainly wasn't built for this particular event."

"Thanks all the same, but I'm sure the old expression among the Irish back home would be familiar to you, 'it's money from America', yes?"

"Indeed it is, it's still true to this day."

"Well my children send me money monthly, so I'm quite well off, thank you. More to the point, what can I do for you?"

"Perhaps you still have contacts that could help me to get away. You see I am with two others but they failed to show up at the park yesterday and as a result I'm stuck until I find out exactly what happened to them."

"Surely it must be obvious by now, besides once out of those gates you should really leave it to the individual to see to themselves."

"But I did say I would see them in the park and they weren't there. There probably is a good reason…"

"Give me one outside of their being captured."

"Well… if they thought they were being followed they wouldn't go to the rendezvous and it's possible that they escaped and will return today."

"You're a great man for wishful thinking but I suppose that I'm no different, particularly when I think how I came to this country with a Polish man I barely knew five minutes. But enough of me; you and your friends need help so all I can do is give you a name and an address. Before she spoke Ian sensed it would be Aleksander's name and address and "of course when you're luck is out it really goes all the way!" Alice was upset but she had no other information that would help Ian and his friends. "There nothing for it but to return to the park and see if they are there."

The park clock became his focus and he determined to move on at 4 p.m. Each minute was an eon in time and felt like a sentence that would never be commuted to solar time. He was on the point of going when a German officer and a young Polish girl sat down. He had failed to spot their arrival and assumed that they had come up behind him, but what to do? The horns of a dilemma seemed pretty simple in comparison with this one—"Do I get up and go or do I sit on making it likely they will see this as normality?" Ian pondered for a couple of minutes unaware that the average Pole or indeed slave worker would get the hell out of it. Too late! Unintentionally he had drawn attention to himself and the officer drew his gun and demanded that he raise his hands.

Ian lifted his hands reluctantly, at one point he thought seriously of making a run for it, assuming that the Gestapo man was unlikely to fire in such a crowded area. A few seconds thought cured him of that notion. Meantime the officer was blowing the life out of his whistle. Eventually three policemen arrived to deal with the dangerous presence of Ian and soon he was whisked off to the city's jail. In the van a policeman informed him that his comrades were in their hands.

Once inside the jail Ian spotted the cause of all his woes, two woe-begotten figures full of sorrow for themselves, "I have you lot to thank, I believe?" Neither of them raised their eyes, "Tell me truthfully was it the issue of which lavatory to use?" Harry nodded and eventually said, "It came to blows—the whole idea was crazy!" Ian couldn't agree, "No, two people with a sensible approach would have had a policy they would stick to *before* they left the camp."

"George is now claiming that he didn't want to use the ladies because he felt his beard was a dead give-away..."

The officer reminded them they were on a serious charge and were not permitted to speak. "Well what's the hold up?" demanded Ian. "There's also a possibility you three will be charged with espionage." Ian couldn't refrain from smiling but knowing how ill this would be received asked when they would know and would they have an opportunity to defend themselves, "In fact the more I think about it, it must be a joke—you can't be serious. These two comedians—spies? No one in their right mind would believe that."

"We Germans are not so naïve to be taken in by this. It could have been a way to distract attention from the person they were meeting, who knows?" The officer gesticulated and raised his shoulders. Ian felt that discretion was the better part of valour, he simply smiled and asked what would happen now. "You'll be returned to your camp and the matter will be dealt with there."

Later in the day the three of them were removed from the cell, where they were held, to meet the guards sent to collect them. The soldiers' faces indicated what was in store for them. "It's solitary for us, for sure," muttered George to Ian—he still wasn't talking to Harry—maybe preparing for the loneliness of the next few weeks.

"How long?" asked Ian in as low a voice as he could manage. "Who knows? Depends on the latest orders from Berlin. Two weeks at the least." Ian wondered if Halle was back there and would she know about his abortive attempt to get away especially after offering him a better opportunity. Certainty on a plate was not what he was after but freedom would be nice but not at the price Halle wanted—not that he knew what that was!

The guard looked at him belligerently and Ian suspected the man must have missed out on his weekend leave because of them. "Let me warn you that they are considering changing the treatment of escaped prisoners—they may be shot for deliberately aiding the enemy in the time of war. Already we are preparing a new camp for constant escapers. This time solitary confinement for two weeks as it's your first escape but you know what will happen if you are so foolish as to attempt it again."

Being held overnight awaiting the guards to arrive from Thorn was a pleasant enough diversion after the previous night in the park. He had visited the house attached to the Church of the Virgin Mary and was fed with an identical soup and with similar black bread as the last time. He wondered if Aleksander had managed to escape the explosion in his house and, if he had, what mischief was he up to now. "Thud!" A huge explosion rocked the cell he and the South Africans occupied, how they weren't killed he didn't know. George and Harry were unconscious but Ian was well enough to make a run for it while chaos ensued within and without the building. Should he go or should he stay? What purpose was to be achieved by staying? He could assist George and Harry to recover but wouldn't the Germans and the fire service do the same? Of course they would and within thirty seconds Ian was on his way, picking carefully through the debris until he was sufficiently in the clear to start running.

Ian never got to know what the people who had turned out to help made of this gaunt figure of a man, covered in dirt and dust, who was galloping down the street as if pursued by all the devils in hell. He didn'tknow where he was, nor where he was going, nor how much ground he had covered when he was suddenly confronted by a woman who pushed, more than directed him into a house. Once inside this small woman continued to direct and push him, this time up the stairs and into a back room. All the while she lay down a heavy barrage of talk, which he assumed was in Polish. Ian sat down on the edge of a bed to catch his breath and the woman stood over him obviously waiting his reply to what he assumed where a series of questions. Eventually Ian shook his head and lifted his shoulders to show his ignorance of what was going on and the woman suddenly looked frightened, realising that he wasn't the person she was expecting. Just as quickly as she had managed to get him into the bedroom she was dragging him, just as quickly, out.

Ian was at a loss as to what to do, as it dawned on him that he was so weak that he had no hope of restraining the woman. "I am British!" he shouted, and the response from the woman was to push him harder.

"Britishski," he yelled as he held on to the banisters. The young woman stopped for breath and for an instant Ian believed that his mutilation of the Polish language had succeeded. He knew he should have known more words, after all he had been with Aleksander and stayed in two different houses but whatever he knew had deserted him.

The woman by now had changed places and he found her below him and pushing him back into the bedroom. This time he went with no force being needed and as he sat down he heard the key going in the door and when he checked he found it locked. "What have I got myself into this time?" thought Ian. "Well it can't be any worse than that prison camp they have lined up for me. Just lie down and rest and see who that woman brings to look at me. Whether it will be Germans or the AK I'll soon discover."

Being held captive by an unknown didn't seem to disturb Ian's equanimity as he fell asleep as soon as he lay back. However, his dreams made up for it and once again he was in Templemore Avenue trying to beat the Lambeg drum that became the size of the Cave Hill. In spite of his inability the noise reverberated throughout the neighbourhood and as the noise dissipated it seemed that he was the sole topic of conversation among the many crowding the streets nearby. It seemed that he was a traitor who was associating with an adult woman called Halle Hegel. As soon as he heard the name he jolted out of his sleep. "That bloody woman still haunts me to this day!"

Another hour must have elapsed before he thought he heard voices downstairs. After a few minutes the sound of at least two people tip toeing on the stairs had him tense and awaiting the worst. He wasn't surprised that the first item he saw was a revolver peeping around the door after the key was turned, "You are British, are you?" Ian recognised the voice and was very quick to reply, "Yes, Aleksander."

"It must be that heretic Patterson!" and Aleksander and the young woman advanced into the room. "My God, do you never give up? Are you on the run again, I assume you were caught the last time, seeing you are here?"

"The battle cry of the Ulster Scots is 'No Surrender' and I have to live up to that!" Aleksander shook his hand and then threw his arms around him and Ian reciprocated. "Can you tell this young woman I'm sorry for the scare I gave her? I did not know what was going on." The AK group leader turned and explained who Ian was and at the same time Ian tried to convey that he had been a prisoner in the jail that they had blown up. The conversation between the young woman and Aleksander seemed to be very intense and finally Ian asked what precisely was going on. "This attack was supposed to have taken place last night and the intention was to create a hole in the wall big enough for our men who are interned there to get away. But we had problems with the explosives and we were forced to do it today but unknown to us the Germans had moved them, perhaps to accommodate you and your friends. Marie here is annoyed because she was not informed about the change of plans. When she heard the explosion she ran out to help those escaping but you were the only one to run in her direction. Naturally she thought she was helping when she pushed you into the house."

"You were not joking when you said you had had difficulties with the explosives—you nearly killed the three of us, as it is the other two were knocked unconscious."

"We are sorry about that but at least you are here in comparative safety. I suppose you are still intent on escaping back to Great Britain?"

"Indeed I am," and he went on to tell Aleksander about Halle's offer knowing that the Pole would be highly sceptical about dealing with anyone connected with the Nazis. Ian went on to ask, "What are the prospects this time of getting to Gdansk, are they any better?" Aleksander took his time in replying, "Perhaps if you stayed in Warsaw for a time, until we have a chance to advise you as to the best time and way to go. It's a risky business whichever method you choose. Many of our men are being picked up and imprisoned and for that reason the chances of you seeing me again are remote. Do not worry, I will see to it that you are looked after."

Clearly Ian was putting a stress on the resistance as they sought a means to help him when they themselves were at their wits end in order to help their own. Ian determined to make it by himself, if they could provide food and some money he probably would get a great deal further than he had been previously—one thing he wouldn't do this time was travel by train!

Later that evening when Marie arrived back Ian told her, by means of signs, that he was going to make an effort to get away. He thought if she could give him some general directions to Gdansk that, with a bit of luck, he would make it, especially as he still had an idea of how to get to Sweden. Marie was unimpressed and pointed to his head indicating his lack of sense but Ian had an inborn Ulster stubbornness that wasn't going to be supplanted by someone else's logic and practical sense. He wasn't going to be beholden to anyone who were endangering themselves on his behalf. He imagines Marie's response to be; "Surely you must realise that you are bound to be caught acting on your own?" Nothing was going to deter him and it was only when he went to bed that he accepted the voice telling him that he was determined to show Miss Hegel that he didn't need her to get out of this mess!

The next morning, still undeterred, Ian sat down with Marie who, remembering his wish from the previous evening, drew up a map for him. Holding the palms of both hands vertically opposite one another over the map he stretched them between Warsaw and Gdansk. Marie was all too aware of what he was asking and she left the room to return moments later with a piece of paper and a pencil, then she wrote '250-300 km'. He held up his hand to hold her there and then proceeded to talk as if to her, "Wait until I work that out in miles—divide by eight and multiply by five." By now he was oblivious of her lack of English and her presence and he spent a few minutes muttering away under his breath as he worked on the distance, "That's nearly 185 miles, that's some distance on foot!" Marie's blank looks brought him out of his reverie, "I'm just going to have to go," concluded Ian. He went into the hall to retrieve his coat and turning offered his outstretched hand to Marie. Clearly she never believed for one minute that he would do anything so outrageously dangerous and probably hoped that Aleksander would return in sufficient time to deter him. Finally she shook it and Ian left.

He proceeded down the street and soon found the main road and once he had worked out where 'north' was he strode out as if he was on a parade ground. "At this kind of speed I'll be there in just a week. March is a good month for this kind of walk," he thought ignoring the possibility of a pun or possibly not being aware there was one.

The traffic comprised mainly of horse and carts with an occasional German Army lorry. He tried not to look at any of them thinking that if he were stopped he would put up a pretence of being dumb in order to bluff his way. The further out of town he went the smaller amount of traffic and he began to feel that the chances of him being caught were somewhat reduced. However, the more he consulted Marie's map the more disheartened he became at the distances involved. She had named a few towns on the way and the first on the map was Plock and it was approximately 50 km away. The thought of so much walking exhausted him and when he came to a bridge over a large river he decided to have a rest by its banks. "This must be the Vistula and according to this drawing it runs right up to Gdansk, if I'm lucky I may be able to get a boat going in that direction." The thought helped him to revive his spirits but the need for food soon superseded all other concerns. He soon had to abandon the riverside and make his way up to the farms that adjoined the river.

Trying to keep an eye on the river and look at the farms for the off chance of food made him careless about checking the possibility of his being observed. On his visit to the third farm he had spotted he failed to see that it was being searched by a detachment of German soldiers and he blithely walked into them.

The officer soon made him aware that they knew who he was and although they hadn't been specifically looking for him they had been on the look out for him since they apprehended his two companions as they attempted to escape from the prison after the explosion. Ian was bewildered at the sudden change of fortune—one moment he was wandering along hopefully seeking a boat and now he was back in custody of the German Army. They soon bundled him into the back of their lorry and he was amazed how little distance he had covered when they pulled into the police station in Warsaw within half an hour.

He went through the usual palaver of warnings and threats of what faced him when he got to the POW camp. In the meantime he was to be transferred to a transit camp where he would be held for a day or two until it was determined which place he had been allocated. Once he arrived it was made clear that he was categorised: "as a recidivist being an escaped prisoner who was beyond reform". Yet he was glad the English-speaking officer explained, although he convinced himself that he had got the drift and that he would be sent to a new camp for prisoners like himself.

Ian was amazed when he met up with a large number of men all of whom had made an attempt to escape but could hardly believe that some had more escape attempts than him. One consoling factor was there was no way that the Germans would have enough space to put all of them into solitary confinement—or could they?

CHAPTER 9

(April 1943)

IAN WAS BEING shepherded along with about twenty men but somehow George and Harry seemed to have been moved to another group. Some guy who was breathing down his neck, literally, kept muttering to himself, and unknowingly also to Ian, about how unlucky he had been. Ian turned, "You know we all think that; I kept blaming my two, so called, friends for all the difficulty I had," he looked the man directly in the face, "and, come to think of it, I was right!" The man laughed, "So you weren't on your own either?"

"No, the escape committee voted these two idiots on to an escape planned for one!"

"Jesus, all these committees act in the same way. I tell you, no more of them for me—I'd rather go out in the middle of winter in my bare feet than get stuck with another idiot—like the one I had this time."

"What happened?"

"Well we had got to Gdansk and I imagined I could see Sweden in the distance, I know it was all imagination but it didn't half give me a lift. I had an address of a fisherman who regularly ran people across so it was going better than fine. Then this idiot, whose whole point of existence was to get off his mark with every woman he met—from six to sixty, as they say back home. How we got as far as there I'll never know because I had to ensure we stayed as much as possible in the wilderness to keep him out of harm's way."

"I suppose he met some dame and drew attention to himself?" queried Ian. "Worse than that, he picked up a woman, OK—par for the course for him—but would you believe she turned out to be an undercover cop sent to stop the smuggling of prisoners to Sweden! And I thought my two children were a handful…" Ian interrupted to tell his new acquaintance how he came to be heading to the same camp at Thorn. Billy, the name of his new companion, sympathised but maintained that Ian had an easier time than he did. It suddenly dawned on Ian that this was the man with whom to do business. "If only he had been with me, or indeed, I had been with him we would have been in Sweden now waiting for the British Embassy to set the wheels in motion for our return to the UK," his mind was working overtime, "Would he go with me? After all he had sworn he would never go with anyone else. I'll ask him point blank."

146

"Billy what are the chances of us making an effort together?" Bluntly Billy said, "No! Sorry and all that but you know the old saying, 'once bitten…'"

"OK, but you could at least give me a list of your contacts so that I could get as far as you did."

"I'll tell you precisely how to get to them but there's no way I would write a list. How good is your memory?"

"Pretty good for life saving details but nothing else!"

Billy proceeded to spell out the directions and the people in the Polish resistance who had been useful to him but he warned Ian that under no circumstances was he to reveal these to any other, whether escape committee or individuals. "Have you heard anything about this place we're heading into now?" Billy shook his head and Ian went on to say that the guards in the police station went on and on about the new regulations and how strict they would be adhered to, "Only those who have escaped more than twice are to be incarcerated there." Ian stopped suddenly as if he ran out of breath, "Lord that must be why Harry and George have been separated from us!" Billy looked askance at him; "You've lost me, what are you on about?"

"It's just that Harry and George have only escaped once so that's why they're not here but to get back to what the guards said, there was a suggestion that the High Command had given instructions for escapees to be shot."

"Normally I don't put much store on that mumbo-jumbo but it's clear the Germans are cracking down and setting up what they call 'escape-proof' prisons. But I'll judge by what I see as well as by what I hear when we get inside." The German guards pushed them to keep the group as tightly packed as possible. Anything that caused discomfort seemed to be the purpose. The 'welcoming' party was awaiting their arrival with the Commandant standing at ease to the front of the main group.

The Commandant required an interpreter, which was a new experience for Ian because each of his previous camps had a Commandant who spoke English as if they had been educated in England. This man, they soon discovered, was an SS officer who had been invalided from the Russian front but who clearly had not got over his fascination for Hitler and all his works and pomps. His speech sounded abrasive and threatening and the interpreter certainly didn't reduce its ferocity, "This camp is here for the three times losers," Ian was confident that the man was trained in the USA, certainly no one at home spoke in those terms, nor did the Commandant in German! The hectoring and the threats were not new to him but there was something that suggested, "Just try it and you'll get a bullet for your trouble."

Billy was none too impressed, he whispered, "I think I'll leave tonight," and Ian nearly burst trying to contain himself and his laughter. Later he asked Billy was he serious in what he had said earlier and the cynical Englishman assured him that he was. Ian asked him to reconsider as he had a proposition to put and after taking some time to think it over Billy returned to say he would wait until the following day.

The next morning Ian, after spending half the night pondering the likelihood of survival in this camp, realised these crack army men had been brought in to toughen up the place but they didn't understand the cavalier attitude of so many of the prisoners. They wanted out and were prepared to take risks that seemed crackpot to men obsessed with logic. It would be a while before these new guards came to terms with this. "I should get out with Billy now before they learn," concluded Ian and he was glad he had asked Billy to postpone his leaving.

It wasn't long before Billy arrived anxious to hear what Ian was going to suggest. "Look Billy I have given this a lot of thought during the night... indeed I thought about it all day yesterday after talking to you. I wouldn't be saying any of this if I didn't trust you. There's a woman touring the camps—before I say another word you'd better give me your oath that you'll not say a word about any of this."

"Look I'd rather not... no harm to you but I dread people giving me their confidences especially around places like these. I thought you were going to ask could you accompany me and the temptation is great because, in a sense, there is a rapport between us but I made a promise to myself that I intend to keep. Sorry, but you know the story..."

"Don't blame yourself, just that I thought... we'll drop it and I'll wish you the best of luck."

"Thanks but I'm determined to make it on my own this time, if it doesn't work too bad I'll have given it my best effort. It's being in places like this one that helps to crystallise your thoughts. I know you sense that we have a lot in common but somehow I doubt it. You see I believe this war is about a bunch of bastards determined that this foreign bunch of bastards won't take control of the markets which they exploit."

"Surely it's more involved than that?"

"Of course there's always something more but this isn't a five-year degree course we're involved in—I don't know about you but I'm here literally fighting for my life and to have a life."

"I agree that life isn't a philosophical treatise. As I see it you live it and if you're wise you learn from your mistakes."

"I wouldn't disagree with any of that but I want to see these chancers get their comeuppance so that none of us have to fight in another war to keep their pockets lined."

"Is this all there is in your philosophy?"

"All I can say is if more people thought the way I do we'd never have been in this mess—and my dad wouldn't have been killed in the last one."

"But you're still not facing up to the competition in life. A lot of the time it's them or us."

"You really have swallowed it, hook, line and sinker. If you play on everyone's ambition to get on by making jealousy and envy the new commandments then we'll be back fighting within five years of this one ending. Do you fancy parading out for the next one? But you're Irish, you don't take a break in between, do you?" Ian let the dig about being Irish pass.

"Where does religion and traditional values slip into this? Apart from the prophetic warnings you seem to have this reduced to two sins?"

"No, if you think on what I said you'll see it's three. Selfishness is the big winner. It coerced me into fighting others like me who only wanted enough grub to eat and a place to put their heads at night."

"This is much too simple for me—and I didn't miss your dig at me— I'm not Irish, I'm British and proud of it—obviously unlike you." Ian was now standing upright like a man on parade and unaware that he was acting as if he was back on a parade ground.

"If fighting for Britain makes you British then I'm one, because my father fought in the Boer War and the Great War for that reason—he was British. Of course he was treated like dirt in between times and still he went on fighting for them. He died in the end leaving five kids, a widow and a war pension, which could barely keep one of them. I've two kids myself and I'm sure my missus is sweating in case I catch a packet before this is over."

"I could name a dozen people who had the same misfortune but they don't bellyache about it."

"More's the pity. Ian, people like you want to live with the glory and honour of the past as if all those who lived the hell of it were important and died gloriously, but it wasn't like that. There was no Golden Age and if people only had a minimum understanding of history they would know that. What your philosophy has brought us is two world wars inside thirty years! However, I don't want to leave you with a disagreement, so shake hands and let us see what happens."

"It's nice to hear others' views even if we can only agree to disagree. But to get down to the essentials, is there anything you need that I can get you?"

"Nothing, unless you have a bundle of Reichmarks."

"Sorry what I had were about to be confiscated in Warsaw so I dropped them into a woman's pocket."

"I'm sorry I'm so like you."

"The best of British, anyway, and I'm not trying to get a dig in," and Ian walked out saddened by the short outcome.

"I wonder why I was going to tell him about Halle's story and the proposed escape. I have no confidence in her or her plan so what was I doing dragging Billy into it?" He paused to consider just what had he been thinking about, "You liked Billy yet you were proposing to involve him in a hair-brained scheme that you ran away from only a matter of days ago." He began to walk about to give the Huns the impression he was exercising when he came across John. "Good Lord, what are you doing here?"

"I've been ill and as this was the nearest camp with a sizeable hospital within its perimeters they sent me here."

"I'm sorry to hear that, just what has been the problem?"

"They haven't found anything yet, so I don't know."

"But how were you feeling that drew your attention to it?"

"I was fainting and apparently foaming at the mouth so the guy that looks after first aid sent for their doc and he arranged to have me moved here."

"Why are you not confined to a bed then?"

"This is my first day up and they turned me out in the air to see if it happened again."

"That's why I didn't spot you when I arrived."

"Look I have to get back, I'll talk to you later about my card playing exploits and how it has managed to keep me from going out of my head," with that he turned on his heel and left.

"One never knows the moment," thought Ian, but his mind turned once again to thoughts of escape and the possibility that Halle held the right cards. "For once in your life don't let prejudice colour this. What did the girl say? Well, she said something about being tied into the German propaganda machine—the radio and using an idea she had to get her out of the country. She was willing to share the idea with me because she knew that she wouldn't be strong enough for some of the activities required to get across borders etc. Did she say this or any of this? Now stop, begin again… she went on about Berlin and the Jews and how she wanted out, nothing about not being strong. Anyway the chances of her turning up aren't exactly rosy and I'm certain she has heard about my recapture and that will cool her ardour in having me along."

Changes continued all day long as it appeared that the Commandant was importing new men but it was only after seeing them that Ian realised that the younger men he had seen the previous day were no longer present. Some of his hut mates had told him that the guards wouldn't be there for long but he assumed that they were stories put about by the administration in order to confuse the prisoners even more than they were already. These guards were much older, indeed Ian thought the majority were in their fifties. "So the Russians must surely be hurting them in a serious fashion," thought Ian, "and that's not good news for me and the boys in this camp. The last thing I want to do is to end up in a Russian POW camp waiting for eternity to pass while they check whether I'm a British soldier. God knows what they'll make of me; born in South Africa, raised in Ulster and British to boot. No, I'd better start preparing to do a job like Billy."

The following day the Commandant's morning speech mentioned that there would be a visitor to speak to each Irish prisoner individually. Ian's head jerked up—it could only be Halle on her recruitment drive and once she saw his name on the list of prisoners he reckoned he would be seen very early. "This is an act of providence—I never thought I would think that about any Fenian and least of all Halle Hegel!" Ian's internal speaker was in full voice, "Only yesterday you were ready for selling her out to your mate Billy, in spite of giving your word that you wouldn't tell anyone of her intentions. 'I didn't believe that story of hers'. Ah! But now you do because it suits you. So you'll go along and play the sweet little angel in front of her, to get her to take you along because you are frightened of the Ruskies. Some soldier, some hero, some Ulsterman you are! 'I'm doing no more than anyone would do to escape in order to re-join my regiment.' And whom do you think you're kidding? At any rate go on, I can't wait to see how you do this without turning red with embarrassment."

He wasn't wrong about how soon she'd send for him. It was early afternoon when he received the call and he pretended to his hut mates that this was the first time he had encountered Fräulein Hegel. The room was laid out in a similar fashion to the room back in Posen—two guards were posted inside the room but sufficiently far enough away to give them the semblance of privacy.

"I had a hell of a job getting authority to visit this place," began Halle. "Why was that?"

"Well you try explaining what good would come of trying to enlist escapees to fight for the Germans on the Eastern front."

"I must admit, you have me there."

"Well it took me a while to think of a reason—eventually I told them that these men wanted action and they weren't being given the opportunity, so what could they do? Wait and starve for excitement or prove they could do something?"

"Did they not want to know how you knew this?"

"Of course they did and I told them about you escaping because you were waiting that long for an opportunity."

"You're joking? Sure you had no idea I would be here before you arrived."

"Nobody knows that better than I do. But I had to get to camps where you were likely to be." Halle could lie with the best of them. "So you expected me to be caught? Why are you bothering approaching me if that is what you think?" The realisation that the somewhat fragile image that Ian had of himself and his escaping had to be massaged. "I'm beginning to wonder myself... I'm only joking; look you hardly think I would be relying on someone who wants to fight for the Germans, do you? Similarly I wouldn't want some idiot who doesn't know his right hand from his left."

"So let's lump this all together; you want someone who knows right from left and that's all? I'm beginning to have my doubts about your sanity."

"This could go on all night, do you think this scheme could work?"

"You haven't explained it yet."

"You mean you have already forgotten what I told you the last time?"

"No, but I'd like to hear it again in full. But before you start, is it true that the Russians are giving them hell?"

"Look, these guys at the door aren't phenomenally bright but you keep mentioning 'Russia' or certain place names and they'll twig on that this is far from kosher—Good God how did that slip out? We can talk about this later, OK?"

"Forget about the joshing I was doing. I remember enough for now and I'm prepared to accept what you said at Posen and I'll go along with that."

"Wait a minute—the last speedy conversion was on the road to Damascus but you've just broken the record."

"I hate it when you blaspheme."

"Ian I wonder do you be as hard nosed and righteous about religion in front of others, particularly in the POW camps, as you do with me?" Ian instantly realised he was selective about whom he tackled and in Halle's case was deliberately making a point about her so-called religion. Recently he had found himself using God's name in vain, a particularly offensive habit, which he associated only with Roman Catholics and now that Halle had nailed his predilections to the door of his conscience he would be more careful in future.

"No, you're right on a number of counts. Yes, I hardly quibble at the use of bad language, it seems endemic in the camps and I want away before the Reds get here because I've heard that many stories about the ruthless murders in that country. As an afterthought you'd be advised to be well away before they arrive."

"Thanks for your truthfulness, I've only began wondering what will become of me if I'm captured by them."

"Can we organise anything right now? You know more about the situation than anyone to whom I've spoken."

"Thankfully these new people in charge are not aware of the rules and regulations. I have papers for the release of prisoners into my custody, which I'm confident, will bluff them into letting you accompany me when I leave. In fact these papers require an authorised stamp but I'm sure they'll overlook it in their haste to get rid of me. However, once I approach them you will be removed from the other men—who undoubtedly will see you as a traitor? Whatever you do, don't speak of this to anyone—the slightest whisper and you'd be amazed how often the camp guards get a whiff of it and that would be that—only I would be arrested in addition."

"OK, it won't be easy to be regarded as a traitor but if this works it will be worth it. I suppose you're organised, plan, travel documents etc.?"

"Yes, I have all the papers but the difficult one will be your papers because they will lack the official stamp from Berlin, but I'm reasonably hopeful it will pass muster. Look, I can't talk fully now but once I've convinced them that this is a genuine case I'll be back."

Ian left trying not to look pleased but by the late afternoon and he hadn't heard from Halle he began seriously thinking of planning a separate escape. If he didn't hear from Halle before six o'clock he would prepare to go.

Halle eventually returned and the expression on her face told what had happened. "The guy I had to deal with was new but he was a stickler for procedure so he wants to hold on to you until he gets clearance from Berlin."

"But that's hopeless! By the time he receives word back the Russians will be at the gate."

"Thanks for thinking about me!"

"For heaven's sake don't let's start this. Is there any way you could get false papers from your escape committee and, of course, help to get out?"

"Why can't I just go with you? Surely if I'm to be this convert to the Nazi army I should be able to go on your say so." Halle shook her head, "I'm supposed to go on to other camps, so normally they would remove you to Germany so there's no other way." Ian's face showed his apprehension;

Halle asked, "Do you still not trust me?" The emphatic shake of Ian's head made Halle demand that he spat out what precisely he was concerned about. Ian tried to explain that the issuing of papers in POW camps was an issue of precedence and there would be many already waiting. Halle was impatient, "Seeing the circumstances couldn't you ask to be dealt with right away…" but Ian's upheld hand stopped her. "I would have to ask someone to step down to enable me to go but apart from that how could they produce forged papers overnight? And then you forget I'll need clothes and a reasonable disguise plus an acceptable story if I'm stopped by your friends in the Gestapo!"

Halle threw her hands up in despair, "Why, oh why did I think of helping you? You are so determined not to lose face by asking—but that's the way with you bastards… sorry I know I'm not allowed to say that in *front of you*; words are such a damnable sin in your eyes as well as being only open to one interpretation."

"Don't you start all this political shenanigans again; I'm all too aware that republicans make words mean different things on different occasions… All right, what do you want me to say to the escape committee? 'I'm back again to ask someone to stand down after having failed twice?' Is that what you want?" Ian wasn't anxious to tell the truth about his three failings because if he went back again no escape committee would be prepared to give him another chance.

"I don't give a shit what you say to those British bastards; I'm only doing this because you're Irish and a neighbour, even if you're a dissenter and a bloody awful one at that! Wolfe Tone has a lot to answer for; perhaps he didn't know about the likes of you when he opted for every type of citizen to be catered for… Sweet God and His Holy Mother, you don't expect me to go in and speak to the committee for you, do you? Just open your lips and the words will trip out; you're Irish after all and we all can talk." Ian's anger at all the ironic jibes at his background of puritanical reticence came to the fore, "You're pushing your luck Halle. If you'd been a man I'd have beaten you to a pulp. Why are you offering anyway? All this gibberish about someone whose idealism is worse than anathema to me, and who was as bad as Hitler in my view, doesn't impress me as to your credibility. I suppose you're expecting me to save your hide from these Gestapo thugs who are after you?"

Halle's response was equally angry, "I'm not going over this again. Perhaps you'd like me to say that I can't help myself and I'm madly in love with you. Well forget it, I'd take one of those murdering Nazis any day before you!"

"Wait a wee minute, why is all the responsibility falling to me? Why can't you go back and tell them that with all the communication problems it will be too late for this man to be of any use, particularly if the front passes him by while I'm sitting here. I'm sure you can embellish the story sufficiently, wasn't it the Jesuits at the time of the Gun Powder plot that put forward the iniquitous idea of a lesser evil being worth lying about!"

"There was no need for you to dig something out of the past about English Jesuits, I have no time for them—they're like all the English they'd lie for the simplest of reasons. But I must admire your standard of truthfulness when it suits you! OK, let's leave it at that, that's a good idea you had and I will go back and put it to them. I have to admit also that you made a reasonable case about your inability to go to the escape committee. Is that enough of eating humble pie to suit you?"

"It's so difficult to follow your thinking, I suppose it's no different from your behaviour when you were young. But I take all compliments with the dignity and humility that one would expect of a young Ulsterman!"

"I see your sense of humour is suddenly stronger than that humility you're always boasting about but I'm away to see what can be done."

It was some two hours later that Halle sent for him and he saw her flush of pleasure before she saw him and it was enough for Ian to realise that she had been successful. "Well how did you manage it?" Halle looked surprised, "You know already?" Ian's smile indicated he was about to launch another mild reproach, "I've always believed I could read you like a book, am I wrong?"

"God but I hate you at times! Yes the Commandant thought it was a logical position and he signed an order giving me permission to take you on to Warsaw where you will be allocated an army unit."

"That's just perfect, the only thing I'm now concerned about is having sufficient money to enable us to stay in reasonable hostels or rooms. I must be getting old, I just don't fancy lying in barns or in ditches. I've no sooner said it than it has dawned on me that John is always winning the poker school on a regular basis. I think he'll let me have it, it isn't much use to him in here."

"I'm glad you thought of it—but where did he and his card playing friends get the money in the first place?"

"Well we're paid for the work we do on the farm, starvation wages wouldn't be in it but over time and with nothing else to do with it there is always a stock of it about. Sometimes they gave it to the escape committee to provide escaping prisoners with some cash and sometimes people like John—all six foot of him—did deals with guards for little tib-bits."

"How did your friend get into this camp, I noticed on his record that he had never escaped?"

"Neither he had, so it was a great shock to me when I arrived and found him here. Apparently he was moved because he has been ill and as this was the better hospital within a reasonable distance he was moved here. We used to argue about whether it was sensible to escape but I think he has been ill for some time and wasn't up to it. Also he had a thing about his height as well, believing that as he stood out in a crowd there was no way he would get any distance from the POW camp."

Ian went in search of John because he knew he was the only one he could confide in. The astonishment that met his request for money was minor in comparison with the look of shock and horror when Ian enlarged on the purpose he had in mind. "Halle Hegel? I can't believe you'd be that foolish. How is she involved with the Nazis? Mind you I always felt that they were of German extraction, possibly Jewish. The Nazis are a different type of problem to these republican bastards. Republicans rate revenge high on their list of achievements, and you would be in her hands, if I can believe my ears."

"I can't spend long and please don't be standing up for me when I'm accused of being a traitor, it's important that the Germans believe that we are both reliable conscripts to the German cause. By the way don't think for a minute that I'm taken in by her. She's holding something back—she's too strong a character to be depending on me; she could have got out before this with her position in the German Army. But I'm going at any rate, so not a word to the others, OK?"

"Don't you fret, there'll not be a word from me. Good luck, you'll need it with that madam!" On leaving John, Ian had an idea and decided to go to the escape committee's chief forger to ask how they were able to forge the stamp on their documents. Jan, a South African from Cape Town, had been in the police and was aware of some ways to copy important papers. "Jan I need to know an easy method of copying a German stamp. Is there one?"

"Yes there is. It's the only one I know anyway. You simply get an egg and peel off the shell, roll it over the stamp and you'll see it reproduced on the egg and then simply roll it over the document. OK?"

"Thanks Jan, I'm indebted to you but I can't tell you about it now. Sorry," and with that Ian went back to lolling near the camp gate where he could be seen from the guard's post. Halle had arranged with the Commandant to have her told in the event of Ian standing nearby. After ten minutes or so a guard approached Ian and took him to the office where Halle was waiting. "I'm about to get the letter from the Commandant and then we'll be off."

"I was thinking, what if the letter is not acceptable to some petty official on the way?"

"We'll deal with that as we go."

"I have a way to put a stamp on that document if you have a copy of it on some other document but I'll need an egg."

"An egg? That'll be even better, wait until we're on the train and you can do it at any of the many stopping points on the way. Is that fine?"

"Yeah, provided you can get an egg!"

Once outside the prison Halle took a coat from her bag and told Ian to wear it to cover up what remained of his uniform. They were driven to the railway station and they boarded a train for Warsaw without any difficulty. "Surely we're going the wrong way?" remarked Ian once they were on board. "How do you mean?" asked Halle between clenched teeth, obviously annoyed at his querying her at this juncture. "Well Gdansk is to the north, we're heading east, does that not tell you something?"

"You've been over this route before?" asked Halle. "Yeah, twice, but not as comfortably as this," muttered Ian. Halle instantly recognised Ian's reluctance to talk about it, "Would you like to say just what was the difficulty you ran into on both occasions?"

"Your tongue in cheek irony doesn't upset me. For one who had to go on the run in England it's a bit much to be quizzing me about the difficulties in an enemy country."

"Much and all as it doesn't answer my question, I should say I was never caught, unlike you. Once may have been bad luck but twice… what was it Oscar Wilde said?"

"You're still comparing camels and sheep. You had the advantage of speaking the language that your enemies spoke, while I had only a smattering of French to help me."

"I know you won't believe me now but I wasn't trying to nettle you, I just wanted to learn from your experience of the past."

"So you say but I know you better; every little opportunity you get there is a dig in it for me… Anyway, the escape committee recommended that we travel in pairs but unless you know the other person through and through you'll run into sticky situations, mostly over disagreements as to the next move. Also I've noticed that you suddenly become erudite when we are almost friendly, explain that."

"Then we'd be as well to stop now; we can't agree on anything and worst of all we have a tendency, well more than that, to argue about everything including how I speak."

"Well we had better decide on the best course at once. I'm only here because you dreamt up this scheme, personally I'd feel better on my own."

"But why did your escape committee suggest that working in pairs was better?" Ian used the old inquisitor's trick by answering a question with another, "Did you work singly or in pairs in England?" Halle barely opened her lips to say, "Pairs" when back came Ian's "Why?"

"Because we battened off one another. If I was in great form and my friend felt down then I encouraged her and vice-versa."

"But you make my point for me, you called her 'friend' and you could tell when she was depressed—we are not in that position, are we?"

"The position is not written in stone, if we agree to stop our political aggressions until we get out of German occupied Europe we could probably make a go of it."

"Is it possible or is this more spitting into the wind?"

"It won't be easy but what alternatives do we have? They are undoubtedly after me and I don't think they'll link us together because of our past history so I think it's worth the effort, provided both of us agree."

"You asked me earlier of my experiences while on the run. Well on one of them I was with another pair of escapees—just what the committee was thinking of I'm not sure. If a pair is bad news, a threesome is the worst possible combination," and Ian went on to relate the story of the abortive attempt to get away. "Apart from that the others had drawn so much attention to themselves that they had been arrested and the Germans were watching out for me," Halle's burst of laughter caused Ian to put his finger over his mouth, "Hush! Keep it down!"

Halle quietened immediately but insisted that he answer one way or the other. "Well there are a number of areas we'll have to agree on. What is supposed to be our relationship? Also if there's a disagreement one of us must have the casting vote if we are to stay together."

"Our papers will have different names…"

"But they don't have to, I can ask them to make them out to Herr Hegel! When I think back to Xerophyte Street and we used to refer to your da as Herr Hegel, little did I think I would be using his name some day."

"Why am I not surprised?" remarked Halle, "Just typical of the juvenile and adult Prods that lived in our street."

"Don't let us start all this again. I think we should travel as husband and wife but if this is a serious concern we could be brother and sister."

"I nearly let my spitefulness get the better of me; I'm sorry, I think husband and wife would be the less suspicious. But in answer to your question about why Warsaw, simply the letter from the Commandant states that we are on our way there, OK?"

"You know it would have been easier if you had said that at the start. And when did you start ending each sentence with OK?"

"I'll not grace that question with an answer, *OK?*" answered Halle with a smile.

The journey continued mostly in silence and only when they reached Warsaw did they discuss what was the next obstacle they would have to overcome. "Should I report to the German authorities now or should we, together, make our way to Danzig?" asked Halle. Ian took a little time to answer, he was aware that he was the one with experience of Poland and in particular of Warsaw. If he hadn't Halle with him he would have made an attempt to contact Aleksander but members of the AK would be none too pleased to have an official of the German Army using them to escape. He daren't mention this to Halle, as she was liable to tell him to go and use his friends—she was much too independent to be totally reliant on him, although he initially believed she wanted to use him for her own purposes. "Take all day if you like!" muttered Halle. "Thinking comes into this you know, or don't you?" was the robust reply from Ian. "OK then, keep you hair on but for God's sake hurry up with an answer. Every last German in this station is watching us and wondering what's going on!" Ian had been about to reply but this outburst caused him to stop and appear to ponder his answer once more.

Halle was exceedingly frustrated by this time and prowled up and down the platform showing her anger to anyone who was sufficiently curious to look at her face. Finally she approached Ian and just before she began to lay down the law he said, "Let us go on, the more time we take the more we endanger our chances of getting completely away." Halle wasn't prepared to bow to his superior knowledge, "No, just a minute, let's talk this over." Ian was already on the move and he spoke over his shoulder, "Well, not here," and walked on through the gates at the end of the platform. 'Furious' wasn't a strong enough word to convey Halle's emotions—"That supercilious bastard better not be trying it on with me. He thinks he's at home and can talk down to that inferior Catholic girl—well he's another thought coming. I'd sooner report him to the Gestapo that put up with his obnoxious behaviour," all this under her breath but she was sure that the smoke was issuing from her nostrils and ears.

Meanwhile Ian marched unconcernedly towards the park of his previous downfall. Once inside he stopped at the first bench and sat down waiting on the red-faced Halle to catch up. "What the…" Halle just about stopped herself from using a word foreign to her vocabulary. "Why are you so ignorant? Does it take a great deal of practice to be as good at it as you are?"

"What do you mean?" asked an over-innocent Ian.

"I did you the honour of giving you a choice in regards to the decision we had to make and when I was prepared to talk over the matter you take to your heels and leave me standing with my mouth open like a stranded fish on a beach!"

"Now look! You were the one who thought the whole world was watching us on that platform, so naturally I moved away just as you hinted we should; so then I'm in the wrong?"

"How the hell are we going to make anything of this escape? You're that determined to undermine everything I say or do."

"Wait a wee minute, you approached me, not the other way about. Consequently when you asked me for advice I thought you meant it, I didn't know you wanted to set up a parliament to have a debate about it. Of course I forgot you do want to set up an undemocratic parliament, Ha-Ha!" Ian's attempt at humour was lost on Halle who had now become seriousness personified.

"Now that you have got all that out of your system perhaps we can get back to what the purpose of this journey is about."

"Fine with me. What objection do you have about *my suggestion?*" Halle gave him a look that could kill. "I'll have to start ignoring your inflammatory responses, you haven't the kind of mind that's required for the job on hand. The fact that you have been caught twice, at least, should have been enough warning for me as to the outcome." Ian controlled himself having in mind that she held a number of aces that he was anxious to play seeing that the Polish resistance could only help part of the way. "Look let's start again and we'll begin by leaving our past just there, is that all right?"

"Just as long as you realise I won't let you push me around. We need each other in this enterprise so let's look at your suggestion."

"I feel that if we make an early move to get to Danzig we'll be able to use your cover on the railway and also in obtaining lodging. Otherwise we'll be forced to take to the roads and believe me that's not only dangerous but it is mighty unpleasant."

"There is a weakness in it though. If I don't report today they'll be on to us immediately, which means we can't use the railways or anything else for that matter. So we're forced on to the road right now. What do you think?"

"If you do show up now, how long is that going to keep them off our backs?"

"A day or two at the most seeing you are with me."

"So whether we like it or not we're on the road?"

"Not if we catch the train to Danzig today before they set the wheels in motion. Provided there is no one keeping an eye on us, did you notice anyone?"

"No, but you've put me off the notion of catching the train. Perhaps we could catch a bus part of the way which would give us some hope."

"I'll go along with that. Ian, I'm sorry about the quarrelling, let's keep it to a minimum, OK?"

"You know you should get rid of those papers of yours before we go any further. After all you had a near thing when the AK kidnapped you on the last occasion."

"Yes but I thought that they would be useful to get into the port area in Danzig. There may be other situations facing us that require us to have some documentary evidence of who we are."

"The truth is whatever we do there is a danger, so whatever you decide I'll go along with. Let's get round to the square and catch a bus."

Ian's knowledge of the area meant it took them little time to get to the bus station. They soon learnt that the shortage of petrol meant that few buses were able to make long journeys and the best they could hope for was a series of hops from one town to another. Plock was the only town on their route to which the bus was heading. Just what kind of accommodation lay at the end of their journey the Lord only knew and Halle's mind was crowded with a myriad of possibilities, not least was her agreeing to act as Ian's wife. Her doubts eased when she realised that she hadn't had time to get the documentation that would 'prove' their relationship!

CHAPTER 10

(May 1943)

THE BUS HAD seen better days and it chugged its way along roads that had never been designed for anything as big as it. Ian and Halle sat together for company as the bus was only half full. Ian attempted to start a conversation on a number of occasions but clearly Halle wasn't rising to the bait. "Can't you talk about anything other than religion or politics?" asked Ian after a period of silence between them. "Of course I can but you manage to get my blood up like nobody I ever met." The silence descended with a sense of perpetuity about it. Halle recognised that the constant bantering between them was a mixture of attraction and real hurt at the other's political position. She knew that for all her anxiety to be Irish she had to acknowledge she looked like her father. Indeed she had his attributes in large measure, which didn't sit easily on her mannered Irish accent and style of living. She had been to secondary school, unusual in a girl and stranger still for a "Catholic working-class" one, a position she claimed but one which her father assured her wasn't up to her to claim, it was the perceptions of others which determined the class position of anyone. Still, he could be wrong but as time passed she knew it was part of the reason she had got rid of Martin with his class-dominated ideas.

Literary pursuits like those that dominated her father's every free minute equally held her in a vice-like grip. However, unlike her father she was more interested in poetry. Tennyson indubitably had dominated her school poetry but in recent times T. S. Eliot, in spite of his Anglophile predilections caught her attention. She knew that among those interested in English poetry there was a tendency to favour W. H. Auden but Eliot's "Prufrock" had all the sense of a time and place with which she was familiar. Even in all of this she felt a traitor not giving W. B. Yeats pride of place but she felt that too much of his work was given over to fairies and spiritualism. An approach that gave a view of Ireland and the Irish, which did not equate with her own, but then again she may not be fully aware of all of his work having relied on the choice of teachers.

Almost as if he had read her mind Ian spoke, "Can we agree to discuss literature and give politics and religion a miss?" Halle was all set to agree but realised that such an agreement would end up as his and that was unacceptable. "No, you have all the last words and here we are again with an agreement, or more properly a so-called agreement that you propose and I'm always forced, from so-called logic, to accept but you will cast up as your property and look as if you are the driven snow."

"OK then, let's go back to religion and politics; anything to please you," this with much gritting of the teeth and gaps in the flow of language which suggested the absence of swear words. Halle realised that she had pushed him to breaking point and decided on this occasion to give way. "I'll tell you what, let us both agree on a subject without one or the other claiming it's their special topic, OK?"

"When do girls turn into women? And why do they have to?" asked Ian of the bus's roof as if he was unwilling to speak to God in such a blasphemous way. Halle was all set to wade into the fray when Ian held up both his hands, a token surrender in the face of the wrath that was to come. "Fine, that's fine with me. So what is it to be? You name it." Halle thought for a moment then decided that to give ground might prove advantageous in the next round. "Let's talk about literature; and don't roll your eyes! I was just making a point, OK?"

With the bickering out of the way Halle proceeded to speak of her attitudes to literature and her likes and dislikes but she acknowledged her deep regard for English poetry. Ian was tempted to go to town on Halle's mixed views about identity but left it alone as he was reluctant to face a tirade again. He purposely agreed with her views although he was aware that he knew little or nothing about poetry or, for that matter, any form of literature. However, he didn't bluff her with his soft tongue and nodding head.

"You know Ian, you can be as nice as nine pence when you like, but when you pretend knowledge and then deliberately ignore opportunities to get at me, sitting there with that smug smile just waiting to get in some snide remark, I feel like punching you. All right just tell me what you're thinking, truthfully!"

"No, I'd rather you'd finish first."

"Very well, you know that we are all part of a mongrel race. I have as many and maybe more English ancestors than you. And when it comes to it even my grandmother was a Presbyterian who returned to that religion on her deathbed. My brother is in the British Navy fighting for you and your likes while you are resting here. So don't think that you can accuse me of bigotry. You and your ilk have the mastery there and always have done!"

"You've admitted it at last! You're a mass of contradictions. You give me how Irish you are but when it comes to literature and poetry in particular, you're an Anglo through and through."

"Wouldn't you just like to be me! None of that strain of wild Irish blood running through your veins; the sense of purity that the Nazis long for! Real human beings are a mass of contradictions, so you'll note that I feel complimented! The real difference between us is that I acknowledge the differences and treasure them!"

Ian in the meantime had pretended that he was listening but he had very early in their acquaintanceship realised they would not last any length of time if the dispute persisted—the horrors of Harry and George would never leave him! "I am different! I'm an Ulster-Scot who has found himself in a part of an island that suits me fine!"

"So that means that not only are the Irish not welcome but the English also? Is that what you're hinting?"

"I'm not hinting, everyone is welcome provided that they accept the custom and practice of the people in Ulster; that's democracy!"

"In other words if the Irish or the English out number your lot it doesn't matter, they just have to tie up the swings on a Sunday and close everywhere for the working classes but let those with dough have alcohol in the golf clubs and their own social clubs."

"You know I don't approve of social division of that kind. The Sabbath should be observed and that should apply to everyone."

"What about those who don't interpret the bible the way your lot do? Many of the English see it from a different angle, don't they?"

"That doesn't mean that they're right!"

"Surely that statement must apply to everyone. The idea that it's democratic is a joke without a laugh. I don't think you can differentiate between a dictatorship and a democracy."

"What are we going to do for digs tonight?" asked Ian, changing the topic before it got too heated for him to keep his cool. Halle ignored the change and persisted in putting another point but Ian wasn't biting and Halle's fear about their nighttime arrangements stopped her talking about it as subject matter.

Plock was a small town and the nearest thing they had to a hotel was a small pension, the equivalent of a boarding house. Clearly they were doing very little business, partly because of the shortage of food and the restrictions on movement meant that there was little or no one journeying in the country. They were asked for identification and Halle smiled smugly at Ian, as if to say, "I told you I was right to hold on to my papers." In the circumstances she was glad to say that while they were travelling together as husband and wife, nonetheless they wanted separate rooms. The host and his wife were only too delighted to have some custom and the fact that they were able to cater for two people separately was a big thing financially. Still they required that the visitors' book be signed, as the Gestapo would ask for it on their weekly visit. Ian signed as Herr Hegel which made Halle smile but not within the vision of her fellow escapee.

Once they had make themselves comfortable they both went down together for the evening meal, which was anything but wholesome. They were afraid to ask precisely of what the main part of the meal consisted. It provided sustenance and that was all that could be said. Ian had, on several occasions, thought that there was a distinct shortage of cats and dogs in Poland but he daren't speak about it now. The night stretched out before them and with nothing to do and nowhere to go Ian agreed to meet Halle in her room to discuss what they would do the next morning.

"Let us begin with the worst scenario we can imagine," said Halle from the comfort of the bed where she was reclining. Ian felt that this arrangement was too distracting for him and proceeded to move the wicker chair so that he had a full view of the street and less of Halle's long slender legs. "What would that be, in your opinion?" asked Ian. "I suppose being stopped by the AK and caught with those papers on me would be my biggest fear."

"Yes, I could have guessed that. But you were right, they did turn out to be useful today."

"What's your biggest fear?"

"Well I had been warned that if I escaped again the likelihood would be a sentence of death. But with me pretending to be joining their Army likelihood wouldn't come into it—I'd be getting a close-up of the nearest wall."

"So we have to make this work; there is no alternative, is there?"

"If we don't get a bus out of here in the morning our chances are not great."

"But you could get help from the AK, couldn't you? I knew you wouldn't go and leave me the other day but the situation changed. While I was in a position to use my German passes I was helping you, now I'm a distinct handicap. So I wouldn't blame you if you upped sticks and left."

Ian was perturbed at the change in Halle. Up to this moment he felt she was a selfish bitch with no other thought but her own survival. In addition he thought that he had kept the matter of staying with her to himself but she had seen through his display of manly concern yet still admired him for it. "No... we reached an agreement and I'll stick to it, regardless. It's an Ulster-Scot's characteristic." Halle knew it was a deliberate ploy on his part to get them to change the topic so she played along asking him what he found different in her and her Catholic friends.

"Well I'm used to hearing people talking about the BB, cricket, rugby, football. Other things as well."

"Such as?" queried Halle.

"The Mother's Union, the Lodge and the Masonic."

"You'll not get much out of me on those subjects, will you?"

"So what do you suggest we talk about? The… what do you call it? The game with sticks… a bit like hockey?"

"Hurling for men, camogie for women."

"Yes, I would be a dab hand talking about it when I don't have a clue as to what is the intention of the game."

"Many Catholics don't play Gaelic games. It doesn't change their views one way or the other," and Halle shrugged her shoulders assuming that her statement concluded the matter. Ian, on the other hand, wasn't sold on her version, "I'm not convinced; you played that game—camogie wasn't it? I'll bet you it affected your attitude, as a young person, to Protestants." Halle was somewhat taken aback by Ian's assertion. "No, I'm certain about that. I hadn't seen, never mind played the game, when I kicked the back wheel from under you."

"Maybe, but I'm sure it hardened your ideas on how to get a united Ireland."

"I can't answer that; we're all affected by the company we keep. You and your Orange family and the fact that you were forbidden to play with Fenians or at the very least discouraged. My brother Brian used to say that Tommy Smith in our street used to get more telling-offs because he wanted out to play with him. More than he got for all his petty thieving."

"The Smiths were a different case. They brought that lad up to be a thief, it was hardly his fault."

"Either you fail to see the point I'm making or you're deliberately changing the subject. As long as he didn't play with a Fenian that was fine but he could rob to his heart's content."

"I'm not trying to be provocative but you're making assumptions as to what was going on."

"Come on now, it must have happened in your house as well."

"None of us thieved."

"You're playing games again. You know rightly what I meant. Weren't you told to avoid playing with *Roman* Catholics coming up to the twelfth?

"I'm sure it wasn't one-sided, was it?"

"Ha-ha! I can remember our Sally going out on the quiet with a Protestant boy from the Newtownards Road. One night he got dragged into the house until she was ready. But she was that late my mother started the family Rosary and the wee lad had to mouth the prayers, pretending he knew them. He was lucky there were so many in that night that only the young ones, like me, spotted he was one of the other sort. Of course eventually someone squawked and he was given the heave-ho."

Question answered, Ian decided that it was time to go as it was well into the night. Once in his room he pondered how congenial he had found Halle and believed he had started to see another side of the Ulster equation. Even as he thought it he knew that Halle would see it as 'typical of the patronising manner of many Prods in the Six Counties'. But he dismissed the negative aspects of this talk, being anxious to hang on to a new style Halle whose whole manner and sense of humour amused him greatly.

A somewhat different Halle awaited him at the breakfast table, "What the hell are we to do? I've just enquired and there's no bus due out of this town in the direction of Danzig." Ian interrupted her, "I hope you didn't say Danzig, did you?" Halle paused in an attempt to remember what precisely she had said, "Yes, I did. I must have been half asleep."

"Was there anyone else around?"

"A few customers leaving and the help."

"You might as well have stood in the street and yelled out 'I'm working for the Germans.' Between showing them your papers and now this, it's a wonder that the AK weren't at the door waiting for us. I thought we had got away with it last night because the people were anxious to do business, regardless of who we were and there was no one else about so they could pretend we were on the up and up. We'd better get out of here pronto."

"As I said, I'm sorry. Where did the 'pronto' come from, I thought you God-fearing Presbyterians didn't go to the pictures?"

"No we didn't but we played Cowboys and Indians with the other wee lads who did. You have a way of turning a conversation that's going against you to your advantage, don't you? Just letting you know I'm not taken in by your manoeuvring. To be as down to earth as you, 'let's get to hell out of here!'" Halle knew when to hold back and she immediately rushed to her room to retrieve her luggage.

It wasn't much of a walk to get to the outskirts of the town and it was only when they got there that Ian recognised the countryside. "I've been here before," he began and Halle reminded him that that was one of the reasons she wanted him to go with her. Finally they stopped so that Halle could catch her breath. The countryside was glorious and both of them lay down to contemplate the joy of freedom from pursuit that they felt had dominated all their moments since they left Thorn. The sun's warm glow permeated skins, which had had little or no time to accustom themselves to its rays. Within a few minutes Halle sat up and fixed her hair and without glancing at Ian asked, "What do we do now?"

"Praying would be a worthwhile pursuit at this juncture."

"I've done that, so what's next?"

"Start keeping your eyes open for German patrols because we're going to have to take to the ditches and trees for cover."

"Is there no prospect of getting a lift?"

"Aye, the Germans will willingly give *you* one, to meet that Oberst, what'shisname?"

"You know damn fine I'm not on the market for going back; is there any prospect that a Pole will drive past and give us a lift to Danzi... Gdansk?"

"No, the Germans don't give the Poles petrol unless they are their paid palookas passing on information to them."

"So what hope have we got then?"

"Little or none is probably the answer but I have an instinct that beckons me on which says that something will turn up." Halle was left without a word to say.

Once back on their feet they walked for an hour before they saw their first human being since leaving the town. He was driving a cart which clearly hadn't far to go because the horse, in spite of looking drained, knew it was approaching home and didn't slow down leaving its driver only the opportunity of waving his whip in their general direction. Totally disconsolate they walked on beyond the road where the cart had turned off. Ian wasn't talking because he had claimed when they first agreed to go on this journey, "If you've nothing good to say, say nothing." Halle, on the other hand, wanted to speak but she didn't want him to think she couldn't control herself and her speech. The silence was pervasive and both felt that they were being undone by an agreement, with which neither of them was at ease. "Look Halle you're forcing me to go back on a statement of mine just because you won't talk. I know you can say something good about people, I didn't say it had to be about me, did I?"

"Clearly you feel at home when you force others to refrain from speaking their minds. If I could say something good about you and your ilk I'd say it, but as I can't I'm not speaking."

"To stop me going out of my mind say something apart from saying nothing."

"I know you're blaming me about having to leave that place so quickly. The damage was done and that was that but then you attribute my showing the papers to the pension host as being as bad as asking for Danzig. You

168

never even brought the issue up last night; if anything you praised me for it and that really is tearing it!"

"I should have warned you to be careful before hand. Let's drop it."

"I'm bloody sure we're not! It's like everything else, when you didn't do something you say, 'Let's drop it!' Well I'm not doing it."

"Tell me one thing that I've said that falls into that category."

"No I'm going to let your self-righteous mind develop that for itself."

Unable to agree on any of the issues Halle suggested that Ian should attempt to find somewhere they could sleep. He found a house down a long lane, which suggested splendid isolation, something for which both of them longed. The house was more in the style of an English manor house than anything Polish they had seen so far. Clearly the house was old, probably dating from the 18th century. There was no one at home and all the indications were that the owners had decamped. The rooms were fully furnished and the amount of silverware and works of art just left were an indication of how sudden had been their flight, probably on hearing of the Soviet successes.

Ian made his way round the premises, intensely driven by his wish to enjoy the beautiful things that he had never known. The staircase, the beautiful oak beams that supported the upper rooms, the magnificent wooden floors polished till they shone, all brought a wonderful sense of life which was meant to be enjoyed.

In a back bedroom his eye caught sight of the huge double bed with its down filled pillows and he threw himself full length on it and found himself enveloped in the softest mattress he had ever come across. He longed to remain but knew he had to look over every possible danger. However, the view from the window was worthy of a great landscape artist's brush. As the eye looked out the swifts, in large numbers, swooped by and for an instant the mixture of hedges was blurred, only to be disturbed once more by a new arrival—a longtail with its more languid movements helping to settle the scene. Just beyond the edge of the garden was a smallish field with a hedge made up of hawthorn bushes and small trees. Beyond these were a series of fields varying in form and colour, from a darkish green to a straw coloured one occasionally interspersed by clumps of trees all heading towards the rushes rimming the lake. But the lake itself was the eye-catcher with the sheen of light emanating from those areas of water not shadowed by trees and rushes. At the far end of the lake a Nordic looking house, at the edge of one's vision, fronted two large barns on a mount in front of a forest. This, in turn, led to a darkened line of low hills on the horizon behind which stood two pillars of clouds standing diagonally on the brow of the hills.

He had stood too long admiring the scene and the urgency to get back to Halle struck him forcibly. Quickly he made his way out of the house and down the lane. He could see the hedge on the far side of the road where they were to meet. As he neared the meeting point his anxiety increased, as there was no sign of Halle. He waited for the best part of an hour before she finally turned up but he was too full of the news about the house to be angry for long. "Where did you get to?" was all he could say. Halle reluctantly admitted that she had gone on ahead to see if there was the possibility of either transport or shelter. "Well I found us a peach of a place!" gushed Ian.

"Please take me there and don't let us talk about it until I see for myself." Her exhaustion was obvious and Ian took her elbow and propelled her gently along the lane until the house came into sight. "What do you think?" Halle stared at the building and its grounds, "My God! You're sure we'll have it to ourselves? Show me the bedrooms, I want to pick out the best, I'm sure you'll not mind." Ian hesitated to say anything, he wanted her to acknowledge that he was the main provider but she failed to comment favourably on his part in obtaining such wondrous accommodation. Halle bypassed the furniture, the portraits and the silver *objet d'art* in her rush to find the most suitable bed. Of course she spied the feather bed on which Ian had languished earlier and that was the proceeding over for the day.

Ian was awake very early the next morning because of the fear of being discovered on the premises. In addition he had given a great deal of thought to the priceless objects which littered ever room in the house. "I'll go into the village—there's bound to be one near here—and try to sell some of these things or perhaps I could barter them for food and transport." He made an effort to clean himself so that he could adopt an air of respectability before trying to do business. Halle came down the stairs as he was about to leave and wanted to know what he was doing with the silver. Ian attempted to explain his motivation but Halle was outraged. "Are we to become thieves and robbers in order to escape? You can, I'm not. You're so materialistic. Can't you see the beauty of this place is something unified by the objects being in these surroundings?"

"I don't pretend to understand any of that. All I'm concerned about is surviving in order to get out of Nazi controlled Poland and with or without your agreement that's what I propose to do!" Halle's horror moderated as she thought over Ian's argument. "I see we'll always have two divergent views on everything. Let me put my view another way, from a different perspective; you want out of Poland and so do I. I suspect that if you go to any of the homes hereabout they'll recognise these beautiful pieces of art and they'll either have the AK on to you or they'll report you to the Germans.

How do you respond to that?" Ian agonised for a few minutes, "What the devil are we going to do for food?" Halle pointed to the window nearest the door, "Look out there, what do you see?" Ian had not got round to seeing the items beyond the door and he was surprised at the cackling of hens and ducks. "A city guy is very slow to see beautiful animals as food," he said by way of excusing his oversight. "Let's get down to breakfast—you wring their necks and I'll pluck them."

After breakfast, which in essence was a perverse kind of dinner, they had to discuss their next line of action. "You know I still think that if we hold on to some of these small items we'll be able to use them to obtain help in the way of transport or food." Halle held her tongue and then looked directly into his eyes, "Putting aside my earlier objections, just be practical. How many of those do you think would buy us our way to Gdansk? Five, six—ten? How are you going to carry them—don't think that I'm going to be burdened further?" Ian knew he was on the wrong side of the argument but he persisted with his suggestion. Halle prepared to leave and went to the door saying, "Coming?" Ian said he would be along in a moment and when she left he proceeded to put small items in his pockets and hurried after her.

The road ahead was a series of bends and Ian was more and more anxious that they wouldn't be able to avoid a German patrol if they persisted in keeping to the road. Finally he put it to Halle that it was dangerous to keep to the road and that they should stay in the fields. He knew before he started that she would be against it simply because he suggested it. "Try to leave me out of the decision making, assess all the information and make up your mind in a logical way. What do you say?"

"I am logical; look, there is no way I can walk in those fields with these shoes and from the state of the ground I don't believe I'd make it in my bare feet."

"If I carried your bag and we kept to the rough paths hewn out by constant usage could you make it then?" Halle stared directly into his face and he felt his temperature rise—it had been a long time since he had been embarrassed but somehow this woman had made him feel uncomfortable, and when he thought about it, in a pleasant way. "That's find by me but the first time you show you're under pressure we're going back on the road, OK? Have you any idea of the date?"

"Not a clue beyond thinking it's about the middle of May."

"It's still 1943 then. I can hardly believe it—this year seems like at least three."

"For you and me both!"

The wandering across fields soon brought exhaustion in its trail and Halle was determined to find something akin to a room, or at least something undercover, in order to get a comfortable night's rest. At one point, while she rested, Ian did a comprehensive search of the neighbourhood. He came back almost an hour later to tell her that there was nowhere suitable. He didn't tell her that there was too much activity in or near the few barns that he came across; he would have been comfortable in them but it was her German papers that left him uneasy about using the barns.

"God you're pathetic! You stay here and I'll have a look myself and if I find one we're stopping at the next opticians to have your eyes tested." Ian let her go on, seeing that she was in such good humour. If she were as bright as he suspected she was, she would be aware of the danger, particularly to herself. When she returned she merely said that he had been right and didn't discuss the matter further. Ian didn't harp on the matter, saying that there was a suitable large tree, which would give them some shelter.

Once the sun went down the ground seemed intensely cold and they talked about sleeping closer together to engender sufficient heat so that they would avoid frostbite. Halle had thought she was long past embarrassing situations with Ian, particularly after their sojourn today, but the notion of touch was an inhibiting new direction. After some thought she agreed as she consoled herself that she would be fully dressed and less likely to be aroused.

Ian, however, despite his weariness and concern about sleeping was already worked-up and eyed Halle in a way that suggested that all previous disagreements were set aside. The circumstances made it clear to both that they would have to prepare for the event. There would be no false modesty; they would cling together and avoid breathing directly on the other's face and finally Halle found the courage to state outright that there was to be no undue fumbling. "Where do you want my arms?" asked Ian with a more than innocent look. Halle chose to ignore the silly boy look, "Around my waist; no higher nor any lower. You get my drift?" Ian nodded, "And before you ask about my arms the same will apply. Stop that sheepish grin now or I'll stop the first German transport and decamp faster than anything you've seen up to now." Ian was more than ever conscious that she had a lifeline in the papers she possessed from Goebbels' Ministry.

Settling under the tree was relatively easy but the lack of covering proved to be more of a hardship that they had anticipated and they were unable to sleep at first. "Have you ever been this close to a woman before?" queried Halle. Ian's slowness in responding encouraged Halle to proceed, "I was known as a 'Falls Road Teaser'—an FRT for short. As you know, I didn't come from there but I think the term is self-explanatory. Is it?" The two words left Ian no alternative but to agree it was clear enough, although he was looking away in another direction when he uttered them. Rather sheepishly he went on, "Does it mean you went so far and no further? But just how far does that mean?"

"I thought you said you understood?"

"I think I do but I don't want to jump to the wrong conclusions." Clearly Ian didn't want to make an issue of it, yet at the same time, unknowingly, was sending the vibrations of jealously which Halle sensed very quickly and encouraged her to play the FRT role in full. "It was a bit of a moveable feast—some girls might let a fellow hold them round the waist at the dance but then I've known others who would have allowed somewhat more than that. But don't try to get me into giving more details, I don't know any more and what I've told you is all second-hand accounts."

"You say all this as if Roman Catholic girls don't deviate much from what's laid down. You seem to think they're different and better than their Protestant counterparts, do you?" Halle recognised that the conversation had taken a right-turn away from the direction she intended it to go. "No!" was her quick response. "What were your experiences Ian?" The whole issue was going to blow up in his face if he wasn't careful—it was much too personal now and he didn't want to speak of his former wife in this context, as it was the only experience he had. "I never had much experience, I only went out with one girl and she was as religious as myself so there was no hanky-panky."

Ian knew that by leaving out the most important detail that he had contrived to make a lie out of a part truth. That was fine because he wanted to indicate an exiguous lifestyle so that his Puritan behaviour, which allowed no sexual contact, was not dissimilar to Halle's own as an FRT. For her part Halle, regardless of the reawakened attractiveness she had found in Ian, was far from won over to that other side of him which she felt resided in that winter grey city of their birth. Her suspicions were raised when Ian hinted, rather than said, he had never known a girl sexually. A man at his age would be expected to be conversant with the subject to a greater degree than he claimed.

As a young woman Halle wondered what value life had to offer and attempted to apply this question to the Descartes quotation which her father constantly used, "I think, therefore I exist." With the passing of time she felt that her version was more appropriate, "I doubt, therefore I am," and Ian's decidedly dubious answer confirmed her opinion that her rendition was the more likely version regarding life as she experienced it. Nevertheless, she settled down to share the coat she had given Ian and the covering of grass that he had provided.

Ian was choked with desire and realised that if she moved against him all promises were off. Exhaustion soon led Halle into a sound sleep while Ian lay holding her and experiencing the worst of all worlds. He wanted her and knew she was attracted to him but both of them were ingenuous in the ways of the world. Later when both had been asleep some time, Ian thought, rather than knew, that Halle had melted into his embrace and, regardless of who thought who was guilty, they succumbed to that age-old enticement which, in their terms, is euphemistically known as the 'temptation of the flesh'.

Some writers have referred to the fullness of a woman's first full sexual encounter as an 'awakening' but to Halle it was more of an awareness of reality which had taken her by surprise and which she now looked back on as a kind of nightmare. Undoubtedly there was a residual sense of pleasure on first waking but the horror of the possible outcome outweighed the previous night's delights. "It all depends on Ian's approach to this," she decided, "he better be offering marriage in the event of a calamity!" The sun had not wakened him and he lay on the broad of his back unaware of the storm brewing beside him. Eventually Halle couldn't wait for him to come round and roughly shook him awake. "I hope I'm going to hear the right words, in the right tone, with a fine line in sincerity Ian."

"Halle you must know that I love you…"

"This doesn't augur well for the rest of this statement. It reminds me of home; your folk—which always reminds me of Hitler and his folk—about to tell us Nationalists and Republicans how much you love us as God's creatures but you must condemn the Roman Catholic religion so…"

"Ah, please not all that again; can't you see I've been trying to see both sides of the argument?"

"I suppose you saw it as honourable to take sides with the minority if it pleased *me* and to see their slights as yours—but I can't see *their* sense of injustice as *yours* because I just can't see it like that. Anyway here you are again getting me off the subject. I had intended to avoid all that and get down to us and what happened last night!"

Matters were moving at too great a pace for Ian's contentment. "Look can we take it as said that I love you and will stand by you no matter what?" Halle stared at him; "You know this sounds more like a verbal contract than someone asking in dulcet tones for the other person's hand in marriage."

"Well, I can't begin to tell you in words how much last night meant to me. I think it was one of the most important happenings in my life. I wonder did it mean as much to you?"

"If it didn't, last night would have been tantamount to rape! I'm sorry to reduce this to my sense of humour but without you speaking out as you did I would be wallowing in misery and despair this morning. Why do you think I woke you? I needed comforting and there you were snoring your head off. I hope this isn't your concept of romance, is it?"

"Of course it isn't, I appreciate the circumstances weren't entirely the ones we'd have chosen but passion isn't inappropriate in love, is it?"

"Nor in other situations as well but I'll just have to learn to bite my tongue like so many other married women." Ian ignored the comment and asked Halle had she any ideas how they could speed up their journey to Gdansk. "I hate this crossing of fields, it slows us down but as you said the nature of the roads means that German patrols would be on top of us before we would have a chance to hide. Still I'd like to risk it; what do you say?"

"Is there anyway we can reduce the risk of being caught, especially you with your German Army credentials?"

"I've been thinking about this and I remembered I still have my pass for the Radiofunkhaus and it mentions Goebbels' Propaganda Ministry, maybe I should dump the Army papers and use these if necessary, what do you think?"

"But what cover story can you devise that fits those set of papers?"

"I suppose whatever I contrive will fall apart if they take the time to check it out. Off the top of my head I was going to claim I was on my way to Gdansk to prepare for a radio broadcast by Minister Goebbels. I was sent ahead to research the situation in a number of towns and to find stories that enhanced the Third Reich's handling of the war."

"Apart from Gdansk it sounds brilliant to me but I'm just the guy in love with you. I think I'm easily swayed."

"For a person who can put such a weak case as the Unionist one, you do fine and I'm sure that in spite of your protestations of love you wouldn't let me tell a story to the Germans that hadn't a chance of convincing them."

"I wondered how long the gloss of romance would keep you off the Northern Ireland situation. You didn't fail me, my love, you're on the ball from the kick-off."

"And for that matter you're calling the north-east of Ireland by a political name your immediate predecessors named it."

"On today of all days let's not go down that road. Sorry about the pun! Just let me wallow in the contentment of being in love—these other issues

175

we'll deal with at another time and place. We've solved your problem but what happens when they quiz me?"

"I think the only way out of it is if you keep just off the road enough to be able to lie down once you hear something coming—you're much more agile than I am."

"It's nice to get compliments but you're arguing a case that's contradicting what we just agreed on. I thought that we didn't want to be slowed any longer."

"But there are limits to what I'm capable of doing, while you are stronger and more able."

"After last night's episode you would have difficulty in carrying that argument with an objective observer!"

"I trust to God there was no such being! But it doesn't prove that you are any less stronger than I claimed."

"Well too prove my love I'll do what you request."

"Much and all as it brings me joy to hear you say it, I'm too much of a pragmatist to imagine that we can always overlook our differences and hope that everything will turn out fine. But this is neither the time nor the place. Let's get on to the road now, because my feet are killing me!"

Ian didn't need any further persuading and, although he wouldn't admit it to Halle, his feet were paining him. Apart from the physical pain, he was also suffering from a sense of guilt through not being able to tell Halle that he had been married and was divorced. Obviously he didn't want to destroy his chances with her because he knew Roman Catholics didn't believe that a marriage could be dissolved, so in her eyes he was married forever or until the death of his wife. It was time to stop this constant thinking about the difficulties and enjoy the moment; what did she call it when she was talking about literature? Was it *carpe diem*, is that something about enjoying the moment or was it seize the chance? There's a major difference in interpretation somewhere!

Keeping in from the road was worse than Ian had imagined, it was nothing to do with the pressure on his feet it was the mere separation from Halle that annoyed him. He constantly had to shout in order to be able to listen to her replies. Conversational topics were also a difficulty at such a distance; he couldn't go on shouting his love and devotion every minute. Then it dawned on him that they hadn't seen a German patrol for the best part of two days. Something big must have been going on to have troop movements reduced to such a level. Halle agreed when he spoke to her on the matter but she attributed the shortage to the increasing strength of the Russians and the German need to bring more troops to the front.

Halle had just finished her reply when Ian indicated that he heard some form of transport approaching. Immediately he lay down and Halle stopped in her stride prepared for anything. Round the bend came a German troop carrier with what appeared to be a full complement; probably a dozen thought Ian from his position some fifty metres behind Halle's position on the road. On seeing her, the carrier pulled to a halt and an officer jumped down and Ian could see, without actually hearing him, that he was requesting her papers. The conversation didn't last long and soon the officer returned to the vehicle and it moved off. Once it was out of sight Ian emerged to ask what had happened. "Oh, it was fine. But do you know what I did? I can only put it down to the state of euphoria you have me in."

"What did you do or not do, for heaven's sake?"

"When he asked me for my papers I instinctively handed him the German Army ones by mistake!"

"Oh Lord, what did he say? From a distance everything looked as if it went well. You see I believed that you had got rid of them."

"He seemed perturbed at my rank and clearly wasn't going to ask me as to my purpose—that's something we had failed to realise when we talked about getting rid of those papers! If you are of sufficient rank they wouldn't dare ask you."

"But you were speaking quite a while."

"Yes, I asked him why there had been so few patrols in the area in the past two days. It was the kind of question he seemed prepared for once he heard my rank. It seems that a large force of troops were sent to Warsaw to put down the Jewish ghetto and it was announced that the temple had finally been erased yesterday."

"So that's why the patrols are back."

"It would seem so. But you better get back to the fields these guys tend to return if they think of something which they failed to ask on the first occasion."

Ian decided that this time he would keep a distance between himself and Halle in case they were caught by surprise. He explained his thinking to Halle and while she would have preferred to have him nearer, understood his desire not to leave both of them open to be discovered by others coming upon them without their being aware.

They had covered approximately two kilometres and Halle had just turned a bend out of his view when Ian heard a number of shots and the sound of a vehicle rushing from the scene. Ian's heart stopped but his feet automatically took him as fast as he could run and to his horror he found Halle lying in a pool of blood in the middle of the road. From the previous night's reconnaissance he knew there was a farm and barn not more than 50 metres from the spot. He hoped against hope that the owners would be down to see the source of the shooting but he was to learn that people kept out of the way when a shooting incident occurred.

As he went he shouted loud and often for help and finally he saw a woman emerging on to the road and he beckoned to her to hurry to him. He rushed back to Halle and it was then that he saw her papers were scattered over the roadway. Whatever had happened, somehow Halle's credentials were part of the cause but the most important problem was to get Halle the right kind of help immediately. The woman rushed past him and knelt down by Halle and put her ear to the girl's chest. She shouted something in Polish that defeated Ian but she continued to point to his shirt and he took it off and gave it to her. The woman continued to point in his direction and he was suddenly aware that she was pointing to the house, which she had just left.

Ian interpreted her sign as an indication that he was to lift Halle and bring her to the house. He was fearful that his manhandling of the girl would make matters worse and he tried to show his doubts by signs to the woman but she ran on ahead as if to prepare for Halle's arrival. By the time he had gone halfway a man arrived and he helped carry her into the farm.

It didn't require great medical knowledge to realise that Halle needed hospital attention and pretty soon at that. The Polish couple seemed to understand the situation and in spite of their being unable to communicate with Ian went on helping to staunch the blood which seemed to flow unceasingly from Halle's breast. Finally the man rushed outside and returned with another who was carrying a gun; they spoke for a few moments and then both of them left.

Ian begged the woman to get a doctor but she could do nothing but shrug her shoulders in a clear indication that she didn't understand. Ten minutes elapsed before the men returned with some form of transport and they left with Halle lying on the back seat and Ian had no choice but to wait there until they returned from heaven only knew where.

CHAPTER 11

(May 1943)

HALLE AWOKE OR had been awake all the time since she was given the sedative. The tunnel was tremendously long and the light at the end was no larger than a tennis ball but the shear intensity of it had startled her. Apart from that there was an attraction, something of a magnet's ability to drag objects to it. So she continued to walk towards the light with an increased sense of need to get there—wherever 'there' was. A sense of being alone in a vacuum prevailed, yet it wasn't the dominant issue… A male voice demanded, in a soft and beautiful tone, "Do you want to die?" Halle wasn't at all taken aback by the question. Indeed the idea of death hadn't entered her head but a sense of otherness that excluded death seemed prevalent. Her analysis of this otherness was a mere acceptance of a reality that she didn't understand but that the word 'death' was a human expression for something which living human beings were kept from. Words were too long to convey the shortness needed to acquire this knowledge, even 'in a twinkling' was days longer. "Does that mean I have to go back the way I came? I mean away from the light if I wish to live?" The voice asked the question again, not in any hostile way but as neutral as any question can be asked, "Do you want to die?" and Halle felt that answers were inappropriate but words were the only means of communication available to her. "Yes, I want to get to the light to get that happiness which I feel and need." Her mind seemed to envelop the wholeness of the situation, which confronted her in a less than tangible way.

The voice never varied in its diction or strength, "What about Ian, your family and friends?"

"I want to get to the light," and Halle proceeded to walk along the tunnel. The light had now grown to the size of a beach ball—the word 'now' felt wrong, as did the variation in tenses, but the happiness had grown in correlation with the brightness. "Do you think you're being selfish?" Halle halted but could not answer. There was an adjustment needed in language for her to understand but the questioning went on regardless, "What did you ever do for them?" A pattern of images rushed past her mind's eye and she saw every incident in which she was involved with Ian, her Mum and Dad. "No, I… I can't think of a single thing." She knew without a word being said that her march to the light had finished. "What will you do to rectify this when you go back?" Halle turned while the voice

179

spoke but saw only a large dark vacuum facing her. She didn't take a step, she was determined to pursue her return to a human voice by answering, "I'll leave the Cumann na mBann because my Mum and Dad would like that. And I'll give up Ian as well."

"But what about Ian, what will you do for him?"

"I'll give him my gun and explosives when we get home."

"He'll be happy then?"

"Oh, I hope everyone will be as happy as I've been this day."

Halle looked around her as the atmosphere changed. The tunnel was gone and most disappointingly, the light. Appearances suggested that this was a sort of field hospital. A female doctor spoke to her from her left-hand side, "You're awake at last." Halle's comment was a little too brusque for her taste, "No, I was wide awake." The doctor bent over her, clearly she was anxious about her and the reply from the girl didn't seem quite the appropriate one. "We were worried when you stopped breathing for such a long time. Were you or are you in much pain? Not that we have much in the way of drugs to relieve it. Some aspirin is about the height of it… is that the correct way of saying?"

"Yes that's grand but everything *was* under control, I knew I was coming back."

"Coming back… I am lost. Look you were shot just above the heart and we think you had a heart attack but we're not sure. The bullet, miraculously, missed vital organs and you should recover in a few weeks."

"Could you tell me how I got here?"

"We're as wise as you. I was told that our patrol came across you lying near the roadway. There were German documents in your name scattered about and they assumed you were German because of your name and your official status, so they brought you here. Of course, they were surprised when they heard you speaking English, so they sent for me as I speak reasonably good English."

"Where abouts is this?"

"I'm not too sure, I only arrived yesterday and it appears to be in the middle of nowhere. My guess is we're on the Polish border or in East Prussia."

"How near are we to Danzig?" asked Halle grateful that she remembered that the Germans still kept the old name.

"I think somewhere between a hundred and a hundred and fifty kilometres."

"You seem to be very busy… Is there a battle going on nearby that I somehow got involved in?"

"I don't think so but there have been some Polish terrorists seen in the neighbouring countryside. Do you think it may have been them that shot you?"

"Perhaps. Perhaps they spotted me going in and out of POW camps and a woman on her own is an easy target. Have you reported this to Berlin?"

"Not yet. The lines of communication are under pressure but the officials here are satisfied with your story and your papers. Look, you need rest not talk so I'll leave you and I'll look in a few times during the night."

Halle settled down to what she knew would be a disturbed night's sleep. Her shoulder and chest ached and the condition of her mind ensured there would be no relief from the anxiety about her condition and Ian's ability to remain free. She hoped he would have the sense to stay away—that is if he knew where she was. Since her 'walk' in the tunnel she was beginning to assess her previous attitudes and behaviour, in particular with regard to her actions and thoughts. She was aware for the first time—no that wasn't true—in the past she had deliberately overlooked her selfishness when she got what she wanted, "Doesn't everybody do that?" began her inner voice but Halle wasn't having any of it. Still change was one thing but she must concern herself, at the moment, about her condition. She must put that first and concern for Ian second. Immediately she was startled and confounded by her supercilious behaviour; she, the changed being after her close encounter with death was putting herself first again. She above all who berated Ian and his ilk for relegating Catholics to third class citizens was doing something much worse—she was acting the hypocrite *par excellence*.

As the night slowly moved on there was an awareness that she was thinking of him as a person—flesh and bones with feelings and concerns. But she had promised to give him up in order to appease her parents. The 'voice' had specifically asked about this and she had given it an unqualified avowal about Ian's place in her life. Now she was attempting to enter a codicil—"What if I'm giving him up for my own sake; avoidance of misery, reluctance to love, honour and obey. What if I'm afraid that in some issues I may have been wrong, prejudice feeds on certainty of superiority. Even if I accept an attempt at equality I know that that wouldn't be enough. What then would he need to do to enable me to put all these to one side? And even if I was able it would only take one aside from him on the Six-County problem to blow our relationship to pieces. I've given my word and that should be the end of it, no more searching for excuses. No, I'd better do it now when I think I love him—I couldn't do it if I was absolutely certain."

Through the night her thoughts moved from Ian to the shooting, there were pieces of the jigsaw missing and only Ian would know the precise details. Yet the more she thought about the event the more uncertain she was that she had been shot by Polish resistance fighters. She remembered being stopped at one point by German soldiers who looked at her papers and got back into their vehicle and moved on. After they left, perhaps anything up to fifteen minutes later she had been shot and naturally she passed out without an awareness of anyone being in the vicinity.

The next morning there was a whole palaver going on. Halle's knowledge of German was small but she heard sufficient words that she recognised for her to understand there was a strong possibility of the unit being moved back to Warsaw. Halle prayed that it wouldn't be within the next fortnight as she was that weak that she couldn't possibly escape the return to Warsaw. She pointedly asked the doctors what was the situation but they were at a loss to know where this story came from. This apart they claimed to be happy with her recovery but said a long convalescence would be required before she would be able to take on any further work.

Ian's impatience with the woman and her lack of English or French had become insupportable and he knew in his heart that she would soon be showing him the door, so it was with great relief he heard the door opening. It was now well into the evening and the men looked exhausted and Ian realised that there was more frustration awaiting him. "How is she?" he began, fully aware that they didn't understand him, yet they were, in their turn, anxious to indicate what had happened. They gesticulated and attempted mime in order to help Ian know what was the situation. The man with the gun indicated that he was leaving and Ian was left more frustrated than ever but he soon returned with an elderly man whose bald head somehow gave Ian assurance that he would be given the information that he anxiously desired.

"Are you English?" asked the old man. "Yes, I am. Can you tell me how the girl who was shot is doing?" The man turned and clearly was interpreting what he had been asked. The two men, who had conveyed Halle, to wherever it was they took her, talked for a long time. Ian watched their faces in an attempt to discern what they were saying but it was hopeless, he was too emotionally disturbed to make out what they were conveying to the old man. Eventually they stopped and the interpreter turned to appraise him of the situation.

"My name is Teodor Korzeniowski and the family in this house are the Czerniawskis. Your friend is in hospital but it is a German military one. We have friends working in it and they will get us all the information that is available."

"How did they get her into it?"

"Well, they found papers which seemed to belong to her and they thought that she was letting on to be German because they had only heard her English friend speak. They knew of the military hospital nearby so they simply left her on the road outside it with the papers lying beside her. They watched and saw her being taken inside for treatment and of course they noticed how interested the German medical people looked at her papers."

"How soon will you be able to get information on her condition?"

"I'm sorry, you will have to speak slower."

"WHEN – WILL – YOU – FIND – OUT – HOW – SHE - IS?" It was only when he saw the three people looking at him that Ian realised he had been shouting very slowly as though talking to someone partially deaf. "I am sorry but I am worried about her." Teodor turned and evidently told the others what he had said because they smiled and nodded in unison. "We will know tomorrow how ill she is."

"Your English is excellent, where did you learn to speak so well?"

"I lived in Michigan in the USA and I taught children of Polish emigrants but I returned home to my family in the early 1920s. But we know nothing of you and your friend, are you British prisoners who have escaped?" Ian was conscious that his pause was creating concern but he was struggling to remember the details of the Sheila Gray story that Halle claimed she had been on the point of telling the AK soldiers when she was 'rescued' by the Germans. "I can't really divulge anything about her. She is working as an Allied spy and I don't know a great deal other than she asked me to help her escape."

His comments, once translated, brought smiles from the remainder of the household. There was a conference and Ian was informed that they were prepared to provide accommodation until such times as Halle had recovered and they could continue their escape, this time, they explained, with the aid of the resistance movement. Ian was unable to find the energy to explain that the AK had helped him in the past and the Poles soon realised that he was exhausted and sent him to the room they had prepared.

Ian was up early, prowling about, anxious to be involved in discovering just how Halle was progressing. He wasn't certain just when they would be able to get the information but he wanted to be there when the news came to hand. Halina Czerniawski was the first to arrive in the kitchen and she made it clear by a series of hand signals that her husband had already left to get the information. Ian was more agitated by this, as it left him conscious that Halle was going to be dependent upon these people and not him. The hours passed in such a leisurely manner that he literally had to bite his tongue to avoid accusing his benefactors of keeping him in the dark.

It was some hours later when Andrzej Czerniawski returned with the disheartening news that Halle was being kept in some kind of intensive care department in a German military field hospital. Worse again was the news that the Polish informant had told him that the field hospital was to be moved to the front in the next few days and that Halle would be transferred to a major hospital in Warsaw. Ian couldn't begin to explain to Teodor Korzeniowski how much danger Halle was in but he soon realised that the second best alternative would be Teodor's awareness of the terrible consequences awaiting an Allied spy like 'Sheila Gray'. He took Teodor to one side and asked what could they do to prevent her being returned to Warsaw. The translator was anxious to be of assistance and told Ian there was a unit of the AK in the area and if the information turned out to be accurate he was certain that they would arrange some kind of rescue. "You don't realise just how successful these units have been right across the country." Ian's smile and nod of the head brought Teodor to a halt, "You *do* know about them?" and Ian proceeded to tell of his time with the Warsaw unit and Aleksander Kosciuszko. To say that the man from Michigan was surprised belittled language; he was astonished and Ian felt disappointed in him, even though he never spoke a word, as he thought he should have kept such knowledge a secret from a total stranger. "Without knowing very much about me you mentioned Aleksander's name, I am amazed!" said Teodor in an agitated voice. "Curiously, I felt that you should not have mentioned the activities of the AK, for all you know I could be a German plant—you never checked us out."

"Like so much else, this war has supplanted trust, never again will it be the live being it once was."

"Back home my parents used to say that very frequently. We stopped talking to our neighbours but I doubt if we will ever get back to that sense of neighbourliness I once thought existed. But now I fear that I never had it and it was merely a mirage and underneath it skulked hatred and fear of the other kind."

"Ian, just what is meant 'by the other kind'?"

"People who are different from my people."

"But is it not a contradiction, surely people are people. Only the Nazis talk like that, usually about those they fear."

"It's not only on our side that the expression is used, both Protestants and Roman Catholics use it to describe the other sort, sorry, the other side."

"Ah, a hang-over from the Reformation is it?"

"Yes and no. Political concerns have added to the divisions."

"Oh, there are more than two sides?"

"Many more and it was much worse at the turn of the century according to my father. Even the various institutions and the churches were divided— well, not the Roman Catholic Church but everything else."

"Do you never get weary with it all."

"No, it has become part of our heritage and we cry 'No surrender!' with gusto, knowing that the republicans have their war-cries!"

"Oh dear, oh dear and we thought we had reserved all the suffering of constant war to ourselves, ... it seems not. And your friend, what is her name?" asked Teodor in a significantly quieter voice. "She is called Halle," began Ian being unaware for a moment that she had become 'Sheila'. Teodor just lifted his eyebrows sufficiently to indicate that Ian's story had now become riddled with holes. "Would you care to explain just what is going on?" asked Teodor his voice now stentorian with concern.

"I'll have to start at the beginning but before I do, it is obvious that you knew something—can I ask what it was?"

"Simply the Czerniawskis and myself were convinced you were lovers and your assertions just did not hold water. I am sorry, I started out to trick you and clearly it was with good cause." Ian told of the hatred that had been part of that heritage he had described earlier and held to what he thought would be acceptable to the Poles. He didn't speak of Halle's work for the Germans other than she was a slave worker who had been captured by the Germans in the Channel Islands. She was posing as a Canadian spy to any resistance groups that came on the scene in order to enable her to get off the continent as quickly as possible.

"You are closer to her than that of a recent lover."

"Strange that you should say that but because we come from opposite religious persuasions we have been bitter enemies since childhood. But here, where we are both in trouble, we have come together to help each other and as I have become familiar with her I must admit that something like love is happening. Mind you I can't speak for her in these matters. We had just reached the point of commitment, maybe I am overstating it, when this terrible shooting occurred."

"That's another strange happening. Tomas, the man with the gun and myself have been making enquiries about AK attacks in this vicinity but there has not been one. So who did the shooting? The Germans? What could *their* motives be?" Ian shrugged with an exaggerated shoulder movement and immediately worried that he had gone too far in showing he didn't want to pursue the subject. Teodor was too wily by half for his comfort; he seemed able to read him without any real effort. Besides what if the group's informant was to overhear the German doctors referring to Halle as a German officer? The game would be well and truly up for both of them and the wall he had heard Halle refer to would be awaiting both of them. "I wish to God I could talk with her, she would come up with some suggestion to get us out of this mess." Talking to one's self can often be therapeutic thought Ian seeking consolation. "On the other hand if this talking doesn't come up with a suggestion it puts you down the slippery slopes of depression." Ian took himself away from the prying eyes of Teodor in case his face gave this strange man more ammunition than he would like to give.

There were a few minutes of silence before Ian approached Teodor and said, "I wonder if it would be possible for me to talk to the person you spoke to about Halle?" Teodor looked uneasy and clearly Ian hadn't cleared the matter of himself and Halle up to this man's satisfaction. "It won't be easy but if it's imperative that you do, I'm sure the person concerned will acquiesce." To Ian's mind the earlier uncertainty in Teodor's English had disappeared but it dawned on him that he was gradually returning to an accent he must have had at some time in his youth, "You know the more I listen to you the less of an American accent I hear." The man smiled, "I was educated in England at Oxford. Of course I returned home for some years and then went to America. Naturally I couldn't have done it without my parents' financial help, they were aristocrats—at least up until the war, and my family, for generations, went to England to be educated. It was a way of life that I doubt will return. I fear that this war will alter the old ways in Europe forever, the era of republics—sorry to be pessimistic—is looming large."

"That may well be the case in the rest of Europe but I doubt if it will hold any sway with the British."

Halle was wakened from her sleep by an odd tiptoeing movement near the end of her bed. It didn't fit with the German doctors' approach, which bore a strong kinship to drilling on a parade ground. "Maybe that's what caused me to waken," thought Halle. She attempted to look round the edge of the blanket but her eyes couldn't adapt to the lack of light. A foreign voice asked her did she speak English and, much as an acknowledgement of such a kind was enough to have her choking on the words, she still managed to say a strangled 'Yes'. "An Englishman called Ian wanted you to know that he is still nearby and if you are in any danger we will help you."

"I don't think I'm well enough to be moved."

"You are not according to these doctors but you should be in a week's time, and it is then that they will move you to Warsaw."

"That's the last place I want to go," gasped Halle.

"Please do not talk, it takes too much energy from you, energy you can not afford. Just listen to what I have to say." The woman told her that they wouldn't let them take her to Warsaw. In spite of herself and her serious intention of finishing with Ian Halle forced herself to ask about him. "He is fine but you will have to keep quiet or the Germans will hear us. They do not know I speak English and I do not want them to know. I will see you tomorrow evening; if there is any message you want me to give him I will take it then." With that she disappeared in a way not totally dissimilar to the way she arrived at Halle's bedside.

After a short nap Halle woke and attempted to look about her. The curtain, which looked as if it was meant to give her complete privacy, was open sufficiently for her to see she was in a room with about five or six men occupying beds at the far end near a door. It dawned on her that the curtain had been deliberately left that way so that any of the nursing staff could check her regularly without having to interrupt her sleep. The waves of sleep kept passing over her and she felt herself drift into sublime unconsciousness once again.

For some time after Teodor left Ian began to put two and two together. At least he considered that was what he was doing. Teodor's manner had changed since yesterday. "I wonder how he knows but somehow he is aware that I'm not telling him the whole truth. But where would he, or could he get the information that would make him aware?" The problem of Teodor's intelligence was upsetting. "I'll have to start piecing together all the various topics we have discussed and particularly those items where I feel the old man has been indiscreet... I wonder was that American accent of his feigned—and he certainly developed an English accent very readily. He seemed to be suspicious of me from the beginning... and then me talking about the AK in such a stupid way... *that's it!* He has been in touch with Aleksander!" Ian paused to consider all the ramifications of his thinking, "I'm sure Teodor has told him about the girl and Aleksander has worked it out that the girl must be Halle—of whom he disapproved; I must say on the basis of my description." The situation was too dangerous for Ian to ignore, but what where they to do? "I'll have to go to the old man and tell him the whole truth—there's no way I can get Halle out of that hospital without their help, and even if I could there's no way she'll be able to go on the run for some weeks."

Just before everyone was retiring for the night and Teodor was about to leave Ian asked him to remain, as he wanted to talk to him in private. To Ian's, not too sure eye, it appeared that the intellectual was already prepared for his approach and consequently felt ill at ease raising the issue of Halle. The shifting ground under his feet was further excavated when Teodor asked him point-blank about his story. "There are a number of flaws in the account of your arrival in this area, young man which I trust you are about to put right." There was more than a hint of repercussions ensuing in the event of these 'flaws' not being put right.

"Let me begin by assuring you that both of us are opposed tooth and nail to the Nazi government in Germany and to its attempt to conquer Europe. But almost equally we are opposed to each other's view of what should happen in our country—even in this I am juxtaposing two countries into one, to which I am entirely opposed."

"Young man you have succeeded in losing me completely! Let us return to your first sentence—the one and only sentence, which I understood. Kindly stick to the sentiments represented in it."

"Very well, I admit I have only told you part of the truth about Halle. Indeed she was a 'slave worker' taken from the Channel Islands but because of her connections with the Irish Republican Army and their fight with the British Government she thought the offer of working for German propaganda by broadcasting to Ireland would help bring about the re-unification of Ireland. However, she soon learnt the true nature of the Nazi Party and became involved in helping a Canadian spy escape, which put her in jeopardy. Because of this she undertook a job supposedly recruiting Irish POWs for the German Army but she only wanted the chance to move around the continent so that she could organise an escape."

"Hold it right there! Where is the evidence for all that you have said?"

"I haven't any. I can only say that I oppose her tooth and nail on her political views and consequently it's unlikely that I would be prepared to believe her if I hadn't seen her efforts to help me escape. I suppose you have an intelligence group inside your organisation?"

"Of course."

"Well perhaps you'll be able to check who is Oberst Hengist and why has he so many men trailing Halle? Indeed I suspect that it was his group which attempted to murder her; mind you I'm assuming that you're being truthful when you say that no one from your group was responsible!"

"Thank you for your sarcasm and your lack of trust! How do you think you would manage if we tossed you out to find your own way?"

"So we're not being put to death then? What part of my story convinced you of our innocence?"

"It added up to the total of the information, which we had in our possession. We never had doubts about you but we were and are fearful lest you have been taken in by a plant, what is the girl's name?"

"Halle."

"Yes, we still have doubts but we will check out the name of this colonel and try to establish what his rôle is in all of this."

"Halle seems to think that he is tied in with the Gestapo."

"The problem is which branch is he tied to?"

"I was unaware that there was more than one type of police in Germany."

"Since the war began the security police have a central staff, the RSHA, they pull the strings of the whole organisation and if your colonel is attached to them there is a fair chance that we would believe Halle's story."

"But why would it not be sufficient for him to be attached to say some local branch in Berlin where Halle first came across him?"

"It would not lend credence to your claim that she helped a Canadian spy, would it?"

"You have me there as I'm at a loss about the whole business. Let's leave it then until you're investigation is finished. Is that all right?"

"That's fine."

Halle's mind was going berserk: "Who was this woman and what was she doing? What if she was another of Hengist's agents? I'm not strong enough to deal with any of these questions. I should be concentrating on getting well and avoiding any distress." She tried to turn over on to her other side but the pain was too much and she had to lie on her back—a position that she never found comfortable.

She dozed over and was startled when she woke, "How long have I been here?" she wondered. "Well... I think I can account for two days; probably this means I have been here at least three possibly four days. What about that woman? If she comes back that is one question I can safely broach without it moving on to who or what I am. If she belongs to Hengist why didn't she kill me? My mind is not asking the right questions. She said something about helping me; that can't hold water, I don't know anyone in this part of the world." She paused to weigh up what evidence she had about the woman: firstly she said she wouldn't let *them* take her to Warsaw— I assume *them* refers to the Germans. Secondly, she said Ian was fine—how did she know about him, I must have asked in spite of all my promises to the contrary! The woman said, '*they* don't know I speak English' and she will see me tomorrow, that's today. It may well be evening already, I must watch carefully so that I will be able to recognise her again.

A noisy buzz of voices suggested that the room was about to be visited by an official who obviously was escorted by the medical team. Halle saw the door open through the half-drawn curtain and she tried to focus on the doorway to see who was the visitor. "Certainly he must be a big noise—I'm definitely going to stop these puns. At any rate he's getting the full treatment—Aw, Lord, now that was accidental!" Once the crowd surrounding him spread out to enable him to visit the first soldier, at least Halle assumed that the patient was one, she saw a little man with a limp to his left leg. "Now there is someone I know. Goebbels! As I'll live and die!" She wondered if he would recognise her from the few visits he made to Irland-Redaktion during her time there. "Please God just let him pass."

As he came along the ward she trusted that the semi-privacy accorded her would be sufficient to put off his coming near her. She recalled his noted charm with people from the conversations with colleagues during her time on radio. However, he left the medical team outside the curtains while he came in to speak to her. "Fraulein Hegel, I heard from the Stabsarzt, sorry I don't know how good your German is, I meant the Captain in charge here. He told me about your circumstances and let me know that you had for a time worked for Irland-Redaktion. Have we met on my visits there?"

"I don't think so Minister."

"Perhaps you would know some of those with whom I was familiar? Men like Menske, or more likely the Irishman O'Driscoll?"

"Indeed I knew both men. Menske actually employed me after interviewing me. O'Driscoll was a friend of mine prior to my coming to Germany. I worked with him in the Channel Islands."

"So you must have been the girl he spoke of who took the coded messages when he wasn't present."

"Indeed I am."

"Well, I am very sorry to see you in such a condition but the Stabsarzt assures me that you are no longer in danger and a convalescent period should ensure your total recovery. And it won't be long before you're back working for the Reich and the ultimate objective of the people of both our countries."

"Thank you, Minister."

He left leaving a bigger opening than there had been previous to his entry. Halle anxiously looked round to see if anyone was watching—if the woman who spoke to her the previous evening saw this visitation it could well jeopardise the whole situation and anger Ian. But there was no one unfamiliar in sight and Halle settled down to await the woman's arrival.

The hand on her shoulder wakened Halle instantaneously. "I am sorry but it is me again," stated the woman. "But who are you?" queried Halle. "It is better you don't know me, then that keeps both of us out of danger. Ian gave me information about you which we know was incorrect and now he has admitted to trying to help you, even though you are working for the Germans."

"That's not totally accurate, even if you don't *he* knows I had stopped working for them a long time ago. I wonder why he did such a foolish thing as confiding in your people?"

"I suspect that he wanted to help you and was fearful of the consequences if my people believed you were a German spy."

"What consequences?" asked Halle trying vainly to sit up. "People have been killed for less!" was the somewhat agitated answer. "So you are saying that is why he did it, to save my life?" again Halle tried to see the woman but was aware that the lady was attempting to cover up the conversation by making herself busy tugging at the pillows behind Halle. "Perhaps he loves you and would tell any lie to protect you." Halle gave a long sigh, "We hardly know one another, we are only together through force of circumstances."

"But surely love does not work on the basis of time, does it?"

"I don't know what it works on, I know I'm confused and fearful about being involved with him," muttered Halle and the woman sensed that she was drifting back to sleep and pulled the pillows towards her in order to waken her. "But you are putting both of you in danger," was the agitated reply. "In what way?" asked Halle. "Well you get favourable treatment from the German Army here in this hospital and then, this very evening, you were selected to be visited by Dr. Goebbels—one of the most hated Nazis in this war."

"He told me that the Stabsarzt told him about me and he came to see me because of my past association with his team of broadcasters who broadcast to Ireland," protested Halle. "Oh, I know, I listened outside the curtains. You must have been an acclaimed broadcaster to merit such treatment..."

"Oh my God, I have just realised, he will mention this to some of the people at Irland-Redaktion and the game will well and truly be up. I must get out of here as soon as possible. Sorry what where you saying?"

"I thought you must be well known..."

"No, it was my association with an Irishman who was seeking armaments for the IRA that brought him to see me—at least I think it was. I'm going to have to trust you; firstly tell Ian all that has happened and emphasise to him that Oberst Hengist will soon be aware of where I am. Tell him to get away quickly as I'm sure that his agents are bound to have spotted him with me since we left the POW camp."

"Wait, just wait. What is this new development? I can not bring messages I do not understand."

"Hengist is a Gestapo man, or something related to state security. Since I helped the Canadian spy he has been watching me because he was aware that the two of us were friends." The woman prepared to leave as she heard someone open the door, "I am going to have to report this but unless they find evidence that you did not help the Nazis it is going to be very tricky."

CHAPTER 12

(May-June 1943)

TEODOR KORZENIOWSKI WAS very quiet when he arrived at the Czerniawskis after hearing his daughter's report from the military hospital. "What am I to do? The story sounds genuine but all this earlier deception has left me very uneasy. Now it is no less than Goebbels who turns up to increase our doubts!" What unnerved him was that Ilona was struck by the girl's fortitude and felt that she would betray herself, if there were anything there to hide, given her circumstances in the hospital. The creases had increased on his forehead in the past few days, his friend Aleksander Kosciuszko had been anything but helpful. Oh, he was certain about Ian but knew nothing about Halle other than what he had heard from the escaped prisoner and at that time he had been struck my how scornful the man had been about the girl. Clearly there had been a change in Ian's relationship with her since then.

When he saw Ian he spoke before the Ulsterman had a chance to question him about Halle's condition. "I have contacted Aleksander Kosciuszko and all he will say is that he will need time to check out Halle's story. I did get the notion that he knew something about that colonel you mentioned. You see, on the telephone it is very difficult to speak when you are reduced to one-syllable answers for fear of being overheard. Questions by their very nature tend to be oblique and rely more on hints and the unsaid."

"What's the news from the hospital?" asked an anxious Ian and Teodor relayed Ilona's statements about Halle's health but left out her comments on the Goebbels' visit, merely saying he had been there. "My goodness! Imagine having a caller of the calibre of Goebbels paying you a visit! My mind can hardly take it on board."

"Just a minute, I know I should remember that expression 'take it on board', they used it quite often in Oxford, but what does it mean?" Ian explained the metaphor to the best of his ability, recalling his talks on literature with Halle. "I know I should have listened more attentively but what was the point you were making about Aleksander and the colonel?"

"You must realise that we can not help without authorisation from Warsaw and in particular from Bór-Komorowski, commander of the Home Army there. The AK has been particularly busy attacking various German posts and troops in the city. I know from the time I was living in the Radon district of the city there were over a hundred attacks in eighteen months.

That will give you some idea of the nature of their work there and its activities. So you see it will take some time to find out precisely who Hengist is but you may be lucky if I am right and that Aleksander has some knowledge of him already."

The days passed very slowly indeed for Ian; while Halle was so exhausted after her operation that time had ceased to bear any relevance to her situation. Occasionally Ilona Scharwenka, Teodor's married daughter, spoke to her— merely to inform her that there was no change in her situation, either in her condition or in the attitude of the Polish underground, nor indeed in the German authorities intention of moving her to Warsaw as soon as she was able. Ilona was as careful as she had been from the beginning and Halle still had no idea what she looked like. Ian's messages of concern for her wellbeing became a kind of tonic and as evening approached Halle waited anxiously for his latest epistle.

Towards the end of the third week Ian had, by now, become part of the work force on the farm. Although he had some experience as a boy picking potatoes in the autumn to help increase his parents' income, this was different. In the main he had to help with the livestock, not that they amounted to many but the milking of the cows and returning them to the pasture was irksome for a city boy. However, he grew to appreciate the work and how it helped in passing the time. More and more he wondered just how far he would have got had he not met Halle; indeed the Czerniawskis, wanted him to go to Gdansk while he still had the opportunity of doing so without worrying about Hengist's agents. They had a friend who operated a boat on the Vistula and he would willingly help him to get there. Clearly, whatever Teodor had told them, their sympathies lay with Ian and they were anxious about his safety. Nevertheless, Ian was committed to her, whether she liked it or not, and he was prepared to stay behind in order to ensure her safety.

One evening after hearing about Halle's continued improvement Teodor approached him and asked would he be prepared to help the AK in the event of their needing him. "Just remember that I was a signaller, not a soldier in some infantry regiment. If there is a need to set up communication lines I'm your man." Teodor smiled happily, obviously having worked out just what he wanted Ian to do. The following afternoon Teodor asked him how he would go about listening to the information being processed from the military hospital. "Is this got something to do with Halle?" Teodor's face had not got used to smiling so often, but he smiled less reluctantly than usual, "Yes." It was Ian's turn to smile, "I'll go with you and you can point out just where it is and when it's dark enough I'll be able to set up a

193

listening post provided you have the materials I need."

"Name them now and by this time tomorrow I will be surprised if I have not got them." Ian called out the various items and Teodor wrote them into some notebook after Ian queried the length of cable needed to set up the post. "I hope you didn't write these down directly? If you are caught with that in your possession they will assume that you are detonating explosives with that amount of wire."

"You are talking to me as if I were the novice instead of you!"

"Anyone can make a mistake, so I was being careful."

"Thank you for your consideration," replied Teodor with heavy sarcasm. "Tell me, do you speak to your young lady in a similar fashion?"

"Firstly, she is not my young lady—well, not yet. I don't think I am dogmatic, at least, I try not to be."

"Has she ever said anything which might make you think that you are?"

"That's different. We are on different sides of a big political question back home, so naturally, she would see me as being pigheaded."

"Ah, what a lovely expression—I do not have to ask you what it means! It is so patently like bull-headed it is obvious, even to a Pole like me, that it means you are stubborn and obstinate! Is that correct?"

"Yes, that's what it means but that doesn't mean that *she* is correct."

"Although you must admit it is strange that I noticed this quirk in your character as well."

"Between the both of you, you'll have me cured before this war is over."

"Let us get down to business and arrange precisely what way we will go about setting up this piece of information gathering."

"That's a phrase that's new to me, it just seems to roll off the tongue. When and where are we to meet?"

"I'll meet you here because I can not be certain that I will have all the materials you'll need." At that Teodor went and got his coat and Ian wished him 'Good Night'.

Much to everyone's surprise Teodor arrived at breakfast time the following morning, "Ilona says that the whole Military hospital is being evacuated next Thursday." His voice was higher than Ian had heard it. "Something had caused him to get this excited," thought Ian, "and it's not over this issue!" Teodor paused to let the enormity of the change sink in, "We knew it would happen sooner or later." began Ian, "More importantly, where are they going and is Halle being taken with them?"

"All of that is secondary to my other news. Aleksander Kosciuszko has been in touch, that man Hengist is in charge of tackling state subversives."

"What does that mean for Halle, and me for that matter?"

"Well someone of his rank and position in the RSHA…"

"You'd better explain those letters. I can't remember what they mean."

"Now according to Aleksander they stand for Reichs-sicherheitshauptamt, that is the State Security Head Office. They are the gods in the whole Gestapo system and are responsible for the detention of people in concentration camps. We know the SS run them but they are the masters. Well someone like him would not be hanging around small fry like your friend; clearly there is something looming larger that they wish to eradicate. We can only speculate that the Germans are hoping to have her lead them to these Allies' spies to which your friend referred. It's not exactly proof but it has convinced the Army Command in Warsaw that she is genuine and they want her taken out of the country as soon as possible. Do you think she knows more than she is saying?"

"I don't know her well enough to say so with confidence," replied an ebullient Ian, "but she is capable of so much that it wouldn't surprise me if she did! At the moment I am bursting with hope now that the AK are committed to getting her out of the country. Oh, you didn't get this information on the telephone, did you?"

"No I received a coded message from HQ which spelt out the dangers for your friend. Goebbels is, sooner or later, going to mention seeing Halle in hospital and then the fur will fly. Is that the right metaphor?"

"Yes, your memory is working well. For a time I thought the single syllables on the telephone were working your imagination overtime."

"I think I understand what you mean," said Teodor is an uncertain voice.

"Well what can we do to get Halle away from them? I'm amazed that Goebbels hasn't spilt the beans already…" began Ian with a smile. "You are pushing the boat out regularly now Ian…" replied Teodor. "I apologise, we Northerners tend to have an impish sense of humour particularly when we are under pressure. You see the effect this woman has on me, I'm that fearful of causing offence to her I didn't say Unionist or Protestant?"

"I am lost now. Please stop all these little games with the language and concentrate on what you were saying earlier."

"Sorry… what was I saying?"

"You are a hopeless individual. You were talking about Goebbels."

"Yes, why has there been no reaction at the hospital."

"According to what I hear he has not been back in his office in Berlin for the past three weeks because he is touring Army groups, obviously trying to keep up the troops' morale. He has been back and forth to see Hitler when he has been summoned but that apart it is doubtful if he has seen any of his cronies in the Gestapo. Regarding Halle, we need to get together with some of our Army men and work out a way of taking Halle from them."

"I notice that you use her name now that she is in the clear!" chuckled Ian. "Well it is understandable, is it not? I would not let myself become involved in case I was given the job of executing her—which I would have if it had come to that."

"Strange, not too long ago I would have given you a hand!"

"I'll never understand you, should you spend the rest of your life with us!" Teodor roared to the amazement of the onlookers. "As that so-called Irish poet of English extraction put it, 'And still they gazed, and still the wonder grew, that one small head could carry all he knew'," quoted Ian and it was Teodor's turn to look surprised.

The next day Teodor's daughter arrived with two young men. "We need to get a strategy sorted out now. Everything is set to go at the hospital and just because they say Thursday next does not mean that will be the day." She introduced the young men as having been sent by the AK to organise and co-ordinate the various tactics that the two groups will undertake. "Which two groups are we talking about?" asked Ian. "Well," replied Ilona, "the local AK men and ourselves."

"I hope your father told you that I was a signaller in the British Army, not a crackshot." The girl smiled in recollection of her father's comments on Ian's anxiety to avoid becoming a soldier again. "I heard all about it but we want to achieve Halle's freedom without firing a shot—that is the reason for this meeting."

"You had better explain precisely what you know about the situation before we begin." Ilona explained to the others in Polish what Ian wanted and they felt exactly the same way. "The Stabsarzt told us that those patients capable of being moved would be taken to Warsaw this Thursday or Friday. At present there are only four men who fit this criterion; the seriously ill are being sent to the local hospital near here under military care. There will be a convoy to Plock and then the military ambulance will head on to Warsaw alone."

Both of the young Poles began speaking as soon as Ilona translated what she had told Ian. "They believe that the best opportunity to get Halle is when the ambulance leaves Plock, what do you think?"

"I bow to your and their experience. The German medics obviously wouldn't expect anyone to be interested in *freeing* wounded German soldiers." Agreement was reached readily on what was required to bring the vehicle to a halt and Ian remarked that it would be his first successful engagement in the war and the others smiled when Teodor's daughter explained.

Over the following days and nights the young men reported back to the farm letting the family and Ian know how they were managing to resource the operation. They got the agreement of a farmer near the agreed point to use his cart to block the road so that the AK could kidnap Halle and bring her back to the Czerniawskis' farm.

The first doubts about the plan came from Ian. Suddenly he could visualise Hengist and his troops arriving at the last moment and the whole thing failing. Ilona begged him not to raise his doubts at the daily meetings. "Just how trustworthy are your guys?" he asked the day before the event. "I've heard there is a lot of political shenanigans going on and I want to make sure that we're pulling in the same direction."

"You could only have heard that from my father."

"No, he never said a word to me but I heard him arguing with some of the young men about communism."

"You do not know Polish, so how can you say that?"

"Some words I know and other words sound similar to the English ones and the heated exchange was all too clear—there is a major disagreement going on and I don't want it coming to the surface right now!"

"All right, there are problems between those giving their allegiance to the government-in-exile in London and some who give theirs to the Soviets. For the most part we get on amicably because we have a common enemy in the Nazis."

"God help you if you can't agree now, what will it be like under a Soviet constitution? It doesn't bear thinking about."

"Then let us leave it. Tomorrow will resolve your concerns but not ours. The Russians murdered so many Polish officers, when the Nazi-Soviet Pact was operating, that it is hard to understand how anyone can trust them."

"Is there any proof of this or is so much assumption? Our own recent history in Ireland, North and South, is riddled with who did what, that each side has its own version of the events and they make sure they tell their children the version they want followed."

"Some say there was a survivor or maybe two who testified to the Russians having done it. But then again I have heard others claim on oath that the Germans murdered them."

"You'll be lucky if you ever find out the whole truth."

197

Halle had just closed her eyes when her unknown friend wakened her. Once again she appeared to have been dusting the rail of the bed and then reached out to shake Halle very gently. "The Germans are moving you tomorrow to Warsaw." Halle became alert very quickly; "I can't let that happen." Ilona pretended to be astonished, "Why? You are in no danger, are you?"

"I am. I don't know whether I can trust you... but you do bring news from Ian, I assume that he trusts you?" During this burst of communication from Halle, Ilona was watching the rest of the room, as she didn't want anyone to recollect her talking with the girl. "I can not speak for him of course but he wants you to know that this field hospital is about to move on in the direction of Warsaw, as far as we know it will be tomorrow or Friday."

"Oh my God, what will I do? He is bound to find me and that means an all out interrogation. You know what that means, don't you?" For the first time Ilona showed herself to Halle, "Indeed I know what that means, I lost my husband to just such an interrogation. Even if you survive you will end in a concentration camp. Now what we, Ian and I, want you to do is rest as we intend to kidnap you from them once they take to the road. If they go ahead as planned then by this time tomorrow you will be with Ian in a safe house. I have to leave now so try to rest and pray that tomorrow goes well."

"Thank you and God bless you."

Everyone involved was on the move early on Thursday morning when Ilona, returning from her night shift, arrived in a state of distress, literally panting from running. "The move has been cancelled and before anyone asks there was no reason given. Just before midnight I, and a few others, sensed a kind of tension in the air and then the Stabsarzt summoned groups of us to his office to break the news." There were three or four conclusions jumped to by the teams—it is a temporary set back; some of those to be moved are dangerously ill; there has been a huge battle and they are waiting for the wounded to be brought to them and Ian's contribution, "I think that it has to do with Hengist."

Ilona was convinced there had been an outside source responsible for the change of plans and turning to Ian remarked that, "It must have been someone of considerable rank but to conclude that it was Hengist is too much of a hasty and rash thought." Ian was not put off by her opinion and insisted that it was better to think the worst rather than sit around doing nothing on the basis that there was no evidence. "I've been having these fears for the last few days and you've heard me state them. I think we tried to kid ourselves that Goebbels hadn't the opportunity to pass on the information about Halle. But the man is no fool, I bet he was asking questions as to why she was where they found her and why the Army was not keeping tags on her."

"Ian you are speaking too fast. Explain your last sentence."

"Obviously Goebbels must have wondered what she was doing near Plock and what was the German Army doing about keeping an eye on her." Ian looked directly at Ilona and she nodded comprehension. "Still I think this is a big assumption Ian. You are jumping from Goebbels to Hengist and back to a backwater Military Hospital, that takes a fair stretch of imagination."

"I've heard Halle talking about Hengist a number of times and his appearances out of the blue have convinced her that she is the person being watched. Personally I think she's right but if so then Hengist must be wrong in assuming that she is involved in spying for the Allies."

"Could he be that wrong; after all you tell us that it is not too long ago that you would not trust her yourself?"

"Trust is a sleekit thing; I'm sorry, I know you're going to ask what it means, it's a mixture of deviousness and slyness that deceives even the possessor of it. People trust the most unbelievable things, like money, just ask the Germans about hyperinflation in 1923. Most marriages are based on trust but a hell of a lot of them fail because it was purely imaginary."

"Getting back to Halle, what are you saying?"

"I'm sorry, please don't let me get on to my hobbyhorse again. Look, we have to act quickly to get Halle out of there before Hengist, or whoever he sends, gets there."

"But she is still ill and it would have been difficult enough for her if it had gone ahead today. Are you thinking of snatching her from the hospital? Because I think you are asking too much from her. Besides you haven't produced any evidence that it is Hengist who changed the arrangements."

"But you're the one who said it must be someone with clout who stopped today's move!"

"I know but it is still a big step from that to Hengist and Goebbels."

"If probability is all we're left with I think, with so little time to play with, we have to try something."

"Well *are you* thinking of snatching her from the hospital?"

"I am if I can get help."

"You leave me in a quandary. What is the term used when you are caught between two impossible choices?"

"Horns of a dilemma?"

"Yes that is it!"

"So you have no suggestion then?"

"I'm not sure what to do—if we attempt to get Halle out at gunpoint the chances are there will be a lot of gunfire and deaths; maybe even Halle's. On the other hand if we wait and you're right, then Hengist will arrive and take Halle to some centre for interrogation. Neither of these are what we want but I think the latter is the better option—at least we could save Polish lives." Ilona's shrug of the shoulders spoke volumes and Ian was quiet for a few moments. "Can we smuggle her out instead?" he asked with a quizzical glance, knowing he was putting the onus on her.

"How could it be done? I am no longer sure as to the purpose of this exercise. Are you asking us to endanger our lives for someone, who—for all we know—worked for the Nazis against us? If that is the case the answer is 'No'! If *you* want to get into the hospital and get her out, I will help you to get in but it will be up to you then."

"What good will that do?" demanded Ian, "I would have difficulty getting back out on my own never mind getting Halle out. Look I need to know more about the hospital and how it works—I mean regarding patients arriving and leaving. Then perhaps—at this moment it sounds like a mighty big perhaps—I'll come up with a plan."

"There is a constant movement of patients, those coming from the front who have been seriously wounded and then those recovered sufficiently to be dispersed to the various parts of Germany by rail."

"How do they arrive?" began Ian, intending to develop the question but Ilona spoke too quickly, "Military ambulances bring the soldiers in and return to the front for further casualties."

"Do these vehicles leave immediately for the front?"

"No, the drivers and any crew they may have stay to be fed or, at least, have a mug of ersatz coffee."

"What about security, do they be stopped coming in or going out?" the girl paused to collect her thoughts; "With such a steady stream of wounded in and out there has been a lot of carelessness—that is the wrong word. No, I suppose their thinking is 'why put a lot of effort into security when no-one is likely to raid a field hospital comprising mostly tents'. Arriving on foot is a different matter, they want to see your pass."

"So if I can get an ambulance the chances are that I'll not be stopped on entering?"

"True, but where are you going to get one?"

"I've thought about it and with the help of your friends in the AK we can waylay one some distance from the hospital and if they hold on to the crew for an hour or so I can get in."

"You have not said it but I suppose you would like me to deliver Halle to the ambulance—and of course that would mean I'd be finished there, I would have to get out." Ian had thought about this and he realised that this was his biggest hurdle and he must be diplomatic to a degree that he had never before attempted.

"You have been living on a knife-edge for a long time in that job, haven't you?"

"Indeed I have. Twelve months I have worked with these people. Most of the time I have been a nurse but all the time I was listening to them and reporting back to the AK on how the Germans were doing on the Russian front."

"If everything had gone to plan you know you would have had your employment ended today? And the odds are that they will end very shortly."

"I know all that but at least I won't be on the run for aiding and abetting you." Ian could see that his 'diplomacy' was going awry. He decided to have a further attempt, "But if you ended your employment today and simply went in tomorrow to collect your bits and pieces you would be in the clear." Ilona didn't rise to the bait, "I will talk to my father about it—no matter what way you put it I will still be wanted and I won't be able to undertake this kind of rôle again."

Ian's aplomb had long since disappeared and the most he could manage was, "Think about it today before you go in this evening and if it is possible maybe your men could get me an ambulance in the morning. You know I'll be grateful and even more so if you decide to come with me. Either way I'm going ahead provided I can get an ambulance. Oh, by the way, a driver's cap and uniform top would be useful."

"You really ask for the moon once you are started and you are not giving me much time to do all that, even if my father and I agree," called Ilona as she started to leave the room. " 'Time and tide wait for no man' or woman," shouted Ian at her back as she left but she still managed to shout the final words, "You are full of these sayings Ian and of course they always support what *you* want!"

CHAPTER 13
(June 1943)

THE SAME AFTERNOOn, when Ilona approached him, Teodor was opposed to her suggestion that she should help the wounded girl. "Any of the corporal works of mercy are fine but given the situation we are in here, we can not afford to lose your expertise and that is precisely what will happen if you have to go on the run because of this." Teodor's hand movements all went to emphasise how strongly he felt about the matter. Equally his daughter showed her concern and anxiety to have his support and agreement, "Look I think I can cover-up my part in the affair but the whole thing needs to be done when I am on the night shift—which means doing it tonight. If your main concern is to ensure that I am not forced on the run doing it this way will avoid that."

"If you are happy and are sure, then I am prepared to do all I can for the success of your mission," answered Teodor in a very uncertain tone of voice.

"So much depends on the hijacking of the ambulance and the disguise for Ian. Can you arrange that?"

"It will be one of the easiest tasks I have been involved in so far!" smiled Teodor, "What have you still to do?"

"Nothing much, I will call on Ian and appraise him of what we are doing."

"What time best suits you for the arrival of the ambulance?"

"The last visit from the Stabsarzt is around midnight, so any time after that should work well for me. However, I have a coffee-break around two so no later than that."

"I will try to make it on time but tell Ian if we have not arrived by 02.00 hours it is off."

"I am confident that you will be able to get an ambulance before midnight so I can not see any difficulties in that area. It is getting the girl out of the hospital is the worrying thing. I have just realised that when the other duty nurse is off, having her break, would be the ideal time and she goes at 01.30. Can you try to be there then?"

"Whatever you say but the more you talk about this the more I suspect that you have a soft spot for that young man," there was a wry look about the smile he gave her. Ilona's wide grin said more about her thinking than the words which tumbled out, "I have no more interest in him than you have, except that I am conscious of your description of his anti-Catholic stance."

"I do not believe he is, it is just a political thing in Ireland," replied Teodor, gesticulating with his hands and arms.

"You would not say that if I took up with a card-bearing Nazi Party member—'it is just a political thing', would you?" Again his hands and body movement spoke volumes. "We are not talking of similar things. They are a world apart," said Teodor as he prepared to leave to see to the arrangements, which Ilona had proposed. "Father, I would not take a bet on you saying 'it is a political thing'!" was her final comment.

Ian was delighted to see the girl arrive because the sight of her convinced him that she was going to go through with his plan. "Everything is arranged as you suggested," began Ilona and she went to great lengths to explain the lead up to the removal of Halle from the ward and she warned him to be ready for the ambulance's arrival some time after midnight. Ian's gratitude was palpable and he found himself unable to convey his thanks for her efforts, "I'm sure your father wasn't in favour of all of this; you must have convinced him, did you?"

"It was not all that difficult. He likes you and from that position he assumes that Halle must have good qualities otherwise you would not get into all this."

"He's right, but you know that it isn't merely 'good qualities', there is an attraction between us that would be there regardless."

"Well, no matter. My father feels he knows you and you won't get us all killed in this business tonight."

"There is no way I am going to sacrifice you or anyone else. Nor would Halle want me to do that. If anything goes wrong I want you to promise me that you will protect yourself and leave Halle and me to our own devices, will you do that?"

"Let us see which way the cards fall and play them from there."

Ilona left shortly afterwards for work and Ian decided to rest in an armchair in preparation for the arduous business ahead. He had hardly closed his eyes when he began to dream of his old composing room in Queen Street where he had begun his apprenticeship. Surreal things happened there! But nothing like what was happening now... the Monotype casting machine was firing single letters at him and he couldn't avoid them and when he collected them they seemed to form words on their own; 'turn coat', 'traitor', 'Lundy', 'Fenian', 'bastard'. Meanwhile the reams of paper, used by the Monotype keyboard, rolled over into galley after galley with the holes spelling out 'Christmas', 'Easter' and on completion they flung themselves at him. In the corner of the composing room two apprentice compositors were using riglettes as swords, trying to imitate the fencing by Louis Hayward in a film.

His thought processes changed direction and he was back in the composing room sorting out the letters from some piece of letterpress work, which had been completed. He felt there was no reality in any of this but he spent time trying to recollect which boxes in the case contained the individual letters—the biggest box is definitely 'e' and the smallest 'z'. The woman said, "Why do people talk about pieing when they haven't a clue how it looks?" He eyed her cagily, "Zane Gray was right when he used compositors as gunslingers in his stories. He was alleged to have said their quickness with a gun was due to their having to set type in a stick in a hell of a hurry." The woman continued with her questioning, "Was it good to get away from the pied pages, particularly those on the stone?" He thought for a moment, "You couldn't make the same mess but you could do much more damage by doing a page the wrong size or use the wrong typeface like Bembo—who had been a cardinal instead of a good English designer of facetype like Baskerville who printed Virgil. Strange how one is so thin and elongated and the other wider set and not so long, is that telling me something?"

"I don't know what it's telling you but it suggests you read too much into everything," said Ilona… Ian woke with a start, how did she get into his dream? "It's the old thing, the last thing you think of before sleep or the last one you spoke to sometimes takes an active rôle in your dreams."

His eyes became heavy again, this time he could see the practical jokers setting the old type at the bottom of his galley and deliberately pieing it to frighten him. Normally he would have had a heart attack and he would have recovered when he saw the old ink on the face types or occasionally, in anger, he would have thrown the rest out with it not having twigged it didn't all need to be dissed. "I don't like dissing, *you* know the dispersal of type into the case," explained Ian. "What is this case, you keep mentioning it?" asked the woman.

"Where the type is kept—you've heard of 'lower-case' and 'upper-case', haven't you?"

He was in the middle of a conversation, but whoever she was had disappeared and had been replaced with an old colleague of his, Sam. "What about Joe's machine?" asked Ian.

"Oh, it still has the same old pulley it had when it arrived the same day Joe did and he's been here for fifty years."

"Is it still giving trouble?"

"Of course it bloody does. Did you ever hear of anything that improves with age? The pulley works sometimes to pull the carriage return across the scale, not a bit like the new ones that operate with air-pressure. At least it can justify itself occasionally, which is more than can be said for you, you turncoat!" called Sam as he turned away. "Before you go, do they all still say to him, 'What do you know, Joe?'" but Sam was gone.

Tommy said, "Guttenberg did us all a favour inventing moveable type, that's how we can read the Bible for ourselves." Pat the interrupter moved in, "There's no two people I know who agree on anybody's interpretation, is there?" Ian kept out and let Tommy carry the load, "Individual conscience! Individual conscience!" Pat the Catholic agnostic asked, "Why then do so many harp on the Old Testament when Christ taught something different from an eye for an eye?" Tommy exited with, "Am I my brother's keeper?"

"Did *you* ever hear of surrealism?" said Ian turning to Ilona. "Surrealism? Of course, I covered many subjects at university."

"Oh, I thought you were a nurse? Do nurses cover art and go to university?"

"No, they don't! What's your definition of surrealism?"

"A bit like what we're doing now. Do you see the artist as a priest interpreting our world?"

"It's tough enough being an artist," she replied by way of saying the final word.

"What about these pages you've left me?" asked Ian.

"Make them 27 picas wide by 42 picas long. What typeface would you suggest?"

"Anything but Cardinal Bembo's long skinny characters—a 300 page book would be lucky to make 180 pages in that! OK I exaggerate but it will reduce the number of pages you imagine it will make." Ilona kissed him, "Thanks for your help," and left. Ian luxuriated in the passionless embrace before being brought to his senses by the clump of Jan Czerniawski's feet. The farmer extended his hand to have it shaken and Ian realised that his host and employer knew of his intention this night. He smiled grimly in a kind of reply—being the best he could do with his lack of Polish.

Teodor entered a half an hour later with an equally grim smile; "The ambulance is ready, are you?"

"What time is it?"

"Almost zero hour—I mean midnight."

"My daughter wants us there around 01.30 hours. How long will it take to get there?" was the rather formal reply.

"No more than fifteen minutes. I was not referring to time when I asked you if you were ready. I meant were you mentally ready for this."

"I'll not know until I face up to whatever is in front of me."

"Ian you are a wise young man; no one can be sure how one will react when under fire. You have experience of it, have you not?"

"Indeed I have but I did more running than fighting when I saw how badly outnumbered we were," answered Ian with a weak grin.

"I suspect you are braver than that; I think you fought as hard as anyone in the circumstances when you were being overrun."

"Thanks Teodor, 'your faith has made *me* whole', to paraphrase an old biblical quotation from Sunday school. How do you suggest we put in the time?"

"A look at the ambulance and its controls would pay a valuable dividend before this night is out. If you come outside I have arranged to have it parked at the back of the farm." They left and spent the next hour ensuring that Ian could drive the vehicle and knew precisely where he was going.

Just after one o'clock Ian drove out of the farmyard and made his way to the hospital. The sentry on duty pulled up the pole blocking the entrance to enable him to gain access. "Everything is going according to Hoyle— where did I get that from? I'll take a bet... Oh no Lord, the effect that that girl has had on me!" He drove very slowly along the side that the girl had indicated when telling him directions. One of the tents had its flap up and he brought the vehicle to a stop just as Ilona appeared and waved him inside, then she had a change of mind and in a whisper said, "You had better bring a stretcher; she won't be able to walk unaided." Ian returned to the ambulance and moments later followed her inside.

"I thought she was in the main building complex," he said in a loud whisper. "Hush! There is a house that she was in but thankfully she was moved out today, perhaps because she is beginning to show greater signs of recovery. And again it may be that they are still under the impression that she will be moved out with the others to Warsaw once the command comes through." All the time she was speaking she walked further into the tent and finally stopped by a bed in which Halle slept soundly.

Together they moved her on to the stretcher and without further ado went directly to the ambulance and placed the sleeping Halle in a bunk. Ian quickly and quietly thanked Ilona and then asked her if she was confident she could cover her involvement. "Just go now; I will be fine. Goodbye."

Driving along the driveway to the barrier Ian felt that few things in his life had ever gone so well. "All done and dusted and it's not a quarter to two yet!" He approached the sentinel's box as cautiously as he had been on entering. This time things had changed, the soldier was standing with his rifle pointing directly at him and Ian decided he had no alternative but to put his foot down and go for it.

The sentry fired and Ian felt the draught of the bullet as he crouched down in the cab. He never got the opportunity to fire again as the ambulance ploughed over him. "Something has gone hellish wrong," muttered Ian as he pushed the accelerator to the floor in an attempt to distance them from whatever forms of transport his pursuers might take. What they would be in didn't concern him, he only knew they would be after the ambulance.

Driving wildly along narrow country roads with such a large vehicle was not the easiest job imaginable and Ian soon realised that there was little hope of escape. Even if he did make it to the Czerniawski farm the chances were that it would be raided within the hour and the family plus their friends and neighbours would be incarcerated in some concentration camp and, possibly worse from his point of view, Halle's life would be in danger. Then, quite suddenly, he agonisingly thought of the dangerous position that Ilona was in because of the foul up. "They must have let one or two of the ambulance crew escape—there's no other way they could have known," thought Ian. "But what am I going to do? I should have planned an alternative course of action just in case of anything going badly wrong; as is the case now."

Although the lights of the ambulance had been greatly reduced by the war time restrictions he still remembered seeing a forest on his way to the hospital. Perhaps if he pulled into one of the forest's roads he could find a place to wait until his pursuers passed. There wasn't much time to compose himself and think it through, so as soon as he saw the road on his left he pulled into it and drove some distance before finding a recess where he could hide the vehicle.

Immediately he stopped he went to see how Halle was and he was pleasantly surprised to see that she was wide-awake. "My God, it's you Ian! I thought the Germans had decided to transfer me to Warsaw in the middle of the night." Her delight in seeing him added to his mounting joy and he unwillingly told her of their predicament and spoke also of the father and daughter's part in the escape. Seeing Halle's contented frame of mind at being out of German hands he asked her which of two options they should choose; return to the Czerniawski farm or do the unexpected by driving past the hospital and abandoning the ambulance further along the road.

Halle deliberated quite a while before settling for the former. "Why that, surely we would be putting the family in danger?"

"True, if it meant that they are unprepared. But the odds suggest that they will be ready with another plan, particularly if they have been responsible for the escape of the crew. Did you hear that?"

"Yes, I was just about to interrupt you when you stopped. That must have been the pursuers passing, we'd better get under way to get back to the farm before they twig what's happened."

The men from the AK, who had been sent by Teodor to make sure that the plan worked, returned in some anxiety. "Everything went well until the ambulance attempted to leave the grounds. There was some shooting and then we assume the POW's vehicle burst through the barricade and hared down the road with a number of German soldiers in pursuit in a variety of vehicles. We followed at a distance but it was clear that the Germans lost them, so we decided to return and report."

"What do you think went wrong? Everything at this end was OK."

"We were discussing this on the way back and it seems to us that there must be something about the time between entering and leaving. The guard took a note of when the British POW entered and he could see him checking his board on hearing the ambulance approaching. We suspect that Ian left too soon."

"You had better wait here, if they have any sense they will come back and in the meantime we will have to prepare to hide them as the Germans will search all the nearby farms. Luckily we have that hideaway in the barn, so go and make it habitable."

The alert was on-going when Ian drove the ambulance into the farmyard. The issuing of orders all stemmed from Teodor and what Ian and Halle suspected as to his position was now clear. Teodor led the rush to the ambulance and once Halle had been safely removed some of the men drove off in the vehicle while others followed in a car. Ian assumed that they had a prearranged dumping spot and the other car was to collect the driver and his companion.

Meanwhile Teodor disappeared and returned minutes later to guide Ian and Czerniawski as they carried the stretcher. They went into a sizeable barn and at the back, under hay, was a concrete slab that had cleverly been made to match the rest of flooring in the barn that hid a serviceable hideaway. "Or perhaps the slab was originally there—which came first, the chicken or the egg? I wish my mind would give me peace!" thought Ian. "It is too late for me to be moving about with all this going on," said Teodor, "I will stay tonight and return home in the morning when the Nazis stop looking in this area."

The Czerniawskis were tortured with the coming and going of the

Germans during the night, however, their three 'boarders' slept throughout with not a noise to disturb them. Next morning the news was grim, fifty people were taken as hostages from their homes in the neighbourhood and posters appeared warning of the consequences should anything happen to: 'Oberst Halle Hegel, a wounded officer attached to the local group command. Anyone with information should convey it to the local army headquarters' and proceeded to give details of its address. Both the Czerniawskis went to the barn to waken their visitors with the news only to find them awake with Ian and Teodor up and about. With much gesticulation, behind Halle's back, they got Teodor to leave and they, making suitable apologies, followed him up the ladder to the barn. In the hideaway Ian knew something was amiss but kept up a conversation with Halle about the joys of being free. Ten minutes must have elapsed before the other three joined them, "Look Halle, we're forced to move you because of the amount of activity created by your escape," began Teodor. "The Germans are implying that you, as a German officer, have been kidnapped and that is why the whole area is under curfew from tonight. You can see why we need you off the premises as soon as possible?"

"Of course I can," and turning to the Czerniawskis, "but I wish it wasn't so, even though I've only spent one night here, the feeling of hospitality and concern are overwhelming and I would have preferred to stay."

Teodor's interpretation lost nothing in the telling and the Czerniawskis were near tears at the dramatic turn of events knowing that they had hidden the awfulness of the Hobson's choice that confronted the unaware Halle. "We had better start getting you ready for the move, Halle," remarked Ian, all too aware that something was afoot and he wanted an early opportunity to speak with Teodor. "What's going on, Teodor?" queried Ian once they had taken Halle into the farm. Teodor was deliberately obtuse; "We are waiting for my daughter to have a look at the girl before we move her." Clearly the girl was already late and Ian could see the tension on her father's face. "You're covering up something, spit it out!" There was a pause as Teodor sought the right opening words, knowing full well there was no glitter he could add to the situation, there just was no varnishing over the circumstances by telling unmitigated lies. "The Nazis are holding fifty Poles as hostages for Halle's return. They are claiming that she is a German officer attached to the local battalion."

"Oh my God! I should have thought this thing through more thoroughly. Hindsight is a wonderful old word. What are we to do?"

"Ilona assured me that there would be no lives at risk in this enterprise but I was thinking more of her and the Czerniawskis. If it was my decision it would be easy—I couldn't allow fifty people to die for the sake of one—even if she were a good Polish girl!" The remainder was left unsaid but it was clear in Ian's mind that he nearly had added, "Not for someone who has worked with the Nazis." While thinking of what was best he prowled around the large living room like a panther waiting to see what it could prey on. "Is there any possibility of a solution other than the obvious one, Teodor?"

"I can't see one that does not involve returning Halle to these bastards… Sorry, I know you worry about the form of words used on such occasions."

"No!… No, that's not quite right. It's blasphemy that is upsetting. Swearing and the abuse of words are rarely done deliberately; has much more to do with habit. But that's getting away from the issue of what's to be done."

Teodor looked at him with concern and some pity, "Only you and Halle can decide this matter. You are going to have to talk it over as soon as you can."

Ilona arrived shortly afterwards, apologising for being late and explained that there had been an investigation into how Halle had been spirited away. "No doubt I am the chief suspect. After all I was on duty in that area when it happened and the other duty nurse was having a break. Luckily for me, just as soon as Ian left I was called to work with a seriously injured soldier. The doctor was present so there is some uncertainty as to how I could be in two places at the one time. Fortunately this particular doctor had no idea of the time and all he could say was that as soon as he called me I arrived."

"Do you think you should be out of there, right now?" asked Ian and was promptly supported by Teodor who asked his daughter if she seriously thought she could go back. Ian pursued this idea by asking her to look at the circumstances through German eyes. "I'm sure and I know you realise that they will be aware that whoever pulled this off was in league with someone on the premises. They'll gradually eliminate the other staff and they'll arrest you!" The girl looked at both of them, unwilling to admit that her position was invidious, and then turned and started pacing the room before speaking. "I suspect that both of you are right but there is a more urgent problem facing us right this minute!"

"You've heard about the hostages then?" asked Ian.

"Yes! But what are you doing about it?"

"I haven't talked to Halle about it; in fact she doesn't know about the hostages." The expression of shock on Ilona's face nonplussed Ian, "What is it? I'll tell her now if you wish."

"You had better tell right now! The Nazis tend to shoot hostages and, in circumstances like these, once they have put out leaflets and posters they start killing one every couple of hours until they get the response they want."

"Good God!" cried Ian breaking into a gallop, "I'm away to break the bad news!"

Ilona turned to her father; "One hope is that if they have not finished putting round the leaflets and posters then they will hold off taking action." Teodor offered up a prayer that such would be the case and suggested that they should plan as if Halle would be given to the German authorities.

Meantime Ian went to the bedroom where Halle was resting in preparation for the journey to the safe house. "Halle things have gone completely wrong!"

"In what way?" Ian went through the whole scenario as Ilona had relayed it to him. "My Lord God... is there any way out of this mess?"

"I've trawled every option with Teodor and Ilona but as far as I can see you're left with the choice between the two horns of this dilemma. Sorry, I hate it when I try to be clever with language," protested Ian. Halle smiled, ignoring his protestations, "The position is clear—I'll have to go back; but how do I do it without endangering others?" Ian wasn't prepared to let his statement stand; he emphasised his love for her before agreeing that in the circumstances she'd made the only possible choice. "We'll have to talk it over with the other two firstly on how to go about getting you there, and then to fit you with a story that covers Ilona's part in all of this."

Ian went to get them while Halle tried to compose herself so that she could put on a brave face to show the others. In the event she did not deceive anyone as they all realised her decision could mean sacrificing her life. Ilona was the first and last to speak: "We all recognise your bravery in this matter but we have no time for compliments. I would suggest that your story should be on the lines of your being unconscious. Say a man, who was not known to you, woke you accidentally as he was giving you some drug—say it smelt like chloroform and you passed out. You have been in and out of sleep since and the first you knew that matters were not right was when you woke at the side of the roadway. How does that sound?" turning to Teodor and Ian. "At any rate the rest of the deliberations don't affect you, so Ian, if you give me a hand with the stretcher we will take it outside and arrange for a car to leave her near enough to the hospital so that she will be found in a short time."

"Wait a minute there is a weakness in the story. Chloroform has a strong smell and I doubt if it would have disappeared so soon, what do we do?" Teodor's daughter smiled the smile of one who had an answer, "We have

211

some chloroform here, do not worry." All of them went to the cart but before they reached it Teodor took Ian by the arm in such a way that it restrained him. "Look Ian, I know you want to go with Halle but we need the room to have her hidden in the hay, after all we want things to look as normal as possible." Ian looked crestfallen, "All right, I'll make my farewells now but I don't know what I'll do if anything happens to her."

"If we get over this difficulty then we can start thinking about another way round dealing with her detention. In the meantime let us hope that the cart won't be stopped by a German Army patrol. They have searched this area that much since the incident it is unlikely they will be anywhere near here," continued Teodor to Ian. But Ian's confidence, already rocked by the present difficulties, said, "Don't let us get over-confident, I've fallen into that trap already! Let once be enough."

Ilona urged them along, as she was worried about the time factor in their calculations. It had been left to her to pick a spot that would be safe for the AK men to leave Halle on her stretcher and she chose a point about one kilometre from the entrance to the hospital. She explained her choice; "Every German vehicle seems to pass this point at least once a day. And with them on the lookout they should find her quite easily... I am just thinking, maybe a phone call would be best in case they start murdering the hostages before they find her. What do you think?" Ian and Teodor looked at each other before Ian spoke: "Do both and then you're covering all eventualities," and Teodor just nodded agreement as he departed with the Czerniawskis.

Ilona's awareness of the German attitude and her familiarity with the area all contributed to Halle's being returned to the hospital. In addition not a hostage suffered more than a night's confinement in the local jail. The local AK was delighted with the outcome but Ian back on the Czerniawskis' farm and Halle, back in her old ward, were despondent. For Halle the one big difference this time was the amount of attention she got from everyone. The German medical staff feared that there might be more kidnapping and they felt they were the more likely candidates for any further occurrence. A permanent guard was placed on Halle's ward, whether for her or the German doctors and nurses or both was never revealed.

Later that afternoon two of the local Gestapo men called to ask her details about the events leading up to her 'kidnapping'. Halle stuck rigidly to the story she had concocted with the others back at the farm and it seemed to be accepted by the two of them. When they left she felt utterly exhausted and fell into a deep sleep. In was early evening when she woke and she was surprised because the German doctors had previously always insisted that she should try to do some exercises, even though she was bed bound. On looking around the ward she noticed that the Gestapo men were still questioning some of the wounded soldiers and she assumed it was about her 'kidnapping' but there was no sign of Ilona and she wondered if the girl would be so foolish as to put in an appearance. There was no doubt in Halle's mind that the authorities were determined to get to the bottom of the incident and with the incessant questioning going on it wouldn't be too long before they deduced Ilona's involvement.

By nine o'clock Halle knew that Ilona wasn't in and she hoped she wouldn't be in. The medical team was frantically searching the hospital and its grounds in case another kidnapping had occurred. But once the Gestapo got a whiff of the situation a whole new angle emerged—they abruptly assumed this woman must be the inside informer who had helped outsiders to remove Halle and that she was now on the run. At least initially that is what Halle assumed but when she started to think the matter over it gradually became clear that they had information which enabled them to get to the heart of the investigation. Their reactions were far too quick. The guard, which had been present since Halle's return, was reinforced and within ten minutes Halle was wheeled out of the ward and transferred to an ambulance. A doctor accompanied her on the journey and at this point she felt that the game wasn't completely up. If they contemplated putting her to death the care and concern would have been missing, yet she knew without being told that she was on her way to Warsaw—but to face what?

Earlier Ian, totally unaware of the situation at the hospital, had been encouraged by Teodor to discourage his daughter from going back and even when he convinced himself that the matter was settled Ilona would change her mind. It soon got to the point where she became shirty and demanded of Ian what it had got to do with him. Diplomacy cuts no ice with her but by persisting with the question "Why?" he eventually managed to get an explanation. "Look, I made a promise to my father that I would do nothing to endanger the work I had undertaken at the hospital by agreeing with you to rescue Halle. Even as you say you are reporting his request for me to leave, he knows that I have made an error of judgement and I do not feel right about giving in to something I suspect may not happen."

"You know, without me labouring it, you are about to compound one error into a bigger one. I was the one who talked you into all of this and I thought if I could admit to a mistake you would see that it must be equally true for you. If you won't listen to me you should heed your father."

"'Heed' is unfamiliar to me. What does it mean?"

"You have heard of 'honour your father and your mother'?"

"Yes, it is one of the ten commandants."

"Well 'heed' is just that, 'listen to', 'respect', 'pay attention to'; it has all these meanings."

"Very well, I'll go to my father and see what he has to say. But that does not mean I will 'heed' him!"

Twenty minutes later she returned to say that she was going to pack the few clothes she had there, as her father said there was no possibility of the Germans not solving the question of who helped Halle's escape. "Where are you heading?" began Ian but Ilona shook her head, "I do not know myself and even if I did it would be highly dangerous for us all if I confided in you or for that matter anyone else." She reluctantly turned to prepare to leave and Ian felt a sudden attraction for this woman who had done as he had requested in helping Halle—this was the price of her help? "Just a minute, do you mind if we say our farewells here where we have some privacy?"

"I must hurry, father is bringing the rest of my clothes over from the house and I need to be ready." Ian put out his arms and Ilona walked into them as naturally as if it were their normal habit of saying goodbye. As she disengaged, Ian kissed her and once more hugged her as he tried to convince himself that this was all purely platonic and a means of expressing his thanks.

CHAPTER 14

(July 1943)

THE AMBULANCE HADN'T moved more than one kilometre when it came to a halt. Halle sensed that this was the deciding moment, Warsaw was not the intended destination. A welcoming party was meeting them and, within a minute, without any surprise on Halle's part she was being greeted by Herr Oberst Hengist. "Herr Oberst, what a surprise! Surely you haven't come all the way from Berlin to see how I was progressing?" Hengist was all smiles and flattery to such an extent that his very stance suggested to Halle that he was an ungulate animal, possibly of the *cloven* hoof type! "Fraülein Hegel, I have been remiss in my duties by leaving my visit to see you to this time. I have but lately heard of your misfortune and I intend to pay my apologies by executing those found responsible."

"Colonel, I only wish that those who did this deed should be punished but I thank you for your concern." Halle was all graciousness behind the mask that the paleness of her complexion provided. "Now, no more talking! The Oberstarzt; sorry are you familiar with the various titles within the Wehrmach, there are so many of them?"

"No, I know just a few, but I recognised the prefix 'Ober' as colonel and the 'starzt' as medical. Is that near enough?"

"Very good; well he said that you should be kept as quiet as possible during this part of your convalescence. And I intend that that will be precisely how you shall spend it." Halle was in the fortunate position of not being required to respond and consequently merely smiled in the hope that Hengist would accept it as her manner of thanking him. She was desperate to ask him where he intended keeping her but couldn't very well initiate a conversation after all that he said.

The ambulance picked up speed once Hengist had left and judging by the time taken Halle was convinced that she was being taken somewhere near Warsaw. Finally it stopped and to her utter amazement Hengist was at the door of the establishment into which she was being carried. "Clearly I'm for the high jump this time!" thought Halle. "What the hell can I do to avoid being found guilty of espionage? I shouldn't have opened by mouth to Sheila Gray, they have tortured her to death and she has told them that I had warned her to leave Berlin."

She waited knowing her other voices would turn up to have their say. "Are you crazy? If he had known all this he would never have allowed you to travel the country, would he?" Halle rationalised this was the more likely of the two scenarios. "But what is *this* all about? If he is still testing me to see where my loyalties lie, he's wasting his time because I can't do much about anything in my condition." Her alter ego was soon back putting other possibilities: "He'll be expecting someone from the Allies to make contact with you and then he'll pounce because he wants the whole network not just you!" Halle felt uneasy about this as a corollary as she was convinced that Ian, with the help of the AK, would attempt to free her knowing that the likelihood of Hengist taking hostages in a large urban area would be remote. With Hengist leading the troops around the building the prospects of a repeat of the Plock 'kidnapping' would lead to a bloodbath or the capture of Ian and the others she had got to know.

After a troubled sleep Halle woke with all the clouds of doubt exacting a price which her health couldn't afford. She didn't need to be a doctor of medicine or a psychologist to know that her recovery was being curtailed by her anxieties, curiously by the two extremes, Hengist and Ian. "What can Hengist benefit by my presence under his wing? Surely if he wanted to test if I have connections with the Allies he should set me free and simply keep an eye on me." A few minutes later it dawned on her that she was there to be the bait for those whom Hengist suspected were her companions in arms. "What way is your mind working? It must be obvious, even to you, that is what this is all about!"

As the morning dragged on Halle kept her voices at bay by concentrating on her pains and the wound from whence they sprang but they had a strange life of their own and when she thought she had them under control, back they came for more of the same. "You're not giving much credit to Ian and the AK, are you? If you've figured it out you can bet that they're just as aware about what's going on." Halle squirmed at the allegation of her lack of belief in Ian's ability, "You know bloody well it's not that. He is impetuous and that's what concerns me! Not that he can not weigh up Hengist's motives. In his desire to free me he is likely to risk everything on a single throw of the dice. What I want is cool calm rational thinking but where am I going to get it?"

After much consideration of the situation Halle concluded that the only way out, for her, was to take matters into her own hands. "That means you have to make a bigger improvement that you have up to now," began her alter ego. "I hate it when you state the obvious," snarled Halle, "you know damn fine I know that, yet you still persist in saying it. It doesn't seem to matter what the situation, you have to put your four pence worth in. Now don't be coming back to apologise in the next five minutes!"

She lay weighing up what she needed to do in order to be fit enough to escape without help. "Firstly, I'll have to make a bigger effort to be up and about. But how do I do it and keep my improving health from them? There'll be no Ilona here to encourage me. Secondly, I'll need to see round this place in order to plan an escape; and thirdly I need to communicate with Ian and Teodor somehow." The more she pondered the 'three needs', as she came to think of them the more despondent she became. However, the biggest concern right now was Ian and she hoped and prayed that he would refrain from 'diving in where angels fear to tread', a description her mother often applied to her. "Maybe he would think more carefully this time and perhaps consult with that man in Warsaw of whom he thought so highly. I wonder why he never revealed his name to me? Perhaps it was the period before he came to trust me."

Teodor took Ian to Warsaw by horse and cart. It took a lot of talk and a lot of convincing to bring him to doing it. The recent fiasco made him determined that, no matter the urgency of Ian's demands, he wasn't going to allow the same mistake to occur. "You do not even know where she is but already you are prepared to blunder into every house you suspect as being used as a private hospital for Halle. I am taking you to Aleksander, not to solve this case, but in the hope that he will talk some sense into you; not for you to browbeat him into endangering himself and others."

Driving along through the countryside it seems remote from the atrocities of the surrounding towns and villages. Ian felt an overwhelming need to apologise to Teodor for the hardship he had brought him, yet he was reluctant to put it into words knowing that Teodor would shrug off any mention of the difficulties he had encountered. Ian missed Ilona and he speculated that if he felt her loss then her father must be miserable at her leaving. "Do you ever hear from Ilona?" he asked as they approached the outskirts of the city. "Not directly but she manages to have someone tell me that she is missing us all and in particular her work at the hospital."

"Has she always been a nurse?" asked Ian. "No, she posed as a nurse while working for the Germans, in fact she is a qualified doctor."

"Goodness bless us! She gave up a lot to bring you and the AK a little information."

"She did more than that. The SS killed her husband when he was on a raid not far from here and she was left with a baby girl. That is why, when she was asked to take on the duty nurse rôle, she agreed but it meant that she had to send her baby to her sister to look after. Of course she got to see her from time to time but nothing like as often as she wanted. Perhaps that is the best thing that has come out of all this, we have set up a home for her quite a distance away and she is able to have her baby to herself."

"I hope she is safe there because I feel guilty at drawing her into the escape, particularly when she wasn't convinced that it would succeed."

"She was not convinced? She told me a totally different story in order for me to agree for her to go ahead. What do you think was going on in her head?"

"I'm the last one to ask! Surely if you were so against it on practical grounds she would have listened to you and not me?"

"That girl has a lot of questions to answer the next time I speak to her! Ian you will have to be quiet there is a Nazi patrol ahead of us."

The Gestapo occasionally stopped the little traffic there was in order to check that the people were bona fide travellers. Teodor was well prepared and he had deliberately postponed their visit to the city until he had all the required documents needed for Ian.

As they moved along at a steady rate Ian couldn't help recalling his past 'visits' to Warsaw: his stay with Aleksander and his friends; the strange pair of escapees who fought over which toilet they should use; the explosion which released him, by mistake, but knocked the other two unconscious. "Why do I return to a place which I only associate with unmitigated disaster?" Rhetorical questions he felt were best when there was little or no possibility of having a sensible answer. His alter ego was none too happy at being categorised in such a way, he had an extremely sensible reply: "It's only the thought of Halle and the possibility of her being tortured or put to death has me here." Teodor's reply startled him as he thought he was still conversing with his voices, "I am not here to save her. It is you that concerns me. Much as I would like her to survive, I fear that she is so critically injured that she would endanger, not only you, but all of us who are involved in fighting for our country."

"You may not have had the opportunity to speak to her much when she arrived at the Czerniawski's farm but I did and I think she is on the road to recovery and I'm sure that Ilona would back me up in that opinion." Ian spoke with a passion and a degree of certainty that mystified Teodor as he had long since lost his assurity about the outcome of the war. "Perhaps you are that breath of fresh air that we all need in times of crises, and although I would be reluctant to be so assertive as you it may be the one thing in Halle's favour that will convince, not only Aleksander but Bór-Komorowski as well."

"I find it difficult to believe that the AK commander in Warsaw would find time for any of this."

"If it affects people in the city he wants to know and Aleksander will tell him his opinion on the possibility of arranging something—but remember it must be a way that will not endanger members of the AK." Teodor's tongue clicking to the horse ended the conversation.

Crossing over the River Vistula, Teodor could see that Ian had the look of someone seeing the unfamiliar. "Aleksander has moved many times since you last visited here." Ian's grin was enough of an indication to the older man that he had wrongly used a word. "What have I said?" asked Teodor as Ian's grin deepened into a smile. "'Visit' isn't quite the word to use. 'Enforced stay' would be more appropriate," answered a more sober Ian. "But you have spoken of your talks with Aleksander with some enthusiasm?" Ian's more sombre mood gave him the air of a philosopher, "It's the endings which determine our views on the whole, not the preliminaries. All I recall are the overall failures. Not one of the enterprises I took part in was a success. No wonder I'm worried about the outcome of this venture."

The horse regardless of its starved looks seemed to put up with the need to continue moving without rest. "Surely the horse deserves some time off, Teodor?" The old man nodded and said they wouldn't be long. "Since we crossed the river I'm totally lost. I just don't know this part of Warsaw." Teodor stretched as if to prepare himself for a long-winded explanation and Ian was almost sorry he had spoken. "Well this is Pragu. When we crossed the river we entered it. It started in the 15th century and became part of Warsaw in the 1790s."

"You sound as if you did this explanation to many another before me, did you?"

"Well I used to take students who were studying Polish history on a tour of the city for a number of years before the war. Just along from here is a zoo but I fear the animals are gone; whether somewhere for safety or used for food, who knows?"

"If I were a betting man I'd say some people are eating them," began Ian but Teodor interrupted, "Perhaps but I'd prefer not to think about it." Ian knew better than to persist. "Earlier you were speaking about Ilona and her daughter. I can't recollect hearing her married name and I know I never heard the full name of the child."

"Her married name is Scharwenka and her daughter's Christian name is Manya—that is an old name in my late wife's family," said Teodor in a subdued voice and Ian realised that the man was moved at the mention of his wife and the associations it held for him with his daughter and grandchild. A few moments of silence elapsed before Ian had the courage to speak again. "Halle seemed to know more about Poland than most people back home," and no sooner had the words poured from his mouth than he regretted them. He looked at Teodor to see if there was any reaction and when he saw none still paused because he didn't want to sound like an apologist for Halle. "Maybe she researched its history before starting off to come here," and his statement sounded more apologetic than an apologist would use. "Once, when I was talking about Thorn... sorry, Torun, she said that Copernicus had been born there. Is that so?"

"Not too many people who have not been to university know of him... I put that awkwardly, not too many non-academics know of him. Curiously the Germans and the Poles both claim him and although he was born in Torun his people were German."

"It's different in Northern Ireland, if someone makes a pronouncement that appears to destroy an opponent's position then you can be sure that they and their friends will know it—but their opponents won't acknowledge it!"

"We Poles say: 'He stopped the sun and moved the earth'. Do you understand?"

"Not entirely."

"Well it was generally believed up to his time that the earth was the centre of the universe and the sun and the other planets moved round it, so you see, 'he stopped the sun' etc."

"Another metaphor! The world seems to be full of them!" cracked Ian and Teodor laughed sufficiently loudly to make the horse whinny and shy. Ian added, when the horse returned to land, "I don't know how I survived without them until I came to the continent!" Teodor smiled and asked, "Is that what you call 'tongue in cheek'?"

"Now we're into a university course in English... but you're right. Back home people would just say 'you're a liar'."

"What, no tongue in cheek at all?"

"You're an analytical devil; you've got your teeth into this and you won't let go."

"Ugh! I'm sick of metaphors!" laughed Teodor as they pulled up to Aleksander's new address. Ian was the first to the door and gave it a thump and despite a few more there was no reply. Neither of them was surprised to find Aleksander out so Teodor took Ian to a man's home who lived less than a kilometre away. Right from the outset Tadeusz, Teodor's oldest friend, was warned that they weren't stopping and he, in turn, insisted that they should have something to eat but both refused knowing full well that, like everyone else, he would be lucky to have enough for himself. Tadeusz was aware that Aleksander would be late but was able to assure them he would be back by 15.30 hours.

During their stay Teodor's horse was tied to a stake on a piece of waste ground and he ate the grass that was in plentiful supply. His neigh of pleasure at seeing them was a surprise to Ian seeing how well the horse had adapted to the waste ground but clearly the horse was anxious to be on his way.

Once they were seated on the bench, which comprised the only seating area, the horse decamped in a hurry.

Aleksander, for all his worries, clearly was delighted to see them. "Ian you are a constant visitor to Warsaw, you must be enamoured of the city." After all Ian had said to Teodor about the place he found it difficult to reply. Finally he thought of words which would be sufficiently diplomatic, "I get around this part of your country, true enough. Maybe if I wasn't so anxious to leave, the opposite would happen!"

Aleksander and Teodor had learnt to enjoy Ian's quips and imagined him to be a humorist in his own city, a claim that Ian would never have made on his own behalf. Teodor spoke before any banter could begin, "I don't wish to hurry you but I want to be well on our way and as close to home as possible before nightfall. These German patrols are more careful in daylight not to parade their murders but once dark descends... I do not have to draw pictures, do I?" He gestured to Ian to start and now and again he would interrupt to add some detail or other to what Ian was saying.

It must have taken fifteen minutes to describe the incident involving Halle and when they finished Aleksander had a well-formed notion of their needs. "So you do not know where she is now?" he asked. Ian quickly replied, "No, that is one of the areas we wanted to seek your advice about."

"And what were the others?" smiled Aleksander, as if he didn't know. "Well..." hesitated Ian after looking at Teodor, knowing how he felt about endangering anyone further. "Yes?" queried Aleksander moving his head to look at both. "How are we to get her out?" burst out Ian before Teodor could get his four pence worth in.

Aleksander paused before speaking and Teodor was pleased that he wasn't going to make rash promises. After all that he had said to Ian he didn't want anything to go wrong, so if the AK in Warsaw could help, well and good but no more of the tactics that Ian had used. "We do have sources who keep us informed of any changes in the city. Someone like Hengist will attract attention—even if it is only his elaborate uniform!"

"You have seen him I assume from your mention of his uniform."

"No, but I have had reports of a new man going in and out of Gestapo HQ and that was the description he had. Is it him?"

"I can't be sure. Halle made no mention of his dress sense. Can you give me an idea of how long it will take for you to provide corroboration of this?" Ian's anxiety to be up and doing wasn't going down well with Aleksander and Teodor. "Hold on Ian," was Aleksander's quick response, "we can not bring the whole war effort to a halt just to provide you with news. What I will do is find the place and get someone to assess the prospects

221

and I'll get the information to Teodor by our usual channels." Ian's face showed his disappointment, "I suppose we can ask no more than that," said Ian and Teodor nodded vigorously. "You are keen to get back before dark," Ian reminded the old man and he immediately rose to make his farewells to Aleksander. "Thanks for your help, whatever it may prove to be," he said in Polish and Ian was left to hazard what had been said.

Halle's plan to get sufficiently well to escape alone suffered an immediate setback when Hengist introduced her to what he termed as, "my own doctor". He would ensure her quick recovery "as she was urgently needed." All of which added up to her finding it impossible to hide her condition from him; the fact of his daily presence became a nuisance of the worst kind. To top it off, the man was obsequious to the point where Halle felt nauseous in his presence. "What has Hengist told this man that he feels the need to be always bowing and scraping? I notice that with any of the others, regardless of how they rank, he is dictatorial and essentially rude; so what has Hengist said? The man must be a spy as well. That's it! He probably is reporting who I speak with."

She looked around the room, " Calm down—this is not like you; sure you don't see anyone and the staff here are that few you can see they've been handpicked. For God's sake—there's barely a dozen patients in here and they appear to be people of rank who are very ill. Which of them is going to speak to you? Certainly I'm the lowest rank in here; they must be convinced I'm important to the Allies and are anxious to discover what precisely it is that I know. They're bound to be thinking I'm mixed up with the AK and that my Republican credentials are mere fiction." Halle contented herself that the more critical voice had not yet appeared, but the emphasis was on the *yet*.

Her positive voice assured her to leave it alone and get well, Hengist was bound to show his hand then. "You don't think he's going to let you out to tour the countryside?" ranted the voice of her alter ego. "Oh, you're back then full of all the joys of life!" She felt she shouldn't have bothered speaking. "Hengist never questioned you about how you got to be on that road outside Plock." Halle had forgotten about that, "Oh God, you're right!" But her alter ego wasn't finished, "You'd already worked out that he knew you were nowhere near where you were supposed to be. Sooner or later he's going to be asking, either politely or when he's torturing you in Gestapo HQ. What's your answer?" Halle gasped, "I'm not going to be here; that's all there is to it—I've no alternative." The voice didn't stop to take a breath, "So he hears you are well—he's here like a shot out of a gun, what do you say?" Halle tried to turn her back on the voice, "I'll leave it until it happens—will you let it alone now?" But her anger didn't stop her voices unsettling her.

When he saw Teodor's horse and cart turn the corner at the end of the street, Aleksander immediately put on his coat and returned to the city centre. The issue of the young woman had become a nuisance. Already he had lost Ilona whose information seeking in the hospital kept the AK up to date on the ongoing battles between the Soviet and German Armies. He had enough to contend with without this.

Bór-Komorowski with all his anxieties about the position of the people in Warsaw had now the additional worry about the setting up of a separate home army by the communists. Of course Aleksander knew that the city commander would think of him when it came to some kind of liaison being required between the various groups. Recently, however, those nationalist groups owing allegiance to the Government in Exile had started taking pot shots at communist sympathisers and what Bór-Komorowski feared was that the approaching Russian Army would take sides to the detriment of everyone.

On the few occasions that the communists had agreed to meet him it was clear that they were determined to follow the strategies laid down by Moscow and were totally opposed to what they referred to as 'the so-called Government in exile'. He was late because there had been an incident the previous evening when some members of the Peasant Party had been in a political dispute with AK members and violence had erupted. Tadeusz, Teodor's friend, had brought him the news and he had tried to contact a few of those he knew among the politicians in an attempt to patch up their differences and fight the common enemy and not each other.

At the meeting place he was relieved to see so many had turned up. He prefaced his opening remarks with an apology for the violence of the previous evening and reminded them that unless they could agree to a joint command there would be more of the same to follow. The arguments went on *ad nauseam* for hours but the communists saw, or imagined they saw, a vast Russian Army pushing the Germans back into Germany and they wanted to be seen as collaborators with the communist leaders in Moscow. Seeing there was no road open to him on the issues and to keep some kind of harmony he asked a series of people to help him establish the whereabouts of Halle. The one thing that gave him some hope for the future was the unity of purpose when it came to opposing the Nazis—he wondered if there would be any of it left if the Nazis succumbed in the foreseeable future.

Once they had returned to the Czerniawski's farm Teodor and Ian talked about the way events had turned. Teodor was slightly the more optimistic of the two feeling that once they had involved Aleksander their chance of a resolution was greater. Ian, on the other hand, felt rather than knew that Aleksander was too preoccupied with other matters and on the basis of that concluded that even if he obtained the information, that was as far as he would be prepared to go. Ian, in an attempt to change the subject, asked about Teodor's daughter and her child. "She has been promised a house in Warsaw because the AK feel there is greater safety there where there is a large population. She is due to move in the next week."

"How do you feel about that?"

"Well, it is better than Mlawa which they first suggested."

"That isn't the most positive endorsement I've heard about moving house," said Ian eyeing Teodor to see his reaction. Teodor looked up and the Belfast man could see the unhappiness, which seems to constitute a father's unease with a situation. "Well the Home Army know their business best I suppose and they are bound to give her a great deal of consideration seeing the risks she has taken over the past year in particular. Yet I'd be happier if she moved to another part of the countryside, away from the city."

"Are you expecting trouble in Warsaw?"

"Only a fool would not expect trouble somewhere in this country in the middle of a world war. The Germans turned the centre of the city into a Jewish ghetto and when a rebellion occurred they sent the entire lot of them to concentration camps and proceeded to destroy the original ghetto. Germans do not forget the hardships they have suffered here at the hands of the Poles and the Jews, believe me. If the situation deteriorates, that is from their point of view, God knows what is in store for the population there."

"At least you would have warning of an approaching catastrophe and arrange to get her and the child out."

"Yes, that is true but I would prefer things to be the way I suggested at the beginning."

"In any event you know that I am more than willing to help her move house. I suppose it's a good distance away?"

"No. It is quite near. She and her husband did not want to be too far away from their native village, so the house is only a few hundred metres along the road outside. It has not been lived in since Stanislaw's death because of the danger to Ilona—being the widow of someone associated with the AK. As it was she had to have a set of false papers to enable her to get the job in the hospital and there was no possibility of her staying there for the same reason. Now it is a question of escaping being captured by the Gestapo."

A few days elapsed before Teodor contacted Ian through Czerniawski and he left the following morning to be of help. On arrival he could see Teodor had already moved some of the furniture out into the yard. "Are these all her goods and chattels, then?" Laughing Teodor wanted to know what the phrase 'goods and chattels' meant. "Your bits and pieces—that's not much help to you either—your furniture and anything else you own that has to go." Teodor laughed even more, "Why could you not say that in the first place?"

"You say what you are used to saying. You haven't answered me—are these all that's going?" Teodor laughed again, "Is this what you think the average Polish family has by way of 'chattels'? No, there will be at least two loads to go." By the time they had the cart loaded Teodor was glad he had Ian to help him, who, in turn, was glad that they hadn't too far to go to get to Ilona's new home. "Where is Ilona staying at the moment?" asked Ian but Teodor was reluctant to specify her whereabouts, or for that matter where she was going to live. "Ian you must realise that the less you know the better. If by some horrible chance you are picked up what you do not know can not hurt you."

Driving the cart for the first time gave Ian a sense of authority but when he saw the first German patrol pass without halting them he asked Teodor to take over, as he felt inadequate to the task of facing the head on stares of the Germans. Teodor navigated all the subsequent obstacles and to Ian's surprise they crossed the river into Pragu and made their way to a street not far from Teodor's friend Tadeusz.

On reaching the house a German patrol passed and for once Ian gave it a hard look. "There's something odd going on here Teodor. I'm almost certain that is the one that I saw first thing this morning. Don't stop!" Teodor slapped the horse a few times to guarantee it walked past the house. "What, are you certain?" Teodor was the picture of anxiety and Ian was instantly unsure, "Well, as certain as I can be. Maybe I'm being paranoiac but I'd almost swear it was that patrol I saw when I got you to switch places with me."

"Very well but do not look round. At the next corner—if there is no one about—I will hop off and you drive on and deliberately stop a few streets away. Heaven help the people in that house, it is sure to be turned over by the Gestapo. I will find you. Remember, no more than a couple of streets away."

Everything went as Teodor had suggested and he soon found Ian. "Is she OK?" quizzed Ian. "Yes, she is gone already. I'll arrange for some women friends of Tadeusz to collect their clothes tomorrow."

"Why can't Tadeusz do it himself, we shouldn't be bringing more and more people into danger." Teodor was on the point of reminding him about how he dragged Ilona and all the others in Plock into his mess but preferred to ignore the young man's rash words. "Aleksander says he had to move house yesterday as the AK informed him he was being watched."

"Well that explains your other arrangements. But getting back to us—now that we've been spotted what's the next move?"

"They are bound to be nearby and I would not be surprised if they have undercover agents watching us."

"What in the name of all that's holy made you go back to warn Ilona? They're bound to have seen you and you have jeopardised her and the child."

"I hazarded a guess that they would be watching the cart and follow it. I took every care to make sure there was no one about when I got down."

"Maybe we're covered on one angle but it doesn't help us with our difficulty."

"No, I'm afraid I am going to have to do this hop, step and jump exercise again." The querulous look given him by Ian made Teodor continue, "One of our AK men operates a stable on the other side of the city. If I get off with my usual panache—do you like that word—and get to him and tell him about the horse and cart. You can circle the streets once again, and we might be able to get rid of these two," pointing initially to the horse and then the cart, "and stay the night in the city."

"You're not thinking of driving this home tomorrow are you?"

"No, I will give it a few days and collect them when things have died down a bit."

The vehicle had crossed the river once more as they made their way to the stables. Ian was relieved to hear Teodor wasn't rushing things and it enabled him to get back to the issue nearest his heart. "Is there any chance you'll see Aleksander tonight?" The old man went quiet then, "I can see him if it is important."

"Well with us being away the best part of a day now and the time it will take us to get back tomorrow, I'm wondering would he have heard anything about Halle."

"In that case I will call tonight after I have got us fixed up with accommodation and see if there is any news on that front."

"Can I go along?" asked Ian with a look of despondency, knowing the likelihood of its happening wasn't high.

"I do not think Aleksander would thank me for bringing a wanted POW to his house at this time. It would be better for all concerned if you wait until I return with the information."

What had now become the usual procedure came into play once the stables were in sight. Ian took over the driving and at the first chance Teodor jumped down and disappeared. It must have been ten minutes later before he caught up with the cart and declared that everything was set. At each turn Ian wondered if the Gestapo undercover men were conscientiously doing their job because they were nowhere in sight. But as Teodor had said on a number of occasions, "Out of sight should not mean out of one's mind." Ian smiled and wondered did Teodor know what the expression 'out of one's mind' meant colloquially in Belfast. "I'll not be the one to break it to him."

Two days after making the first of his inquiries Aleksander had a message delivered to him by one of the delegates he had spoken to at the meeting. He confirmed that the name of the new officer seen in Gestapo HQ was Hengist. However, he was unable to obtain any details of his accommodation or if there was a private hospital being used by the Nazis for special patients. Now that he had this information he felt he needed to consult with Bór-Komorowski and put him in the picture about the latest Gestapo man to arrive in the city and what he believed was his mission there. Later that day he passed a message to one of the commander's runners and the following morning he received an invitation to meet the General at a house not far removed from the old museum.

Aleksander was particularly careful in going to his rendezvous with the General. Too many of his people had been captured and tortured in the past eighteen months and he didn't want to be one of them—not because he feared captivity or, for that matter, torture but the fear that he would reveal secrets which cost lives. Bór-Komorowski was anxious to see him and summoned him into his presence once he heard his liaison officer had arrived. At first the General thought that some breakthrough had been made with the communists but Aleksander had no further information on that front but when he mentioned the name 'Hengist' he saw the General's eyes light up.

"I have had the rather dubious pleasure of meeting this man before the war—that is, if it is the same man. At one point in the night, when he was drunk, he let it be known how the Nazis would obtain lebensraum in Europe. Of course the open countryside in Poland and the Ukraine was the attraction and my how they lived up to their word! Hopefully we won't give them any 'living space'."

"I have attempted to find out what rôle this man is playing in the life of an Irish girl named Halle Hegel," and Aleksander went on to give the details of her life, as he understood it since her arrival on the continent. "She may well have been working for the Nazis at one point but it seems that she had a conversion but kept it from her employers. Later, whether accidentally or deliberately, she warned an employee that the Nazis were onto her and consequently she decided to plan her escape from them." Bór-Komorowski, obviously enthralled with the story, wanted to know what had become of the girl. Aleksander explained as well as he could, considering his lack of knowledge as to her whereabouts. "You must find her urgently! She must, knowingly or unknowingly, have information that they regard as terribly important. Have you anyone working on this?"

"I have but so far there have been no developments."

"I think we need to increase the numbers working on this. If I thought it would be productive I would have Hengist assassinated but the question of hostage taking and large-scale retaliation comes into the equation. See what can be done in the meantime and keep me informed as to progress." Aleksander left feeling bewildered, after all he had initially advised Ian to steer well clear of the young woman and now here was Bór-Komorowski taking a personal interest in the case. "I wonder how Teodor will react when he hears the news!"

After returning from the meeting Aleksander prepared to meet the area commanders to pass on what the Warsaw commander wanted. He was reluctant to give the coded news to Teodor as there was only so much he could put into it and there would be countless questions left on Teodor's mind. He had just prepared to sit down and write the details when he was shocked to have Teodor shown in to him. "My God Teodor! I was just preparing this message for you to get in the morning and here you are. Could you not wait?"

"Not me but you know who. I told him not to expect too much this early in the proceedings and in any event we can not risk people over this matter." Aleksander laughed and went on give a full account of all that had happened. "I just do not believe it. Bór-Komorowski wanting this dealt with immediately; well who would believe it! I will have to hurry back and put Ian in the picture. There is going to be one happy man in Warsaw tonight!"

Halle, in her determination to get well, was impressing Doctor von Berlichingen, Hengist's doctor with her efforts to walk. Certainly there was a weakness in her overall health, which would continue for some time. Later she would obtain some mobility, as he constantly reminded her, but that shouldn't deter her from her present policy. He was full of praise for her Nazi devotion, which he saw in her determination to overcome the consequences of her shooting—an incident he attributed to the AK terrorists.

Halle, taking advantage of the situation, asked to be allowed to walk further each day and when he gave permission she used the opportunity to spy out the land. In between times however, she realised just how badly time was dragging when she started looking forward to Dr von Berlichingen's visits.

After the best part of a week Halle deliberately engaged in conversation with the platitudinous doctor. The fact that he indulged in trite commonplaces by way of conversation did not deter her. She sensed he was the only route to the outside in terms of being aware of what was going on—whether he was prepared to divulge any information she would have to put to the test. After the first occasion she was pretty confident that she could extract little tib-bits of news that might seem petty to him but would be useful to her when taken in the round. Items about the various injuries the officers in the hospital were being treated for, was the first step then what did Dr von Berlichingen think of the auxiliary staff and their numbers. Piece by piece she gradually built a picture of the place and its inhabitants.

Halle knew that her condition was improved immeasurably by the walks and the exercises the doctor had recommended and such was their relationship he would occasionally walk with her. On one of their journeys round the hospital he spoke of Hengist and mentioned how much he admired the man and his achievements. "What achievements do you mean precisely?" asked Halle throwing all precautions to the wind. "His restructuring of the police in Poland and the fact that the Führer has recently honoured him."

"That is tremendous indeed. I suppose he has been in Berlin for the presentation then?" There was a moment's hesitation, "No, I suppose with the war being so drawn out presentations only take place when men are on leave."

"Of course, I had forgotten that. Do you see much of him then?"

"Every day…," and the doctor immediately dried up and made an excuse about his need to get back to the ward. Halle's voices started up, "He must live on the premises in order to keep an eye on you!" but Halle didn't want an orchestrated pessimistic cry from her alter ego. "He probably lives near where the doctor is staying." The voice gave a jeering kind of laugh, "Come off it, he's here and you know it!"

"But why would he remain here?"

"You just think about it. All this began with Sheila Gray and your big mouth. If you hadn't opened it we'd be in Ireland having the good life."

"It's only speculation on their part, if it is that."

"What else could it be? She was an admitted spy for the Allies and she was a friend of yours; you know damn fine what comes after that!"

"Let's add this all up. Firstly, Sheila was a spy; secondly, she was working on something important or there wouldn't be all this fuss; thirdly, they think I know something about it, so what is it?" Halle stormed her brain trying to recall every word that Sheila had said but nothing came out of it. "I need to talk to someone trained in espionage who could see what is going on from the little pieces that I have."

The stable owner had provided Ian and Teodor with a room for the night and in addition had organised a lift to the bus station in the morning. Teodor's visit to Aleksander seemed to take an eternity. Ian waited impatiently for his return and when he eventually showed up he greeted him with the anticipation of a child anxious to see what his parent has brought. Even Teodor's removal of his coat added to his impatience: "For heaven's sake, Teodor, tell me what's going on!" Teodor tried to tease him by describing the journey to the house—"Stop it now! Come on, get to the point!"

Teodor gave his exasperating smile, "Good news and good news." Ian threw up his hands in horror, "I trust this isn't going to be a jokey kind of report, is it?" The smile froze on Teodor's face, "Jokey? What do you mean?" Ian turned, "Come on, you know what that means? I hope you're not going to make a joke of all of this. Is that clearer?" and the exasperation showed in his voice. "I'm sorry, Ian. I did not mean to be infuriating. The word is that General Bór-Komorowski is aware of the situation and has ordered as many men as are necessary are to be allocated to the search for her."

"What? Repeat that last sentence." Teodor spelt out what Aleksander was to do but could not enlighten Ian as to what had changed their approach to the issue of Halle. "All that he said when I was leaving was: under no circumstances were we to interfere in this matter."

"Which means precisely what?"

"You, yes you, are to keep out of this. Whatever has happened must be important or why would they go to these lengths?"

"But what has happened? I know as much as anyone or more about Halle and her life in Berlin but for the life of me I can't see what it is with the Gestapo and now the AK that's of interest."

"You can bet your life—to use your phrase—that brighter minds than ours are working out what is going on."

"That phrase is not mine—it's a saying more often used by the Fenians at home than the Protestants. At least it was before I left, everyone could be using it by now I suppose. I think we're been left in the dark and they'll keep us there until it suits them to tell us—maybe sometime, maybe never!"

A few days elapsed before Aleksander got the information he wanted about Hengist. The man was escorted everywhere he went by a company of troops.

So seemingly he was easily followed until the man given the task of finding his address discovered, more by luck than good judgement, that there were undercover men keeping an eye on Hengist. But, in addition, they were interested in anyone being inquisitive about his comings and goings. Fortunately the man backed off immediately or the 'whole gaffe would have been blown', as Ian so indelicately put it to Teodor. Stephan Sobieski, the local commander, took it on himself to be at the same point where his man had been the previous evening, only he had a car, which discreetly followed Hengist at quite a distance. Once he had the address he soon had his men take over from the local window cleaners and it was they who noticed that the people inside the huge house appeared to be veteran officers recovering from wounds.

Putting down the notes he had been handed Aleksander muttered to himself: "So he is staying in the so-called hospital to be as close as possible to any staged kidnapping! The General seems to have got it right, the security there is beyond belief. So what is it that girl knows? They are going to have to make a move of some kind soon. Not that I'm going to say any of this in my report; I will watch his reactions when I give him the details."

Aleksander trooped around the room preparing himself for a grilling from the General; "Will these details be enough to satisfy him? I doubt it. He will want to know what is happening to the girl and the way Hengist is handling her. I better get back to Sobieski and see if he can penetrate the security around her."

Next morning he reported to Bór-Komorowski and was pleased to get out before the General had an opportunity to digest how little information there was in the report. On his way back to the river he decided to see Sobieski there and then; "There is no point in waiting for the kick up the backside from the General. I need to have someone who can talk to the girl and is sensible enough to bring out all of the information she has."

The local commander was surprised when Aleksander suggested, through an intermediary, that they meet. They had a policy in Warsaw of avoiding having commanders being in the same place together. Local units were constantly being eroded by the work of the Gestapo and it was generally believed that much of the information was coming from men who had information tortured out of them.

Sobieski was a man used to planning each move carefully and saw this unusual step as an opportunity to draw his strengths directly to the attention of the Commander-in-Chief—being aware that Aleksander Kosciuszko was known as Bór-Komorowski's chief advisor. Aleksander wasn't familiar with the man but was aware of his growing reputation as a person who wouldn't lose a soldier if he could help it.

Compliments didn't come easily to Aleksander but he began his meeting with Sobieski with one. "I want to thank you for your unremitting efforts to conquer the invader in this city. It has not gone unnoticed, and because of that and other factors the Commander-in-Chief has particularly requested that you should take on an important investigation for him." Aleksander didn't mind the white lie if it motivated the man sufficiently to see that this was extremely important.

"The fact that we are meeting in person emphasises the point. The man you and your men have been trailing is called Hengist. He is reputedly close to Hitler and the General has been informed that this man is holding a woman prisoner because of her ties with the Allies." The exaggerations were beginning to stick in his throat but he wanted to direct Sobieski's mind in the direction he wanted.

"By the way in our informal meetings I would prefer that you call me Aleksander, not sir. OK?" Sobieski's response was immediate, "And I would want to be called Stephan." Kosciuszko stood up but turned to face Stephan, "Before I go, please do *not* repeat a word of what I have said to anyone. There is enough conjecture going on, on a variety of subjects already, we don't want to add to it." Stephan nodded in acknowledgement of the compliments he had been paid and then said how grateful he was on being trusted with such an important piece of information. "There is no need for thanks, you deserve to be treated in this way. One final thing, as soon as you conceive of a plan to get a trusted individual to this woman I need to know. The General wants to be kept up to date on your progress and in addition still wants to be kept informed on Hengist's movements. Is that OK? I appreciate what a great deal is being asked of you, it won't be easy finding who are the people servicing this 'hospital'. What we do know is that the Germans wouldn't have enough personnel to do the cleaning and the auxiliary nursing, so there has to be Poles in there who would be happy to work for the homeland."

By now Sobieski was anxious for Aleksander Kosciuszko to leave to enable him to get on with the business, so he got to his feet and thrust out his hand which Aleksander shook vigorously; as he left he felt confident that he had chosen the right man for the job.

CHAPTER 15
(August 1943)

Stephan Sobieski left a message for his runner in the local shop. In the neighbourhood it was understood that no one questioned his credentials and when he sent for someone it could mean anything from a bit of spying being required, to: 'the next time we will put a bullet in you!' Only the recipients were in a position to deduce as to why they were wanted. By mid-afternoon Konrad Poniatowski was in possession of the message and the shopkeeper assumed from his cheerful disposition that he had somehow become a man of some standing in the community. Konrad knew exactly where he was to go and when; so after letting his comrades in arms know that he had to see the local Commander, he set out for the prescribed meeting place.

"What is it Stephan?" he asked after assuring himself there was no one positioned where they could hear their conversation. "That building we discovered the other day is a hot-house of spying for the Nazis and the boss wants us to keep an eye on that same guy we spotted. Also he wants a list of all those Poles who are employed in that place—don't ask me why, I haven't had a chance to ask him, so I don't know."

"I thought you said that we would only be dealing with the difficult cases in the future," Konrad was making a cheap point at Stephan's expense. He was all too well aware of the Commander's ambition to climb the promotion ladder and his anxiety to take on work which would draw the attention of the top brass. "Anyone of our guys in this neighbourhood is capable of putting the strong arm on some of the punters working there and getting the details."

"That's precisely what we don't want. There must be no drawing attention to us or for that matter to anyone inside that building. You get the drift? This is too serious to be making cheap cracks at me. Once we get that list we have to have a clear picture of all these characters because we'll be expected to know them backwards and I mean just that!"

"OK chief! A nod's as good as a wink, etc. etc."

"Why do you keep on with these sayings when you don't know what they mean?"

"It's a habit, I have a kind of sense of what it means."

"We'll not go down that road—you have me as bad as yourself. One more time then: the names of the punters working there; their backgrounds—in other words can they be trusted; the same men to work on this Gestapo guy, we want to know his every move. Is that everything then?"

"I can't think of anything else."

"OK then. Tomorrow here, mid-day without fail. Cheerio!"

"I'll do my best to have all the info you want," he said to Sobieski's back.

Halle's determination to undertake her escape alone and without help was beginning to crumble. In just over a week she had been to every part of the hospital and found every outside door was locked or guarded. "I'm in a bad way here. It looks like it's going to take a miracle to get me out and that's before I start thinking of what I'm going to do once I get through those doors." Her alter ego had been strangely quiet for days, as if well aware of these insurmountable objects and he had no need to pursue his usual pessimism. "Damned if I know why I refer to it as male! I'm going to have to re-think the whole position. I need help here and outside." Her voice was only waiting the opportunity to start, "You should have realised that after your experience the last time."

"Come on, give us a chance! The last time, as you so quaintly put it, I was unconscious for most of it and, in addition, took no part in the planning."

"I knew you'd have an answer! Not a very good one seeing that you heard all the details from Ian and why he needed the help."

"You never make allowances for my being ill."

"Here come the excuses again!"

"Give me a rest and keep your mouth closed."

Once she got down to thinking the matter through Halle realised that she would have to make contact with some of the non-German staff. But whom could she trust? There was no Ian on the outside to organise an escape, perhaps if she were clever enough to word it properly to some of the cleaners; it would look as if she only wanted to get some fresh air. "For God's sake do I have to point out everything, these people don't understand the Germans, how, in the name of all that's holy, will they understand you?"

"Oh my God, I was right when I said this is going to take a miracle— and what a one it is going to have to be!"

Stephan and Konrad met at the appointed time and their deliberations were longer than they needed to be. "How many people are there in that place?"

"Thirteen—they don't seem to be worried by an unlucky number!"

"It's only the Anglo-Saxons get on like that—what about these people's characters?" asked Stephan looking particularly guileless. "There's a few bogeymen among them," answered Konrad with a large grin. "Here we are again! What's that supposed to mean Konrad?"

"I suspect there's a few German lovers among them, at least from what these reports say."

"For God's sake let me have them, otherwise we'll go on and on all day. What about the other business?"

"Your man has been following the same route and going to the same places daily. There was only one change, he went to that big army camp outside the town and as far as we know he met some high-ranking generals there. What they discussed, heaven knows."

"Well I'll be in touch as soon as I have a chat with those whose names I dare not mention. Here, the same time tomorrow?"

"OK but I was asked a few questions by our friends."

"Such as what?"

"Is there someone being held in there, seeing that we're wanting to set up contact of some sort?"

"Anything else?"

"They claim there's only Germans in there, so what the hell is going on? They're the two main questions."

"I'm glad you asked so I'll take it up with the bosses, OK? Cheerio."

Later that afternoon Aleksander got a message from Stephan requesting a meeting. "Either Stephan has had difficulty concocting a plan or he has found out something about Hengist," he thought. "I better see him this evening because the General won't be too happy with the delay." Within an hour of getting the message to Stephan he received an order from Bór-Komorowski to contact him immediately so he had to abort the other meeting with Sobieski.

"Aleksander what, in the name of all that's holy, is going on?"

"I'm sorry sir. When Sobieski and me drew up the initial plan, as you requested, we thought it would be as well to test some of the areas where we anticipated trouble before bringing the final plan to you."

"That's not what I asked for, did I?"

"No sir."

"So in effect you ignored an order?"

"I don't believe we did sir. We tested issues, which we felt could be weaknesses in the overall approach. As you were aware, sir, I was not at liberty to reveal all the information to him. But he sensed that his men would ask the purpose of our proposals—this is not like army conditions we are operating under sir."

"You had better explain just what you have done."

"Well Sobieski's men maintained that those they have spoken to say there are only German military people in there and they are being treated for injuries. They also noted that none of the workers they have contacted—nor indeed none that they knew—spoke German or any other second language. We had to rethink the problem of communicating with the girl, it will be a handicap but not an impossible one."

"How do you propose overcoming it?"

"If we have the messages written in English and leave space on the paper for a reply."

"Well that explains one part of the reasons for your testing the plan. What else have you discovered? By the way, do you think Sobieski is capable of finding someone who could liaise with this girl, she is bound to be suspicious and, if your information about her is correct, they'll need a contact whom she'll trust?"

"Starting with the last question, sir, we think that if we got the Belfast man to write the notes we could overcome her doubts. He's bound to be able to say something that no one else could possibly know. Regarding the picking of a person for the job, I have decided to make the selection myself, after I have seen and spoken to them. That's another advantage of the information being in a foreign language, it cuts down the chances of facts being bandied about and it safeguards both parties and it makes the job of finding someone with English as irrelevant."

"You've made a good case for yourself and Sobieski. But I warn you don't try this again! We'll meet in two days time and hopefully you'll have everything in place so that we can do the most damage to Hengist's plans—and I'm not referring to freeing the girl."

On leaving the General's presence Aleksander paused to take a deep breath. This had all been too close for his liking—most of it down to Sobieski and his putting the plan into action before it was talked over. It was only then he was taken aback when he realised the importance of the General's final remark. "I wonder if he intended setting her up as a double agent—or maybe a double double-agent? I can't let this out of the bag or I'll have Ian and Teodor on my back."

Next day, at a different rendezvous, he repeated his needs and those of the General to Sobieski—that is, only those that applied directly to Sobieski and his men. "You want to correspond in English? Is that meant to stop my men knowing what's going on?"

"It works both ways, it's a cover for the person delivering it and the woman receiving it."

"How is it a cover for the person delivering it?"

"Simply this, if there is a leak, and God knows we've suffered from any God's amount of them in the past, we know it can't be them, understand?" It took Sobieski a moment to grasp the point. "Now don't be asking me how it covers the person receiving it—remember I'm acting on orders myself. What the General needs from you is to obey and also remember that mum's the word." Sobieski smiled and jocularly replied, "Just as you say Aleksander."

That evening Sobieski repeated just what was required to Konrad, who by now had given up asking questions when it was clear the big brass were not going to be forthcoming. "Have you picked one of these characters to do messenger?" Sobieski wasn't going to admit that someone further up the ladder had made the choice, "Yes, I had narrowed it down to two but on reflection I feel it's a job for a woman. The name is Maria Wieniawski and I would need to speak to her about it."

"When do you want to see her?"

"Make it tomorrow as early as she can make it. You had better come along as well." Konrad was on the point of making a cutting remark about Sobieski's prospects being enhanced by all of this but refrained at the last moment and merely quoted the Bible, "Thy will be done."

Konrad left a note for Stephan late that night saying all was arranged for 0930 hours and mentioned a safe house for the meeting. The next morning the first thing he noticed was a middle-aged woman entering the house just in front of Konrad. "She must be just finished a night shift, she looks exhausted," thought Sobieski. The woman listened attentively as she was told what she had to do and when all was explained she nodded agreement. "When do you want me to deliver the first message?"

"Tomorrow will be the first of them and in all probability once the woman is at ease she will give you messages on the same piece of paper to bring back to us. Whatever you do, don't let any of these fall into the hands of the German staff—if necessary eat them. You understand it could cost you your life if there's a mistake?"

"Yes, I am prepared to do this for my dead relatives."

"Remember it is more important that you live for Poland rather than to die for it. Dead you're worthless, living you can have a part in overthrowing our enemy."

"I'm glad of the opportunity and I will remember what you said."

Aleksander was relieved to hear that everything had gone well and he sent a coded message to Teodor to contact Ian as they needed him in Warsaw. Ian was shocked when he was bundled into a car and rushed to the city later that afternoon. The AK took him directly to Aleksander where he was told the gist of the story and asked to write a note to Halle in as few a number of words as possible. "Do not forget to mention something that no one else would know so that she will accept it as genuine."

Ian handed over the note and Aleksander read it with some amusement: "'The wheel has never been the same.' Be in touch soon. Ian. Any comments write on this paper and place it under the water-jug on your locker."

"Is that OK?"

"It sounds fine but will she be sure that it is you?"

"No one else on the continent knows of it bar one and he's in a POW camp."

"The General will be pleased that this is at last underway. For the first time Halle has become a priority for the AK and that is because Hengist is known to the Commander-in-Chief." Ian bubbled with enthusiasm finding it difficult to believe that they had found her in a relatively short time—something he knew he would not have achieved on his own. "Where am I to stay?" he asked and Aleksander put his hand to his mouth in horror as if he hadn't thought about it. "The room above the stable where you stayed the last time you were here. But do not get too comfortable you will be moved from place to place for security."

Halle was close to despair when the lights were put out, which left only the low glow of an oil lamp to enable the staff to get about the ward. She settled down to sleep and, as was her habit from her childhood, she slept, or attempted to, with her arms outside the blanket. Much as she tried to get to sleep the uncertainty of her situation prevented her. Halle had begun counting in an effort to make her doze off when she felt a hand taking her right hand. At first she thought the nurse was taking pulses really early but then she felt a piece of paper being pushed into her hand. She instinctively pulled her hand away and almost screamed—indeed if it had been anywhere but there she would have. Then it dawned on her that it was a note and the excitement was almost too much—one moment despair the next exhilaration!

"What shall I do?" she thought. "Read the bloody thing!" shouted the voice. "How? When?" The voice rose like a scream, "In the toilet. Now!" She almost did as she was told but she restrained herself long enough to enable the person delivering it to get clear. The excitement reached a crescendo when on opening it she spotted Ian's name and when she read it, the reference to the bicycle wheel from childhood made it absolutely genuine. "Now where am I going to get a pencil, there must be one about the ward. I'll find it no matter what."

Maria Wieniawski had been warned that she wasn't to make direct contact with Konrad; she was to leave it to him and that could be anywhere on her way home, or on her way to work. These were the only two methods to be used as there was great danger that Hengist's undercover men would be watching—not necessarily her but it wouldn't take much to draw their attention. In the event of a major change in the circumstances affecting Halle she was to place a note under a specified tree in the nearest park.

Maria was glad that everything had gone according to plan. The note was in its right place and it was relatively easy to get when she was renewing the water. Halfway home Konrad, after checking that they weren't being observed, pretended to find something she had dropped and handed it to her and she slipped the message to him. She hurried on; unaware of what had become of her contact.

Sobieski waited impatiently for the first message to be delivered and hoped that it wasn't going to add to his difficulties. He knew, no matter what he told Konrad, that there was no way the messenger wouldn't look at the piece of paper, so he didn't mention it and merely grunted in a feeble attempt at acknowledgement. Once he had it he rushed to meet Aleksander, making sure he had a look at it himself. "It may just as well have been written in Chinese," he thought as he crossed town on his bicycle. The liaison officer had discretely kept Ian in the background, as he wanted him to see the note and to prepare another.

Ian checked out Halle's message of thanks. She was grateful to be in touch with loved ones once more and thanked them for their concern. A little later Aleksander made contact with the C-in-C, telling him that the message had been delivered and a reply received. He knew that the C-in-C wanted to be involved as much as possible but wondered at the pressure of work he was under. Within the hour Aleksander was summoned to a meeting in one of the 'safe houses' in the city.

Bór-Komorowski was in high spirits and he greeted Aleksander affably— a somewhat different meeting from the last one looked to be in prospect. "Congratulations, well done. At last we can get down to the real purpose of this being set-up. I want you or your English friend here to ask Miss Hegel a series of questions in your next letter. Firstly, why did the Germans think it was important for her to hold a high military rank? Secondly, who was the General directly in charge of her? Thirdly, where did she stay during her tours of both countries? I'll leave it at that. Perhaps Mr... excuse me I do not know your name..."

"Patterson, sir!"

"... would be willing on another occasion to talk about Miss Hegel and hopefully cut down the amount of letter writing. It would obviously be better if I had her here and she could talk directly to a number of my advisors. I can not take a chance on revealing what is precisely on my mind through these messages. Would that suit you?" looking directly at Ian. "Certainly, sir!" was the reply, "Thank you," and turning to Aleksander, "Please thank all those involved for a remarkable piece of work." The both of them muttered their appreciation and withdrew.

Back in Aleksander's home base Ian was given the task of writing the note in as short a way as possible so as to enable Halle to give as full an answer as the paper allowed.

The whole performance went like clockwork and Maria passed the reply to Konrad early in her journey back home. On opening it Ian and Aleksander were struck by the capital letters: WHY THIS? which prefaced Halle's responses. Both of them took their time to read and re-read her replies and finally Ian said, "This must be what my old schoolmaster meant when he said, 'read and inwardly digest'".

"I have to take this directly to the C-in-C. For the life of me, I have not a clue where this is taking us. Have you any ideas Ian?" Ian looked at him in wonderment, possibly at the suggestion that he could have solved such a riddle, "I haven't a baldy notion." Aleksander looked bewilderedly at him, raising his eyebrows to the ceiling, "What does that mean?" It was Ian's turn to be uncertain, "I've no idea; and that's what that means!" Aleksander laughed, "These idioms of yours are more and more ridiculous. Just get ready, you had better come along, I have a feeling the General wants to talk to anyone who has had any dealings with Halle."

Bór-Komorowski read the message avidly. "Can I presume that you gentlemen read her comments?" Ian had ceased to be surprised how readily both men starting speaking in English in his presence.

"We did, sir," replied Aleksander, "but we are as wise as ever, as to what is going on. Are you any the wiser yourself sir?" The C-in-C gave him a hard look and proceeded with what he was about to say, "It is pretty clear that this young lady is as unaware as you two." Ian didn't know whether Aleksander was being foolhardy or courageous raising the issue again when it was clear to him that the General would not be drawn on what was going on. "Are we to be let into the secret, sir?" Bór-Komorowski gave an enigmatic smile, "I do not yet…," he paused, "I have not been informed myself. However, we need Miss Hegel out of there without delay. Can that be done? Now do not tell me you will plan it and let me know—this time I give you *carte blanche*, use it wisely."

On their way across Warsaw they spoke once again about Halle's answers. Ian asserted that Halle was convinced she had been given the military rank in order to get Camp Commandants to agree with her approach to the talks given to Irish prisoners, which she wanted to be done individually not in groups. "It makes a kind of sense, do you agree?" asked Aleksander. Ian didn't respond to this but asked, "That General's name she gave as being in charge of the Commission, did you recognise it?" Aleksander shook his head, "No, I never heard of him." Ian went on to the question about the places Halle stayed in on her journeys, "Did her answer make any sense to you at all?" Aleksander paused before speaking, "I think that that answer was the clincher for the General—it was that which made him certain she wasn't involved in whatever it is that is going on." Ian was slightly puzzled, "Are you referring to the point about staying in hotels and rarely in officers' quarters?" Aleksander nodded and drew the discussion to a close, "What is more important now is, how the hell are we to get her out of that place? But we had better postpone our talk until we are in a more secure place."

Shortly after their return and they had been fed, Ian raised the question again, and Aleksander was still without an idea but suggested that both of them should see Konrad and Maria. "That is something, anyhow. They know more about the institution and how it works than we do. I don't doubt there is a way round these problems but they'll see them quicker than we will," began Ian, "perhaps we could start by getting paper and some pencils so that we can draw out the hospital, or rather so that they can do it. Again it may be an idea to ask Halle's thoughts on the matter when I write tonight."

"All that sounds good and hopefully it will not be long before she is with us, and more importantly with the General so that whatever is darkening his skies will be brightened."

The message from Halle the following day was discouraging, Ian paraphrased it for Aleksander, "Apparently she has been right round the place and she says if the doors are not locked they are guarded. Seems they are determined to keep her!"

"I have been thinking over the idea of meeting the other two involved and had begun to come to the conclusion that it was too risky for all concerned. But after this letter we will have to risk it." Ian wasn't about to disagree, "Needs must when the devil's driving." Aleksander gave him one of his looks, "I wish to God you would not start with a metaphor. Does that mean you agree or disagree?" Ian smiled in a superior way, "Ah, I agree."

Maria left work and was almost home when Konrad made contact. This time she was taken by surprise when he spoke openly to her without any kind of pretence of being a stranger. "The big brass wants to see you." Maria's start indicated her shock, "What about? I don't want attention drawn to me directly." Konrad, never the garrulous one bluntly said, "You won't!" He gave the details of time and place to meet him and told her he would then take her to the house.

Later that day Aleksander and Ian made their way to the safe house and were told that Maria and Konrad were already present. Aleksander had arranged for Sobieski to be there also but without the others being aware of his presence. "It's important that he be kept informed considering his rôle in the hierarchy of things." Ian was confused, "It's my turn to ask about a word; I thought 'hierarchy' was something to do with the Roman Catholic Church. Has it not?"

"No, not especially, it is a word like any other word. It can be used in a number of ways—it means 'position' or 'rank'. We had better go and meet these two." Konrad's description had intimidated Maria so much she almost went to pieces. Aleksander reassured her that she would not be expected to endanger herself any further than she had up to the moment and he went on to ask her about the hospital's security. It didn't take long for them, after the interpretation for Ian, to see that Halle's assessment was identical to Maria's. Konrad was only aware of the security outside the premises and thought that it wouldn't be difficult to get someone away once they were outside the building.

Ian addressed Maria, leaving it to Aleksander to explain, "This business of them locking doors must cause problems from time to time. For example, say someone has to be moved urgently do they unlock any of these doors?" Apparently they never used the doors during Maria's hours but then again she was on constant night shift. Aleksander could see where Ian was going with his questioning and suggested that Maria should ask someone she could trust where the keys were kept. She agreed and the meeting ended in quick time. After Maria and Konrad left, Aleksander explained the situation to Sobieski and their intention of getting the keys to enable them to make copies. "I wish you had spoken to me before getting Maria to speak to anyone else. I have a contact whose wife, I've only discovered, is an auxiliary nurse in the place."

"Quickly! Run you on and tell Maria not to bother. Say we don't want her involved any deeper than she is." Sobieski rushed out and came back shortly afterwards to state all was well and he would take care of the matter. "Explain, in what way?" quizzed Aleksander. "I'll get my friend's wife to get an impression of the keys in soap and have them made. Then it's only a question of having them slipped to Halle and organise a time that's suitable all round."

"Excellent, how soon can all this be done?"

"Tomorrow should see her get the impressions and the following day I'll collect the new keys. Is that soon enough?"

"Grand. One thing, make sure that the original keys are cleaned carefully to leave no indication how we spirited the girl out of there. We want to leave the notion that she got up and left by herself. Also see Konrad about the outside security. When we spoke to him he was confident he could get past them easily enough."

"I wouldn't be too certain it will be easily done but it can be done if there is enough care and attention given to detail."

Ian stood uncomprehending during this exchange and when Sobieski left he wanted to know what all the problems had been. Aleksander assured him that they were on top of the situation and in a few days he would see Halle and Ian left with his friend feeling that all was well with the world. Still he knew that a report would be forwarded to the C-in-C and he wondered just what the man had been up to in the interim. Even in his happiness, at the turn of events, he felt there was more to come from that source.

Halle was making good progress according to Dr Berlichingen and he said he would recommend to Oberst Hengist that she should be sent to some convalescent home, probably in Germany. "I knew this would end in tears," began her voice. "Give over, things are progressing on the outside." Still her illness left her more readily open to despair, "'Too late, too late shall be the cry!' You've heard that, haven't you?" Halle buried her face in the pillow to hide her tears from anyone nearby and the rest of the day passed like eternity. That evening after each visit by the nursing staff she looked under the water jug because she still had not made contact with the messenger. It was after 0200 hours that she discovered it and made her way to the toilet to read it. Ian was explicit as to what was going on but couldn't give time or details yet. She wondered if she would still be in the hospital the next day and her voice piped in with a pessimistic appraisal, "It's good of them to try but they're going to be too late."

The doctor's morning round was just completed when Halle noticed a piece of paper sticking out from under the water jug. The excitement was too intense to be good for her yet she went immediately to the bathroom so as to have the privacy to read the note. "Sometime today you will receive a key and a drawing showing a door to which it belongs. It's important to destroy this note and the drawing when it arrives. Make sure you know which door the key opens before you destroy the map. Love Ian. See you tomorrow."

An overwhelming surge of love for Ian swamped all her other emotions. This man could have been home in Belfast but he remained here to see that she came to no harm. It took some time for her to realise that she had no clothes other than the nightdress the Germans had given her. "To hell with the clothes! I could care less! I'd run out of here naked if need be!" she proclaimed to her inner voice. "You're all talk. It would be one sure way of attracting the Germans' attention, wouldn't it?" Halle shook herself back into a re-evaluation of the position. "I must not rush out the moment that the key arrives. Just take my time and pretend I'm going to the toilet as usual—it would be great if they knew about that door next to the toilet. Now I want everything, isn't that the way—never contented."

"It would be the thing if the key didn't work!" Halle put her hands over her ears to drown out the voice of her alter ego that was clearly back in business. "I'll be out the night for sure—working key or no working key!" By midnight panic had started to set in, "Where the hell is the messenger? They are extracting the full pound of flesh!" Halle lay down but could not sleep; occasionally she would doze and then jump up angry with herself for letting her weak body jeopardise any hope she might have had. After one of these bouts she noticed the piece of paper and something behind the water jug. "The key! At last, I'll have to go to the toilet to see to which door this belongs. It's amazing what you don't think of when you're up to a hundred!"

She took a moment to adjust her eyes to the light and was delighted to find that the door beside the toilet was indeed the one earmarked on the map. "No more hesitations, straight out and take your chance. Don't let that voice get an opportunity to speak."

Halle turned the key at the first attempt, gingerly opened the door and looked agonisingly round the corner, then looked right and left and turned left relying on her instincts. She had only taken two steps when she had a blanket tossed over her head and she was lifted off her feet and carried bodily to a waiting car. There were massive noises all around but she had concluded that this person had been sent to collect her and although she was frightened to death it was a different fear from that she had experienced in the hospital.

The car was purring before she reached it and pulled out as soon as she was laid down in the back. "Are you all right Halle?" and she felt Ian's arms round her in a reassuring circle. "God Ian, I never knew anything to go as perfectly as this. I owe you everything—even life itself!"

"Please Halle, you don't think I am capable of all this do you? The AK pulled every trick in the book, even attacked the place across the street to pull the German security men away from the building!" Aleksander, who seemed to take pleasure out of driving everyone in it to despair, was driving the car in a rather sedate fashion. "Can you not get this old jalopy to go any faster?" yelled Ian. "What exactly is a jalopy?" was Aleksander's quiet rebuttal. Of course Ian never answered that question but instead plied him with another, "Are we going to see the General at this time of the night?" Halle noticed the smiling dimples of Aleksander even sitting in the back seat. "Hardly! He would have us all before a firing squad first thing in the morning! No, a safe house has already been organised as we are expecting wholesale searches tomorrow morning."

"By any chance is this part of the C-in-C's plan? If the Germans make no effort he'll assume you're a plant," speaking to Aleksander and at the same time looking at Halle and making her aware that there was another dimension to her arranged escape, "On the other hand if they do, he could still assume you're a plant! That's the life of a double agent—take it or leave it!"

"Come on, he discarded that idea the day we got Halle's answer to his questions. Do not have us at each other's throats. I know you are wondering what is going on, just like I do…"

"What are you two talking about?" interrupted Halle. "It goes back to those questions he asked us to pass on to you," said Ian, "The C-in-C will not say what the relevance of those questions is. We know he has had previous dealings with Hengist and sees him as one of the most dangerous of the Nazis, as he is aware that the man is a personal friend of Hitler. Is any of this information you already knew?"

"It's completely new to me, sorry about the pun, it's the nature of the language," she said directing her apology to Aleksander. "I can see now where Ian got his anxiety about speaking to a foreigner. Look, leave this all until tomorrow when we see the General and by the time he has questioned you Halle, we will have a better idea where this is heading."

The decision as to where Halle was to stay had been left to the General and he had sent an AK commander to have Halle housed just outside the city. Ian was thoroughly put out by this and anxiously asked Aleksander was he permitted to attend the session with the C-in-C. "He has not said no, so I presume that it is quite all right. Just go back to your room and have a good night's sleep."

German activity was great early the next morning and Aleksander was left with the job of finding a safe meeting place. He came up with the idea of their meeting him in St Hyacinthus' Church on Freta, close to the Maria Sklodowska-Curie Museum. "Why there?" enquired Ian. "It's a well known one and many people pay visits to the Blessed Sacrament and the Museum so both she and him will easily be lost in the crowd." Stephan Sobieski arrived at the house saying that the Germans had intensified their search and it was going to be very difficult to move Halle anywhere in the city.

"How the devil are we going to get her through the city centre when she is still so poor on her feet? We can't push her in a wheel-chair, it would be too obvious," stated Ian to the two men. "Yes, you are right," said Stephan, "but if we reverse the situation and have her push Ian through the streets." His look bore the hallmark of one who knows he has come up with a gem of an idea. "But could she walk that far pushing the chair?" queried Aleksander while looking at Ian.

"I'm confident that she could manage that but won't the wheel-chair draw attention to the both of us?"

"I suspect that you will be the one drawing the attention not her and that should be fine," argued his friend. "But to be on the safe side should we not have them dressed as a nun and a priest…?" enquired Stephan but was unable to finish because of the hard laughter of the other two. "You should have kept quiet," laughed Aleksander, "your first idea was brilliant but now you have lost our admiration of your brilliance! Still the chair will enable Halle to walk with support. No, I can't take it away from you, it is a brilliant idea!"

General Bór-Komorowski and his aides greeted Halle warmly in the sacristy of the church. "I'm sure you are exhausted pushing that wheel-chair," and he smiled wanly at Ian. "How did you hear about it General?" enquired Halle.

"My aides keep me informed of everything! I must admit that early this morning I laughed heartily but it has worked and that is the main thing. May I now congratulate you on your enterprise and initiative in managing such a daring escape." Halle could feel the blood rushing to her face, a totally new experience for her, "Thank you, General."

"Secondly, we in the AK appreciate how much you have tied up the Gestapo and the German Army here in Warsaw by their attempts to recapture you. Finally, I am keen to put as much pressure on Hengist as I can because

I suspect or rather more than suspect that he was one of the Nazis who helped plan the attack on our country." Halle sat back and enjoyed the glow of self-satisfaction at the congratulations that flowed her way.

"Perhaps we could begin, Miss Hegel, with you giving us a brief outline of how you got involved in all of this." Halle didn't know where to start and the General, spotting her dilemma, suggested starting at her first association with the Germans. It seemed strange to be relating her story to people who seemed to find it increasingly interesting but she proceeded, explaining her decisions and how they affected the direction she found herself heading. Once or twice some of the General's aides stopped her in order to get her to enlarge on a specific area of her story—Halle began to sense that her tale bore more interest to them when she mentioned places she had been and in particular places she had stayed.

When she had finished the General asked her if Sheila was dead or alive, "I'm convinced the Nazis murdered her when they failed to get whatever information she had." He then asked her permission for his aides and himself to withdraw to discuss what they had learnt from her story. Ian spoke to Aleksander on their leaving, "Did you make anything out of what Halle said?" Aleksander took his time to reply, "I'm certain by their looks that they have found something, even in the way they questioned her," nodding in Halle's direction, "it was clear that they were working with other information which they wanted to combine with her story."

"But did you make anything out of it?"

"No, I didn't, but then I had not got the information they had." Ten minutes later the General and his aides returned, "Has my story been of any help, sir?" asked Halle.

"Indeed it has, with what our intelligence team has told us we think we have a much clearer picture of what is going on within the Wehrmacht in Germany."

"We have no notion of how that story of Miss Hegel could have been useful…, sorry sir, but do you think you could enlighten us now?" asked Ian.

"Indeed you have been useful. I met Hengist at an army exercise prior to Hitler coming to power in 1933. He was full of hate for the Treaty of Versailles, even when we were just conversing in the bar. I marked him then as a potential irritant for the future, but what I did not realise was that he had already aligned himself with the National Socialists."

"You say he was in the army in those days. How come he is now with the Gestapo?"

"We are not sure just when the transfer took place but as we get more and more information it appears it was just prior to the attack on Poland."

"Sir, what way did Halle's story help your understanding of the situation?"

"From the answers Halle gave me the other day I knew she was not involved. Today as she told us how she began to work for German propaganda and then how she applied for and got promoted in order to get more troops for the German Army we were interested in her movements around Germany and Poland."

"Is that all there was to her story?"

"Basically yes. From the details we have gained from Miss Hegel's account we will pass on to the Allies who will be able to work out the implications."

Halle was disappointed at the General's answer but realised it was unlikely, even if he knew precisely what lay behind Hengist's hounding of her, that he would have passed it on to her. She forced a smile and said, "I'm glad to have been of service to humanity—whether my friends will see this in the same light is another matter, which I won't speculate on now."

Ian realising that the audience was almost at an end spoke directly to the General, "Sir, may I ask a question." The C-in-C's look clearly showed he was none too anxious to be drawn on any more detail. "Yes, what is it?"

"Well when Halle, Miss Hegel, was shot I assumed that the German patrol did it. Later our information from the hospital indicated that the Germans thought that the patrol had come under attack from resistance fighters..." Halle interrupted him, "Even Hengist believed that, and we have been wondering," waving her hand in the general direction of Ian, "if you have heard just what was going on?"

"Yes indeed. It was Aleksander's telling of the story of Miss Hegel's experience that started me wondering what had happened for there to be such confusion. Initially I felt that the local resistance had taken matters into their own hands because they had overheard the German patrol querying her German credentials, or something like that. In any event I ordered an enquiry and I recently received the report from the local commander in Plock. According to him you had been stopped by a German patrol— everyone is agreed on that—and you showed your papers," looking up to see Halle's response, "I think that's true," she responded. "Your papers indicated that you were in the Wehrmacht with the rank of Oberst. This report indicates that the investigator found that a day or two after the shooting a band of AK men successfully attacked German troops killing all but one of them. Our soldiers had been anxious to capture some Germans so that they could hear their version of events at the time of Miss Hegel's shooting."

"Sorry to interrupt sir, but if they knew they didn't do it why bother to ask the Germans?"

"That is precisely why we had an investigation, our men there knew they did not do it but who did and why? If you will bear with me I think the report clears everything up. In any event, the wounded soldier survived long enough to tell his version of what happened. Apparently the patrol, after stopping you, returned the way they came and stopped until you were out of sight. They discussed what a full blown colonel was doing in that area and they assumed that you," pointing to Halle, "were there to assess their fitness for the Eastern front and they convinced themselves that you would be recommending them to be moved. There and then they returned to kill you but they must have heard the calling of your friend and left in a hurry."

"Why did they not wait and kill him?" asked Halle.

"The commander does not make this clear and it would only be conjecture in any event. They could not possibly know if there were one or one hundred on the road but that is the best we can do."

"Thank you for that," replied Halle, "much and all as I regret the death of anyone, those men were bent on murder and God knows how many they have killed. Anyway it's a weight off my mind." General Bór-Komorowski stood up and the whole company rose. "At any rate, whatever tomorrow holds, I want to thank you on behalf of the Polish Government in Exile and myself," he proffered his hand which Halle shook with some vigour to indicate her thanks for all that he had done for her. The rest of the company applauded them both.

CHAPTER 16
(August-September 1943)

NOW THAT HALLE was free from imminent arrest by the Gestapo, Ian found his mind returning to the differences in their backgrounds and beliefs. "You don't think these unbridgeable differences can be bridged?" his voice asked. "You know full well that by definition 'unbridgeable' means just that! Evidently you are against Halle and me having a successful relationship."

"You're kidding yourself again—it's your thoughts that have brought us to this point." Ian attempted to blank out the voice's assertiveness but gradually came to accept there were many issues to be faced when he and Halle eventually got together. From the height of rapture at Halle's escape, he had now descended to this depressing scenario of having to deal with his voice and its pessimism.

He had hoped to have more time with her but the inevitable need to make it difficult for the Gestapo to find them took precedence over their feelings—that is if Halle felt as he did. Still he shouldn't have been cast into such a depression so early. Perhaps he was prejudging Halle's response. Inwardly he realised that he had avoided telling Halle about his former marriage to Vera. The question still needed to be put—why had he ducked thinking about it, never mind not telling. There was an ugly type of certainty and this was it: "You know darn well she's going to run a mile when you tell her about the divorce." Ian persisted in churning the matter over in his head and his alter ego was having a field day, "Give it up it's hopeless!" was a phrase it never ceased to use. "That aggravating voice makes certainty seem like a bad taste in the mouth and boy is it destructive!" remarked Ian to the nearest wall.

He concluded that the excessive amount of time on his hands only added to his depression. Even praying with more concentration did not stop his voices from giving vent to their corrosive assurity. "You know you have a terrible temper and sooner rather than later someone's going to feel the edge of your tongue!" Ian begged them to take a rest and give him some peace and at one point he was shouting aloud, but the voices persisted, "Don't you be taking it out on Aleksander just because he is the only one here. Look at how much he has done for you." Another voice started the ball rolling in a different direction, "Watch him, he's pushing a Romanist agenda. He's got under your defences and now he'll take advantage of your friendship by getting you to agree to tenets that wouldn't stand up to scrutiny back home."

Ian was close to total despair and his memories of the women in his life took on an existence outside of anything that had really happened. "You should have stayed with Vera. That Fenian Republican isn't fit to tie her laces but just because she wanted sex and it suited your craving, you've turned it into 'love'!" Aleksander opened the door and Ian, glad to see anyone, greeted him as if he were the Prodigal Son.

Ian was anxious to return to Teodor's farm to arrange accommodation that would be safe and allow Halle time to recuperate. Aleksander smiled at the naiveté of the suggestion and had to remind him that to move out of Warsaw at the present time would be asking for trouble. Hengist had the city in as tight a circle as there had been when the German Army moved in to destroy the Jews and the Jewish Ghetto, "There is no way out at present and you will just have to bide your time and wait as patiently as you can. Is this anxiety being pushed along by the two of you being separated?"

"Of course not! We've been apart for a long period already and I suppose we can manage another but I don't want her pushing me around in a wheelchair again!" Aleksander laughed as he recalled the return journey and Ian squirming while Halle did all the work, "You must admit it worked like a charm!" Ian glared at him, "You weren't the subject of everyone's pity. Some of the people even spoke to me in Polish, what was that about?"

"That was even funnier, they thought you had been crippled in the army's attempt to throw the Nazis back."

"So one can only be a hero if he's crippled in your army?" laughed Ian well aware that there was a grain of truth in his question. Aleksander wasn't bluffed by the laugh and treated the question seriously: "Do you think that Christ would have had a bigger or lesser impact on this world if he had died a peaceful death in his own bed?" Ian hated these types of questions, only liberals and Micks without concern for Christian principles asked others to defend or attempt to outguess what history might have decided. "I've no idea." Aleksander applauded, "Congratulations, you have taken your first step on a liberal journey into the unknown! But the fact that you thought about it at all, even if it was for barely a few seconds, is the most promising part."

"You know Aleksander that sounds patronising; whether you meant it or not that's what comes across. I never was a born again liberal—I'm an evangelical, I take the Bible literally. I don't want to make guesses on the might-have-beens in history. Black and white is all that I want. It's true or it isn't. I am aware that you university types can run rings around me with ideas and imaginative suggestions but all that does is add confusion to confusion and the end is perdition!"

"I am sorry if I hurt your feelings, it was not meant. Education to me is important and all I ask of my students is to consider as many possibilities as they can, otherwise I feel they will never sort out the day to day problems everyone faces. Now if that injures your perception of the world, once again I am sorry but it shall not stop me believing that what I say is the proper way."

"Let's leave it. We'll never agree on this one and you are too much of a friend for me to insult you in any way." Aleksander was reluctant to let the topic drop but he saw there was no leeway towards give and take, so he let go.

The days following this conversation were long and devoid of any humour. Occasionally Jerzy, a friend of Aleksander, would turn up and everyone in the household would assemble to ask him to play on the upright piano in the back room. One night, when Jerzy was a little under the weather, Ian sensed his friend's uneasiness as the former sat down at the piano. Whether it was at his inebriated state or his remembrance of him at a grand piano in a concert hall Ian didn't know, nor did he know what to expect. Jerzy's expertise on the keyboard was such that even Ian's limited knowledge appreciated his undoubted talent, yet he was quite surprised to recognise a tune and started humming. Suddenly he realised that he and Aleksander were the only people left as there had been a sudden surge of bodies to the door. Rather bemused Ian asked what was going on but the piano player played on with some passion and Aleksander smiled like a Cheshire cat. There was no response to the question and finally Ian told Aleksander that he knew the tune, "That's a song called 'I'm always chasing rainbows'." Aleksander convulsed and began pulling Ian from the room. "What the devil is going on?" demanded Ian. "We have to get away from here."

"Why?" shouted Ian, noting that the street appeared deserted. "When Jerzy is drunk he tends to do this."

"I'm at a total loss as to what's going on," began Ian. Aleksander urged him to hurry, "Jerzy will be arrested but the Gestapo are well used to his drunken bouts and they'll keep him overnight until he's sober."

"Arrested for what?" asked the puzzled Ian, "For playing that song, 'I'm always chasing rainbows'?" Aleksander laughed uproariously, "No, for playing Chopin."

"But he wasn't, was he?"

"That, so called song, is the Impromptu—fantasia in C sharp minor, opus 66, and it is by Chopin."

"So what? What's the problem?"

"He's banned in Poland because of the emotional quality of his music, particularly for Polish people. God knows what would have happened back there if Jerzy had played the Polonaise!" Someone must have informed the Gestapo because no sooner had they turned the corner at the end of the street than the police arrived.

Aleksander could exercise his mind with reading, a form of recreation from which Ian was excluded because of the lack of books in English. "At least you would think he would have the King James' version of the Bible!" thought Ian. After a series of silences over a week Aleksander consulted Marie, whose home was being used by Halle and was told that a similar situation existed with her. Whether this was the final crunch or not, it was decided to return the two escapees to Teodor.

The return journey took place without a hitch, each one of the Belfast 'twins', as Aleksander had christened them behind their backs, was taken by an AK member to Plock where they were collected by Teodor at different times on the one day.

Their excitement at being together again convinced Teodor that he would have to get a priest to perform the marriage ceremony before their behaviour became too outrageous for the very conservative people in his neighbourhood. Luckily he didn't tell them what he was thinking for he would have well and truly set the cat among the pigeons, as Aleksander informed him when he appeared to discuss the next phase of getting the pair out of the country.

Although they were happy to be together Halle wasn't altogether certain about the sensibility of their early return. Talking to Teodor she expressed her reservations but he also was in turmoil. Ilona had replied to his letter and indicated indirectly—clearly afraid of the message being intercepted—that seeing the Belfast pair had returned to the immediate vicinity of the field hospital she also was considering returning but this time with her daughter. Teodor went on about it being uncharacteristic of Ilona to put her daughter in danger, "Indeed she is excessively careful when she has the child with her."

Later that day Halle mentioned Ilona's letter when she returned to the subject when speaking to Ian. "I don't believe, for one minute, that Hengist has decided that we have got away. He is like a fox waiting in his lair until the pursuers have passed before starting out again in search of a meal. Nothing convinces me that he has given up—it's as unlike him as Ilona's returning home with the little girl at this stage. Maybe Teodor's feelings are an omen. Do you think the AK have underestimated Hengist and his group?"

"Perhaps we should be making our own arrangements to get away," said Ian, speaking with less than conviction. Halle guessed he was less than keen so she gave him an opportunity to withdraw, "I don't think we can insult Bór-Komorowski after all he has done, apart from anything else it will insult our friends here and in Warsaw if we should now ignore them. It may be a difficult tightrope to walk but in the meantime I don't think we have an alternative."

"It's enough to be on the run without living in the shadow of Hengist, waiting for him to turn up!" Ian realised he was beginning to reflect Halle's attitudes which wasn't appropriate given Halle's need for convalescence. Halle, for her part, could see how she was affecting Ian. His was almost a proprietary claim on her, constantly agreeing with her and unwilling to put an opposite view. Even his questions led to answers she knew were inevitably in agreement with her. "What can we do? Are you strong enough to go on the road again?" Halle spoke, as if to another person, "Well the AK have promised to help but I don't like the idea of sitting here leaving it all to them. We need to ask them what ideas they have. After all you have a name in Gdansk who can help us get to Sweden." Ian searched the ceiling for patience; "You have half answered my questions. Are you strong enough?"

"I'm nearly there; I couldn't go at this moment but say in a week's time. Anyway let's enjoy the summer weather."

After a few days of this romantic interlude Halle began to be anxious about their future together. "Look Ian, we'll have to settle these differences of ours one way or the other."

"How do you propose dealing with them?"

"Well I thought, seeing that we are stuck here for some weeks, if we could agree to openly discuss whatever issues there are, which are separating us."

"Is sex one of them?" asked Ian in a voice that couldn't be taken seriously.

"If you wish to make it a topic by all means—but don't think that gives you *carte blanche* in your approaches to me!" Halle meant to be humorous but she sparked off the serious side of Ian's nature. "No, I just want to know what are the parameters—are there any topics excluded?" Once the Rubicon had been crossed Halle determined to stay with its possibility of grave implications but, like Ian, didn't bring the issues into the light of day. "No but there does need to be a time limit on proceedings, otherwise issues could drag on for days."

"What do you say if the maximum for any session is two hours and they can only occur once a day?"

"Well what should the first session be about?"

254

"About us and the future."

"Are you giving any hints about which angle you're coming from?"

"No, I'd better leave it until tomorrow evening."

Halle was agitated all day wondering how she would reconcile her promise when she was in the tunnel with what she expected would be a proposal from Ian. "If hell hath no fury like a woman scorned, what about men then? If I tell him about offering him up as a sacrifice so that I would please my mother... at any rate, he'll be pleased I agreed to end my association with the Cumann na mBan at least." Also she concluded that if she were agitated today then Ian would be ten times more so. "He can't wait to get this business of ours out in the open—I wonder what's going on in his head? I suppose I can only wait and see what he has to say."

Halle put the matter out of her mind but when Ian came in at lunchtime she resumed her worrying. "You want him to ask you, don't you? So that you can tell him you can't, is that it? You're worse than a FRT, you give in to sex but pretend you're not emotionally involved. Has this to do with religion, politics or just obstinacy?" She got up to do her usual walking exercises and it dawned on her that her health could well be one of the critical areas; she must arrange to meet Aleksander and discuss their being moved. It wasn't fair putting a family in jeopardy having the pair of them. Part of the answer was for her to be well enough and for one thing not have to go to bed in the afternoons.

Ian had gone back to helping the Czerniawskis and had his evening meal with them, so he was later than Halle anticipated. When he arrived Halle sighed unintentionally, "Can we talk now or do you want to wait?"

"Let's begin. Where do you want to start?"

"Do you think we have a future as partners, husband and wife?" Ian internally winced at the words 'husband and wife'. For all his determination to tell her about Vera he still hadn't done so. "Look Halle, I have to clear up one point before we talk about this further."

"OK then, just one and no getting off the subject."

"Do you remember, right at the outset, when you talked about being a Falls Road whatever..."

"A Falls Road Teaser. Yes, go on!"

"Well I said truthfully that my experience was limited, as I had only been out with a girl who was as religious as myself... Well I didn't go on about it..."

"You're starting to stammer, Ian."

"None of this is easy, Halle. Give me a chance to tell it my way." There was a longish pause; "Well I ended up marrying that girl..."

"You are a *liar* in every sense! You deliberately deceived me! Do you

255

think that for *one* moment I would have let you near me if I had known that? I'd have frozen to death that night rather than let it happen!"

"No, I didn't, I only answered the question you put."

"Ah! The great politician—that cuts no ice with me. You told less than half the truth and by saying nothing further implied that you were single and unattached."

"But let me explain myself, you see we're split up and divorced so that is why I didn't feel I needed to go to the point of telling you then. I put off the telling of it 'til I could decide my feelings about you."

"Ian you're making things worse. There's no way I could marry a divorcee at any time. So you see there was no point in going on about this relationship—there never was a place for it to go."

"I'm sorry Halle, I thought we could have got round it. The Pope is always allowing annulments, isn't he? Couldn't we get one?"

"Look, I don't know anyone who got an annulment. Yea, there's plenty of stories but when you check them out most of them are rubbish and the others are based on canon law and have stood the test of being tried before they were given. How would your divorce stand up to that test?"

"Well we never consummated the marriage. Is that not sufficient?"

"I... I... don't know. But you never had any problems with me, did you...?"

"Halle it was more complicated than that. The girl was so religious she just found it too much of an 'indignity', I'm using her words, 'to have intimate relations.'"

"Oh, my God. I wondered at that myself when I was young; yet we, such enemies, didn't seem to take that on board."

"Do you think there's a chance?"

"Ian I think we should forget this. I know I'm in love with you in spite of the harshness of my criticism—but face reality, there's no hope of an annulment so let's call it quits now."

Having almost reached a terminal crisis in their talks Ian proposed that they let sleeping dogs lie. "Perhaps tomorrow evening we should look at areas we can change." Halle was disgruntled with the way their discussion had gone, feeling that there was no hope of agreement and wondered why they should bother discussing anything else. "Are you proposing that we wait and see what the Church's response will be when we get home?"

"Yeah, something like that."

"I'll not say no but don't you go getting your hopes up."

The next day Halle considered the position once again and could find no way out, "You're only digging a deeper hole, one from which you'll never climb out." Halle clicked her tongue in disgust, he was back: "I thought I had got rid of you." The voice of pessimism had reached his zenith, "Are you going to go through with all this gobbledegook?" She knew she had heard this word before, "Where did you dig up that one?"

"You don't listen to Ian when he talks. The story of the American Negro has that word in it somewhere." Halle disagreed but allowed that it might be a newly coined word that is in use since they left Britain. "Is it back to the good old Irish way of dealing with questions?"

"No, I thought you had begun making your own words."

"Does this mean you are not answering the question?"

"Yes! To both."

Ian arrived somewhat earlier than the previous night. "I hope there are no more areas of disagreement that can't be resolved."

"You're asking a lot. We haven't begun dealing with each other's views on religion and politics."

"But they're matters of choice."

"Oh! Then what *do* you choose, Ian?"

"You; what else?" the quizzical nature of his voice caused Halle to look sharply at him.

"Without all the paraphernalia of the past?"

"Can *you* give *me* some guarantees on your part?"

"Look, your commitment was to God and Ulster—that's nothing like mine!"

"I know my Da signed the Covenant in the City Hall in Belfast in 1912, and signed it with his own blood but I didn't!"

"No? You're still avoiding the issue. You answered a question with a question."

"For someone who bombed people in England because of a belief, you have some gall to compare my beliefs with yours and then ask me to cast off 'my paraphernalia' as if they are some old clothes to be dumped."

"You've said enough!"

"Does that mean what I think it means?"

"I know we don't have one-way streets in the centre of Belfast but you must have lived in one in a past life."

"You're making less and less sense!"

"Then you should be relieved to know we haven't to spend that much more time together."

"I'm sorry it had to come to this. I think we could have made it, maybe not in Belfast but either in England or the USA. The truth is neither of us could give up enough to satisfy the other."

"Ian, I have feared this from the beginning. I know what I'm going to tell you will be difficult for you to accept."

"You've said enough as it is."

"Ian it's not so long ago when I was near death that I decided that I loved you for yourself and the person you have become while we've been together. I never told you about promising to change…"

"You're good at asking others!"

"Please, I know you're angry with good reason. Perhaps I'm still that FRT at heart—I hope not."

"Look, can you make this short, we need to get out of this room before Teodor returns."

"All I'm saying is—putting you first, not myself—won't work. I know I'll never love anyone the way I love you but above all else I don't want it to turn to hate because of our differences…"

Ian turned and left the room. Halle's voices went on the rampage; "You lied again!" Then a second voice echoed the first in essence, "You know you promised The Voice to give him up that time you were wounded. Why didn't you tell him instead of deliberately searching for a way out that hurts both of you."

That night, before turning in, Halle went to speak to Ian and asked him to allow her to finish all that she had to say the next day; somewhat reluctantly Ian agreed. Each night both of them made a point of saying "Good night" to Teodor, which he duly reciprocated but this time he had news of Ilona. "She is back with Manya in her old house and hopes to see you both tomorrow." Teodor felt their cordiality about the news was forced and wondered what was driving them to put up such a front.

Early next morning Teodor departed for Ilona's house leaving instructions for Halle on how to get there. By now she was starting to take her long lie-ins for granted and it was nearer lunchtime before she arrived. Father and daughter were in the process of tidying and dusting a cottage that hadn't seen human habitation for weeks. Halle offered her services but Ilona was happier with Halle playing with her little girl. It was a new experience for the Belfast girl and she was surprised how much she enjoyed it. It must have been a similar experience for Manya because when her grandfather and Halle were departing she ran after Halle and asked her for a kiss in Polish—which required a new kind of interpreting for Teodor.

Ian arrived with the intention of leaving the disputes to another time. There was too much unnecessary aggravation—or was there? These issues need to be decided once and for all, pussyfooting around didn't help the matter. Halle came in shortly after him and was so full of life that Ian temporarily forgot his pledge to leave the thing alone. He thought, "If she raises it, it means she believes there is a chance so I'll have to go along with that. But in any event I can't spend the night on whatever issue she has in mind because I told Teodor that I would call on Ilona."

Halle's bubbly mood continued right through dinnertime and when they went outside to get the air, it was she who initially talked about the future. "I can't visualise myself as a wife and mother. Probably after all we've been through it's hard to imagine anything so normal."

"If I have children I'll never tell them the dreadful part of this story. It's better to stick with the funny side of it—there's no way I'm going to describe to anyone, never mind my children, the heads of friends of mine being blown off by German tanks. Even that American killing the pig with his bare hands is horrendous."

"You don't mind telling me though!"

"You're as hard as nails; you've seen it and given it... sorry, I didn't mean to bring it up again."

"Oh but you're an old woman bellyaching on and on; the worst kind of nagging. Especially when you're full of praise for the AK fighting for their homeland. But *the others and me, fighting for our* homeland, we are guerrillas and terrorists." There was a belligerency about Halle that Ian had not seen before and he trod softly.

"It's a weak argument all round, I agree but what are we Unionists to do? Surrender and be trod into the ground because of our political and religious beliefs?"

"No one is asking you to do that, all we want is justice all round."

"But on your terms."

"What way do you see it, then?"

"If you would accept the majority rule and try to work for Northern Ireland the balance would naturally return."

"Wait a wee minute, when did it ever balance back home? Maybe before the Plantation but certainly not since. As it is, your people have a set-up majority and you use it as a justification for your treatment of the people opposed to you, don't you?"

"I notice you ignored the rôle of the Presbyterians in the 18th and 19th centuries when they attempted to unite the various factions!"

"Sorry, it was an oversight, probably because I was getting hot under the collar. Still there was no balance even then. Why could you not be like them? They were men of conviction and courage—unlike your bigoted, twisted group of b... sorry! You're getting me riled deliberately!"

"It's hard to take. I raise an important point but you're off immediately blaming me for your oversight—*as you describe it*. Anyway I'll have to leave it, I promised Teodor that I'd visit Ilona this evening after work. Did you see her today?"

"Ian I try not to be unpleasant but there is a kind of inevitability when we get on to these subjects."

"Forget it, I doubt if we will ever reach agreement on anything."

"Don't say that just yet. I haven't given up hope that we'll find some grounds we can agree on—maybe not enough to be lovers or husband and wife but at least be friends."

"Do you see 'lovers' as distinct from people who are married?"

"No, did I say that?"

"It wasn't clear anyway but now you've eased my mind!" and they both laughed as Ian went indoors to prepare to go to Ilona's.

It did not take long for Ian to get there, it was only after he arrived at her door that he realised how anxious he was to see her. "Ian! I am glad to see you," and reverting to Polish called, "Manya! Come and see who is here to see you!" The child timorously approached from the other room and Ilona told her that this man was the friend of Halle's and came from Ireland—the thought crossed her mind at the time that it was a good job that Ian didn't understand what she had said! Ian noticed Ilona's embarrassment when he entered slightly disturbing, but he wasn't to know the by-play that had gone on about him between father and daughter earlier in the day.

The evening passed pleasantly with each of them having a series of questions to put to the other about how they managed to survive without working for such a long time. "Thankfully, I'm back working with the Czerniawskis and with it being the height of the summer I'm kept busy every day. How do you put in your time?" Ilona gave him a long stare, which suggested 'what a stupid question to ask of a mother with a small child', and then she merely pointed at Manya. "Do you miss the activities at the hospital, particularly those which the Germans considered illegal?"

"Curiously, in a way I do. Although the nightmares have abated there are still times when I wake up thinking the Gestapo are breaking the door down." Suddenly she missed Manya and went looking for her only to discover that the child had fallen asleep on her bed, obviously bored by the adult conversation. Ilona woke her and prepared her for bed and finally knelt down beside her to say her night prayers.

"Does she ask about her father?"

"Occasionally but she always prays for him every morning and every night." Ian looked distinctly uncomfortable, waited a moment and moved the conversation back to areas that were more familiar to him, "Can you go back to medicine here in your own community or is it too dangerous?"

"I would like to but my Father is frightened at me being home again. So I haven't the nerve to discuss it with him. But that's enough about me, what about you and Halle?"

"What did she say on that score?" Ilona gave him what he considered was an old-fashioned look, "That really would be telling—it is your story I want to hear." Ian briefly explained that both politically and morally they were on different wavelengths and in an attempt to ameliorate the situation they had agreed to talk matters over but their differences were still too great.

The night passed quickly once Manya had settled down to her night's sleep. Apart from Halle, it was Ian's first experience of talking with a truly intelligent woman and he promised himself that if he ever got out of this mess education would be high on his intended list of things to do. All his life he had been associated with the seriousness of the Lord and the need for salvation was the predominant concern. The people here, outside of Halle, were more concerned with life and enjoyment—this in spite of the many deprivations they had to endure. Ian tried to avoid finding fault with his own people and asked Ilona: "How do you view the belief generally that the Germans are massacring the Jews?" Ilona's face changed immediately from one of a humorous disposition to one of despair. "I have no doubt that it is a genuine belief; they are murdering those they sent to Treblinka in thousands."

"Are the Poles generally sympathetic to the Jews?"

"I am afraid world-wide there appears to be little sympathy for the Jews, and in this country we have had a large anti-Semitic group over the years. Don't ask me to explain it, it is there and it is a shameful thing. For myself, I see these peoples as Poles of the Jewish faith and as a result the Nazis are murdering my people." Ian didn't pursue the matter it had all the hallmark of events he recalled as a boy, maybe not in the scale that they happened here but with the same intensity of hatred.

Later, walking back to Teodor's, some of the old issues from home arose in his mind. "Could we accept the others' differences and still accept them as fellow-countrymen? What is the definition of traitor that makes it such a heinous offence? Can we find common ground where we can agree and leave the rest to posterity to sort out?" He soon realised he was on dangerous ground as he heard the angry mutterings of his alter ego, "You shouldn't be giving these people excuses for their behaviour; it implies that we must be wrong if they are right!" Ian tried to wave them away as he proceeded into Teodor's house but again the old questions raised their ugly heads: "Are you only attracted to Fenians? There are millions of Protestant women in Europe and you manage to find two Taigs—you'll have some trouble being made Grand Master in the Orange now?" His voices were having a field day—"There you go again using all these betting metaphors. Roman Catholics belong to Satan and to drinking and gambling and the more you associate with them the more in danger you are. Hitler and Hengist can kill you but these so-called Christians can steal away your immortal soul!" Ian attempted to answer them but the torture of his mixed feelings towards both women proved to be too excruciating and he got up and went outside to see if he could find Halle.

Ian was considerably worked-up when he met Halle. He was only too aware that it wasn't a good time to have a heart-to-heart discussion but his voices wouldn't be silent, "You need to confront her now!"

"Look Halle I'm being tortured mind and body over all these issues. Whether it's nationality or religion we can't agree." It was clear that Halle wasn't going to leave him room to negotiate his way out. Her opening remarks were intended to draw him into further arguments: "Nationality is a trick of perception. Think of those who immigrated to America. Some saw themselves as Americans from day one, others wrapped themselves in the flag of the country from which they had left and became more Irish, German, Polish, Italian etc. over the years, while Ulstermen rarely retained any vestige of their background—that is outside of their religious convictions. Why is that?" A reluctant Ian was finding himself being forced to respond: "It's a question of identity. The more they associate with their country of origin the longer the ties will remain firm but Ulster Presbyterians have their identity spread across a series of loyalties and try as they might, once they've immigrated they seem to adopt to their new country."

"Then how do you explain their ancestors' differences in Ireland?" asked Halle with a supercilious smile. "Some of them fought the British in 1798 and others fought for them. A darn sight more of them fought the British than their so-called Roman Catholic compatriots," answered Ian with more vehemence. "What about the majority of them then?" asked Halle with a smirk. "Surely it must have been the fact that Ireland was controlled by the English and it suited them."

"So it doesn't matter if the native Irish were deprived of their rights and their country?"

"It never was like that. The English in England and the Scots in Scotland were equally mistreated but only the Irish saw it as discriminatory."

"You mean that the Irish were the only ones who weren't prepared to put up with it!"

"Now don't make it out that the Irish stood up to the establishment on their own. The Welsh and the Scots had many battles with the English as to who controlled these islands…"

"The way you're talking you'd think we were in the middle of Belfast having an argument. But to get back to the dispute—the Welsh and the Scots were like Birds' custard, they were mopped up very easily."

"Halle you have the most evil way of insulting people. Give it and me a rest."

Not another word was exchanged the rest of that evening and Ian dreaded the confrontation that awaited him the next morning. Halle, on the other hand, cried all night but knew in her heart that there was nothing she could do to keep the romance going and she was prepared to destroy whatever there had been between them in order to justify the promise she made in the tunnel.

Early the next morning Halle made her way outside in an attempt to stop Ian going to the Czerniawskis' farm. Her determination to blow the relationship out of the water was fixed and she only sought the opportunity to place the blame on Ian for bringing matters to a head. "What about taking the day off Ian and we'll settle down to solving the issues that Teodor wants resolved?"

"That's fine. Can you wait 'til I nip over to the farm and let them know the situation?"

"Go ahead."

Twenty minutes later Ian returned and was full of chat about the children he had seen working in the fields. "Back home they would be back at school by now. You were the same, weren't you—back by the end of August?" Halle nodded, "But school times are different in war time, aren't they?" Ian wasn't sure but recalled his father saying about helping with the harvest when he was a child during the Boer War. "War is a terrible thing. I remember this old teacher of ours, a survivor of the Great War, would read a poem by Wilfred Owen. It was called *Dulce et Decorum Est,* did you ever hear of it?" Halle was disgusted by the question; "Of course I have but never at school! Never liked it much, it's so pessimistic—it seems like a coward's poem." Ian thought for a moment, "I suppose I was like that when I was young but recently, especially since I ran over that German soldier, I've been rethinking my attitude to war."

"Do you remember any of the lines?"

"He used to beat the poems into us but not that one, yet curiously I remember some of the lines… 'If you could hear, at every jolt, the blood come gurgling from the froth-corrupted lungs' and then there was something about an old lie. What was that? Wasn't it in Latin? Right up your street."

"They're the lines I couldn't stick because I believe that it is a good thing to die for your country!"

"So that's what it meant—how do you say it?"

"Dulce et decorum est pro patria mori."

"I remember him saying that it had been handed down from Roman times but he warned us that 'patriotism is the last refuge of the scoundrel'."

"Samuel Johnson."

"I thought he was talking about Irish Republicanism."

"Trust you! You must have been taken in by every word these bigots said."

"What are you on about?"

"Your real God is Unionism—everything that ever happened, everything you want to be has to follow a set formula."

"That's rich coming from you—you dance to whatever tune your parish priest plays!"

"That's it, enough's enough! Can't you see there's too much in our history that separates us? All I know is that this constant friction is killing me—something Nazi bullets couldn't do! I can't sleep; think straight or get away from you and your continual hatred of all that I believe!" shouted Halle.

"All that you believe? That's a good one! Of course all I believe in is rubbish in your eyes—but that doesn't matter—my feelings don't come into it. I agree with you—at least on this one issue—we're not good for each other. I'll ask Teodor to find us separate places until we can organise an escape, separately or together," Ian regretted the words as soon as they issued from his mouth.

"I know we are attracted to each other and that's unlikely to change but together we are bad news; so go ahead," for a moment Ian thought he heard a huskiness in Halle's voice. A moment later he was prepared to be reconciled, "I'm sorry it hasn't worked out but we're lucky we've had this chance to find out what life together would be like."

"I'm too angry to be sorry! You are too insulting to be concerned about me or my feelings!"

"There you are, away again. You can't let the hare sit, can you? Apologies just don't work with you."

They parted and went off in different directions each of them aware that they still hadn't dealt with the main issue on which they agreed—the desire to escape! During the night the upset caused both of them to rest uneasily and it was Halle's turn to be remorseful. She went to his room and knocked gently not wanting to waken Teodor. "Yes," whispered Ian obviously aware that there would be only one person who would be knocking his door in the middle of the night. "May I say a few words to you?"

"Come in," sitting up at the same time. "What is it?" he queried as Halle entered the room. "I'm sorry about yesterday evening and I want to talk to you again in the morning. Perhaps we can deal with the train without getting sidetracked—sorry, the pun was unintentional—but you know what I mean." Ian smiled in the dark knowing she could not see. "That's fine. At least you apologised!" Halle turned on her heel and angrily slammed the door entirely forgetting about Teodor.

Ian slept well after his visitor left and she soon went to sleep mainly through vexation at being so silly as to apologise to an Orangeman who took no account of the difficulty it had been for her. Both were up and about early next morning but Ian was the first to speak, "Do you still want to talk?"

"I don't! But I promised Teodor to get this matter sorted out and that means having to endure this."

"It's a beautiful morning perhaps we could go down to the river and sit and talk there? The peaceful surroundings may help us to be the same!" Halle disdainfully nodded her head in preference to opening her mouth. "I hope this doesn't mean we are going to communicate by sign language?" grinned Ian knowing he had the upper hand in the confrontation so far. Making their way along the riverbank it was obvious that they wouldn't be able to agree on a place to have their discussion so Halle abruptly sat down and Ian, who hadn't noticed, had to turn back.

Neither of them spoke and seemingly each of them was enjoying watching two birds that sat on the very apex of a nearby conifer. At first Ian thought he had been mistaken as the birds had sat motionless making it hard to differentiate if there was one or two. But suddenly both turned their heads in opposite directions and he turned to look to see what was distracting them but having turned 180° he realised that the birds were being cautious, watching for hawks and other birds of prey. He drew Halle's attention to them wondering did she see them in a similar way to him. "The birds are nerveless in one sense but are on guard nearly all the time," remarked Ian, hoping to spark Halle into saying something that would correspond to his own position. "Do you mean about us being on the run from the Nazis?" Ian was anxious not to force words into her mouth and hesitantly said, "Partly."

"Oh, you're into symbolism now we've taken the edge off our dispute with literature as the punch bag? Be a man, spit it out. What do you think that little dumb-show meant to us?"

"No, I don't want to put ideas of mine into your head… you're right about symbolism. So what do you think?"

"It's beyond me—symbolism is like beauty, it's in the eye of the beholder."

"Ah, come on, you're opting out—the critics you're so fond of quoting often see perceived symbolism in a similar way."

"It's good to get on to literature but at the moment my mind's full of my parents. I wonder how they're surviving German bombing."

"I certainly hope they're OK, just as I hope my parents and family are the same."

"But they've been through so much in their lifetime it's a bit much that they now have to put up with bombing."

"Was it all that different from everyone else's grandparents?"

"I just don't know—everyone nowadays says 'it's all relative'. But I only know these experiences that my family have related to me."

"OK, point taken, but can you relate a story without a raw political point?"

"No difficulty. When my granny was small, she was the eldest of seven children; there was little or no room. Apparently you couldn't swing a cat— God I hate these clichés. Anyhow her grandmother came to live with them and space ceased to exist. But worse than that, from her point of view, her granny only spoke Irish—didn't have a word of English..."

"How could that be the worst part?"

"For God's sake, will you let me finish this story. Well when her mother went shopping the granny had no control of the children simply because they couldn't understand her. So when her mother came home granny reported every move they had made and she, who had previously been in charge, was relegated to being one of the rest of the family; see?"

"Well that's a first... not a political point made..."

"I could if you really want one..."

"Save me that. I can spot it from a hundred miles—British imperialism comes into it?"

"Exactly—so I'll leave it to keep the peace!" the emphasis in her voice coincided with her rising to her feet and Ian knew that the prospects of getting anything discussed, never mind the escape, were pretty negligible. As they made their way back Teodor appeared and announced that Aleksander was due to visit them in the next day or two. The sense of guilt hung in the air like a suspended sentence. As Teodor departed Ian turned and asked if they could start again, an innocent remark made in relation to the discussion they were supposed to be having. Of course Halle deliberately misinterpreted it and went on the attack once again. *"Start again!"* she roared, *"You have the unmitigated gall to suggest that!"* Ian held both hands up in surrender. "Hold it! Hold it! I was only referring to our discussion about the escape, nothing else!" Now Halle was completely flummoxed and put her hands over her face to hide her embarrassment. "I'm sorry, I've become so used to seeing offence in every word you say that I assumed you were doing it again."

Ian, anxious to take advantage of the new situation, acted to ameliorate the position, realising that if he acted as a helper in her difficulty in determining how they would handle the escape he could earn kudos. But despite all his efforts they failed to come up with a likely rôle for her.

Aleksander's return meant that there was to be some movement about their final escape plan. Ian didn't go to the Czerniawskis' farm that morning and waited for Teodor and Aleksander to complete their discussions. Halle didn't appear and Ian wondered if she was aware of what was going on, but dismissed this thought realising that she probably was lying on in bed as usual.

Teodor went outside looking for Ian and Halle but after a search only found Ian. "Where is your girlfriend?" and Ian was tempted to say something about the lack of relationship between himself and Halle. "I assume she is still in bed resting." Teodor walked with Ian for a moment before saying that Aleksander had been sent by General Bór-Komorowski to suggest a possible escape route, which had been put to him by his intelligence officers. "We were hoping that you could get us to Gdansk because I have a contact there." Teodor smiled, "Sorry about that, but Aleksander has been talking about the number of prisoners who never make it across to Sweden. Apparently there has been money put up by the Nazis to encourage our fishermen to inform." Ian couldn't believe what he was hearing, "I doubt if the guy I was told about was involved."

"Let us put it like this, if he wasn't, he was one of the few!"

"This sounds more like a story the Nazis would put about to discourage prisoners attempting that route."

"You may be right but if the AK are giving an assurance to get you and Halle to Sweden, I would take that rather than an uncertain character who may or may not be in league with the Nazis."

"You've sold me on it—wait until we hear from Halle."

It was the best part of half an hour before Halle appeared, weak and drawn. Ian felt guilty at her appearance thinking that the dispute with him was setting back the prospects of her making a full recovery. Briefly he told her that Aleksander wanted to talk to the both of them but he didn't attempt to influence her one way or the other.

They walked unhurriedly into the room where Teodor and Aleksander were waiting to give them the details of the General's plan. With a hug for Halle and a handshake for Ian, Aleksander greeted them as if nothing had happened to them in the interim between the escape from the Warsaw hospital and their return to Plock. "I trust that you are improving Halle. Going by your looks you certainly have improved considerably since you have left Warsaw." Halle shrugged and made a point of thanking Aleksander and his men for all they had done to save her. "But getting to the point of your visit, you must be desperate to have us on our way because we have been a constant thorn in your side the whole of the time."

"Nonsense, the General made a point of thanking you for all you succeeded in doing—even if you were not entirely aware of the implications. You gave us more than we could pay you in return. Anyway, to get to the point, the General, from a sense of obligation, has had our intelligence officers looking at a variety of ways of getting you out of the country. Ian had spoken to me about a man who operated a boat between Gdansk and Sweden. They made enquiries about him and found that he had been arrested by the Nazis on a tip-of and nothing has been heard of him since." Ian threw his hands up in horror, "It's unbelievable what people will do for money!"

"That was that possibility destroyed. However, not to be outdone, the men involved in finding a solution discovered that recently the German, British and American Governments have reached an agreement to exchange prisoners who are ill, probably close to death, either mentally or physically, on or around the 19th October. There are to be three movements, the first one is called the North Sea Movement; the second one is the First Western Mediterranean Movement and the final one is the Second Western Mediterranean Movement. The North Sea one is what concerns us as it leaves from Gothenburg in Sweden. Apparently a British hospital ship and transport are being prepared. They are carrying German prisoners from camps in the UK, USA and Canada; on the return journey they will be joined by a Swedish ship and bring back to the UK over 4,000 men who are to be brought to Gothenburg by the Germans. The great majority are British but there are a few Canadian and seventeen Americans. Our intelligence group thinks that this could be the perfect solution to our problems. It is evident that you, Halle, are still not fit enough to travel cross-country with Ian, even with our help—which, to put it mildly, would not amount to much as we are finding it increasingly difficult to travel around by road. So they have suggested this as the likeliest way of getting both of you to a neutral country, and the fact that it will be the Germans who will transport you there is the icing on the cake!"

However, the AK officers had warned that Halle needed a story round which they could forge the requisite papers but she had only a few days in which to come up with the scenario. Aleksander did not have the time to sit and go through the likely stories for them but promised that he would keep Teodor informed of any developments, particularly any in relation to the conditions, which would exist on the train. Teodor had been silent during Aleksander's speech and didn't mention that he had asked them for suggestions.

When Aleksander left Halle couldn't think clearly and was constantly going back to Teodor asking for ideas. His only contribution was to suggest that the story should be elaborately woven round how she came to have such a horrendous wound. In bed later that night Halle's imagination went berserk as she imagined herself as Hengist's mistress about to have his baby and attempting to get away from all the horror that her previous nightmares had concocted. Eventually she woke, drowned in her own sweat, and had to give herself a rub down before returning to bed in another attempt to get some sleep. Her second attempt wasn't any easier, she didn't know what brought this story to mind but was aware that it was slightly based on Ian's telling of meeting a black man on a train. The man had related where he had been and how he had been sent from place to place, as the Germans wanted to segregate the various races during their incarceration. "They soon gave up that notion when they started having problems with space. Still I suppose they did divide the areas in the camps to separate them." Surprisingly, she was relieved to find herself in a concentration camp but despaired when she discovered Hengist was the Camp Commandant!

The next day Ian had to call her a few times before she answered. "Have you anything worked out yet?" he wanted to know and rather than say 'no' she hedged her bets with 'some'. The next day it was a similar story: the nightmare and no answers to Ian's constant queries. Teodor had learnt there was a possibility that Aleksander would be able to produce a list of prisoners to be exchanged. The resistance groups had been informed so that there would be no accidental attacks on the train carrying those very ill men.

Two days later Teodor produced the lists of British prisoners to be exchanged. "God it's more like a gigantic book than a list," proclaimed Halle. "Surely there is going to be more than one train involved in this. Apparently there are four thousand two hundred men and already sixteen have died during the journey so far. Those that are dead are starred. If you can see a name listed as dead who was from the same area as you we can produce false papers that will pass. We have been making papers for both of you already so it won't take much to remedy them."

Across the room Ian's voice reached a high pitch, "I can't believe it, John Dickson is among those listed as dead! He and I joined the Army together. I knew he was seriously ill but to think he got this far and has now died!"

"I do not want to intrude on your grief but how did you compare with this man. You see your accent—coming from the same part of the world— would sound alike to a foreigner."

"He was taller than me but if he has been stretchered this far they wouldn't have a clear notion of his height. I can give you every detail you need to prepare the papers."

Ian, seeing that he was to pose as his late friend John, suggested that Halle should be his nurse both on the train and on the boat trip across to Sweden and the suggestion clinched the ideas that had already been developing in her mind. "There is only one difficulty with that, you're going to need a great story as a cover. You see the agreement calls for other prisoners to act as doctors, medical orderlies and stretcher-bearers and they will be repatriated as well. Which means that she will be the only woman on the train and possibly the only one on the ship."

Halle began telling the full story she had concocted to Teodor, which helped her to feel secure in the telling: "I was a nurse who had been captured at the fall of Tobruk last year but the German authorities accused me of spying, saying I had crossed between two armies carrying information on troop movements. Eventually I was cleared of all charges and was sent to work in a prison hospital in Poland. During my time there the AK had attempted a mass breakout of Polish prisoners and I was accidentally wounded. The German prison authorities had recommended that I should be repatriated and seeing that I have made such a remarkable recovery in the interim they wanted to use me as a nurse during the movement of the seriously ill. How does that sound?"

"There may be some difficulty but I think there should be enough experts to ensure you get them." commented Teodor. "I can only pray now that everything turns out well," said a tearful Halle, and Teodor putting a comforting arm around her, assured her that, "Given a little luck all should be well."

Ian was seen by an AK man who felt that his scars and thinness would help him to carry off the impersonation. However, if there were any detailed checking he doubted if Ian could bluff it but Ian told him he would consult Halle and see if she had any ideas. She, in turn, thought a great deal about the matter and decided that she had enough experience to carry off a deception of the Swiss Red Cross team who were looking after the prisoners on their journey. "The only difficulty is that they will have the prisoners' documents with them in order to show that the repatriations are genuine. The one big advantage we have is that the Germans have to stop to take on supplies, as some of the prisoners have had to travel very long distances indeed and she would be able to board the train at that point."

The plan she devised was simplicity itself, a cliché which she managed to choke back when she explained its ramifications to Ian. She would use her German credentials to speak to the officer in charge and she would tell him that she had information that implicated John Dickson in spying for the Allies and that therefore he would be held until he appeared before the courts. "Of course the officer will protest that the man is dead and I will demand proof. He'll show me the evidence and I will take it away to show my superior officer and tell him I'll return in a few hours with the papers. Hopefully the AK will have their experts there to make sufficient notes on which to base their reproduction of these documents, *voilà!*" Ian looked at her with apprehension, "You know it's always the simple plans that go awry! True?"

"We have been a mite unfortunate in the past. But we're too near getting away for me to allow anything to go seriously wrong! Do you think I'm a big head? Don't answer that!" smiled Halle.

"No I won't, but answer me this," turning to Teodor who had just entered the room, "When I finally get on this train and present the documents, which you and the AK produce, do you think that the Germans will have forgotten that John Dickson is dead. Especially if Halle draws attention to his having been a spy?" Halle, who had a pale pallor since her wounding, went even whiter. "Oh my God, you're right! What the hell are we going to do?"

"When this matter first saw the light of day, Aleksander thought that the best solution to the problem was for the AK to launch an attack in the vicinity of the train and in the subsequent panic the guards wouldn't notice a change in the numbers."

"But that has its own brand of weakness."

"Explain just how," said Ian looking wearily over her head. Halle started into the problem, "To begin with we're still going to need documents when it comes to the exchange, aren't we?" Ian's look of disdain was replaced with a look of despair, "This is rapidly becoming incapable of being solved. Any other ideas?"

"What if the AK simply steal all the papers from the train. For a group as good as they are, that doesn't sound as if it is beyond them, does it?" Ian held his hand up, "Wait a moment, we have not analysed any of the possible answers sufficiently, we need to give this more thought and stop jumping to possible conclusions. Are we agreed?" Teodor, who had been keeping out of the discussion, nodded and Halle wanted to know how much time they had.

"The AK, and more especially the General, want the information as soon as possible," commented Teodor in what he thought was a final authoritative remark. Ian in his normal, undemonstrative way said, "We're going to need help to sort this out." Teodor wearily replied, "I am going to Warsaw tomorrow to see Aleksander and I will tell him that we are having problems and we can see what they come up with."

The following morning just after Teodor left the house Ian made one final attempt to talk the issues over with Halle. "Can we talk about all these things that separate us in an objective way?" Halle's weary response didn't suggest there was any hope of a rapprochement. "Is this about the escape plan?"

"About anything you care to mention," answered Ian, tactically unaware of how much scope he was giving her.

"I still haven't figured a way round the difficulties. With all the silences between us it's very difficult to think straight," was the response of a somewhat withdrawn Halle.

"You wouldn't like to make a prophecy on what's going to happen?" innocently asked Ian.

"No. But then you don't take anything like that on board, do you?" said a rejuvenated Halle.

"You mean 'prophecy'? Depends on whether they're believable or not."

"I suppose you've heard of St. Malachy's prophecies?" asked Halle, knowing that it was unlikely but aware that she was leading him into an argument.

"No, I haven't and if he was a Fenian I don't anticipate any good news," Ian began to suspect he was being led into something and consequently his reply was more aggressive.

"He was a bit before them, that is the 19th century Fenians, but you're right as usual. Well he forecast that when the slips down at the shipyard are covered in moss the British will leave Ireland," Halle's sarcasm didn't escape Ian, and his reply spelled out his awareness, "Just how long ago did this Malachy prance about?"

"I knew the nasty words were just waiting to bounce out of your mouth. I think it was the 9th century," her high dudgeon left her unaware of the opening she had left.

"Ah! And Harland and Wolff didn't arrive in Belfast 'til the 19th century, so he would know a right lot about it. Halle I continue to be amazed at how someone as well educated as you could talk such prattle. Harland and Wolff will see us both into the grave, so why should a good Unionist worry? In other words do you never think before you open your mouth?"

"When I hear you talking about 'civil and religious liberty' I realise why the British are regarded as the greatest liars unhung." Having been wrong footed Halle couldn't resist another attempt to label the British as the cause of all of Ireland's woes.

"I can see we're agreeing to disagree again. That's fine provided you don't give me the silent treatment for another two days," were the wrong words if Ian wished to dispel the anger in Halle.

"If only you could find a sweet word in that evil mouth of yours that would compensate for your ignorance," made it clear to Ian that there was no room to manoeuvre but she took his ground from under him with, "Let's quit while we're in front. You know that I wouldn't hurt you for love or money." Even at this point she has to use horseracing parlance, thought Ian but instinctively said, "Ah! but you would for religion or politics!"

"You're determined to keep this going. Well, I'm away so that I can't be accused of being the one to foment this situation further," which was ironic, thought Ian considering that she had deliberately staged the whole row. He then went back to his room and Halle determined to find somewhere else to stay even if it was only a matter of a day or two.

CHAPTER 17

(October 1943)

ILONA WAS RELUCTANT at first to take Halle into her home, even though she knew the child would love it. She didn't want Ian to see her as taking sides in their dispute—whatever it was about. However, on reflection she decided that she could do nothing else and seeing it was only going to be a couple of days at the outside thought it would do nothing but good as she and the child could do with the extra company.

Manya and Halle already had a good relationship and Ilona put her uncertainties to one side and welcomed Halle wholeheartedly. Curious as she was to know why the two Belfast 'lovers' were no longer together, she held her tongue and accepted her father's version of events. According to Teodor, "They had had a lover's tiff," whatever that may mean. At any rate it was something he had elicited from Ian but didn't have the nerve to ask what precisely it meant.

"There are great advantages from having Halle here, not least her ability and keenness to look after Manya—it is wonderful to hear them converse in a strange mixture of Polish and English with the odd colloquial word from Ireland tossed in. Another thing, it enables me to get out to visit you," she explained to her father but in her mind the dominant thought was: "It won't be long before Halle would be on her way to Gdansk."

Halle's first day there was idyllic—the summer days were already deepening into autumn and brought memories of home, her parents and her brothers and sisters travelling to the more remote parts of Ireland; journeys which invariably ended with them riding on jaunting cars to their destinations.

A memory, which came to mind constantly, was of their trip to the Aran Islands. Each day the family walked to, what seemed to be the permanently isolated beach. But on one occasion, while her father and mother went timorously out into the water, she fell asleep only to be wakened shortly afterwards by a loud call from a young Irish mother to her children playing nearby: "An bhfuil ocras oraibh?" Halle, almost instinctively responded, but just stopped herself in time from shouting, "Ta ocras orm!" The recollection brought her back to the present and her hunger, which had probably sparked the thought, causing her to return prematurely to Ilona's cottage.

Teodor was in the cottage talking to his daughter when Halle returned.

He greeted her with a smile and a hug. "We're having a final meeting in my place to go over this plan that has been sent from Warsaw to get the both of you on to the train. That means Aleksander and myself will be there as you will be leaving immediately afterwards. So tomorrow, make your way to my place, around eight o'clock."

"*In the morning?*"

"Now do not be joking about it; you will forget if you do."

"Teodor, that's a condition which occurs at your time of life!" she said laughingly. But Teodor was quick with his answer, "'Do not mock the afflicted', is that the expression, 'because one day it will be your turn'?; if I had Ian staying a few days longer I would be spending the rest of *my* days translating these expressions into Polish!" He didn't stay long as he was expecting his friend's arrival at any moment and, sure enough, when he got home he discovered Aleksander talking to Ian. "Are you staying the night here?" asked Teodor. "Yes, if you do not mind and I would like to make it an early night as we all have to get back there before tomorrow afternoon."

The next morning, when all had gathered, Aleksander began: "The General and his aides have agreed on a strategy. They won't attack the train but will blow up a small piece of the line and stage a mock battle. We have had the carriage identified which contains the documentation of all the prisoners and we intend to set it on fire—nothing excessive, just sufficient to destroy some of the records to cause confusion in Gdansk and also in Sweden. At the same time, another group will be making sure that you and Halle get aboard and are settled. I have the nurse's uniform for Halle somewhere among these things," and he hunted among a collection of parcels he had. "I will find it before I go to bed and give it to you."

"Won't we look out of place, especially Halle, because she's bound to be noticed in that uniform," argued Ian.

"What you must remember Ian, is there is a constant change because at some stations they will pick up new patients and you will be taken as a recent addition. In any event you won't be able to speak—for God's sake remember you are seriously ill." Aleksander turned to Halle, "By the way, Teodor told me that you and Ian have had some disagreement—I trust that you patch it up soon because the last thing we need is discord, especially as you will need to act together." Halle acknowledged the truth of his assertion by dropping her eyes, while Ian looked carefully away from her.

Aleksander continued, "So far the train has been held up on a few occasions by air-raids, the need for additional medical supplies and of course, the need to change crews and guards. Naturally it is making our job difficult assessing where and when it will be close enough for us to get you to the train. It should be here, near Warsaw, this evening. Most importantly, I hope you have not forgotten Hengist is still trying to find you," looking at Halle. "Ian you will need to be back in that bundle of rags you call a uniform leaving here. I am sure Teodor can lend you a coat to cover it. Any questions?" For the first time in days Halle and Ian looked at each other. Ian indicated with his hand that she should speak first but she had nothing to say and Ian mildly said, "You seem to have covered everything."

The embarrassment Halle had felt being addressed by Aleksander in such a way soon turned to shame. After all that had been done for her by the AK, and for their representative to have to speak to her in such a disapproving tone left her determined to do something about it. The breach had to be healed—not through any romantic aspirations as one of her voices had suggested—but to ensure that the whole programme concocted by the AK would work. After the meeting she waited in the hope that an opportunity would arise naturally for her to broach the subject. She was pleasantly surprised when Ilona arrived with Manya to wish them well. The child rushed to her and threw her arms around her and the suddenness of it all left Halle breathless but when Ian re-entered the room the child made a dash for him and gave him the same treatment. Ilona chuckled at her child's handling of the pair, having meted out the same punishment to both. "How did you manage her and you so weak?" enquired Ian of Halle, and she, determined to be amenable, spoke with kindness, "I'm fine but I can see that you are as scrawny as you were that day when I saw you for the first time in years," laughed Halle, to which Ian, maintaining the camaraderie associated with memory replied, "I shouldn't have any trouble bluffing the Germans into believing I'm seriously ill at any rate." Seeing the way things were going between the two, Ilona called Manya saying they were there to see the child's grandfather as well before he left.

On their departure from the room the rush of words suddenly dried up as each eyed the other in their somewhat dishevelled state. Ian eventually stuttered into words, "I... I suppose you came to see how we're going to manage?"

"That's it! Aleksander meant it when he said he wanted some sort of an agreement to be hammered out... No! No! Not that word. To be found."

"Halle we can get along just fine, provided we avoid those areas which we both know cause arguments." Ian looked outside when he heard the child and her mother approaching. Ilona apologised before making a request, "Halle would you mind looking after Manya for about half an hour. I have asked my dad to get me some things for decorating while he is in Warsaw so he wants to see exactly what is required."

"Not at all, go ahead," and then realising about their need to be ready for Aleksander, shouted after her, "I hope he's cleared this with the boss?"

"Oh yes he has," shouted Ilona in reply. Manya ran after her mother waving her farewells and once she was out of sight she resorted to play, hollering and whooping about in her grandfather's garden. Halle immediately ran out to see if the child was in any trouble but she was just enjoying herself. Manya thought Halle was pursuing her and ran harder to avoid being caught and Halle soon realised that she wasn't only amusing Manya but that there was another pair of eyes following her every move. Although she knew she was not exactly helping the situation that she wished to exist between them, she was reluctant to stop but did when she felt that the issues could not be left to a few sentences. When eventually they returned to the house it was clear that Ian, who insisted that she should get ready, was fearful that their isolation would turn into some kind of confrontation and he was uneasy as to how they should begin, especially with the child present.

In an attempt to keep the tensions between them low, Ian asked Manya would she like a drink of milk and a biscuit and when the child accepted offered Halle a similar treat. They sat down and talked freely in the presence of the young girl. "I think we have too much to lose to be constantly at one another's throats," Halle tentatively began. "When I thought of the efforts made by so many people to free me, and that includes you, from the clutches of Hengist and then I had to be spoken to about my attitude by Aleksander— I don't think I've ever been so embarrassed in my life. It is not enough to be sorry, I am distraught at the pain and suffering I've caused."

"Please Halle, don't. There's nowhere to go with this. Both of us must be the laughing stock of every Pole who has met us. I'm certain that when they're stuck for a topic of conversation they bring up the shenanigans we've been up to while here." They were interrupted by Manya asking could she play outside: "I'd better keep an eye on her, she's capable of running anywhere when she spots something new," responded Halle. Ian followed her out and together they spent most of the half hour playing with the child and as a consequence enjoyed each other's company, Ian, particularly feeling a glow of contentment at what he thought was a renewal of Halle's interest in him. But his alter ego was far from happy with this revived Ian, "She's here to ensure that the escape works, not to re-engage the emotional traumas of the past!"

Halle knew she needed to start packing some of the clothes she needed, "Is that everything we had to discuss?" Ian wondered aloud and in the same moment wished he had not spoken words that he knew would hasten the

277

end of their conversation. "Yes, I think that that's everything; are you happy with it?" Clearly she was making a concerted effort to keep the talking going. "Yes, I know there will be problems we can't foresee but with our intention to work together we should be able to overcome many or all of them," replied a confident Ian, who went on, "The child seems to have enjoyed herself at any rate." Halle was quick to give him credit, "I suspect it's your presence—a young man is something she must miss in her life."

"I hadn't thought of that—you're probably right but I suspect she will be one of millions when this war ends—that is if it ever does."

"It will be no consolation to her as she grows up…" The shooting was loud and clear; the sharpness of a single crack at odds with the burst which followed but Halle reacted instantaneously throwing the child down while Ian, reacting just as quickly, threw himself on top of Manya as Halle attempted a similar feat. "Where is that coming from?" yelled Halle. "I've no idea," yelled Ian getting slowly to his feet and helping the child up. Aleksander burst into the room wanting to know from which direction the burst of gunshots had come. Ian shrugged and turned his attention to the child, "Are you all right Manya?" he asked while at the same time gazing round the garden and the house trying to assess the likely origin of the gunfire. "She doesn't understand English," cried Halle and she spoke to the child in the mixture of languages, which seemed to mean something to the both of them.

"I've never been able to establish the direction of shooting, even on a shooting range!" explained Ian to Aleksander.

"It's bound to be near," said Aleksander as he made his way to the door. Halle, in a more even tone, attempted to control her more immediate fears; "Perhaps both of you should check around while I look after Manya, she is disturbed more by our reactions than the shock of the shooting." As Ian and Aleksander left, Halle returned to trying to pacify the child. Leaving the investigation to someone else was somewhat alien to her but she reminded herself how she had left so many things for them to do when she was confined to hospital, "Please God, don't let it be anyone associated with me. I couldn't deal with the guilt of being responsible for whatever has happened!"

Aleksander and Ian very cautiously left the garden and went along the road where they imagined the sounds had come from. The only habitation in that direction was Ilona's cottage and Aleksander couldn't believe that anything horrible could happen in such an idyllic place. They were about to retrace their steps when Aleksander saw the Czerniawskis running towards them, some hundreds of meters on the other side of the cottage. Aleksander immediately hid behind a hedge, "I do not want any of the locals to see me because if this involves the Nazis there will be revenge attacks of a worse order if they know I was in the vicinity." Ian nodded and began running towards them now convinced that somehow Ilona and Teodor were involved. He, being younger and closer to the house, was the first there. Ilona and Teodor lay on the kitchen floor covered in blood while the remains of a green distemper, which Ilona had been using to paint the walls, was spilt and it looked as if the falling bodies had knocked the tin over. In her hand Ilona had a revolver of some kind and although he was aware of it Ian was more concerned to see if either of them was alive. He quickly knelt beside each of them in turn to check if there was any sign of life but dissolved into tears, as the horror of what had happened suddenly hit him. A home which Ilona had been decorating intending it to be a place of happiness had been turned into a slaughterhouse. Andrzej Czerniawski arrived breathless and gave a howl of anguish when he saw the figures stretched out in front of him. He yelled and screamed at Ian but the young man could not understand and he continued to cry and by now he was much closer to hysteria. Andrzej shook him to stop him screaming and once he got control of himself he instinctively reached down and lifted the gun from Ilona's hand.

The old man turned and left obviously attempting to stop his wife seeing the terrible orgy of bloodletting which had been let loose. "Halina! Halina!" he called but Ian knew that the man wasn't capable of words and rose to go outside, automatically putting the gun into his pocket. Once outside he realised how hopeless he would be in preventing the woman going in and as he turned to go back he hesitated when he saw neighbours coming along the road to investigate not only the shooting but also the noise of the shouts and the crying. He knew it was time to get back to Aleksander, Halle and Manya—there was too much to be done and above all they needed to get away.

As he rushed back he paused, thinking he should attempt to explain to Andrzej and Halina where he was going and why but he knew it would take an eternity to explain by means of sign language and undoubtedly some of the neighbours would be upon them and he couldn't distinguish between those who were aware of his existence and those that weren't. Instead he rushed on but decided to stop just before entering in order to calm himself and not upset the child. "Lord, what am I to do?" he begged, "Halle is bound to be distraught. How will I be able to break the news?" The door opened before he had an opportunity to think the matter through and Halle came out wide-eyed and anxious with eye-brows raised in a questioning mode. Ian beckoned her further out—away from the child—not because he thought Manya would understand but in order that if there should be any outburst of emotion from Halle he could attempt to stifle it.

Ian staggered from what he intended to be a gentle revelation of what had happened to a forthright description of the slaughter of Ilona and Teodor. Halle went from total silence to sobbing in its worst form—from the long sigh to the sounds of the voice cracking under the stress of emotions, which had already been strung out during the wait for Ian's return. Ian's attempt to comfort her was in vain; instead she pointed to the door, which he took to be an indication that she wanted him to see to Manya while she tried to stop the retching shudders which had taken over her body.

As Ian turned away her voices gave full vent to their bile: "Hengist has been after you—you knew it and you didn't attempt to stop Ilona returning!" another voice pre-empted her attempt to excuse herself because of her illness. "You never take responsibility for your actions, do you?" The rhetorical nature of the question didn't stop her voice from demanding a reply. Halle summoned up her stock answer, "I've always let others make decisions, that's the nature of being a soldier—obey the commands of your senior officer." The voice didn't allow her a moment's respite, "That's a great get-out isn't it? Right or wrong no moral responsibility—just the same as those who deposited the dead bodies outside that camp. You know they'll apply the same argument to what they've done, don't you?" and the remorseless pursuit of her went on in a fashion which she considered not dissimilar to that undertaken by Hengist. The tears began to flow but they did nothing to suppress that voice which continued to accuse her of guilt and reminded her that even Peter's tears didn't diminish his culpability in denying Christ three times. The thought had, intentionally or unintentionally, the effect of stopping her immediate concern with the self-loathing and the self-pity in which she had been indulging.

Now, with her emotions under control, she returned to the kitchen just as Aleksander returned. "I have been looking round the back of the cottage and I suspect that a German troop have been there. What was the situation you found inside the cottage?" he asked turning to face Ian. The Belfast man was still aghast at the slaughter but did his best to graphically describe what he had found, "You say that Ilona had a gun in her hand?" Ian nodded and Aleksander hazarded that she must have attempted to fire on them when they burst in and they shot her and Teodor. "I suspect it was against their orders which I imagine would have been to take her alive. Whatever the reason, we will have to get out of here." Halle was determined to speak her mind on the situation, "It's as clear as daylight that Hengist has sent his gunmen out to find me and somehow stumbled across Ilona and Teodor."

"No," began Ian vehemently, stopping in his striding about, "someone's pointed the finger. They have probably seen Ilona about and were aware of the situation in the hospital and the Germans' suspicion that she was involved in your escape. I would imagine it was someone who has worked in the hospital."

Halle's strong sense of guilt was somewhat ameliorated but she didn't want a debate as to how and why: "Please don't let us get into the realm of speculation at this point on who pointed the finger, if there ever was such a person. Do you agree with Aleksander's opinion as to what happened?"

"I do. You remember we heard the single shot fired first? It's pretty clear that they have burst in on them in an attempt to take them alive—after all they had more to learn from them alive than dead."

But Halle was more analytical and questioning: "Why didn't they comb the area there and then?"

"I can only assume that they were taken aback by the shooting and I suppose that it's possible that one of them was shot, so they withdrew to take stock probably assuming that it was the preliminary to an AK ambush." The more speculative Ian became the more agitated he appeared. Aleksander let them talk the issues out of their systems.

Halle now concentrated on what action was needed and asked Aleksander what they were to do: "For if you're right they'll be back shortly and where can we go?"

"I already have transport laid on to take us to Warsaw, I think that is the thing to do."

But already Halle's mind was on other matters, "Once Hengist gets a report on what happened here I'm sure, knowing him, he'll want to lead the search himself." Ian who had been tending to the child all this time agreed, "So we'd better put our best foot forward. Do you think we can placate Manya—or maybe that's the wrong word? Can you make her understand what we're doing?" Halle, in spite of all her practicality up to this, shook her head and began sobbing in spite of herself. "I can't tell her—even if I spoke Polish fluently I couldn't do it! What do you think, Aleksander?"

"I do not think the child could or would take it from me, even in fluent Polish!"

"Well can we just go and we'll figure this out later?" it was clear that Ian was beyond being able to determine what to do with the child. Aleksander left first in order to collect the transport, which he had deliberately left some way away. The others started for the Czerniawskis' farm conscious that the Gestapo could be around the next corner. However, they got to the farmhouse without any difficulty and Ian's familiarity with the house enabled him to find the cat, which he knew would keep Manya busy.

After a few minutes Andrzej came into the house, Halle, with a few words and many hand signals, conveyed Ian's and her own emotions at the death of Ilona and Teodor. Andrzej was no longer the man who had made them welcome all those weeks ago, it was obvious that he and all involved with him saw the both of them as the cause of their friends' deaths. "The quicker we can manage to get away the better," thought Ian and was glad that it was Halle who was doing the communicating. Andrzej was more concerned with Manya and Halle had made a number of attempts to get him to tell the little girl about her mother and grandfather but he too could not bring himself to explain their deaths to Manya.

At this point Ian intervened in an attempt to hurry the process along by writing Ilona's name and her sister's name, 'Wislawa', beside it. Andrzej spoke to the child and it was clear that he was telling her she was going to her Aunt Wislawa's house. But Halle stopped Ian to point out there were items in Ilona's house that they would require for the child: "Perhaps her baptism lines and photographs of her father and mother are there; but also any photographs of any of her relations plus her clothes." It was evident that Andrzej was not going back, at least not then. "He will collect them later and forward them to Wislawa," said Halle. "We have to get down to the road and meet Aleksander as quickly as possible."

Once they were some distance along the road Andrzej, with a great deal of caution, walked slowly back towards the cottage. He spied a half-track parked outside Ilona's house and was about to do a quick turn around back to the farm when he noticed approximately six Gestapo men on the road, seemingly carrying the bodies of Ilona and Teodor, which they quickly deposited on the floor of their vehicle. Other men emerged from the hedgerows and soon the half-track was heading away from him. Once the vehicle had disappeared around a corner Andrzej trotted up to the cottage and as soon as he was convinced there was no one there darted inside.

There was no trace of blood; indeed the painting of the walls had been completed. Andrzej recognised there was something terribly wrong with the whole set-up and suddenly realised that his wife Halina had not returned and he wondered where she had got.

Once on the main road Halle asked Aleksander if he knew Wislawa's address, "Yes, she lives in Teodor's family home on the outskirts of the Old Town near the Krasinski Gardens and Palace, we will take the little girl there." Aleksander drove at a steady pace and Halle assumed that the German soldiers didn't stop them because they assumed they were important citizens.

Halle and Ian were taken aback when they saw Wislawa's home. It was huge and set in grounds that were at least two acres in area—in essence it was a mansion but the greater shock occurred when they met their friend's sister and saw how similar Wislawa was in looks to Ilona. Manya was the first to react; running to her aunt with outstretched arms but Aleksander was the first to speak after Wislawa had put down the child. He began hesitantly and Halle warmed to him as he approached the subject sensitively, breaking the news of the deaths of Teodor and Ilona to the girl in a soft voice but she immediately crumpled, fainting with shock. Aleksander managed to catch her and Halle helped him bring her round but the girl was devastated and wailed continuously without anyone being able to console her.

CHAPTER 18
(October 1943)

STEPHAN SOBIESKI ARRIVED the next day when he learnt of the tragedies from Aleksander. "What happened Ian? Does anyone know exactly?" Ian immediately thought that the story must have been limited to saying that Ilona and Teodor had been murdered. "I can tell you what we found when we went to the cottage," but before he could enlarge on the story Aleksander arrived. He had received a message from Plock saying that Andrzej Czerniawski discovered Nazis removing the bodies when he returned to the cottage. But the most amazing part of the message was that Andrzej had found the interior had been completely decorated.

"What do you make of that?" asked Aleksander turning to Ian.

"There's something strange about the whole affair but I still suspect that someone in the hospital spotted Ilona and reported it to the Gestapo."

"Look Ian I haven't much time, nor do you, but I'd like your written assessment of what you think were the reasons for their brutal murders before you leave and if you can throw some light on the other events at the cottage I'd be grateful."

"I suppose I could write what I think happened initially but what happened later is beyond me," added Ian with much lifting of his shoulders and the spreading wide of his hands.

Stephan, who had been merely an onlooker, was more bemused than he had been at the outset, "What the hell is going on in that neck of the woods?" he asked in a loud voice in his own language. "You can bet your life that Bór-Komorowski will be torturing you with questions," he continued.

"Sorry?" began Ian but Aleksander was quick to translate it into more moderate English. Turning to Stephan he said, "I don't know what is going on in Plock. And I do not know *how* the General is going to take this." Turning, almost in despair, once more to Ian he asked, "Have you any ideas at *all* about the clean-up?"

"I haven't an inkling, this is away beyond me and I had hoped that we had merely to get on this train and say good-byes and that would be that but clearly it won't be!" and once again Ian's hands conveyed his feelings. Halle arrived after seeing to the child as Wislawa was still in a state of shock. It was her turn to be quizzed by Aleksander. She couldn't add any more than Ian had but thought it was unlikely that the slaughter had anything to do with Hengist. "It makes no sense to have these two people killed," ended her comments. Aleksander drew a line under the matter: "Forgetting that for the moment—come hell or high water—both of you will be on board that train this evening. Everything, in regard to papers, is ready and we will move the operation closer to Warsaw than had previously been planned but in other essentials nothing had changed."

When Aleksander left Halle had just settled down in one of the sitting rooms to study the documents when Ian came in, "I'm trying to study these papers before we get on the train this evening." Ian knew it was less than a subtle hint that he should leave but he persisted. "You realise that you will be in trouble with the British authorities once you land in the UK?" Halle put down the papers; "As a matter of fact I think I'll be in trouble with the Swedish customs and the police when we land there."

"You've thought about this and you didn't think of asking me about it?" Ian was trying not to let his fury overcome him. Halle could see his annoyance, so in a somewhat lower tone replied: "You haven't been very interested in me in the past few weeks, have you?" Ian immediately changed his approach: "But this is a different business altogether—leaving aside our differences I don't want you jailed over your past activities." Halle smiled, "Well thanks for that anyway. If you want me to spell out what I intend to do when we reach Sweden, I can sum it up 'nothing'!" Ian was surprised; "You're just going to chance it?" Halle shrugged and made a face, "I figure there is a better opportunity for me to escape in England than in some foreign country where I don't know my way around—besides what would happen to me if the Germans invaded Sweden? After all they have done it to other neutrals. Apart from that hypothetical case, if I'm caught *there* I'll be interned for the duration of the war—how long is that going to be? No, I'll take my chances in England."

"I know I'll go with whatever you decide but I want you to take the worst case scenario that can happen to you in Britain and weigh up what is the best choice. Sweden may be a heaven in comparison to what awaits you in some of those British jails."

"Well I've heard stories of terrible treatment being meted out to Republicans and I suppose it's possible that I could get up to twenty years but I've never heard of anyone actually doing the time."

"But you're basing that on those who have committed terrorist crimes in the UK, your case is different."

"How do you mean, different?"

"They can charge you with being a traitor and working for the enemy in addition to the IRA charges. You said you came up with the idea of getting Irishmen to join the German Army from someone in the Great War, what was his name?"

"Roger Casement." Halle knew before he spoke that he had asked the question despite being aware of the answer. "*Sir* Roger Casement and what sentence did he get?" Ian's emphasis was not lost on Halle. "He was executed," this said *sotto voce,* "So you see what I mean?" Halle couldn't take much more, "I can't think of it now, I have too much to do before we leave for the train and that thought is quite enough for the moment. By the way, Ian, what did you do with Ilona's gun?" Ian looked perplexed, "Nothing, I was thinking of giving it to Wislawa. Why are you asking?" Halle's intense look suggested that she had already thought of a reason, "I was thinking it mightn't be a bad thing to have on the train in case we have to use force to get away." Ian's quizzical look also portrayed his anxiety, "You're not seriously thinking of shooting our way off it if anything happens?" Halle smiled one of her tight-mouthed grins, "Of course not." Ian still was not happy, "OK, I'll hold on to it."

"No, remember that you have to be a patient and where are you going to hide it? It's better if I hold on to it." Ian left to write the report he had promised Aleksander.

Konrad Poniatowski arrived shortly after Ian and Halle agreed to leave things as they were. Konrad and Stephan had been sent to go over the arrangements with them. Stephan drilled them by numbers because of his limited English and because of his training in the Army: "One, we will be at the track side; two, attack takes place; three, board train when told; four, keep up appearances—patient and nurse; five, have papers ready for guards; you boarded at Warsaw if asked." He then warned Halle to make herself familiar with her own documents but, more importantly, to memorise the details that the AK's medical people had suggested for 'John', namely that he had mental problems and was unable to speak properly, a condition which dated from the time he was captured and confined in hospital. Stephan then had to go through much of the same information for Konrad, this time in Polish.

Ian felt that he was being patronised and was amazed that Halle didn't show a similar reaction. For her part, Halle was agitated by Ian's facial expressions which she felt must antagonise Stephan—of course she resented the didactic method used and of course she felt there was little need to elaborate on what appeared to be obvious but here she was, once again, indebted to the AK, so why would she show impatience in the face of people risking their lives for them?

The Belfast man knew all this but he wanted away without any fuss. He had endured enough because of Halle and often with no regard for his own interests yet he was treated like an enemy. Even now she couldn't support him by telling Stephan to quit.

Afterwards, when the two men left, the day dragged by for Ian while Halle was totally involved with Manya and her aunt. The little girl was easily amused and she proved to be a godsend in distracting her aunt from the depths of despair she had reached. Halle consoled the aunt as best she could but noted the considerable differences in strengths between the two sisters in spite of their lookalike appearance. She also took advantage of the circumstances to ask Wislawa about her husband and her beautiful home. "I assumed that your husband was wealthy but I just remembered your father telling Ian and me that he came from an aristocratic family, so it's possible that you are the wealthy one!" she laughed, more at her insolence in asking than at anything humorous in what she had said.

Wislawa was slow to respond, "It is difficult to talk about these things when so much has happened. You were right in your assessment of things but no longer is it true. My husband, although a Christian, comes from a Jewish family and just a few days ago he was arrested by the Gestapo in his little jewellery firm in the city. My father's wealth came from estates in the country but because things are the way they are we have less and less income each year. Now the Gestapo closes my husband's business and he is interned in Treblinka concentration camp. I am at my wits end as to what to do."

"Can you afford to keep this place?" asked Halle sympathetically. Once again Wislawa took her time, "I had given it a great deal of thought before the latest news about my father and Ilona and I had made up my mind to leave here but where was the question bothering me then."

"Perhaps you could go to Teodor's cottage in the meantime," suggested Halle and the look on Wislawa's face indicated to Halle that it hadn't dawned on her before. On leaving her with her dilemmas, Halle reconsidered her opinion of the two sisters as having been made on too little evidence. Since hearing the problems Wislawa has to contend with she now thought that they were much more alike than she had realised.

Meantime, Ian was continually leaving the house to walk about the grounds in spite of having been warned more than once on the danger of being spotted. As the day wore on Ian was conscious that there was a sudden deterioration in the weather, "It's not a bit like home—October is a kind month in Belfast." The drop in temperature made him more aware of just how scantily he was dressed and the likelihood that it could get colder as the evening progressed. Inside once more, he remarked on the change and Halle wondered if she would be strong enough to stand for any length of time waiting for events to unfold beside the railway line. Ian, voicing his recollections of Belfast in September, interrupted her thoughts. Halle made a feeble attempt to be humorous: "It's pleasant back home then because there's a drop in the number of Orange parades!"

"I take it that this is a joke this time. Is it?" he asked with a tone of heavy sarcasm. "Of course it is—aren't you happy we're about to set off for home?" giving him a smile that he hadn't seen for a considerable time. "Yes I am but I'm frustrated that things haven't worked out the way I'd hoped." If it hadn't been for the nearness of the events of the evening, Halle would have insisted that he spell out what he meant by the phrase, 'haven't worked out the way I'd hoped'. However, she was determined not to let him undermine her happiness, "Ian don't let us drag up our past. Tell me this, what have you missed throughout this war?"

"Do you mean like family, food and frustrations?"

"No, I hear you on about them, like myself—no, your individual pleasures, your pursuits, the things you do when alone."

"Well I have an old gramophone, which I wind up occasionally and play old records—singers like Florrie Ford, Paul Robeson and Gracie Fields—they were records belonging to my parents and my older brother, from the late '20s and early '30s. When I had a shilling or two to spare I bought Crosby and Sinatra—they are my favourites and I certainly miss listening to them. What about your interests?"

"We had an old stand-up radiogram, I don't know what they called it when my people bought it but just like yourself I played their records, John McCormack, Al Jolson, Al Bowley. I didn't fancy Bowley much."

"Was that because he was English?"

"Partly, but I think it was more to do with his imitation American accent. Come to think of it—I didn't like Al Jolson."

"Break it to me gently, to whom did you like to listen?"

"If the truth be told, I used to buy, when I was flush, records about Ireland; ones like: *Who fears to speak of '98* and *O'Donnell Abú*."

"That would be the equivalent of a good Prod listening to the *Sash* or *Dolly's Brae*." The distaste on Halle's face conveyed her feelings but she still had to say something, "I hardly think so. That claptrap is part of the bigoted attitude to one side's religious beliefs, hardly the same thing." Ian could spot a row developing. "I can see you're getting het-up about it nevertheless." But Halle was adamant that she wasn't, "I'm not, as you so colloquially put it, 'het-up'. I'm merely stating a point that many another made before." Ian was keen to keep their conversation going and couldn't think of another topic, "I'll drop it if you like but anyone can see the major differences in our 'raring'." He thought that placating Halle was never going to be an easy task and he proved to be right, "That doesn't add up either, my father influenced my reading but he didn't affect my ability to think for myself. If it had have gone on 'raring' I would be English—am I glad I'm not!" she replied with a tight grin. "Ah, please… not that road again," complained a despairing Ian.

"You brought it up, didn't you?" and all Ian could do was to nod. "I never learn, do I?" while Halle tossed her hair and left to see to the child.

A car called for them that evening and took them a short distance past the railway station, Warszawa Gdanska, in the northern section of the city. The sun was just going down and Ian was aware of an eerie feeling about the countryside as the shadows grew longer and created an atmosphere of uncertainty caused by the illusion of changing shapes. From the constant movement of Halle's head he concluded that he wasn't alone in feeling this way. The rustling sounds as men crunched their way over fallen leaves into the places allocated to them for the 'ambush' added to the general discomfort already being felt because of the coldness that had set in.

"I'm damned if I understand these people putting their lives at risk," muttered Halle in Ian's right ear. "What are you on about?" irksomely replied Ian, content to deal with his discontent and nothing else. "It's been bugging me for the last few days. These people are at war, they're not members of the Red Cross." Ian tried to adjust his mind to this new concept of Halle's, "And your point is?" Halle took a deep breath, which Ian knew to be a condemnation of whoever was at the receiving end for their stupidity, "Why are they playing games out here when thousands of people are dying? Probably Wislawa's husband is one of them."

Ian deliberately sighed to show his weariness with the topic and with Halle's attempt to imply he was educationally sub-normal, "Do you want answers or guesses?" Halle perked up at his response knowing that she had touched a nerve and had managed to get him thinking about the issue, "I'll accept any one of them that gives even a sense of a near thing."

Now that Halle was starting to talk to him as if he was a human being Ian reverted to form by putting his next statement as open ended as possible, "Well, to pass the time—you go first with an idea." He couldn't see Halle's eyes flash with annoyance, "I'm bloody sure I don't. It was me that thought of it in the first place." Even if he couldn't see her eyes her tone of voice told him that he had hit a sour note, "OK, OK. How about this—it has got something to do with your friends the Brits." There was a distinct pause as Halle weighed the odds whether Ian was serious or joking, "You're pushing the boat out a bit, aren't you?"

In reality Ian had been joking, now he had to make a case for something he didn't believe or he could really annoy Halle by telling her he was joking— he stuck with the former. "Well the General indicated that there were Allies spying on the German High Command, so that's the Brits isn't it?" Halle began to sense that Ian was flying by the seat of his pants, "You know there's speculation and outright stupidity. Which one are you indulging in today?" A small titter of laughter indicated she had hit the nail on the head. "Look, I met a Canadian girl, not a Brit in the tender loving way you use the word. A Canadian working for her country in a way that I'd do for mine." Ian laughed to the annoyance of the men standing in the shadows. A chorus of "Shoos," greeted his outburst. "Do you think…" began Halle as the chorus grew louder as the sound of a very slowly moving train could be heard in the distance.

The 'shoos' echoed around them as each man moved to his allotted position on either side of the line. Aleksander appeared out of the gloom taking a last opportunity to wish them well. It seemed that eternity had taken over prior to the train reaching them. On the other side of them Ian heard movement and he nudged Halle and then pointed to the barely discernible figures moving on to the line. Both of them grew tense as they awaited the sound of the explosion.

The explosion when it came, although expected, still caused them to jump and Ian heard Halle counting out the order of events to herself and thought that she was a trained soldier—more than he ever was. They both stood still as the train chugged to a halt with the driver and fireman waiting on the report from the guards on the damage to the line. The German soldiers dismounted and ran helter-skelter in the general direction of the explosion. As soon as they were a sufficient distance up the track the AK set fire to the carriage, which someone had earmarked as being the one containing the documents.

At this point Ian and Halle were bundled towards the train and Ian felt hands pushing him down on to a stretcher. "So much for the counting of numbers …" he grumbled as two hefty looking individuals lifted him and the stretcher aboard the train. They didn't travel far inside the coach before they were set down on a pre-prepared bed. Ian immediately placed himself under the bedclothes and Halle took off the coat, which concealed her nurse's uniform, and handed it to one of the stretcher-bearers. The two men rushed to the door and no sooner had they left than the rifle fire ceased. The German soldiers soon regained their composure and rushed back in an attempt to save the carriage, which held the documents. However, there was nothing to save and they were forced to stand and watch the flames devour the carriage.

An hour later they uncoupled the burnt out carriage and manoeuvred the train back to a junction where they were able to shunt the unwanted debris to one side. They then stopped the train where they could wait 'til morning, when there would be sufficient light to check if there was any damage to the line. Ian fervently hoped that the AK had done something, otherwise there could well be an official investigation and that was the last thing they wanted. He wasn't to know that the AK were well versed in the art of dupery and although the line was damaged, it was superficial and it had been made to look as if the device had only partly gone off.

Once the train came to a halt, doctors and nurses went on their rounds checking how the patients had managed during the 'attack'. Halle was quizzed about herself, so she produced the papers which entitled her to be on board the train. Regarding 'John's' health she was adamant that his papers had already been forwarded to the authorities in Berlin and that she was only provided with her own documents. She explained that she had been appointed to take care of John but he had a mental condition and she was not specifically trained in the care of that type of patient. The doctors proceeded to take Ian's blood pressure, temperature and pulse before leaving. Halle gave a sigh of relief, "Please God, let that be the end of the questioning!" she prayed and patted Ian on the back as she passed.

It was only when she walked down the corridor that she saw how much effort the AK had put into the job of convincing the Germans that it was a genuine attack. The windows were shot out in such a manner that it would have been impossible to know that the bullets were aimed high deliberately. Whether some were stray or otherwise did not concern her: she was on her way home and that was all that mattered!

Although it was only a matter of an hour or two for crew members to repair the line the Red Cross officials were hugely put out by the 'attack'. They were anxious to send a communiqué to the British that the agreement on repatriation could not be upheld if there were any more attacks on the train containing prisoners. Naturally the German officers on board concurred with the sentiments proclaimed in the message, so they were able to get the Gestapo to act quickly and relay the messages through intermediaries.

Back in Berlin, Herr Oberst Hengist received a request from a staff officer who wished to see him about a message that had been intercepted from the British to the Red Cross. The staff officer appeared looking nervous and told Hengist that the contents appeared genuine on first reading but the speed of the reply was worrying. "Just how quick was it?" asked Hengist.

"Herr Oberst barely a day. From the message it is clear that the German Army Group in charge were told of the Red Cross's concern about the attack." Hengist didn't betray his feelings but it was obvious that he was startled. "Is there anything odd about this train other than it is the first exchange of prisoners?" The staff officer fidgeted with his tunic buttons, clearly he was uneasy about the whole business. "Come on man, out with it!" He cleared his throat; "Well we just received information about the affair from those officers on board but the damage to the line was so small that it was repaired by the train crew..." Hengist interrupted him, "But these amateurs are forever setting the devices wrongly; there is nothing new there. Is there anything else?" By now the man was sweating profusely, "There was a considerable number of windows shot out and the carriage containing the documents relating to the prisoners and their illnesses was destroyed. The officer on board is very suspicious that something is going on. His experience of the AK suggests they don't bungle operations of this nature, unless they are up to something else."

At this Hengist stood up and began stroking his chin with his right hand and suddenly changed the direction of his questioning, "To whom, in the Gestapo, was this message passed initially?"

"Sir, do you mean the reply?"

"Don't be bloody stupid! You're here telling about the bloody reply—so it's unlikely to be that, isn't it?" Hengist's anger began to abate. "To whom in the Gestapo did the Red Cross pass their message?" he asked in a slow measured voice hinged with heavy irony.

"I don't know his name, sir."

"Do you know who received it here?"

"Sir, I received it."

"Look man, I could tell by your demeanour that you were involved. Did you not think it sufficiently important to tell me?"

"Sir, I thought it was merely a bureaucratic note of complaint, nothing more."

"You may still be right. Did the officer on board say anything else?" The staff officer continued in an agitated manner where he had left off, "He pointed out that with the constant addition of new patients throughout their journey it had been difficult to deal with their papers. But now he says it is almost impossible to keep track of anything seeing all the documents were destroyed in the attack."

"How did the interpreter react to the intercepted message?"

"He said that it was a very feeble response, which he instinctively felt was a cover up which is why he drew my attention to it immediately."

Hengist looked the man directly in the eye, "What does the officer on board the train recommend?" For the first time the man spoke with conviction: "He would like us to send an investigating officer to Gdansk to meet the train."

The train took almost twenty hours to cover the three hundred and thirty kilometres from Warsaw to Gdansk and Halle who was familiar with European measurements worked it out roughly as being nearly two hundred and ten miles. When the opportunity arose she whispered to Ian that they had arrived but it would take some time to take the prisoners off the train. "How long have I lain here?" he asked and when she told him and the distance travelled he was at a loss. "We had to stay out of stations at night and so during the hours of darkness we couldn't move in case we were accidentally strafed by the RAF. It didn't mean much to me the Brits are always after me! The Germans and you Orangemen are not used to it!"

Ian realised Halle was taking advantage of his curtailment to get a series of humorous digs about the tie-up between the Germans and the Orangemen prior to the start of the Great War. "And you being so British that you'd fight them!" Ian spluttered his answer as he realised that some nurses nearby were listening and obviously wondered what was going on between the two of them. Halle was quick to tell the German nurses that she had been told to remind him occasionally of his past life in Belfast in order to encourage his recovery.

When the nurses moved on Halle apologised about her sense of fun but told him how lucky he was to have slept through most of the boredom. She, on the other hand, never slept because of the tension and the uncertainty of what awaited her in Gdansk and wherever the boat would dock in Sweden. A German officer came round to inform the various nurses and the Red Cross officials that there was some hold-up and the vehicles which were due to meet the train would be at the railway station within the next hour or two.

Halle told Ian at the first opportunity and he was more annoyed at having to be accompanied to the toilet than at the time involved in waiting. In the small cubicle at least they could speak openly, even though they had to speak in whispers.

"What do you think is going on?" began Halle. "Probably nothing; why are you so determined to make something out of nothing?" Ian's irritability was starting to show. "I'm suspicious, is that all right with you?" Halle's anger was as much to do with Ian's unsympathetic approach, as it was to her nervousness about the on-going situation. "Are you clairvoyant

293

or what?" came back Ian in a voice breaking with the effort needed to maintain a whisper. "Will you move outside, I'm desperate to go here?" Halle smiled when she realised why he was so edgy, "I'm sorry I thought you wanted down here to have a conversation!"

While the train had been on the move, even if it was very slowly making its way to Gdansk, there seemed to be calmness in their carriage. But with daylight and the knowledge of their being in the terminus, the patients were clamouring to be outside in the air. If the first hour dragged by the second one was too much for the doctors and nurses, never mind the patients. Eventually they demanded to be unloaded and put on the platform.

The Red Cross officials had no difficulty with their demands but Halle noticed that the German guards were particularly edgy at the suggestion. "I hope you're watching Ian. The Gerries are up to no good—they *are* deliberately holding things up!" Ian had learnt to put some faith in Halle's sensing things that were in the air—it could be frightening if she was accurate all the time but that's what made it difficult, he never quite knew when to heed her and when not. The movement of her hand to the waistline of her skirt caused him to forget his rôle as a patient and he grabbed her hand aware that she had the gun in it. "For heaven's sake, what are *you* up to?"

"Hengist has just arrived on the platform outside!"

The German nurses, en masse, launched themselves on Ian convinced that he was attacking Halle. In the melee Halle was dragged down the corridor to the 'protection' of the nurses' carriage. Eventually, when they had Ian 'under control', another struggle occurred when they attempted to put him in a straitjacket and remove him to an isolation section further down the train. While there had been some doubt, in the minds of the German officials, and indeed among some of the Red Cross team on board, about their authenticity, Halle and Ian were in jeopardy. Now it was patently obvious that the prisoner *was* seriously ill and that Halle *was* doing a job for which she had no training!

"How are you now?" asked the German doctor. "Pretty shook up," answered Halle, "and I have this mark on my face which I suspect I got when the nurses rushed to my rescue." She nearly asked about Ian directly but remembered just in time to change the name, "Is John recovered?" The doctor explained about his needing to be detained in the isolation room until they got him off the train but he doubted if the Red Cross medical team would contemplate his release from the straitjacket until they reached Sweden. "Have you any idea what caused him to go berserk?" Halle hesitated knowing it would be interpreted as her trying to remember precisely what happened but instead it gave her the opportunity to make-up a story. "I think it was the delay in getting the patients off the train that upset him. I found it hard to keep him on the stretcher and I was attempting to make him comfortable when he grabbed me. I really don't think he knew what he was doing." The doctor sagely nodded his head; "In such a situation disturbed patients are likely to act in a violent way. You are lucky you were not hurt more seriously. I would like you to stay away from patients until you feel better. Indeed stay here until you are moved to the ship."

Halle was relieved to be away from the crowd that Hengist would undoubtedly be examining. "Something has gone terribly wrong! How could he have possibly associated me with this repatriation train? Everything has gone so perfectly up to now. Clearly the train was held until he arrived. What does that mean? Perhaps it means that he has heard something that made him suspicious or worse, from our point of view, would be if the AK has a spy in its midst. It must be the latter, how could he have known about us boarding the train?" She fell asleep and woke a few minutes later; "Does Hengist know Ian?" She couldn't remember them ever meeting, "But that doesn't mean that he hasn't seen him, he could have been spying on him when I was in hospital!" Her thoughts went on torturing her the whole time that she was on the train.

The process of removing the patients from the train was a painfully slow one and apart from this slowness an objective observer would have been overcome by the state of each and every one of them. Some were blind, some had missing limbs, others were suffering shell shock and the vibration of their bodies told of some of the horrors their minds were having to deal with each and every day. Finally they took Ian off the train under guard and Halle watched his departure down the platform to be placed in a military ambulance from the safety of the nurses' carriage. The doctor who had treated her returned to escort her to the truck, which was provided for the medical staff. Halle was conscious that Hengist was somewhere in the station and pointedly used a towel to cover her face. To the doctor and others it was to cover the scars of 'battle' or as a protection against the cold wind which whistled between the platforms but in essence, it was to hide her identity from prying eyes.

Once through the gate at the end of the platform Halle felt more secure and less concerned about her face. She was about to leave through the main entrance hall when she noticed a German soldier looking at her with above average interest. Suddenly he sprang to attention and in a loud voice began, "Heil Hitler! Herr Oberst," then mumbled something under his breath, "Frau Oberst." Halle knew it was Boehme, the solid Saxon, who had driven her to some camp or other. She decided, on the moment, to avoid any involved explanations, which would require lying of an exceptional standard and was relieved, in the middle of a weak wave to Boehme, to see that the doctor was saluting assuming that Boehme was paying him some respect. He had assumed that the salute was for him and thought that the man had been somewhat confused about his rank and consequently the mumbling.

Halle's walking improved immensely in the short walk to the truck and she was thankful that there were no delays on embarkation at the docks. Once on board she asked permission to see her 'patient' and although the new doctor knew little or nothing about this man, he warned her not to release him from the straitjacket until he was confident that he posed no threat to anyone on board. Reluctant as she was about his conditions she agreed knowing that the prospects of her seeing Ian were remote otherwise, seeing that she herself was a prisoner, if not a *bona fide* one.

"Thank you very much for this confinement!" began Ian when she reached the ship's prison. "And I'm not talking about this room! Come on get me out of this jacket, it's the most damnable experience of my life."

"Oh, it's a bit like what we Nationalists and Republicans endure. Ignore that Ian, I'm sorry—I was trying to be facetious. I asked that they permit you to be released from it, seeing that you were locked up but they wouldn't hear tell of it. The doctor on board says that once he is convinced you are not a danger to the people here he'll release you." Halle was anxious to both placate and distract Ian, being conscious that she had been responsible for his predicament.

"Once again thanks very much. Once again I try to save your life and I'm the sufferer for it. How many times have I said, 'I'll never learn'? Well put another tick at it. As sure as God made little onions that's the last—you can do whatever you want, on your own, leave me out of it. You're a danger to whatever side you're on. Us Unionists can never be defeated as long as you're on the Republican side! The day you decide to leave them let me know; I want to leave the country before all hell breaks out!"

Halle's loud laughter brought the guard to the door to enquire if she was in any trouble. "Far from it. I think your prisoner is getting his senses back, although it may not seem that way." As the man turned away Ian begged her to ease the straps so that he could get some circulation going in his arms. "It's not often I get the opportunity to do a good turn for a Prod so I'm taking it now, because once I get home I'll be accused of being a traitor."

"I don't doubt that at all. Christian charity is in short supply on your side of the fence!" Halle pretended to be aghast at this reply, "That's bound to be a joke! You who rely on the Old Testament for your dictums accusing us of not being Christian! I think you're short of digs if that's the best you

296

can dig up! Whoops! I didn't mean that to be a pun." Halle's struggling attempt to keep the conversation on the light side was almost on the rocks to judge by Ian's straight face. It was crystal clear that he wasn't seeing the humorous side of things.

"Halle, do you think I couldn't have brought up more issues? Of course I could have; things like the Roman Catholic Church's insistence on children of a mixed marriage being brought up as Roman Catholics. Your insistence on being called Catholics as if your religion is the only worldwide church is abhorrent to most Protestants. What about the suffering of those whose marriages have failed and are unable or more likely not allowed to settle-down with someone else; is that not dictatorial? The list goes on and on ..." Halle's approach changed and she began to mirror Ian's: "Am I not allowed to answer?"

"You can once I've finished—I held my tongue so you try doing the same. OK?" Halle wavered for a moment and then agreed, "OK." But her echoing of his last word sounded weak.

"The list goes on and on—since the formation of the Free State in the south in 1923 the Protestant population is going down and down—is this just a coincidence? None of *us* believe that! Yet you want us all in a united Ireland—some hope, some joke!"

"Am I allowed to speak now?" Ian just pausing for breath was quick to respond, "Of course, we believe in freedom of speech, freedom to worship, freedom to think for one's self. Roman Catholicism on its own as a religion might be defensible. I say 'might' I don't know, but once it allied itself to some political group or nationalist opinion in any country then it seems to be capable of every evil one can think of." Halle, not aware that Ian had finished, took a little longer than usual to respond. She realised the subtlety of Ian's approach, knowing that if she condemned the Church for its attack on nationalism then Ian would claim that the whole Republican movement was hypocritical. But if she refuted his claim that the Church was connected to her Republican ideals he would ask 'why not' and she would be caught on the horns of a dilemma. "Personally I feel that every human institution is imperfect in some way or other..."

"Ah! You don't subscribe to the dogma that the Pope is incapable of being wrong?" What Halle took to be a malign glint in Ian's eye told her he saw an opening but this time she felt she was able to shut it, "But he claims no such thing. If he said Glasgow Celtic would beat Rangers the next time they meet, I might want him to be right but it's only a matter of opinion on his part. The Pope is only infallible when he speaks on faith and morals."

Ian immediately attacked her ability to spout out the formula given to her at school. "You're all indoctrinated. You have told me many a time about the evil of the Nazi propaganda system but your people introduced the term 'propaganda' to the world with all its propensity for diluting the truth!"

Halle felt that her strong position was being shot out from under her because of Ian's constant altering of the focus of his attack. "That's a different question from the one on infallibility; I could go on all night refuting your claims and then you would dig up some other disreputable argument that has been answered a thousand times."

"But not acceptable answers!" Ian, without the use of his hands, realised the whole argument was getting too serious and smiled at her in his best apologetic stance seeing how restricted he was. Halle managed to turn her back while she smiled, "OK, shut up or I'll tighten your straps for you."

The bantering had to cease at some point and Halle turned to more serious matters when she related her meeting with Boehme, at once Ian sat up from his slumped position. "Is that the big German on guard at the entrance?" Halle described him and Ian nodded, "That's him! He smiled and nodded to me when I was being escorted to the ambulance. One of the German nurses told me that I must be someone special, Jacob seems to be fussy about who he speaks to."

"Is that his name? I never was aware of that but then I only met him once before this," said Halle. "Didn't his name strike you as one that you've come across before?" asked Ian. "Jacob Boehme? No, I can't say that I have." Ian shook his head as if to enable him to remember where he had come across it, "I might be just imagining it." Eventually the guard knocked the door and told Halle that the doctor wished to see her.

In his puny little room near the patients Dr Johnston heard Halle's footsteps along the metal corridor outside his door. He immediately stopped writing and put the paper in his desk drawer. The knock came soon after, "Come in," he hollered to overcome the noise emanating from the ship's engines. Halle assumed that he was going to question her about 'John's' mental health and she wasn't disappointed. "How is he now, nurse?" and Halle enlarged on his improvement since boarding the ship. "I'd be happier if you took him out of the straitjacket. It's bad enough that he is imprisoned but both punishments are too much."

"I will be reviewing the position in the morning once I get an opportunity to see him for myself. But he is not directly the reason why I wished to see you. The captain was approached by, what he took to be, a Red Cross official just before we sailed and informed that you and the patient were bogus prisoners and that you were using the repatriation scheme to further your own escape. He, in turn, came to me to see if there was any way I could prove that you were not a nurse. Now I do not want to get involved in any of this but I want you to know that there will be an enquiry once we dock and both of you will be held until the matter is decided. Have you anything to say?"

"I can't believe that any Red Cross man would make accusations like that. Where is his evidence? Apart from anything else John and myself have documentary proof of who we are."

"I am not disputing anything, I am merely telling you what is the situation. As to the Red Cross man I can point him out to you when you are on deck for your hour's airing this evening."

Halle left in a distraught state. "I warned you that it wouldn't be all plain sailing!" her alter ego was back in full flow, puns and all. "Someone pointed you out, it's as clear as a bell!"

"OK, who? You're so clever give me a few names. You're slow to respond this time, aren't you?"

"Let's wait and see who this doctor has in the frame for it. I'm patient, not like your other patient!"

Once on deck Halle recognised just how the weather had changed. She shivered with the cold and with the apprehension that there was someone who could ensure that Ian and her would be interned for the duration of the war. Dr Johnston was slow to appear and those patients capable of walking were few in number, so those on deck could easily be identified as prisoners or Red Cross officials. Halle scrutinised each one but could not find who was likely to be the person responsible for her predicament. The doctor finally arrived accompanied by a man dressed for the conditions, a fedora hat pulled down over his face with a fur coat, which reached to his heels. Dr Johnston turned from the man and went directly to Halle. "I haven't seen anyone that I recognise," she said. The doctor was quick to correct her, "I did not say that you would know him. You asked me who would do such a thing and why. That man I came on deck with is the person concerned."

Halle stood back from the doctor to take a better look at the tall man who had reached the end of the deck and was turning towards them. "I can't see him because of the hat."

"Don't worry, he has a habit of removing it from time to time as if he is not used to wearing it. Just wait, you'll get a good look at his face." At that moment the official turned to walk back to the opposite end once more and Halle impatiently waited on his return. Halle was using the doctor to shield herself from the man and occasionally peered over his shoulder. Once more he removed his hat and a totally shocked Halle grasped the doctor's arm to stop herself from falling into a faint, "It's Hengist!"

CHAPTER 19
(October 1943)

"YOU MUST BE mistaken," was the initial laconic response of Dr Johnston. Halle was still in shock, "I'm not mistaken; he is an important member of the Gestapo hierarchy and I have met him on a number of occasions. Indeed, he is a personal friend of Hitler's."

"So you are admitting that you are not a genuine repatriated prisoner?" Halle was slow to respond so the doctor continued, "I have been to the captain and he assures me that his papers are in order and when he checked with a number of officials they said he had arrived from Sweden the week before last with a contingent of others. By the way his name is not Hengist, it is Eckberg."

"Doctor, I don't suffer from delusions; what I've claimed is that this man, known to you as Eckberg, is a dangerous person and yes, I am admitting that I'm here under false pretences because I'm attempting to get away from him. I wouldn't be saying all this if I wanted to keep up the pretence. However, John is a genuine prisoner."

Johnston was perturbed by her insistence, "I am merely a doctor and I am not here to take sides. You give me no evidence to support your statement so what am I to do? Now that I have informed the captain about you I can not retract my story."

"You ask what are you to do but what am I to do? My life's in danger; this man is capable of getting to me no matter where the Swedish government put me," replied Halle in a tone of fear. The doctor's calm dispassionate appraisal was antagonising Halle, "Paranoia—you insist that you are right but you present no evidence in support of your story. You make accusations, which seem to me to be highly improbable..."

"Such as what?" asked Halle in a heightened voice.

"According to you he is 'a friend of Hitler'—almost head of the Gestapo. Also you said he was in Poland but according to the evidence given to the captain he was in Sweden and then in Gdansk!" Halle was becoming more and more agitated: "I want to speak to those Red Cross people who said they came over with him. Someone is lying and it isn't me!"

"Are you asking me to go back to the captain and ask for names?" demanded the doctor, adjusting his jacket as he stood up.

"Yes, otherwise I am going to make one hell of a fuss whenever we dock!" Halle finished by abruptly standing up and the sudden action in such a small space exaggerated the possible violence that she threatened. "Very well! I am going and please calm down. Stay here until I get back."

Halle's act of defiance was just that—an act. Inwardly she was quaking with fear at the possible consequences awaiting her. She just hoped that she had found the one weakness in the story that could save her being interned. "What if the captain is part of the conspiracy?" began her voice. "Oh my God! I'm totally sunk if that's the case. Trust you to find a possibility I hadn't considered." The calmness of the voice's logical assertive certainty was maddening, "Sure it's logical; if you're telling the truth and I can testify to that, then some Red Cross officials are involved in helping the Gestapo. I can't take that on board—sorry about the pun—or it's got to be the captain. OK?"

Halle's mind closed down for a few moments, then it sprang back to life as panic set in. "I'll need help to get off this ship when it docks!" A lull occurred before her next thought, "At the moment I can't see the captain locking me up because I think the doctor would object—he suspects I'm on the verge of a nervous breakdown." Talking over matters in her head helped her to deal with complicated issues but the negative and soul destroying propositions put forward by her alter ego was a balance she didn't enjoy, "If the doc speaks to the captain about this you're done for. You know that the captain and Hengist will have to deal with you themselves—you'll never get near a Swedish jail!"

Halle's worst fears were systematically being built and by now she had come to believe that internment in some isolated part of Sweden would be more acceptable than this nerve crunching predicament suggested by her voices. Not all of them had come into play, yet! But then, there was no guarantee that they would speak again; she hoped against hope that that would be the case.

The footsteps approaching the room indicated that more than one person was about to enter. "If it's the captain with him you're dead meat…" began the solitary voice of despair but Halle quickly banished him from her mind. The doctor entered followed by a man she didn't recognise. "Before you get any more edgy, let me explain. This is a Swedish official who accompanied the Red Cross group from Stockholm to Gdansk. I thought that it would be wrong to approach the captain seeing he could be one of the people you suggest could be lying. Not quite how you put it but not bad for a Swede?" Halle agreed, "That was very sensible. I only thought of that after you left the room."

"I am more than a physician I am a head doctor, is that right?" Halle laughed, "I understand but the word is 'psychiatrist', you could be putting yourself in charge of all of this!"

"Good! If you are right and someone is lying I did not want to warn him as one of the wrongdoers. So I remembered this man who I had met when we were going over the details of the prisoners. I took him to see the man you say is a high official in the Gestapo but I will leave him to tell you what he knows." The man offered his hand and introduced himself; "My name is Eckberg and I was told that the man Dr Johnston pointed out to me was an overseas observer to ensure that the agreement was carried out to the letter."

"But surely that was your rôle along with the Red Cross men?" Halle's quizzical look indicated her lack of confidence that she had acquired in Berlin. "Yes, we were highly suspicious of him and the officials with me have already written a report for their HQ." Halle looked at him with horror, "Do you realise that I am liable to be killed by this man and all your friends can do is write a report?"

"I have nothing to do with that and I am not in a position to enlarge on what my rôle is. However, because of what I told him, Dr Johnston has changed his view of your behaviour and we have agreed—provided you agree—that you will be the first person taken off the ship and handed over to the British authorities." For a moment Halle was pleasantly surprised but her voice resounded through her head, "Personally I would rather take my chances with Hengist." Mr Eckberg spoke to the doctor as he left and immediately Halle asked the doctor what she had missed. "Mr Eckberg said we will probably find the captain is of German origin or has relatives there and is being blackmailed—on the other hand, as I pointed out to him, he could be a Nazi!"

"How can he speculate on such matters? Why doesn't he add he could be a traitor or a mercenary?" Halle was roused by what she suspected was a typical neutral's response. "I suppose he could but I suspect he is a policeman and he is telling what he thinks is the more likely situation." Dr Johnston's placidity was adding fuel to the fire and Halle was quick to voice her concern at the standing back of so many, "My God, this war has touched the depths of depravity in so many ways that I can scarcely believe that human beings could do such things. But what hurts is that so many watch and merely raise their hands in disgust!"

The doctor was getting annoyed with this 'patient' who had been quick to seek his aid, "You are not referring to yourself?" Halle backed off when she saw how her remarks were being interpreted as an attack on him personally. "No, although I've been through quite a bit. But what I've seen by way of murder and carnage I'll never reveal to my children—that is if I ever have any!"

"You never answered Mr Eckberg's question. Will you go along with his suggestion about leaving the ship before the others?"

"I've no alternative, so it has to be it!" Her voice was quick to respond once the doctor had left, "I see you've taken to quoting Ian, 'I'll never reveal etc.' what game are you playing? I suppose you'll be back outside asking the doctor's permission to see him and to have that straitjacket removed? Don't you think he looks more attractive in that thing?"

Ian was wakened by the new nurse, who then removed the straitjacket. "What brought this change of mind?" he asked and was surprised to hear an answer to what he had thought was a rhetorical question: "Dr Johnston ordered it. It was a strange decision, we thought he would have at least examined you before setting aside the judgement of the German doctors." Ian tenderly rubbed his arms and stretched himself in an attempt to restore his circulation. "Where am I to be kept?" The nurse looked at him before asking where he had been held prior to his incarceration. "I had a bed in the carriage I shared with other mental patients. I mean I shared the carriage with them."

"I will show you where the others are being kept."

"Are you not amazed at the remarkable recovery I've made?"

"We were given talks on dealing with mentally unbalanced patients before we left. Apparently some prisoners playact at it and they are sent home, unfortunately none that we heard of regained their sanity."

"I've only been playing at it for a couple of weeks, sorry I should have said days. I'm confident that I won't end up being confined to Purbysburn mental hospital in Belfast. Where is the British nurse that was looking after me?"

"You have a serious problem recognising a problem! Is that the nurse you attacked on the train?"

Halle duly paid Ian a visit and was told by the medical team in that area that she was welcome to resume working with her patient if she felt confident that she could deal with his tantrums. Halle smiled as she told Ian their views on him. "Do I look surprised? No, because whatever you do, you come up smelling of roses; while I'm regarded as the chief troublemaker on board!" Halle broke into a laugh; "It serves you right for all the hassle you've brought me in the past few months." By this time Halle had settled herself on the bunk.

"How can you laugh at such a thing? Truly you've a conundrum!" Ian was getting rattled at the constant barrage of seemingly funny comments each with a sting in their tail.

"No I'm not. You're the conundrum, not me!" argued Halle deliberately provoking Ian to see how long he could endure what she considered repartee.

"I am straightforward in all I do. I tell the truth as I see it—nothing could be further from a conundrum than that!" Ian, by now, had lost the thread of their conversation and could only resort to dropping the chit-chat and becoming serious.

"You see! You don't even see it! Where are the forty shades of grey in your make-up? You *boast* about being one complete colour—and I don't mean Orange!" Halle, in spite of being the initiator of this, was returning to her true colours and stood up more as an indication of temper than an intention to leave.

"Then what colour does that make me?" retorted Ian, knowing full well that he had left himself open to a lunge that he couldn't parry.

"A very dull monochrome grey! Particularly when you can't see that ninety-percent of the time I'm pulling your leg! Anyway let's leave it alone, I've too many important things to tell you."

Halle then gave a detailed account of her meeting with Dr Johnston and Mr Eckberg and their decision that she should be the first person escorted off the ship and handed to the British authorities. Ian was back in his element, preferring the serious comment to the comedy of manners, which he wrongly attributed to the bluff censorious comment commonly used by Halle. "How do you feel about that? Do you think you can bluff it out if those two keep their mouths shut?"

"The papers look genuine enough but once they realise I'm not on the list they'll make enquiries and it will be no time before they arrest me," Halle shrugged.

"They'll not be able to check these things out from this end and if you can slip off the ship from Sweden quickly enough in the UK you'll be gone before they can locate you."

"Look, on board this ship is a man who is determined to murder me and you're talking about the niceties of escaping the cops in England! Let's get our priorities right. What do you suggest we do, or more realistically, what should I do?" Her face spoke of her worry, her tired eyes lacking the sparkle which Ian always associated with her.

"As long as you are with the prisoners and medical staff I don't see how he can get at you. Apart from that the more I ponder the whole business of Hengist and you the more confused I am as to what is going on. *But* I don't think he wants to kill you—he's had too many opportunities all along to do it, so there seems to be a reason for keeping you alive."

"I wish to God you had told me this before, I think I would have slept better and had fewer nightmares. OK Sherlock Holmes, give us a clue about what's he's up to." Halle sat down once again.

"If only I knew I'd set up my own detective agency."

"In Belfast? You wouldn't even get a case of divorce to investigate there.

The only things the judges get when they open a session, is a pair of white gloves. So that should give you a clue as to how much business there is."

"I don't follow you. What's this about a pair of gloves?"

"If there are no cases to be heard the prosecutor symbolises how pure we all are by handing him a pair of white gloves." Ian shook his head, he always had a problem with gestures but Halle was anxious to get back to his speculations; "Come on you've given this a great deal of thought, spill the beans; out with it. When did you first make this deduction?"

"I suppose it was when you were moved to Warsaw from that field hospital near Plock. You know you should have died. Even the average soldier with such wounds would have been regarded as not worth all the trouble. But you were taken to a special hospital for top field officers— there were generals and colonels in that place."

"But wait a wee minute, I was a colonel and so was entitled to be there." Ian leant forward, almost as if he had anticipated her bringing this point up; "That's another part of this I wasn't happy about. Who made you a colonel?"

"General Eckhard, the head of the commission set up to find more recruits for the German Army."

"From the stories you've told me I would say he was nominally head of it, but the whole caboodle was run by Hengist. Eckhard may have handed you your papers with the commission to colonel but if I was a gambling man I'd bet a lot of money, if I had any, that it was Hengist dug up the idea."

"You're going from one idea to another without the least evidence to support what you're saying. It's all speculation, give me some hard facts so that I can rest in my bunk tonight!"

"OK, that story you told about the AK holding up the passengers on your bus and he rushed to your rescue. From whence? You suspected he was in Berlin but that would have been impossible in the time he took to get to you. You said it was then that you felt that something else was going on, didn't you?"

"It was a train I was taken off and *of course* I did become suspicious when he turned up with a squad of German soldiers when the AK put me on a bus. I'm not entirely a fool but I'm not going to add two and two and make twenty-two like you!"

"Do you want to go over the various things that don't add up?"

"We'd never get through it, there's that many. But let's make a start."

"You said that this began after you went to see Sheila, what did you call her?"

"Sheila Gray was her maiden name, I think. I'm confused now, she was supposed to be married to some French Nazi—Gourmont I think his name was but he died. Although she was English she had lived a long time in Canada."

"Did you believe that she was a spy?"

"She fitted the warning that O'Driscoll gave me and I warned her they were watching her, that's all."

"What was going on in that radio station that she would be spying there?"

"I've gone over this time and time again in my head to the point where my voices think I'm Sheila! We'd need to make a list of all the people she could have made contact with while there." Halle tossed her hands in the air, "I'm sorry I said that, there's no way I'm starting that. How long is there left before we dock and where is it going to be?"

"I've no idea... how often have I said this since we met? No, don't answer that, it's purely rhetorical. Do you want me to go up and ask the captain seeing that the doctor had second thoughts? Oh, you can answer that one all right."

"There's a devil got into you which your brethren back home will have a job to cure. Of course I don't want you going near him! Ask somebody, maybe one of your friends among the mental patients—I take that back, ask someone!"

"You are cruel to those who can not defend themselves," said Ian with a smile

"It's gone past a joke, give it a rest," growled Halle, as she stood up once again but Ian was determined to have the last word on this occasion; "Who said, 'ninety-percent of the time I'm joking'? Anyway, I'll be back shortly," and promptly left the room.

Ian never got an entirely satisfactory answer to his question and Halle remarked that it would probably be like the Channel Island boats in peacetime—two days between sailings. "The best information I was given was by Dr Johnston. The way he put it was this: 'If we are putting into Gothenburg it will only be a matter of a few hours; if we have to go to another port God knows'. The only thing is we have to be wherever it is no later than the 19th October for the handover of the German prisoners and, of course, we to the British."

"What date is *this*, have you any idea?"

"Not the slightest but the way the good doctor spoke I took it to be the eve of the handover, the 18th."

"Wait a minute, there is something you said that doesn't sound kosher," Halle's puzzled features indicated that something was very wrong.

"First of all, what is 'kosher'? And what is it that I said?"

"It's a Yiddish word which has come to mean 'genuine'. I heard Sheila use it a few times. It was a real touch of irony to hear a word used by Jews about the preparation of their food being used to mean genuine and there we were in Berlin at the height of the Jews being put out."

"What did I say then?"

"It was: 'we were being handed over to the British on the 19th October'. Then who is Mr Eckberg handing me to in a few hours?"

"I wasn't there when you were told. But you definitely said that you would be the first off the ship and you would be handed over to the British, which you felt was a mixed blessing."

"There's another strange thing—Hengist used the name 'Eckberg' is that merely a coincidence? God my mind is going berserk! Do you think this man has taken in the doctor?"

"What if he has—what in the name of God are we going to do?"

"I still have the gun and I think it's time to use it!"

"Hold it. I want no part of gunning this man down, nor for that matter do I share your enthusiasm for having Hengist murdered. It's only a moment ago that we were trying to work out *why* he didn't kill you with all the opportunities he had!"

"You had better come up with a suggestion quickly. There's little time left before we dock."

"What if we dragged Hengist into one of those cabins that aren't being used and force him to tell us what is going on?"

"And you imagine that he'll tell us, just like that?"

"I'm sure you could convince him that you'll kill him if he doesn't. You could convince me!"

"We're only given *carte blanche* about the deck and the cabins we are assigned to, not to the whole ship. So we can knock that one on the head."

"Suppose we go at this another way… don't interrupt for a moment. I'm trying to think this thing out on my feet. Say for a second we have worked it out that he means you no harm. What are his intentions in Sweden? He can't do anything to you without dragging the authorities into it and I'm sure that isn't his intention. So if we agree to go along with whatever he has in mind perhaps we'll get a solution acceptable to both of us."

"Wait a wee minute 'til I take this in. You want me to go to him and say,

'I know you mean me no harm so can we work out something that will be to both our benefits'?"

"What have you to lose? What can he do to you here?" Halle climbed off the bunk and stretched herself to relieve the aches of having spent so long in the one position and moved to the door, "What are you going to do?"

"I'm just going to confront him and demand some kind of answer."

"Wait, he'll just give you the cold shoulder and you'll be no further on," argued Ian. Halle glared at him, "Where did that fellow go who was here a moment ago who was pushing me into facing Hengist?" The sarcasm was too bitter and she changed her tone, "It's better doing it this way than just sitting here going off my head!"

"Do you want me to go with you?"

"They're all watching you, waiting for you to have another outburst. No, you sit tight and if the doctor turns up quiz him about his saying that 'they', whoever they are, would hand me over to the British in Oxelösund or whatever you call the other place; you know what I mean?"

Halle began searching the upper deck around the funnel, a spot where she had seen Hengist previously but was surprised to find him on the poop deck staring back in the direction of Poland, which was long out of sight. She stood for a moment looking at him and pondered what made a man do the things he must have done to reach such heights in the Gestapo. He must have sensed her presence because he turned and didn't show any surprise at her presence. "You should not be here, there is a storm expected at any moment. Get back to your patient!"

Halle almost did as she was directed, then the pointlessness of coming to see him struck her and she stood where she was. She became acutely aware of how cold it was and she wasn't dressed to ward off the Siberian winds that took the ship into wintry climes. "I need to talk to you, can we go to your cabin?" Hengist was clearly exasperated, "No; I'm having a last look back, enthralled at the idea of further adventures when I return." Halle hugged her body to steel herself against the bitter cold and to stop every part of her body shaking, "Just tell me what's going on—I'm powerless to stop you engineering whatever it is that you have set up for me. I know you have no designs on my life, so what is it you want?"

Hengist thought for a moment before responding, "I need to keep you alive and out of Britain for a few months more. It might be less but I can't forecast events; all I can tell you is that it is not in my interests to have you dead." Halle's anxiety to get to the truth caused her to pay less attention to the sudden swell which began to rock the ship. "It still doesn't make sense. Any of this: Eckberg, your presence, your attention to me in hospital, are they all part of the one thing? None of it adds up." Hengist held up his hand, "Please get back, don't you realise the ship is pitching at a steeper angle now?"

Halle was determined to get some sort of response and tried to get nearer in order to hear him. Just as she got alongside him she was thrown off her feet and Hengist grabbed her and pushed her back in the direction of the funnel, "Go now before it is too late!" he shouted, and he turned to grasp the handrail but the ship lurched with its stern pointing skywards and to Halle's horror she watched him disappear over the side. It took a moment for her to react and then she began screaming for help. The crew in the vicinity rushed forward to discover the reason for her hysteria and eventually grasped, from Halle's sign language, that there was a man overboard.

CHAPTER 20

(October 1943)

HALLE WAS ESCORTED to the Captain's cabin where she was held and then searched by a stewardess and the gun was taken from her. The stewardess departed and Halle was left with the two sailors who had held her while she was being searched. All told she had to wait about twenty minutes before Captain Borg arrived. His red face and bulbous nose spoke his feelings before he shouted, "You've murdered that man!" and before Halle could respond, "You had a gun and you had a motive and Mr Eckberg, who is the policeman responsible, will hand you over to the authorities as soon as we dock." Halle protested and tried to explain what had happened.

"Where are your papers? I looked for them because I was informed that the documents from you were not damaged by the explosion on the train but could not find them." Halle explained that she still had them and they were with a few items of hers beside her bunk. Turning to a sailor called Jan the captain told him to go to Miss Hegel's bunk, "Bring back the papers first and then go and find Mr Eckberg and politely ask him to join us." Halle asked him to repeat his order in English, which he did. Again Halle complained, this time about dragging a known associate of Hengist's into the investigation. Captain Borg was astonished at Halle's vehemence and explained that the man was attached to the Red Cross although he was employed full-time by the Swedish police and that he was the person they would have had to contact even if the death had occurred in Gothenburg.

Halle looked at him in horror, "I don't know how he has bamboozled you but he's a Nazi agent working for the Gestapo!" It was obvious that Captain Borg was struggling to keep calm, "Can you clarify which of them is the Gestapo man?"

"You mean *was* the Gestapo man!" said Halle through clenched teeth. "He is overboard and dead by now—it's the other which concerns me at this moment. They must have been acting in unison—or how did Hengist have papers with that man's identity on them?"

Borg was becoming more and more disgruntled with Halle's reaction, "I can understand your wishing to cover up your crime... but to invent such a story in such a short time is beyond belief. For your own sake I suggest that you say no more and let me get to the bottom of this." Halle was about to make the point that it was beyond her to concoct such a story when she decided to hold her tongue.

310

Captain Borg took up his questioning of Halle once more. "Who do you say was the man who you claim fell overboard?" Halle drew a deep breath and started: "This man was called Hengist and he was very important in the hierarchy of the Gestapo. He has been hunting me for some months and I'm not totally convinced that he wasn't involved in having me shot a few months ago."

"Just how badly were you shot?" Halle cleared her throat and told her story with some conviction and finished with a rebuttal of Eckberg's statement. "Dr Johnson spoke to me about you approaching him to see if I was a nurse. He said that a man, supposedly from the Red Cross, had pointed out the patient I am with and myself as not genuine, do you recall any of this?" The captain sheepishly acknowledged that he had a vague recollection of the event. "Well," continued Halle, "the doctor pointed out the person who had made the allegations and it was then I recognised Hengist, a member of the Gestapo."

"Miss Hegel, I can see that you have no regard for the Gestapo but you must remember that my country is not at war and we see them as the legitimate police force of a friendly country."

"Captain, you are missing the point, it was *he* who purported to be a member of the Red Cross."

"No, his papers indicated that he was a policeman."

"I'm sorry but we're talking at cross-purposes, you have mixed the identities of the two men."

"I am confident that the first Mr Eckberg showed me papers that showed he was a Swedish policeman. Do you think there was some collusion between them in order to prevent you gaining entry into Sweden?"

"Well how do you account for Dr Johnston saying the man was part of the Red Cross team sent from Sweden?"

"I did say that he *came* with the Red Cross. Not that he was one of them. I think this is taking us away from the purpose of this enquiry. By the way where is Mr Eckberg and where is Jan?" And the argument went on much as before. The captain appeared to hear a knock at the door, which no one else heard and opened it, then he conversed in a whisper with one of the crew. "That was a message from Jan saying that he has searched around your bunk and can find no trace of your papers. He has been round the ship once already and can't find Mr Eckberg. He is now in the process of completing it for the second time and he will report the success or otherwise when he is finished."

"If you are honest with yourself that should confirm what I've said all along, he *and others* conspired with Hengist to have me taken prisoner for a purpose that I haven't figured out." The whistle from the bridge was an indication that the ship was nearing the harbour and that the captain was needed. "Captain," said Halle, "you're going to have to come to some decision as to what you are going to do."

"Oh, I have already decided that I am handing this matter to the police in Gothenburg. It is going to take more than one detective to sort this out. Just what is going on seems to depend on the last person you hear. Your version is at odds with Mr Eckberg's and probably will be the same with regards to Dr Johnston's account when he arrives... Ah, Dr Johnston you have arrived too late to alter my decision but I suspect that if your evidence is anything like the rest of the stories I have heard it will only add to the confusion!" The captain left leaving Halle and the doctor with a member of his crew to await the return of Jan and what he had discovered.

Jan arrived five minutes later while the doctor and Halle were discussing their varied recollections of what had brought them to this point. "Where is the captain?" enquired Jan. Each of those present spoke in their own language; "He's on the bridge." Jan looked at the other sailor, "What am I supposed to do?" The sailor shrugged, "I am here to see that Miss Hegel remains until the police come on board." The doctor suddenly became aware that Halle's 'patient' wasn't present. "You need to get John Dickson up here; he seems to be tied into this as well."

"I can not move as long as Miss Hegel is here; what about you Jan?" The young man looked at the doctor; "I can not order him here without an instruction from the captain." The anxiety in the doctor's voice and his wild look at the others propelled Jan into rushing for the door, "I will go to the bridge and ask him what to do!" he shouted back.

Dr Johnston asked Halle to enlighten him about what was going on and she attempted to be as objective as she possibly could. "Are you positive that Hengist and Mr Eckberg are two different people or is it possible that they are one and the same person?" Halle was adamant that they were two different people, "The way I see it is, Eckberg lent his documents to Hengist to have me interned in Sweden or possibly worse. They didn't think of the captain asking your opinion of me as a nurse and the possible consequences of me telling you what I knew."

"I doubt if I can sway Captain Borg to let you go with the repatriated prisoners but I'll try." Halle was grateful but warned him that there were other agents on board and related the story of her missing papers. Dr Johnston was intrigued, "I was in the vicinity of the nurses' station during that time and the only person who went in and then came out some minutes later was Jan." His comments brought an immediate reaction from Halle: "Are you sure about the length of time he was there?" The doctor was obviously surprised by the question but he thoughtfully said: "He could not have been very long because I was moving around the various patients and I was still with the one I was examining when he went in and I was still with him when he came out. It could only have been a matter of a few minutes."

Halle turned to her 'minder'; "What is your name?" The sailor was somewhat taken aback, "My name is Rune."

"Rune you've been here all the time I've been here, how long would you say that Jan was missing before the sailor turned up saying he couldn't find the papers?"

"Possibly fifteen minutes. The captain was getting annoyed at the time taken."

The doctor was trying to be more accurate with his assessment of the time Jan was at Halle's bunk but couldn't. "You are implying that Jan is one of the people working for this man Hengist?"

"Not only him but Eckberg as well. I still can't fathom what they are up to—although a remark of Hengist…" her voice trailed away as she realised there was no certainty that these men were not involved with Hengist.

The door opened and Ian appeared accompanied by Jan who told Dr Johnston that the captain had instructed him to bring Mr Dickson to the cabin and leave him under the supervision of the doctor and Rune. Jan apologised because he couldn't stay, as he was required on deck to help with the ship docking. "How long will it be before disembarkation begins?" Halle enquired of Jan, as he opened the door. "I heard Captain Borg say that he had sent a wire to the British authorities and I think he will keep everyone on board, except the very ill, until they arrive."

"What is going on?" demanded Ian. Halle, now thoroughly upset, attempted to explain all of the happenings that occurred in the past hour. "How do you manage to bring the world to an earth shattering end each time you are out of my sight?" asked Ian in an effort to lighten the atmosphere. Halle couldn't manage to summon sufficient strength to maintain the tone that Ian had created. Dr Johnston however hadn't missed the humour and enquired of Ian, "Is this the norm in regards to Miss Hegel?" Ian began to banter Halle, "Tell the good doctor how you got shot just rounding a bend!" But she couldn't, and silence fell as if all had entered the monastery of an enclosed order of monks.

Ian who was more used to having silences being used against him for various infractions outside of his knowledge knew better than to disturb the deep thought, which Halle was prone to from time to time. What he wasn't aware of were the number of voices, which beset her when she was in dire trouble. "We're in it up to our necks this time! By the time that British consul gets here you'll be charged with every crime committed by the Nazis in this war and in the last one!" Halle withdrew more into herself hoping that from this extremity she would be able to extract herself by the shear logic of her position. "Logic! You are raving mad! They're already preparing a charge sheet on you in London—within a month you'll be swinging at the end of a rope!"

"Give it a rest!" said Halle suddenly to the amazement of the others in the cabin. "Sorry, I'm having a discussion with myself."

"Don't you start dwelling on all of this. If she had killed Hengist, she's the type that would have admitted it!" Doctor Johnston looked on with something akin to incredulity at the antics of both of those in his charge. He was beginning to be seriously concerned about Halle's sanity knowing how some people crack under severe pressure. "Rune how long does it take to dock this ship, normally?" Rune replied immediately, "Fifteen to twenty minutes, sir." The doctor began pacing about the small room; "Will it be much longer now?" Rune smiled, "Well the engines have stopped and we should be along side any minute now." Once again a hostile silence took over.

Captain Borg returned to the cabin in a deep quandary contemplating how long would this undesirable turn about endure. "Doctor I trust you've given this business some thought; I can tell you now that I want this sorted out ashore and not on board this ship. Up to this moment I haven't lost any time and that is the way I want it to continue. Have you any suggestions that will take this dispute away from me and my ship?" The doctor looked at the two prisoners and turned to the captain, "I would suggest, after all I've heard, that this is a matter for the British. If you report the missing man as a suspected murder victim you will hear eternity knocking on your door. The police will want to speak to each and every member of the crew and all those passengers and medical team who were on deck at any point in the past two hours. How long do you think that will take—a day, two days…"

"Say no more, that is more than I require to reach a decision. I am not about to let the authorities on board this ship if that is what is likely to happen. I have sent a message by wireless to the British and they hope to send someone to sort this out before the exchange takes place. I have also informed the police, this is the message I sent: 'A man has been reported to us as having fallen overboard. On checking our passenger lists we find we have a full complement.' any suggestion from them that involves the Swedish police having to interview passengers will be opposed by me. How is that with you?" He had pointedly turned to Halle, anxious that she would accept this compromise. "I am not terribly interested in any kind of compromise," she began but when she saw the look of brutal hostility on the captain's face she backtracked, "but in the interests of all I think that it is the better of the two alternatives."

Ian smiled at the doctor by way of acknowledgement of his part in saving them from another period of incarceration. Halle was in a different world seeing herself doing a life sentence in England or, as her voices assured her, swinging from the end of a rope. However, the captain received a telegram, which read:

WE WILL MEET YOU IN GOTHENBURG. THANKS
Philip Drain (British Consul)

Captain Borg was relieved although he read the telegram with aplomb in front of the others. He had been aware that he had left the consul little opportunity to get to Gothenburg from Stockholm and consequently the message was a surprise. His main gain—from his handling of a tricky situation—meant that he could get home and leave the preparation for the ship's next voyage to others.

Shortly after this the disembarkation of the worse cases began. The captain left the two suspects in the hands of Dr Johnston and two Red Cross officials—the latter being totally in the dark as to what was going on. They believed that 'Dickson' was mentally unbalanced and needed a doctor, a nurse and two helpers to deal with him if he became violent.

Halle fell asleep in the ambulance, which conveyed them to the temporary hospital where they were to spend the night. She woke at the touch of Ian's hand on her arm and immediately was relieved; for no other reason than it came at a point in her nightmare where she had just heard the sentence of death pronounced by a man wearing a wig which was surmounted by a black cap.

"How are you now?" whispered Ian. Halle still partly asleep paused before beginning her explanation of her contradictory emotions. When she had detailed the events in her nightmare Ian smiled and Halle wanted to know just what in her story he found funny. "You *are* determined to see nothing but happiness ahead!" he said laughing in an attempt to get her mind away from the dangers that lay ahead. "Please Ian, your sense of humour seems to come at the most inappropriate times." Ian took her hands in his, "You need to stop dwelling on these matters. Who knows what the future holds?"

The awareness of how close he was to eventual freedom caused Ian's emotions to heighten and he remembered, with deep affection, gradually falling in love with Halle. He pondered their future unaware of her

315

commitment to God to give him up. Now, having done his best to alleviate the situation, it was his turn to wonder about what had happened to Hengist's agents. He had expected some attempt by them to kidnap Halle prior to her being handed over to the British, yet there had been nothing. He couldn't recollect accurately what was said by Hengist to Halle, and his best shot at it was: "I have to keep you out of British hands for some months" which left him all the more perturbed at the lack of an effort by Hengist's men.

Halle seemingly had read his mind, "Why has there been no attempt by them to get me?" she asked. Ian was quick to respond, "I was just wondering about it myself. Someone else must be pulling the strings now that Hengist is dead." The idea of another person taking over the mantle of Hengist hadn't occurred to Halle and the tremor of fear that ran through her body was not missed by Ian who rushed to say, "I can't see, for the life of me, another Gestapo agent being involved over here. Those two guys—Jan and Eckberg—were Swedish and neither of them struck me as being capable of handling an operation of the kind that would be required to capture you and, *more importantly*, keep you captive for a number of months," he prognosticated in his most commanding voice.

"That's a consolation all right, but the obvious way out for a new comer would be to have me shot, or killed in some other way," speculated Halle. Ian had considered that but hoped that his confident manner and tone of voice would have been sufficient to discourage Halle thinking of it. "How would it be done? If you can suggest possible ways then we can organise some kind of protection on board the ship."

"Well it would have to be some crew members. Do you think the British authorities would arrange to have the crew scrutinised?"

"In the circumstances I think they would; but my mind is off in another direction. Say, for the sake of argument, that this new guy has received instructions, why are we concluding that he is bound to break them?"

"What you're saying then is: whatever rules made Hengist avoid killing me must be still applicable to the new man. Is that it?"

"Yes. It seems logical to me."

"Oh, don't let's bring logic into it, especially from an Orangeman who doesn't see that parading up and down nationalist areas is offensive!" Halle's attempt at humour wasn't appreciated by Ian as he tried to unravel the machinations of some military mind. Halle hurried on, "If it isn't the Germans running this, who is and what have they to gain from keeping me out of sight for months?" Ian didn't get an opportunity to reply as the ambulance stopped and they, and many others, were set down.

Halle saw the officials steadily wending their way through the crowd of prisoners towards them. Everything about them screamed 'British'! Whether it was the Homburg hats, the long black coats and the brief cases or simply their air of superiority that set her heckles rising she didn't know but whatever it was she wasn't about to be put down by them. Dr Johnston was the first to speak, asking them for some means of identification. The group as a whole seemed to be reluctant to produce evidence of their position and Dr Johnston had no difficulty in maintaining his dignity while he waited for them to sort out their act. Eventually one of them, whom Ian took to be Philip Drain, showed some kind of document to the doctor who promptly asked him, "What do you propose doing with these two prisoners?" Drain was not about to be put down by some upstart medical and told him that the matter had nothing to do with him and that they would determine the next step without any outside pressure.

"Very well, if you will be kind enough to wait here, I will summon the Swedish police to sort this matter out." Drain immediately apologised and requested that they be given a moment to consider the position. When he returned the British Consul suggested that the prisoners should stay in a hotel they had booked until they were given instructions from London.

"I am sorry but that is not acceptable to me or the Red Cross. From the story they have told me it is clear that both of them are too ill to be dragged into some furore or other as to being genuine or not. We in the Red Cross went along with both countries involved in this repatriation—not that we agreed on the conditions imposed—but in an attempt to save as much suffering as we could. Both of these prisoners have gone through hell but you are so anxious to keep to the letter of the agreement you are prepared to endanger their lives. I will hand them to the Swedish police where I am sure they will be well cared for."

The Consul's team must have been prepared for this possibility as they abruptly did a *volte-face* and asked the doctor for his recommendation. Johnston, unperturbed by the shenanigans of the British diplomats, said he wanted the two of them to be given the same medical attention, which the other prisoners were receiving. Drain instantly gave his assent and they moved off and left the Red Cross officials to continue helping the stretcher cases into the fleet of ambulances provided.

The return trip to the docks the next morning took an excessive amount of time; the loading and unloading seemed endless, particularly to those who were lying supine on the stretchers waiting to be dealt with. Those in the immediate vicinity of Halle were distracted by her stories of her primary school days in Belfast under the iron rod of the nuns. Those Englishmen well enough to pay attention asked her about the attitude of her parents to the series of punishments to which she and her classmates were subjected. The age-old excuse, 'spare the rod and spoil the child' was a serious misnomer according to Halle and of course, as was her intention, it stimulated a heated argument as to which was the better course.

Once on board Ian and Halle had much to consider. "We've got over the biggest hurdle we're likely to meet," exuded Ian. "Would you care to enlarge on that and stop drooling at the mouth at the same time!" responded Halle seeing the world through the underside of a glass. "No more or less than I said! I can't visualise a bigger difficulty than Hengist and his gang. He's dead and the group looks to be a pale imitation of their master," remarked Ian as if satisfied that the whole world was his oyster.

"You're jumping to conclusions. Firstly, because they're not doing anything within our vision doesn't mean that they're not doing anything. Secondly, you were the one who said, that someone was manoeuvring Hengist—would you care to name him or her so that I can keep a weather eye open for them? Thirdly, the British aren't going to disappear, you can bet your life he has been 'on to London', as he so quaintly puts it, to make sure that I'm taken prisoner when we land and charged with the death of 'someone unknown'."

"You have an ace which will cause all these doubts to disappear!" Ian replied with, what Halle called, his forked tongue being deliberately unhelpful, wanting Halle to ask him what it was to which he was referring. "Go ahead, your moment of glory has arrived. Do you want a trumpet fanfare before you begin or will it do later?" Ian would not be undone by the pessimism, which exuded from very pore of Halle's body. "Come on, get on with it or are you waiting for the King to present you with a knighthood using his orange sword?" asked the amused Halle and continued. "You see, that's where we really differ; I do a thing because it needs to be done—you on the other hand, want everyone to acknowledge your brilliance before you begin!"

Ian, using his tongue and mouth made a drum-roll and then in a voice used by a master of ceremonies at a boxing bout announced the details. "And now for your edu-mic-ation and enlightenment, Ian Patterson, alias John Dickson, will present you with astonishing information, which will shock you into humour."

"Don't stop now when you're in front!" shouted Halle. "Tell the world so that everyone will be aware of your exceedingly brilliant deduction." Ian couldn't bring himself to shout the details and instead leant closer to Halle and said, "The AK!" Halle's hysteria was infectious, particularly with the mentally unstable. She began singing the letters A and K in a variety of notes

318

that brought everyone within hearing range to their carriage. Soon it seemed that the whole ship echoed with the two letters and the medical teams were called upon to restore order so that no one would be ill with hysteria.

The pair had to move out into a gangway to continue their more serious discussion. "I get your drift, fine. You think that because General Bór-Komorowski organised our escape that that will be sufficient to impress the British authorities as to our genuine credentials. You're nuts!"

"It's bound to be useful particularly in regard to you. I have only to convince them that I'm Ian Patterson and not John Dickson—which shouldn't be too difficult seeing that poor John is dead."

"OK, outline in detail how it's going to help me once I'm arrested by your lords and masters."

"Well leaving out the nasty implications of your final words, let me put it this way. The AK, through its commander in Warsaw, acknowledged your help in distracting the Gestapo to such an extent that the commander summoned you to see him to be personally thanked..."

"For what? We still don't know what the hell was going on, do we? For all we know it was some internal deal between the Nazis and the Poles preparing the ground before the communists sail in. I can't see the Brits buying that load of horse manure as an indication of how I opposed their enemies. I tell you what... maybe I shouldn't, it will only jeopardise you."

"It's too late if you're worried about me. What do you intend to do?"

"I'm going on the run again, I'm well used to it by now."

"You can hardly get from one end of this boat to the other without help and you think you can do what you did before? They'll get you through the Mental Health Act before you get off this ship!" Halle laughed uproariously and Ian was convinced that he had shown her the error of her idea but she persisted that she would not leave it to the British to determine her fate without some resistance on her part.

"Leaving all that we've said aside there is another aspect of this matter which I know that you're deliberately ignoring. If I go before a court and 'recognise it', I use the term advisedly knowing full well the both of us know what that means, I will be abandoning all that I believe in and ending my association with the Republican movement. And my friends will promptly abandon me. Again, if I recognise the court, you will be called on by whoever is representing me to give evidence in my support. I know you well enough to realise that you will present me in as good a light as you possibly can—what will that mean to you and your family back home? I'll tell you, you'll be ostracised at the very least! Can you see now why I have to go on the run?"

"Surely everybody will see there are mitigating circumstances..."

"You're kidding yourself, and using the big words from the newspaper reports that you've read won't alter the situation for either of us. If you think about it, you have heard that many stories in the papers about people trying to distance themselves from their past that you use the jargon as if *you're* a lawyer. Say we do what you suggest when I'm arrested in England; there'll be such a mixture of cajolery and threat we'll not know what end of us is up. No I'll stick to my original idea, it has more prospects of success."

"You realise that if you attempt to escape and are caught that constitutes another offence with which you'll be charged?"

"I need to sit down, I'm exhausted with all this serious talk. By the way are you a lawyer in your spare time?" Halle made her way back into the carriage where the noise had simmered down. "No, but I work with the BB, the Boys' Brigade, and sometimes when a youngster gets into trouble I have to advise them what to do. So I do know about these things."

"I'm starting to think you're Mr Know-it-all. Every time I open my mouth you are the voice of the negative—don't do this, don't do that—say I go along with what you suggest and I get twenty years or I'm sentenced to hang, will you be as quick to take the blame as you are to rubbish every idea I put forward?" Halle's exasperation was taking her closer to breaking point.

"On the other hand, to show you the optimistic side—which I've been trying to put and for which you give me no credit—say the British agree that you have been of help to their allies, the Poles, and give you some kind of suspended sentence, what then, are you going to refuse?"

"No, but I'm going to have to find somewhere else to live."

"When your people learn about the events that have been happening in Europe, the killing of the Jews and the massacres of millions of people right across the continent, the right thinking Roman Catholics will see that the world was right to oppose the Nazi government in Germany."

"I'll tell you something for nothing—the British have been pouring dud propaganda into Ireland for centuries and I'll bet the nationalists will see the stories as just that. Dud propaganda."

"My God, what a mess we're both in—the only consolation is that we're in this together and if we hold our nerve we'll see it through." Once again Halle didn't enlighten Ian about her promise to God.

On board ship neither Halle nor Ian could get any indication as to which port they were due to dock. When Halle saw some sailors working on deck she left the cabin she had been assigned and went outside. She hoped to hear the crew discuss the port or harbour they were heading for but either they didn't know or were being particularly evasive in naming the port.

Now, more than ever, she was determined to escape and, later, when she was told that the severely disabled were to be driven to special rehabilitation centres, she felt that she could readily go with them and not be picked out to be specially interrogated. She was still dressed in the nurse's uniform provided by Aleksander and she hoped that it—plus the forged papers if need be—would get her out of the docks area.

Finally she asked the first sailor she saw resting, "Where are we bound?" The deckhand stood up, "I'm only guessing but I think it's Newcastle-on-Tyne. But things change in war, so where you start for isn't necessarily where you end up." For a moment the man's down-to-earth view wrong footed her and she merely nodded while she continued contemplating the sea in all its dark foreboding. It was then she recognised that she had undergone a deep philosophical change, "But you've ended up where you started—back in England on the run!" Halle was irked by her own thoughts, "No, I haven't, I have changed. At this moment I'm thinking seriously of facing the British and arguing my views in their courts." For a moment her voice held its breath as it contemplated what negative position it could adopt. Once it spotted that it had only one direction to take it started: "More fool you. Do you think they'll report anything you say? Of course they won't! They'll call it 'national security' and it will have one of those notices posted on it making it a criminal act to publish your views."

Halle felt a sense of destiny as she searched her way to an answer, "I'm not going there to have my opinions in the press, I want to challenge the hypocrisy of all those who advocate war as a solution and send the poor and the downtrodden to fight their battles for them!"

Her alter ego soon found her Achilles' heel—a belief that her 'solution' was unique. "I suppose you think you're unique? Well I've news for you—that argument is as old as Methuselah and it never saved one life yet! Because no one thinks that the character spouting these lines is sincere but is another politician making a speech, not a warrior converted to peace."

"But you know I'm not a pacifist nor a warrior; what I've seen in the past few years has taught me that we have to search for another way." Her voice chortled with disbelief, "Your views won't last long after the Brits have swung you from a tree!"

Halle tried to breakaway from the angelic mode she had adopted, but she still persisted in speaking in a martyr's tone, "That's a risk I'll have to take; hopefully there is a way out that balances their prejudices and mine."

Back at the gangway, where they had just been told to gather, she saw Ian looking decidedly edgy. "Thank heavens you're here! I was imagining all kind of things."

"Such as?"

"You diving overboard and trying to swim ashore."

"No—Oh! I have been looking at the sea and I have decided to face whatever it is that awaits me." Ian could see despondency ahead and attempted to lift her out of it, "A conversion on the road to Damascus?" he joked. Halle, turning to face him, didn't see it like that; "Your approval is a dispensation I can well do without. I have changed nothing but the method I'll use to put my case."

Ian's tone changed, "You mean you're going to recognise the court?" Halle looked at him with disgust, "What am I after saying? Clearly you didn't grasp what I'm on about. I won't be recognising it in any form of words and if anyone construes that by arguing for myself I'm paying allegiance to a British system they'd be wrong. Imagine a British citizen before a German court; defending themselves wouldn't suggest that they had accepted the German system of justice, would it?"

Ian's attempt to warn her of the likely consequence fell on deaf ears and he was more direct in his reply this time, "I suppose it wouldn't. But you're not in Germany and Republicans won't see things the way you do now, will they?" Halle shrugged indifferently. "That's their problem. I've come back with the intention of stopping war and establishing peace." Ian's disbelief was unmeasurable, he well knew how physically ill she had been but now he was convinced she was mentally unhinged.

"You're off your rocker! It will end up being interpreted as you wanting Ireland for the Irish, isn't that what Sinn Féin means?" Halle's calmness, in face of his passionate appeals, made him aware how much she was over the edge. "No it doesn't mean it the way you say it—'Ourselves' is inclusive of everyone on the island—it isn't meant to exclude anyone."

Ian attacked her view in an attempt to bring her back to some form of rationality, "No one believes that; you attack Britain and everything British, and that includes us Protestants." But Halle was disconsolate at his lack of support, "God, I thought that if I could get through to you there was a chance but you've knocked even that thought on the head!"

Ian persisted in his view and told her she needed rest and added, "You should be thinking of a proper defence—like having a good solicitor to advise you." Halle was no longer able to deal with Ian's counter arguments and admitted, "I've only come to this decision on the ship and I haven't thought it through. The odds are they'll arrest me and God knows in what prison I'll end up."

"Just a minute, come over here, I want you to see this!" and Ian pointed to a considerable number of police lining the dock as the ship tied up. "They can't all be there for me!" exclaimed Halle.

CHAPTER 21
(October 1943)

H ALLE PUT HER hands over her face and repeated herself, "They can't all be here for me!" Ian, in a despairing attempt to calm her said, "You want to bet? I shouldn't be saying things like that especially as I will be going home in the next day or two. But I have said this time and time again—you must be involved in something big. Whatever it is it seems to spark an immediate response from governments and armies across Europe!"

Halle smiled, "I have to admit your sense of humour has improved since you fell into my company." Ian threw his hands up, "You can be so obtuse when it suits you. No matter what happens you keep seeing it as a normal response but I haven't seen anything normal about these responses right across Europe, from Germany into Poland and even in Sweden. And now in Britain they've the red carpet laid out for you!"

"You're a devil for exaggeration, aren't you? God knows I realise there are mysteries at every step but then a good Catholic expects that!"

"That's tantamount to blasphemy, even in your Church!"

"What do you want me to say? You keep implying that I have influenced something important. You tell me, how could that be? My story is an open book—you know all that's in it—so go ahead and explain to me, I'm all ears—and don't be making any cracks about that!" Ian hesitated, "I admit I don't know but you don't have to be Sherlock Holmes to see there is something going on—a platoon of police to arrest one ill young woman. You often said when we first met in the POW camp that I lacked imagination so it's not that, that I'm suffering from."

"Ah, you've come a long way since those days—now I'd say you're full of imagination." Ian, who was already on to another aspect of the situation, missed the twinkle in her eye. "When they take you in you'd better remember all this, particularly when you speak to a solicitor. In fact that's just given me an idea. I'll try and find a politician who is still a practising solicitor. He would be in a position to ask the right questions of those who organised this unbelievable welcome."

Finally the ship came along side and the nursing and medical teams began preparing their patients to be taken ashore, Halle however persisted with her conversation with Ian. "For God's sake Ian, you're a terrible man for overcooking things!" Ian knew she had deliberately drawn God into the discussion because she was aware that he felt it was morally wrong but he decided that this time he would avoid a confrontation knowing how close Halle was to a breakdown. "Look Halle, I won't be there when you speak to this solicitor, so don't leave anything out—you'll need all the help you can get."

"Whatever *you do* don't get me one who is totally opposed to Irish unity. I don't mind one who is not fully committed one way or the other but *don't* get me one of your sort... I'm joking—OK, in a half-hearted way." The Tannoy buzzed with an indistinct message, which Ian interpreted, saying there would be at least a half-hour wait as most of the ambulances had been delayed because of the previous night's blitz.

Ian went on to ignore Halle's instructions, merely remarking, "I'm not about to hire someone who'll wash his hands of you before the trial begins."

"By the way, where are you going?"

"I'm being sent home to recuperate and then I'll be brought back to England to be tested as to my fitness for military duty."

"How long will you be in Belfast?"

"A month at least."

"What am I going to do without you? I know I never seem to be agreeing with you on anything but you know in spite of it all I love you."

"I never thought I'd live to hear you say that but you know that I feel exactly the same way about you. I think I'll go and see the medical officer and ask if I can remain with you."

"Don't you dare! You need to see your people and rest properly so that you are as strong as you were before the war. I don't want to take back anything I said but at the same time I don't want to build up your hopes that there is some future for us."

"Well I haven't given up hope that we'll solve this, in spite of what I've preached to others in the past."

"Just remind me how bigoted you were—I jest!"

"Look Halle, meeting you has forced me to go back on a philosophy which I preached to others on more than one occasion. John Rainey, a lad from the Shankill came to me just after he got engaged to a Roman Catholic girl. He said he was having second thoughts, as he was afraid his relatives would dump him. I advised him that if there was no accommodation in her allowing him to bring up the children as Protestants then he should call it a day as there would be nothing but rows and disagreements all their lives."

"Oh, so you're a prophet to boot!"

"No, I always rationalised situations and tried my best not to let religious bigotry influence what I said."

"Yet you were telling Rainey to demand that the children be brought up in his religion? Nothing bigoted about that then?"

"I didn't issue an edict requiring Roman... sorry, Catholics to be sure that the children of mixed marriages should have to be brought up as Catholics, did I?"

"No, you just issued an edict of your own! Christ when I think of the times you criticised the Pope for claiming infallibility, when you claim it every day in the week without setting any limits on your power, while the poor Holy Father has to be speaking on faith and morals to be infallible! Now who or what was the other guy I heard you bumming about?"

"Bumming?"

"Yes bumming!"

"The one whose girlfriend tried to kill herself when he dumped her?"

"Ah... well she was unstable in any case... that's all that proved."

"You and your gang of lay preachers nearly sent that girl to Milltown Cemetery."

"I'm sorry. It was never my intention to do that. I was trying to save him from himself."

"Well you'll be glad to know that just before I left Belfast he left his wife—the Protestant girl who would make him happy!"

"I don't believe you. You'd say anything to make me look bad."

"I don't have to try. You succeed admirably on your own! No I'm sorry, I shouldn't have said that—it's just me being bigoted. The chances are the things that broke up his marriage would have done the same to whoever he was married."

"Aren't you glad the ambulances weren't able to make it on time? It has given you the opportunity to tell me you love me, that I'm a bigot, a wrecker of marriages and a potential cause of suicide. Apart from all that I've changed and am more a Fenian than you, so I'm all right then?"

"You better forget all those kind of words when you get home or try to remember the expletive that goes before them!"

"I beg your pardon but I am not the type who uses expletives."

"No but you admit you've used your philosophy to proselytise those members of the Protestant faith that you felt were wavering just because they were thinking of marrying Catholics. You're not going back on that, are you?"

"You're doing me less than justice. I only wanted to warn them that they risked losing their children to the Roman Catholic faith which we don't consider Christian."

"Are you still like that? In spite of telling me that you love me and would marry me if I got a dispensation? It's as well I put that proviso in when you first raised this. So I'm not a Christian?"

"Of course you are, you've seen the light and have changed."

"I thought that you were joking when you spoke about a road to Damascus job but now you're telling me that you weren't?"

"Now I didn't say that. I meant only that you weren't going to try to escape as you had proclaimed all along."

"Let's just drop this, it's obvious what you think of me and mine. What in the name of God was I thinking about when I got involved with you? Just say cheerio now and disappear, we've both had a lucky escape."

Ian's travel voucher allowed for his journey to Belfast and he was given sufficient back pay, which enabled him to travel to London to search out a suitable solicitor for Halle. It didn't occur to him that Halle might have decided to make arrangements of her own now that they had 'finally' broken up. Given that he had been the main mover in all of this and bearing in mind the conditions laid down by Halle he had concluded that the Labour Party was probably his best starting point. He didn't know how he knew that their headquarters was sited in the General Transport and Workers' Union building, Transport House, but he made his way there. It was only a matter of minutes before he was given a name and a telephone number and he didn't waste any time contacting the MP's office and making an appointment.

No sooner had he made an arrangement to meet the Rt. Hon. Hugh Maxwell KC MP than he began to have major doubts about his own involvement—particularly since Halle had been so emphatic about their break-up. Another issue that particularly galled him was having to resort to a Labour MP who was anything but Unionist—still he fitted within the parameters laid down.

The next morning he made the same journey once more. Maxwell was already there to attend a meeting later that morning so he quickly ushered Ian into a small office on the second floor. "I'm intrigued by having an escaped soldier seeking advice so shortly after escaping, please go ahead, the floor is yours. Oh, can I assume it's not to do with the war?" Ian's negative reply shook the MP; "Can you explain more fully what it is about?"

Ian launched into a précis of Halle's story, leaving out the parts which he felt were dubious or could be better explained by her. "I thought that this matter would have related to you, so I am surprised." The man's public school voice rattled Ian as he had expected someone with a strong working-class accent, "I'll arrange to see her tomorrow in prison." Ian apologised for not being able to enlarge on the details, "I haven't been given authority by her to explain this matter; I can say that it touches on all the intelligence agencies—at least that is our considered opinion." His sudden usage of jargon associated with the legal profession wakened him as to his openness to suggestibility by dint of a cultivated voice.

"I failed to ask you where she is being held?" this in a tone of reproachfulness about his forgetfulness. "I honestly don't know but she herself suspected she would end up in Holloway."

"She would only be there on remand."

"Where are those found guilty held?"

"Aylesbury in Buckinghamshire. And you can't add anything else?"

"She specifically said she didn't want anyone representing her who was sympathetic on the Union."

"So you picked on me on that basis and now, at least, I can see one aspect of this case—which is better than none. I will contact the police and make enquiries about the charges facing her. Will you be in touch with her in the interim?"

"No, we've fallen out—not over this—and I'm heading home to Belfast for a long overdue leave."

"I wish you well and do your best to get back your strength and for heaven's sake try to put on some weight."

Ian left feeling that if anyone could save Halle it was the one time junior minister in the 1929 government under Ramsay MacDonald.

Halle, in the meantime had been transferred from remand in Newcastle-on-Tyne to remand in Holloway Prison in London. No matter how prepared she had been for the trials and tribulations of solitary confinement the continual procession of drunks, prostitutes and the dregs of society shocked her. The one hour's exercise per day proved to be the greatest luxury afforded her, apart from the long sleep she had without interruption in her first few days there. It was on her third day that she was told that her solicitor was waiting to see her in an interview room, but they would be under the scrutiny of a guard.

Her first sighting of Mr Maxwell left her feeling absurdly lost without Ian. "I've used the word 'intrigued' when talking to your friend about you and the situation in which you find yourself." Maxwell went on to make it clear that she would be charged with being a member of an illegal force, viz. the IRA, carrying out bomb attacks on persons and property on the British mainland. But he went on to say that the police were investigating further charges of her (i) joining the German Army; (ii) preparing broadcasts

327

and taking part in treasonable radio talks as part of the German propaganda machine; (iii) attempting to recruit British troops for the German Army; (iv) killing a British spy.

"There is something going on! My friend Ian thought so while we were in Poland and he tried to warn me when he saw the streams of policemen coming towards the ship. No one in Britain could possibly have the information that would enable him or her to point the finger at me for anything unless they were involved themselves. But what's this about killing a British spy? I have never taken a life anywhere!"

"You have to be aware that there is so much secrecy in wartime that it's unlikely that we'll ever get the name of the actual informer."

"It doesn't have to be wartime for that to happen at home."

"In any event let's begin with those charges which have been laid against you." Halle admitted her involvement with the IRA, "Actually I was in the Cumann na mBan, the women's branch of the movement. I was a courier delivering explosive to various parts of England." Maxwell calmly took notes without giving a sign of a reaction to anything she said but she did notice that now and again he watched her hands and in the remaining time his eyes rarely left hers. "Would you say you were young and naïve in getting into such an organisation?"

"No, on the contrary, I felt that I was fighting against a pernicious evil which turned the meaning of the word 'democracy' on its head." It was evident that Maxwell was interested, "You didn't view the 1921 Treaty agreement as democratic?"

"No! The northern nationalist voice was excluded."

"But surely you would be seeking to do the same thing in reverse if you wanted a united Ireland against the wishes of a large section of the people in the north…"

"Who had been planted deliberately there by Elizabeth I! I thought Ian would at least have followed my instructions instead of planting an English unionist on me!"

Maxwell looked at her dispassionately, "He was quite specific about requiring that I should not support the union of Northern Ireland and Gt. Britain." Halle's look mirrored her consternation, "Then why are you pushing a unionist message at me?"

"The prosecutor, in all likelihood the Attorney-General, will be trying to get you to admit what you're just after admitting to me."

"What precisely was that?"

"That you are of sound mind and capable of taking such a position by deeming it justifiable in the circumstances as you see them."

"So? I'm not withdrawing any of the things I've said to you… Is it that you want me to refuse to recognise the court?"

"No, indeed I don't. But let's leave this issue for a few days—the possibility of your case being heard within the next few weeks is extremely unlikely.

"I want instead to pursue the story from your involvement with Germany. If you would relate the main details as you see them, firstly and then we shall go over the minutiae when we get the opportunity."

Halle told of her escape from the British police by going to the Channel Islands—she deliberately left out O'Driscoll's part in it. Her applying for a radio announcer's job in Germany after the islands had been invaded; her work and her decision to attempt an escape by acting as a recruiting officer for the Wehrmacht. The series of events which culminated in her being thanked officially by General Bór-Komorowski and the over active attention she received from Hengist, a high ranking Gestapo officer. She went on to mention his accidental death almost in the last hour before reaching Sweden.

Maxwell paused while he thought out his next move, "I think we've covered sufficient ground already, I'm sure you're exhausted, and I will have a lot to explore before I see you again tomorrow at Bow Street Magistrates' Court." He stood up and they shook hands and then he left without a backward glance.

The next morning Halle was remanded and charged with the first two counts, which Maxwell had read out to her the previous day. Although the magistrates gave a date for the trial—27th of November—Maxwell told her that the average time taken for a case this serious to be heard at the Central Criminal Court was four months. "Why did they give me such an early date then?" Maxwell was quick and very assured with his answer; "The magistrate has to ensure that justice is not merely equitable but is swift. But there are other problems confronting the judge when we get to the Old Bailey, the police will seek to continue holding you on remand because they will claim that they are still collecting evidence on additional charges to be put to the court."

"But in my case there are additional charges still to be made."

"Yes but the police are not beyond tilting the scales in their favour by imputing that these are a series of major offences waiting in the wings."

"How would the police obtain evidence for offences they claim happened in Germany and Poland?"

"That's the crucial part of this case; you probably will get five to ten years on the IRA charge but the death penalty would be a possibility if they could prove you colluded with the Germans in wartime. As to *how* they would get evidence?" and he raised his shoulders to show his lack of knowledge, "You're going to have to put on your thinking cap. However, there is one I can foresee—the broadcasts. The intelligence services record all they can receive from Germany and her satellites, so they'll have information based on the items you read. If you just read them as an announcer I doubt if that would seriously alter the length of your sentence but if they could prove that you wrote it, that would be a different case. By the way, talking about length of sentence—I suspect that when the war ends all these sentences relating to the IRA will be reviewed and the prisoners eventually deported."

"Do you think the end is that close?"

"Perhaps a year or two down the line but the Nazis wouldn't be able to withstand the pressure on two fronts."

"From my experience they'll be fortunate to hold the Russians never mind defeat them. But getting back to my case, I can't see how they would get evidence against me."

"Don't assume that they can't. You'll need to assume that they'll find a way so that you're not caught unprepared. I'll talk to you in a few days but think the matter over." Maxwell left Bow Street with a deeper frown than he had shown Halle. He didn't wish to alarm her too much but he was convinced that the police had something, especially when they had disclosed so much to him.

Halle knew Molly would have been in Aylesbury with those also sentenced. When she returned to her cell from court, she discovered a note under her pillow—it was from Molly: "Only heard of your arrival. Got a friend who was being sent up to Holloway to deliver this. Sad for you but hope you can beat the rap as this place is wild. I'll hardly contact you unless you end up with me."

Halle asked for permission to exercise at the same time as any of the Irish being held but the female guard told her she would have to put in a formal request to the Warden, which she promptly did and equally promptly she was refused. "I suppose they think that we will launch a German invasion," she remarked to the guard who brought the flat refusal. "No, but over the years the IRA have managed to free a few prisoners and the Warden hasn't forgotten when he served in Lincoln Jail De Valera escaped!"

Ian was glad to be home after such a long sojourn abroad. His last encounter with Halle had been the final straw; the fact that he left without the slightest effort on his part to poultice over their differences was indicative of the drain on his emotional resources. At first he intended to call on Halle's parents but he knew he wouldn't be welcome, particularly if they thought there was a relationship between him and their daughter. He was a curiosity among his friends and relatives but to the others living nearby they assumed that he was just home on leave. "It just shows how little people really know about their neighbours," he explained to a few friends whom he met in the Lodge on the Monday after he arrived. He looked at each of them in a new light—it dawned on him that he was attempting to see them through Halle's eyes but try as he might he saw only the love and concern they had for him. He wondered how would they feel if the newspapers reported the Halle story and his involvement. "Lord, please don't leave me to choose between them and Halle."

As the evening ended someone stood up and began singing the National Anthem and as Ian joined in with the others he recognised that his Britishness was a part of him that he would never relinquish, even if it meant losing Halle, which was a curious decision seeing that their parting was regarded as permanent by her.

Maxwell's expression was grim from the moment he arrived and Halle knew that he was perturbed about something involving her; or at least sufficiently upset as to display a side of him that she never expected. "We may be in further trouble—I'm sorry, it's my fault, I didn't think of warning my secretary about the dangerous nature of this case."

"My God! What's happened?" demanded Halle; not able to imagine what had occurred which left him in such a state. "Apparently a female came to the office and showed her some kind of official identification and asked who had arranged for me to represent you, seeing that you were in custody at the time.

"She gave her Ian's name and regiment and his home address which he left in the event of me needing him. I immediately smelt a rat when the girl gave me the message on my return from court and I made enquiries because I was going to lodge an official protest at the tactics being adopted but the woman did not belong to the police."

"So where do we go from here?"

"You tell me! I can only say that there doesn't seem to be any recognised governmental agency involved—that doesn't mean there's not but the probability is that the information I got was accurate."

"Let's think this through. She didn't ask what prison I was lodged in?"

"No, but the morning papers would have given that detail or in fact it wouldn't be much of a guess given that women who are a security danger are housed there."

"That only leaves Ian as the person she is trying to contact—obviously she didn't want to speak to you, nor me for that matter. Well, given that I'm in here to the end of time I didn't make the first team. She was quick to work it out that I hadn't arranged a barrister or a solicitor. By the way don't you normally work through a solicitor?"

"Ninety-nine percent of the time but if I'm approached and I like the case I'll use a colleague of mine as the solicitor. But go on with your deductions."

"I'll have to stop short because I'm becoming too excited at the prospect of having someone on my side who I'm hoping will be able to explain all, or at least part of this mystery. Can I make a suggestion?" asked Halle and proceeded as if consent had been given. "Perhaps you should write to Ian and warn him. It may be nothing more than a nosy reporter but then again it may not." Maxwell gave her what she considered a hard look, "You're trying to cover up what you really think; you know that a letter of such a kind from me would be a clear indication to him that there was a new development."

Halle smiled, all too aware that this man was not easily fooled, "You might be right or my speculation may be a long way off the target. But seeing as I'm making the suggestions it would be better if you make it a letter of apology for inadvertently divulging his address and regiment." Maxwell looked disgusted, "What did you think I was going to do? Blame him? Just stop labouring the obvious." Halle apologised but went on to mention her uneasiness, "What if this is not the innocent enquiry I think it is? Say its some ultra security group poking their noses into this to cut me up—I'm preparing you for just such an eventuality."

"But what makes you think that you would be of interest to them?"

"If you knew the various aspects of my story I'm sure you would be saying, along with me, 'I need to suspect everything'."

"You know that you will have to divulge what thoughts you have on these matters if I'm to save you from the rigors of a long prison sentence." The querulous tone of his voice was not lost on Halle, "I know we haven't got down to dealing with some of the oddities I've encountered in the past two years."

Maxwell suspected that she was weighing what to tell and what to leave out so he came at it from a different direction, "My work load is heavy this week but with this sudden turn of events I'll have to put some things on the back-burner and get your queries dealt with—that is, if anyone's capable of dealing with them."

Halle didn't like the idea of this man suggesting that it may not be possible to represent her successfully. "Perhaps you should spill all the beans and leave him to advise you, after all he can't divulge what you've told him as it's privileged information," smugly rejoined her alter ego. Halle had learnt to distrust its direction and advice but on this occasion she couldn't find from which direction it was coming; still she wasn't going to tell all. Having reached this conclusion she thought she heard the sound of a gloating laugh in the background. "When do you propose talking about them?" asked Halle.

"We'll start tomorrow and I'd appreciate you documenting some of the incidents which you now feel, on reflection, were odd," and turning to pick up his papers and deposit them in his brief-case Maxwell bade her farewell and asked the guard to let him out.

Ian woke with a start, "I should be in London seeing Halle and her lawyer, this watching from the sideline is not my style. I'll have to get back." It was only when he was sitting down to a breakfast of bap and butter that he recalled that it wasn't enough to turn up at the ferry to Heysham, he needed a pass stamped and dated. He was still wondering how he would talk his way into getting his boarding card altered when he heard the post drop through the letterbox.

Normally he simply lifted it and sat it on the table for his parents; but this time he looked at the postmarks and discovered that two of them were posted in London—an unlikely venue for letters to his home. He simply was not used to receiving post and it took him a moment to spot that both of these were for him. He dithered over which one to open first and then abruptly opened the top one. The writing was difficult to read and he assumed that the writer wrote it in a hurry and in a somewhat disjointed fashion. "I read of your Bow St. hearing. I'll be in touch at whatever posting you are at. Tell Halle not to worry. Sergeant S. Gourmont."

"Who is this sergeant and what does he mean 'she wasn't to worry'?" thought Ian and tried to put it to the back of his mind whilst he opened the second letter. The heading indicated immediately that it was from Maxwell. He read the apology with alarm, at first he didn't see any connection between the two letters, then the penny dropped and it was clear—at least to him— that the person who wrote the other letter got the address from Maxwell's office.

He shouted up the stairs to his mother that he was away to make a phone call to his regiment about an early return to barracks. His mother was naturally concerned as she thought he wasn't well enough for active duty but he reassured her that it wasn't likely he'd be sent abroad in the present situation. When he entered the phone box at the bottom of the street he assumed that he would be able to make contact immediately but he had forgotten how difficult it was in peacetime to make a trunk call and how much more difficult it was in wartime. Of course he wasn't able to get through as the operator told him that the line to England was busy and if he wanted to put his name down on the list it could be the best part of an hour before there was a line free, so he pressed Button B and got his two pence back.

He walked towards Bridge End conscious that the blitzed houses in Thistle Street were the first changes there had been in the city for about thirty years. "They're going to have build new homes now or as soon after the war as they can get things up and going again—'up and going' is not exactly a description of the Belfast Corporation that anyone in this part of the country would recognise! Lord have I changed? I never thought I would criticise anything run by my own people." He continued walking past Seaforde Street and the Short Strand aware that the Fenians lived there besides St. Matthew's Chapel. He began thinking about Halle and how she attended services there and how she resented him referring to it as a 'chapel' saying it was a derogatory remark making out that Catholics couldn't have real churches. But when he argued that Roman Catholics called it 'a chapel' she brushed it aside saying it was only the ignorant ones who couldn't tell the difference between the two. She also talked about the area as being Ballymacarrett like he did which he thought was ridiculous and told her she had a nerve claiming the name 'Ballymacarrett' for the Catholic area. She would say, "Oh yes, that's a real British name being in Irish and meaning the town of MacArt," and he smiled at the recollection. "There's been no change in my attitude to things." But the more he let his mind wander the more he saw the immensity of the difficulties that confronted Halle and himself. "The devil take this, I'm just going to walk over to Donegall Quay and chance my arm. I'm bound to know someone who works to the Cross Channel Ferry who'll put me on the right road to getting a boarding card."

Halle spent the following day after Maxwell's visit writing down what she considered were the various episodes which suggested to her that she had been used by some group or other in Germany and Poland. Looking back the first thing which came to mind was the odd way she was sent to POW camps, particularly in Germany. Why the out of the way places with so few Irish prisoners? Then again her results were so poor why did they persist, after all it was her idea not theirs? Initially she had felt that General Eckhard was attempting to dictate to her who was in charge but now, on reflection, she saw Hengist's hand in so much of it. Indeed the very title of Colonel given to her made no sense. At the start she was so excited at being able to plan her escape that she failed to see that the story they had told her about being put on the same level as the camp commandants to enable her to do her job more efficiently didn't stand up—in the last analysis she had no say in regard to prisoners, so what was that about? The only benefit she had gained from the title was being able to stay in some of the officers' quarters of various army groups near the POW camps.

Another thought began to bother her: Hengist could have had her removed by having her killed or having her thrown out of her job but he didn't, why? Other strange things struck her as well in regard to him: why didn't he question her about being outside Plock when she was shot? "It's such an obvious question but he didn't ask," and she spoke out loud without being aware that she had done so. Then again, she remembered Ian mentioning how they discovered where she was being held in Warsaw. Surely Hengist couldn't have been that stupid as to lead the AK to her? And the actual escape—could anything have been that simple? Sobieski was standing outside without the Germans spotting him—very unlikely!

The whole issue of Hengist's behaviour on the ship convinced her that he was under orders *not* to kill her. The fact that he said that she would be held prisoner for some time until he got instructions to free her could have been a ploy to encourage her to go without a fight but the more she tried to rationalise all the events the more she felt that Hengist was playing with a different ball than she and Ian were. "What will Maxwell make of all of this? He'll probably think he'll be able to get me off as a likely psychiatric case who's coming down with conspiracy theories!"

CHAPTER 22
(October 1943-January 1944)

IAN TOLD HIS mother and father a white lie about getting back to Lancashire to his regiment. Once he reached Liverpool from Heysham he made his way to Lime Street and took the London train to Euston. He felt that there were issues hanging in the air which would be resolved if he could find out precisely who was this Sergeant S. Gourmont. The only person who could throw some light on the identity of the sergeant was Halle and he was sufficiently aware of prison conditions to know that outsiders would never get leave to visit those in jail. This left him with Maxwell as a conduit to Halle, so that was the reason for his heading to Maxwell's office. The quicker he saw him and got back to his regiment the sooner all these difficulties would be resolved. Of course he wasn't in when he enquired at his office in the Strand. "What are the prospects of seeing him today?" he enquired of his secretary. "I'm sorry sir, but he is visiting clients today and has a late court appearance. This evening he is due to be present at a sitting of the Commons. I can arrange an appointment for tomorrow at noon; I'm afraid that's the best I can do." Ian reluctantly accepted and left heading towards Paddington to find accommodation.

Halle read and re-read the notes she had prepared for Maxwell's arrival knowing that he would be ready with a series of questions or answers which would minimise the effect of her assertions. She was determined to show him that she was no mad dog Irishwoman intent on visiting the ten plagues on the House of Hanover. "He'll never like that, especially in the middle of a war with the Germans," responded her alter ego with enthusiasm, which promptly made Halle change the term in her mind to the 'House of Windsor'.

Thoughts of home plagued her now that she felt that she was so much closer to it. "Maxwell will get a message to your mother and father and your brothers and sisters if you'll only write one that doesn't get him into trouble." The voice was so persuasive that Halle decided to put that on the top of her agenda but she would tell Maxwell that they were not to put themselves out by the expense of travelling over to see her. As usual, once her mind started darting about there was no knowing where it would next alight. A thought suddenly emanated from just such a quarter: "My name is as much English as the royal family's." But the supposition that she was

336

indirectly claiming some form of Englishness soon blew the spark out. The banging of cell doors indicated that the exercise hour was about to start and she looked forward to it as a means of trying to get back to full fitness after her long illness.

She had just returned when she was informed that Mr Maxwell was waiting and she must go to her cell immediately. He noted how flushed she was and asked with a smile, "Are you working on some daily rota of exercise so that you can scale the outer walls?" Halle chose to ignore the humour, "I am attempting to regain my health not my freedom, the latter I leave to you."

Halle's mind just couldn't see any connection and she assumed it may have been Ian's former wife, Vera. Maxwell gave a visible sigh of relief thinking that at least the damage had been little, "About your health, perhaps you could detail how it has been affected and then we can go on from there," and Maxwell drew a fountain pen and a propelling pencil from his waistcoat pocket and placed them on the table in preparation for taking notes. "My time in Germany, although not pleasant, was fine but I was badly wounded in Poland when I was in the process of escaping with Ian."

"What brought that about and who initiated the escape?"

"I suppose you'll need Ian's confirmation but I thought that with his record of escaping and my ability to pass myself as a German officer—you know that part of the story—that we could complement each other's strengths and make it to Danzig, as I persisted in calling it until Ian taught me to say Gdansk. Perhaps we should get back to this hearing on the 27th November?"

"I hate this jumping about from one issue to the next but whatever makes you feel easier."

"Do you think there is a chance that they'll now process the other charges?"

"No, as I explained originally, they'll hold back those charges as they'll ask for you to be held on remand."

"Even if they have 'proof'? I suspect they have but I just can't figure out where they got the information."

"They'll go the usual route regardless of what they have, unless of course they feel it's politically useful to put you away for a long period. But IRA activity has practically ceased in Britain so that won't be an issue."

"Is there any other purpose being served by putting this on the long finger?"

"If there is something going on, and that's a big 'if' going on this list of items you have given me, what do you think it is that will change the nature of this case?"

"I'm sorry. Ian and I have talked this into the ground and can do no better than say how suspicions grow and grow with each incident but we haven't been able to put two and two together."

"I'd suggest we tackle our position on the charges of IRA membership and involvement in attacks on property in Britain."

"Perhaps I should plead guilty," suggested Halle but Maxwell explained that effectively it would mean the end of the case. He wanted to be in a position to argue mitigation but brutally stated that he felt her prospects were negligible. "I realise that but although I'm not happy at the idea of a long custodial sentence, it's better than facing a death sentence on a charge of treason or taking the rap for some death I had nothing to do with!"

"Having come this far perhaps you want to look at the charges which are likely to follow?"

"Having scanned them what do you think is going on?"

"I tend to see them as oddities but not necessarily tied to the charges which they suggested to me will come later. Take each point and tell me what bearing each of them has on the charge of treason." Halle went through them and explained her suspicions and how they grew with what she thought initially were coincidences.

Ian was shown directly into Maxwell's office the next day at noon. He was greeted like a long lost friend, which shook him as he had a perception of solicitors as being class conscious and extremely unbearable. Then he thought that the man knew he had been in the wrong over the issue of providing a total stranger with his name and address and he was convinced he had hit on the reason when Maxwell began by asking him about it: "I was wondering if this woman has been in touch with you yet." He was clearly anxious to get the matter out of the way thought Ian. He searched his inside pocket and produced the letter and threw it on the desk and immediately regretted his action. "Sorry about that, normally I'm more careful about the niceties of behaviour, but I seem to be acting out of character since I returned to the mainland."

"It's understandable, you have been through the mill and it will take some time for you to settle down. I went through the same experience after the Great War."

"How did you deal with the pressures afterwards?"

"Well I had been wounded at Passchendaele and it took me a long time to recuperate and I suppose that helped but my wife and I were still young and committed and we pulled through." While speaking Maxwell read the short letter from Sergeant S. Gourmont, "It's hardly a woman's handwriting is it?"

"I never thought of it being a woman—I suppose it could be given that there are sergeants in the ATS. No, I had presumed that the woman had passed my details to this sergeant. Do you think this is the person your staff handed my address?"

"It seems probable, at any rate the quicker they get in touch with you the sooner we'll be able to make an assessment of what help they can be in Miss Hegel's case."

"Well I'm heading back to my regiment in Stafford this afternoon and I will telephone you in the event of anything important turning up, otherwise I'll just write. Is that OK with you?"

"That's fine, we'll leave it like that."

Halle had forgotten to look in her cell in case there was a note from Molly. "The distraction of Maxwell's visit was chiefly to blame," she told herself. It had only dawned on her much later in the day and she found it almost directly. Whoever delivered it made no attempt to try anything ingenious. Again it was under her pillow and as she only knew of one person who had the ability to get messages into Holloway it must be from her.

"Heard from Vincent today. Will try escape for you if life is in danger. Love Molly." Halle didn't want anyone risking their life for her, particularly as she felt that there was a combination of things favouring her being released. She had no idea what they were but her intuition told her and that was sufficient reason to reject any outside help. "God it would be desperate if Molly has been able to get a message through to my people back home before Maxwell makes contact with them." Once again her mind was going for a jaunt and the longer she remained interned, as she considered it, the worse the condition would get.

Ian, on arrival at the camp, had just been enquiring if anyone had been seeking him when he got word from the front desk that a Canadian woman in uniform was at the front gate wanting to see him. He rushed round and he saw a woman about as tall as Halle waiting in the guardroom. "My name is Ian Patterson," and he extended his hand, "are you Sergeant Gourmont?"

"Yes, but please call me Sheila." The name echoed in his mind and he wondered if this was the 'dead' girl that Halle talked so much about. "I thought you were supposed to be dead…" but the tinkle of laughter from her halted whatever he was going to add. "I'm afraid that was the deliberate intention to protect me and others including Halle but it went wrong, not in every detail but in its effect." She went into a catalogue of incidents which made up the whole of her story beginning with her recital of being Sheila Gray who had adopted the pseudonym Gourmont. She made it clear that she had no permission from the Canadian government to speak on the matter but when she saw the report in the *Times* of the charges of IRA membership she knew she had to contact someone to explain that she owed her life to Halle's passing her information. "It's doubtful if I'd be allowed to go to court—so much of my story is regarded as needing to be under wraps that even if there should be a miscarriage of justice I'm sure the authorities would rather let it happen than endanger whatever scheme they have afoot."

Ian was taken aback, "For the life of me I can't see how anything Halle did involved any of the Allies." It took the best part of an hour for Sheila to tell her story and answer questions from Ian and as she left she told him that if need be she would file an account dealing only with the events that directly involved Halle.

Maxwell was surprised at Ian's telephone call so soon after leaving him the previous day. "None of this appertains to the possible charges she has yet to face," he explained when Ian had finished telling him Sheila's account of the events, "Even if it did would this woman be able to testify on any of it?"

"I doubt it from what she said."

"Can you come up to London for a few days?"

"I still have leave due to me so that should be fine. I'll see you the day after tomorrow."

On the strength of the information given to him by Ian, Hugh Maxwell thought that he couldn't wait to consult his client and determined to see the Attorney General, Sir David Southerby as soon as he could and with that intention rang his office to make an appointment. He realised almost as soon as he got through that he couldn't tell the person at the other end what the meeting was to be about because of its nature and he hung up. Instead he rang the prison and asked for the Warden and was put through very quickly, "What is it Mr Maxwell that has you telephoning at this time of the night?"

"I wonder would it be possible for me to see my client urgently tomorrow morning?"

"That's fine but let me organise things at this end first and I'll give you a call in five or ten minutes." In no time at all he received confirmation of the appointment.

Halle had been prepared for his coming but was surprised that it was arranged so hurriedly. "What brought about this sudden visit?"

"I shan't keep you long. I just need confirmation that you knew or had dealings with a woman named Sheila Gourmont, or as she was more commonly known as Sheila Gray?"

"Yes, I had. If you recollect when I told you my story of events in Berlin she was the girl to whom I was referring. But I fear she is dead, murdered by the Gestapo."

"Could you give me some details about her and a description please?" Maxwell showed an intensity that Halle hadn't seen before in him. Normally she would be asking for reasons but on this occasion she merely answered: "Well she was about as tall as myself—if I'm totally honest she was slightly taller. She had blue eyes and bobbed fair hair. Oh! She was very athletic looking. Apparently she had been married to a very right-wing French man who had been killed accidentally by the Germans."

"At one point earlier you told me you had warned her—about what precisely?"

"I can't tell you who told me, I don't wish to jeopardise his life—sorry but I shouldn't even have said that much! Like everyone I suppose when suspicions are aroused they naturally think that the finger is being pointed at them, so in a selfish attempt to extricate myself I turned to the one who was closest to looking like me and that was Sheila. Then, assuming I was correct, I suddenly found I was putting myself in her shoes and it was then that I decided to tell her of the rumours going round the building."

Maxwell had been busy writing a longhand synopsis during Halle's account. Halle couldn't wait on him finishing, "What is going on?" she demanded but Maxwell continued writing unhurriedly and when he completed what he was doing put down his fountain pen and in a somewhat laconic manner related to her the story which Ian had conveyed to him on the telephone. Maxwell realised that the emotion was building in Halle and he paused, "Are you all right?" Halle merely nodded but this didn't satisfy her counsellor. "What has upset you at this juncture?"

"I suppose it's the combination of knowing Sheila's alive and that Ian still cares for me enough to continue working on my behalf." Maxwell was not at his best in comforting people but he tried and succeeded in getting her to stop long enough to agree to his putting this evidence to the Attorney General. "What will it mean?" asked Halle. Maxwell sighed, "Very little, I'm afraid, on the two charges that you're facing but perhaps it will succeed in getting them to drop their proposed charges on aiding and abetting the enemy."

When Maxwell left Halle pondered the new information and realised she was no further on in unravelling the morass of 'evidence' she felt that she had dug up. "I need a Rosetta Stone of my own to interpret all these incidents," she told the wall.

Sir David was none too anxious to be involved in weighing evidence, which he felt should be left to the jury but agreed to see his old sparring partner on the basis that Maxwell wasn't the type to play a flanker on him.

"There's going to be some difficulty with a great deal of the evidence I'm going to present to you. Mr Patterson has been told, by an intelligence agent—who is unable to testify on behalf of my client—that Miss Hegel helped her," began Maxwell, "and I would need her present to confirm parts of the story which Mr Patterson will tell."

"What information will this Mr Patterson give which will have a bearing on Miss Hegel's case?" Clearly Sir David was anxious to limit the issues to the charges already made and he could see that Maxwell was uncomfortable. "He has been given details of issues that arose in Germany." The Attorney General's response was sharp and to the point: "What have they possibly got to do with this girl's IRA membership?"

"Nothing directly but certainly indirectly. But I'm led to believe that there are further charges pending and this evidence will have a bearing on them. Oh! May I add she was never in the IRA!"

"So you think that this new information will force the police to withdraw the possible charges they're considering?"

"Yes, I think the authorities would be an ungrateful bunch if they proceed with all these charges."

"Hugh you are prone to exaggeration!" and Sir David stood up and excused himself. "Where is he going?" wondered Maxwell. His voice somewhat cynically rejoined, "He could be going to the toilet for all I know but I suspect he is ringing someone from the other room asking them for details of the other charges." Sir David returned and settled himself behind his desk, "I have arranged for Miss Hegel to see me tomorrow morning, provided you can be here with the young man and perhaps," looking sharply at Maxwell, "we'll be able to get back to the original charges."

The Attorney General waited for Maxwell to enlarge on what he considered was a desperate barrister's attempt to get his client off the hook. "Just a minute, David, I want to say this without my client and the witness being present. I have given no undertaking that I will refrain from mentioning any of this in court. Indeed if my client refers to it I doubt if the judge will be able to stop the jury hearing all the details."

"Hugh, what do you expect to gain from such a line?"

"Justice! An item which is more difficult to find during war than in

342

peacetime and in the present circumstances perhaps I'd be better searching for the Holy Grail." Maxwell's voice was gruff and clearly he meant that he wanted a *quid pro quo* which Sir David had to offer if they were to proceed any further.

"I would have to hear exactly what this is about and from the way you are speaking it is clear that I'll probably have to consult with a number of departments, including the Foreign Office, not the easiest to deal with."

"So can I leave all this until tomorrow morning?"

"Better leave it until I get in touch with you. Just one thing more, he did not witness any of these events he is going to relate?"

"No, and I know that, if this was a court case, it would affect its worth but this is merely painting a picture of what may occur if this sees the light of day in the Old Bailey."

"Very well," and the Attorney General stood up, signalling the end of their talks.

A few days later Halle was wakened and handed a note from Maxwell telling her that with Ian she was to see the Attorney General and that he would also be present. Normally she was very lethargic early in the day but the news had given her hope that she would be able to present a case, which would considerably alter her position.

When Ian arrived at the Attorney General's office Maxwell was already there with Halle. He went directly to her and she gave him a hug and a peck on the cheek but their conversation kept to talk of her health, prison conditions and the weather and, inevitably, was somewhat stilted. Maxwell assumed his presence was the reason but Ian realised that nothing had changed between them. "How was Sheila?" asked Halle, "Did she say how she got away…"

"Good morning, come in everyone," said Sir David, who had just arrived. "Take a seat and we'll start as soon as I hang up my hat and coat." Maxwell introduced Halle and Ian and the Attorney General asked Ian if he was ready to begin. Ian was somewhat hesitant, "I'm afraid you'll have to be very patient because as you know I am not the person who witnessed these events. I can only tell what I think has been going on, on the basis of what I've been told." He paused for a breath, "Sergeant…"

"Hold it for a moment! I don't think it's advisable to mention names in this situation," said Maxwell looking at each person present. "Sorry, go on."

"This person was and is working with a Canadian intelligence agency and she was working in Berlin on an important matter," Ian was struggling to tell the story without naming people. "She had to make contact with another person in the city but somehow, without her knowledge, she landed a job in radio, she assumed that it was because of her alleged background as the former wife of a French Nazi who had been accidentally killed by the Germans."

"Well it's at this point that Miss Hegel, Halle, arrived on the scene at Irland-Rekation, the radio station in Berlin, and there unwittingly became friends with an English girl who, she later discovered, had Canadian citizenship as well. Perhaps Halle you could explain this part better than me." Halle was reluctant but seeing Ian looking anxious she began: "I was in a position to hear the rumours circling the building and I warned her that she has been spotted as a likely spy or double agent. 'Your friend has died suddenly' was the word put out by the bosses but you can imagine my surprise when I learnt, just a few days ago, that that was not the case. I guessed someone had spirited her away knowing that the German authorities would do a cover-up in order not to frighten the staff at the radio station. In the days and weeks that followed I was determined to get out of Germany, as I had, by that time been convinced they had murdered my friend. But I had only a limited knowledge of German and had no friends in the country, it was then that I thought up the idea of recruiting for the German Army as a way out."

"A likely story!" remarked Sir David.

"Please let her tell it without interruption!" demanded Maxwell.

"I was somewhat surprised to be offered the job so readily but was shocked at being given the title of colonel because as the general put it 'you'll be able to deal more readily with the camp commandants'. I soon discovered that the title only gave me a little access to officers' messes and overnight accommodation.

"But the next move caused me a great deal of anxiety. I was directed to various POW camps in Germany but in such a way that I frequently bypassed those which were more important."

"Sorry to interrupt, Miss Hegel, I just don't follow the point of that," remarked Maxwell. "I never figured out the reason," said Halle. Ian rushed to support her, "I don't think we'll ever know what precisely went on, but I was at the meeting between Halle and General Tadeusz Bór-Komorowski..."

"Excuse me once again, are you referring to the Commander of the AK in Warsaw?"

"Yes."

"What brought that about? A man, no, a leader in the middle of a war takes time out to see Miss Hegel?"

"Please Ian, don't say anything that will embarrass me. I didn't know I was doing anything of importance. If anything, up to the time I escaped and indeed afterwards, the Germans saw me as their ally against the British."

"That's another mystery we haven't solved," replied Ian, "but I was about to say, that at one point I thought he was going to tell us what was going on but at the last moment decided against it. At any rate, he had brought her to him to thank her for the help she had given to the AK by distracting the Nazis with her attempt to escape." Halle was far from satisfied by Ian's description and added, somewhat ironically, "He was so grateful that he didn't tell me what was going on."

"Maybe because of what you said earlier."

"What did I say?" queried Halle her forehead furrowed with wrinkles. Ian deliberately was slow in responding, "'The Germans saw me as their ally against the British' is what you said. And if you remember Aleksander and the General told me that they had grave doubts about your reliability at first and although Alek came round I don't think there was any possibility of the General taking a chance by telling you the truth, whatever that may be."

The conversation entered a phase of aimless discussion on what may or may not have been the General's motives. "Excuse me," said Halle, interrupting, "What was the point of Hengist holding me prisoner until he got instructions?"

The others were slow to respond, as they hadn't worked out the motives for Hengist's other tactics. Inevitably Sir David intervened, "I'm at a loss— one moment Miss Hegel is *allegedly* working for the Allied cause, next she is regarded as working for the Germans against *us*. Neither of which she denies, which suggests she is a double agent! Hugh you and your client need to make up your minds what it's to be! This is all very nice but I haven't the time to unravel it, basically Hugh, your view relies on what these two people here have said—and one of them is totally relying on the word of someone only one person in this room knew. There's too much supposition in all of this to make judgements. Let me add another difficulty I find hard to deal with," turning to Ian, "I believe you're a Unionist, why then are you supporting this young woman, who, if the charges are correct, used explosives in an attempt to change the political position in Ulster?"

Halle answered before Ian could speak, "Ian's saying no more than I am, you meet evil with sufficient violence to do away with it." Ian, more thrusting than anyone there had ever seen, "I never attempted to defend the republican ideas of Halle and her partners in crime."

"So we're going down that road again!" roared Halle, "You and your

British cohorts, by the use of violence, tore a nation apart and you didn't care with whom you associated to bring it about," turning towards Ian, "Did your father and his relatives not deal with the Germans to get guns before the First World War?"

Sir David intervened and then turned to Maxwell; "It's not so simple is it?"

Halle was quick to take up the cudgels for Maxwell, "I lived in Germany—the people there were under no illusions about the Gestapo's involvement in killings of all kinds. People were afraid to speak because all too many friends and neighbours had been deposited in concentration camps and never heard of again. I thought this was common knowledge in Britain—at least I heard people discussing the Nazis during the time I stayed in England and although I believed it was typical British propaganda they didn't, otherwise why would they have gone to war? They were convinced it was happening, on the other hand I had to learn the hard way."

"I take on board all you say but we still have no evidence to support it," was the calmly presented answer from Sir David.

"I thought that what I said about the German people would have been evidence of a kind but clearly you want someone who has survived a concentration camp to give you a direct account before you'll accept its legitimacy. Is there *no* weight given to circumstantial evidence when the other type isn't available?"

"Of course you're right," said Maxwell, "what Sir David is trying to do is place a political slant on all of this." Sir David shrugged and brought the proceedings to a halt by standing. "I'm afraid I have to leave for a meeting but I'll be in touch, Hugh, within a few days with a response to all of this," waving his arm to encompass everyone in the room.

Halle and Ian left the room somewhat dispirited in that their intrinsic differences hadn't abated one iota in the time they had been separated. Ian did not see Halle's justification for the use of force in the same light when it came to the issue of Northern Ireland. Their farewells were somewhat formal involving the use of handshakes, which had no meaning. Maxwell viewed the pair in a mixture of despair and helplessness feeling that whatever the outcome of these talks there was little hope of any reconciliation for them.

CHAPTER 23
(October 1943-January 1944)

THIS OCCASION WAS different; the boss did not wish to speak directly to Mr Maxwell but merely wanted her to pass him a message about one of his clients—a Miss Hegel. She was to say that Sir David had taken advice, both political and legal, from his colleagues and others about the matter they had discussed and the consensus view was to proceed with the case against his client. He would be in touch regarding other charges. Her experience of Mr Maxwell told her that neither of these answers would be acceptable and that he would demand to be put in touch directly with Sir David. And there was the rub! She had been warned that on no account did he want to speak to Maxwell and that, in essence, meant that she would be the one to take the drubbing that the MP would undoubtedly have ready to give Sir David.

The telephone rang in Maxwell's office and his secretary answered it. She had been waiting for two days to hear from the Attorney General, her boss had been adamant that she should contact him if she didn't hear early in the day from him. No matter what, she was to find out how Sir David's exhaustive negotiations had gone. But she didn't know what she feared most; whether it was her reluctance to face up to being pushy or the dread of being given the news which Maxwell didn't wish to hear without talking directly to Sir David. As she reached out to lift the receiver she prayed that this would be his secretary with good news. "Good morning, Mr Maxwell's secretary." The earpiece seemed to stick to her and the expression on her face told its own tale of woe. The news was bad, "Just a moment and I'll put you through," and she rushed to insert the plug into the switchboard but her colleague at the other end had replaced the hand receiver. Angry and annoyed she rang back immediately only to discover the engaged tone—a despicable act of cowardice, and suddenly she smiled at her caustic judgement knowing she had used the same tactic from time to time with that same office.

She knew better then to give in, she persisted until she finally got through. "Excuse me may I know your name, please?" The pause indicated that Sir David's secretary was wondering what way to handle this. "After all these years? Why?"

"Well I've been up to high doh waiting on your call and it's just dawned on me that we shouldn't be such slaves to our masters that we have to adopt their tactics to each other and thus condemn each of us to a hell on earth every time we have to be in touch," Maxwell's secretary was more than forthcoming and evidently she had touched a nerve.

"Well I'm known to my friends as April—in fact my real name is Avril Hill but I hate my Aunt Avril so I don't use it," chuckled Sir David's secretary.

"That's curious—because my Christian name is Catherine but I've never liked it so I told my friends in school that my name was Kathleen Turner and I've stuck to it ever since, even though it's got me into a few scrapes along the way," and both of them laughed.

"Sorry Kathleen but you rang me because I put the telephone down promptly to avoid having Mr Maxwell breathe fire and brimstone down the line. Let *me* tell you what he wants. He would like to speak to my boss because he's unhappy about the shenanigans that he and his cabinet colleagues have been up to. How near is that?"

"Pretty much spot on and in addition *I'm to persist* until I get Sir David on the line. Any suggestions as to how I get round this? By the way I'm in plenty of trouble already with him because I gave out a name and address of a witness without consulting him."

"I'll tell you if you'll cover for me."

"You can depend on me when I know I'm on to a good thing."

"Well recently the police have been compiling a list of those they consider to be traitors who are at present abroad. I'll not go into the names on the telephone but some are well known for their broadcasting. Others belonged to Mosley and his group before the war—all told there are more than a hundred. Well the gang wants to test the legislation before the whole troop of them is caught. So your client is the victim of that witch hunt."

"I can't tell Maxwell any of that. The whole bloody lot of us would be on a charge with the hundred others. Sorry about the language. What I'll do is exaggerate the number of times I rang and how you gave me a different excuse for his absence each time. How's that April? It gets him off my back and at the same time you get the credit of keeping me at bay, OK?"

"That's fine with me. I could be doing with some credit for my work. He's always implying that I'm too easily swayed and fall for every line that's used to get him to talk on the telephone. I'll get him to write and confirm the message I gave you earlier."

"Thanks again April. With the both of us co-operating this work will be a thousand times easier."

Maxwell was not surprised at the answer awaiting him when he returned from court. "How often did you try to arrange for me to speak to him?"

Kathleen told how she had lost count and how amazed she was at the number of excuses her counterpart in the AG's office had made. "Put me through, I'll speak to her myself."

April took the call from Kathleen and for the first time in all of their dealings she felt prepared for Maxwell. "My dear, what is your name?"

"April, sir."

"You realise that you, single-handedly, are putting the life of my client in jeopardy! Undoubtedly the AG is acting out some rôle given him by his political masters and you in your concern to do your imagined duty have brought an innocent woman to the steps of the gallows."

"I thought she was an active IRA terrorist," replied April, wishing he would keep his speeches for the High Court. "Young woman there is a very considerable difference between being something and *alleged* to be that thing. Tell your lord and master from me that he may mistreat my secretary but he better not go any further with such behaviour with me. He forgets I was a minister of the government some years ago and I haven't forgotten how to get the ear of the right person."

"And who would that be, sir?"

"The Prime Minister, no less!" answered Maxwell with emphasis. April realised that the matter was getting out of hand and told him she would inform Sir David as soon as he arrived but couldn't guarantee he would be able to reply today. Maxwell hung up fuming at his so-called 'learned friend's' behaviour but he meant what he said. "Sir, what happens if the PM agrees with Sir David, where does that leave Miss Hegel?"

"I'm afraid in a potentially dangerous position; I'm also afraid, that no matter what angle we take, it could mean that the judge may decide not to allow Patterson's evidence as it is totally based on hearsay from a person we cannot name nor say how they are in a position to give such sensitive information. And even if we could get him to reduce it to two charges we still wouldn't be allowed to bring up material not directly dealing with the charges before the court."

"Surely it's only a question of getting that Polish general to testify how important the girl was to them—everyone knows the government are in touch with them, so what's to stop them?" Maxwell looked thoughtfully at Kathleen, "I think you may well have hit on it but leave it with me and I'll see how the hare sits."

Sir David praised April for her ability at keeping Maxwell at bay before he learnt that his opponent could be approaching Churchill. Indeed he had forgotten Maxwell's time in office under Ramsey Macdonald. He knew

Privy Councillors, like himself, assisted the King in his governmental duties and of the unspoken convention that they could see the PM on issues, which *they* considered of national importance. "Perhaps I've been less than wise in not seeing Churchill about Miss Hegel's case."

But his alter ego had always been more abrasive than the cool logical side of his nature. "But you have dealt with it—you are going to prosecute her on all the charges. Besides it has been agreed at a higher level to test the legislation on treason at the earliest opportunity," all very reassuring he felt, yet his mind would not rest, "Maxwell will crucify you in Downing Street if he gets admitted. In fact he'll make mince meat of the way you've handled this!" The two-stage argument in his mind was now totally developed, one querulously asking, "Do you think I should speak to the PM even at this late stage?" while the other attempted to change ground while still holding on to a vestige of nastiness, "Better you than that mean bastard!"

Going back into the reception area, Sir David asked April to contact Mr Maxwell as he wished to speak to him urgently. She felt, but controlled the urge to tell him, how easy it was for him to change his mind while she had no opportunity to make a point. "Sir David for Mr Maxwell, please." Kathleen giggled, "How did you do it?" April put her hand over the mouthpiece and told the AG that his secretary was attempting to get to him but he had a client. "Ah! A bit of his own back!" muttered the AG. But April didn't wish to foul up a situation which she felt was more promising from her viewpoint, "I believe it's genuine enough, sir. Yes? If you pick up the receiver in your office Sir David you'll find he's there."

"I see you received my threat," said Maxwell, taunting his political adversary. "What threat was that?" innocently asked the AG, as if he was hearing the words for the first time. Maxwell went on about having the opportunity to put his case directly to the PM and the inherent dangers for the AG—if it was made clear that his client had helped the Polish people and this was how she was repaid. "Not only your head will roll but never mind that; do you think that the old man will be rewarding you by increasing your tenure in office?"

The AG was somewhat nonplussed by the outright attack from Maxwell, still he wasn't going to lie down and roll over. "You're turning this whole issue into a political one and that is not the rôle intended for the Attorney General. I'm here to see that justice, in all of its manifestations, is carried out. I can't turn my back on criminal acts because they may—and for all I know, may not—result in some cheers from the sidelines."

"You have a remarkable sense of humour telling me, of *all* people, what is your rôle. I know damn fine that you play politics deciding who and what you will prosecute, this time you'll have to choose which cap you are wearing! Oh, by the way, who was it left word for me that he 'had taken advice, *political* and legal'? I don't want to get you into trouble with your lord and master so I'm hoping that we can find a solution that bypasses all of this."

"Perhaps you could call on me and we'll put our heads together to resolve this."

"I'm available now, if that's OK?" replied a more amiable Sir David. "Fine, I'll see you in the next half-hour."

Maxwell was surprised to find the AG awaiting him, "Pull up a chair and let's talk things over," said Sir David and Maxwell hid a smile as he did so, thinking he had been wise to hold Kathleen's suggestion back until he reached this point.

"David, I haven't the time to go over all of this with you. But let me put it like this—both of us are patriotic Englishmen and if we spend the rest of our lives looking at Ireland and its problems we'll never get it sorted out, never mind this part of the case against my client.

"A great many things in Miss Hegel's life in Germany are contentious but I'm sure you'll accept that she was attempting to escape from the country and certainly wasn't interested in promoting Nazi ideas."

"No, but she was pushing out propaganda attacking the British Empire." Maxwell's look of disgust was sufficient indication to Sir David that he was ploughing a furrow that would yield no harvest. "What the devil would you expect from a Republican?" demanded Maxwell, "As soon as the Nazis tried to get her to attack the Jews and Communism she made her attempt to get out but not before she had warned a Canadian agent that the Nazis were on to her."

"You have evidence to support this?"

"You can be a blithering idiot at times; of course I don't! Can *you* imagine the Canadian government giving permission to one of their agents to go into court and be identified as a spy? Come on David, I thought this was an attempt to rationalise the situation."

The Attorney General stood up, a nervous habit that Maxwell recognised as a sign that he had touched a nerve, he began to pace the length of the room and eventually he turned to face his opponent. "Hugh, I would like to put my cards on the table but I can't, the intelligence people won't talk about this with anyone—they all suffer from buttoned lips. But worse than that they are intractable and I can't get past them."

"Let me put a suggestion to you which might resolve all our difficulties."

Sir David raised his eyebrows at this sudden change in Maxwell. "This is a somewhat different tack from the one you have been adopting up until now. Why the sudden change?"

"Well, if the truth is to be told the idea or more accurately, the suggestion came from my secretary."

"Go ahead, what is it?" Hugh Maxwell realised then, that Sir David was willing to give more credence to a suggestion from *anyone* else than to anything emanating from himself. "Well, she simply said that it must be easy for British Intelligence to get a message to and from General Bór-Komorowski. So why couldn't they ask him for a character reference for Miss Hegel?" Sir David rubbed his beard as if he was thinking long and hard about the implications then finally, reached out his hand and shook Maxwell's as he nodded his agreement, "Provided I get *their* agreement to do it and I can't see them refusing."

"April, how are you? Is my boss still there?"

"Yes, it looks like it will take the rest of the morning. Hold it a moment...," there was a brief pause and April came back on the telephone, "They've just come out smiling! Someone has sorted it out. I wonder who?"

"Do you want to meet at lunchtime so that I can tell you?"

"OK, see you outside your place then."

Halle's wait for the decision was proving to be more difficult to deal with than she had anticipated. Up until recently she had been preparing for a lengthy sentence but with the appearance of Sheila and her story she felt the odds were now more in her favour for a considerable remission in this sentence. A message, which she daily expected from Molly, failed to materialise and the breakdown in communications made the waiting unbearable. She thought she had better resume contact with Ian and wrote two letters but on reflection realised she was using him as she had no intention of entering into a so-called marriage—as she saw a registry office ceremony—so she tore up the epistles. Yet her determination to put Ian from her mind suffered constant rebuffs. Logic couldn't account for his presence throughout her imprisonment—the hell that they had shared; his refusal to put himself first when he had an opportunity to escape; the contacts he had made and then used to enable her to get out of the clutches of Hengist; the list appeared endless, yet their intimacy that one night did not loom large in her thoughts, if pressed she would have had to admit that she had deliberately buried the memory because of the degradation and shame it had brought.

Since her imprisonment she had been visited by the prison chaplain and she had confessed her sin in terms which had taken days to compose and which, initially, she had attempted to hide in a host of venial sins—like her forgetting her morning and night prayers on occasion. Somehow it had been easier to go to confession in Berlin to a German priest whose familiarity with English would be such that she could be confident that he would miss the nuances in her account of such things as 'bad' thoughts. Equally she could present her involvement in attacks in England as good patriotic work to restore justice. To confess similar misdeeds to an English priest would have stuck in her gullet, as he wouldn't see it in the same light, yet her conscience forced her to tell him about it because she feared that she had taken advantage of the German priest and obtained absolution on the basis of her own conscience at the time.

However, the adultery was a different matter, it was a real sin in her view and she knew that if it had happened in Germany and she 'played it down' she would have needed to go back to confession and do it properly. With all these thoughts her prison cell became more of a hell than the hospital one she had left behind in Warsaw and she struggled to keep her sanity.

"Mr Maxwell is here to see you," shouted the woman warder through the opening at eye level. Halle leapt to her feet glad to be able to turn her thoughts from Ian and their sin to the possibility of good news. Maxwell smiled and Halle attempted to interpret his seeming happiness as an indication of word from the Attorney General.

"Well how did you get on?" was Halle's greeting. "Sit down for a moment; it's not all good news. The AG has agreed to drop the charges relating to your time in Germany." Maxwell sat down and took a breath and instantly Halle said, "So I 'wasn't helping the enemy'? I don't know whether to feel sad or happy."

"Just a minute," and Maxwell stood once more, "the other two charges are still on the list for trial in the Old Bailey."

"I knew I wouldn't be let off with those. How long do you think I'll get?" asked Halle in a more subdued tone. "Well your friend Molly got five years, so that's probably what they'll ask the jury to hand down. On the other hand she didn't recognise the court."

"But of course I won't," said Halle knowing full well that this was probably the end of her association with Maxwell.

Maxwell looked at her long and hard. Halle knew he didn't suffer fools gladly and thought, "He knows I'm no fool!" but the doubts were already setting in before he spoke. "I think you'd be foolish to take such a course, it may re-open the whole issue of the other charges and one of them could lead to the death penalty," argued Maxwell in an even more subdued tone that the one used by his client moments earlier.

"Oh I didn't understand that, I thought that there had been an agreement reached on the other counts."

"So there had. But you see they would have believed you were using the law to fight the other charges as you were using me as your advocate."

"I see that now—it's at moments like these that you can appreciate a cliché such as, 'the horns of a dilemma'."

"Why does it have to be? Surely your friends and members of your organisation would understand." Again Halle thought for a moment before answering, "I'm sure the advice they would give, if circumstances turn out the way you suggest, is for me to have representation. But then again perhaps not." Maxwell walked the length of the cell before speaking; "I'll have to go. Perhaps you'll let me know in the next forty-eight hours your decision."

"Regardless of my decision, I want to thank you for all you have attempted to do on my behalf. You know how much I value your opinion and I'll take into account what you've said in making up my mind." Maxwell stooped and kissed her on the cheek, "Yours has been as an intriguing a case as I've come across in many years. I wish you well, whatever decision you make."

CHAPTER 24
(January-July 1944)

ONCE BACK IN her cell Halle had to ponder deeply on her course of action. She really needed help—the kind that her friend Molly would be in a position to give—but how was she to reach her and tell her *all* of the circumstances? A simple message wouldn't be enough and there was no way of contacting her in person.

At the outset she felt that she shouldn't recognise the court because it was tantamount to turning her back on all that she believed. However, as the day progressed she thought it the height of folly to die for something she didn't do. Someone was trying to blame the death of Hengist on her and she wasn't giving a British agent that amount of pleasure. "They've probably worked out that I won't recognise the court and they know that the likelihood is that the other charges will then stand as well. It won't happen and that's that." Later, as darkness descended, she changed tack again; "I have given my oath not to recognise any authority that the British may claim to have over me. So I'll let it stand."

The next morning she prayed, before being taken out for her exercise period, that whoever had been collecting and delivering the messages would return. It was risky but it had to be attempted—what more could the prison authorities do to her? However, when she returned, she decided to put aside the one in a million chance of being able to contact Molly. "I'll have to deal with the problem myself," but she reassured herself that she would use the traditional Republican approach in deciding what to do. As the day progressed she changed her mind countless times; finally she recognised that whatever action she took she was going to be a loser. If she didn't oppose the AG's charges about the so-called murder of Hengist she could end on the gallows. But if she did go to court she would find herself ostracised by the Cumann na mBan and the rest of the Republican movement, as they would be unaware of the other charges.

"The Brits have me over a barrel—I'm a loser whatever way I turn. I wonder who's pulling the strings? Probably the same people who employed Hengist and they're determined to have their pound of flesh. I'm going to have to explain all this to Maxwell—perhaps he can put this mess back into the frying pan."

"Can you reach my solicitor, Mr Maxwell, and ask him to come to see me as soon as he can?" asked Halle in a surprisingly undemanding voice. The hours of desperate decision-making had left their toll. The female guard was taken by surprise and quickly nodded and motioned to a colleague and he went and made the arrangements. "There's no going back now—at least I can't see me doing an about turn."

Later she was told that Mr Maxwell would see her the following morning. The relief was tangible and she sat down on her bunk wondering if there was a possibility of her being released on bail until the court hearing was concluded. "You're unlikely to get it," began Mr Pessimism but Mr Optimistic was convinced that if they could squeeze a guarantee out of her that she wouldn't talk to the newspapers about her 'exploits' in Germany and Poland and, in addition, return to face the proceedings there was a possibility.

Maxwell looked the picture of happiness when he arrived. "Can I assume that you are going to fight this?"

"Indeed I am," and she proceeded to give her reasons for taking up the issues but when she then proposed that he should apply for bail on her behalf he was less cheerful. "On what grounds would you suggest I should make this application?"

"I am no danger to them and I can give them guarantees on secrecy and on my returning for the trial. I just need to get the hell out of here before I have a mental breakdown."

"I think I can make the AG listen to those three good points—Ah! One other thing, who will put up the money?" Halle was in a quandary, she knew her people would rather be left out of the matter, even though they would have been confident that she would have kept to the terms of the bail. "Ian will do it, I'm sure!"

"Very well, I'll contact him and see what he says and in the event that he agrees I will make arrangements to employ a barrister for the trial."

Ian sent a telegram to Maxwell agreeing to go guarantor for Halle's bail, which relieved the solicitor as he saw that the court might act favourably to a request from a serviceman with an impeccable record. It was only afterwards that the penny dropped with Ian. "Oh you're a fool! That's the end of you in Belfast! Putting up the money for a tall Republican pin-up girl! I can just see the reaction back home in the Lodge. That's another place you won't be able to stick your nose into! God you're a fool, she isn't even interested in you, but still you persist. It's curtains all round and I hope you realise it!" Ian attempted to block the alter ego's dominance in his thoughts—"Who'll know? This kind of thing never sees the light of day back home. And the English papers don't bother with news about Northern Ireland, the war's

356

the whole thing; it's as if our place doesn't exist. The other day an educated man asked me to give him any stamps I got from home as he was saving those from abroad! It will be all right!"

Halle sat in the dock in the Old Bailey frightened out of her wits. The dark forbidding woodwork and the centre like a pit for dogfights were meant to cause deep foreboding—and they did! The black-cloaked lawyers and the clerk of the court added to the sense of an imperial justice system, which, to her republican mind, suggested there was little likelihood of any for the downtrodden or the poor.

Judge Jessel was barely seated before Mandeville, Halle's barrister, was asking for bail for his client. The judge, sensing there was the danger of a battle royal in his court, asked the Attorney General and Mr Mandeville to accompany him to his chambers. Halle prayed that her lawyer would be the bearer of good news when he re-appeared but his visage was anything but comforting and the fact that they had barely been away five minutes didn't bode well. Mandeville approached the dock and leaning forward told her that there had been no objection from Sir David and that she could go. Halle's relief was immense and she left immediately in the company of Ian and Maxwell telling them and the world that she would "never understand what goes on in this country—one moment I'm fighting for my life, next I'm out on bail!"

The weeks before the trial passed with her being chiefly on her own, as Ian had to return to camp immediately after the hearing. However, he did manage to get a weekend pass and they spent most of it wandering through the cold and wet streets of a London bereft of any social entertainment that would have appealed to them both. Even the cinemas were reduced to showing old films for the most part, as the U-boat war in the Atlantic meant there was little room for goods that didn't help the war effort. By far and away the worst part was the refusal of Halle's landlady to let Ian on the premises with her and so they found themselves out and about in the foulest of weather. "Why can't we go back to my place?" enquired Ian. "I wish you'd grow up and stop being so naïve! What do you think they'd make of me? And don't answer that!" Ian shook his head and acknowledged that the least she would be was compromised.

After his visit she realised that the time had flown by and nothing had been accomplished, so she determined to pay more attention to the many beautiful buildings that still remained in the heart of the city. But the more she saw the more she was depressed at the devastation of a once proud city and on returning to her lodgings was struck by her feelings and confused by her earlier wish to destroy anything British.

Maxwell made arrangements to meet her before the actual trial began but later sent her a telegram expressing his regret at not being able to see her but assuring her that he would pick up Ian and then collect her on the morning of the trial. Everything went as planned and the Judge soon got the proceedings underway. Halle couldn't concentrate; she had succeeded in having the charges relating to Hengist dropped by this—what she considered a mere device—and the charges of membership of the Cumann na mBan and delivering explosives would ensure a five-year jail sentence at the least so she felt there was little could be done to alter destiny.

The judge called for evidence from the prosecutor and the RUC and the English police duly read from detailed lists, which showed her involvement and Halle knew that Mandeville had nothing on his side of the argument to refute the case being made. Inevitably the judge called an adjournment to the next morning to allow the jury to consider their verdict—on what Halle considered an open and shut case—and to give him the opportunity to look at the details before deciding on a sentence.

Halle and Ian left the court together and were delighted to see how little interest there had been, both from the general public and the national newspapers. There was one photographer there but he appeared to be taking photographs at random and seemed more interested in the comings and goings of others. "He won't make sense of a British soldier leaving the court with an Irish Republican girl friend. We'll be all right even if he takes a photograph." And as they left they noticed that the photographer continued taking photos.

The next morning no sooner had the court been seated, than the judge began his summing up to the jury, making it pretty obvious where the balance of probability lay. In less than an hour the jury returned with a guilty verdict and Judge Jessel sentenced Halle to a year's imprisonment, following which she was to be deported back to Northern Ireland. Both Halle and Maxwell were astonished at the leniency of the sentence—Mandeville was astonished but his acting ability was great and his demeanour suggested that he had pulled all the rabbits out of the hat and by his indubitable wisdom and ability had circumvented the system and Mr Maxwell! Ian rushed forward to greet her before she would be ushered back to prison. "Aren't you surprised at all?" asked Ian, undoubtedly taken aback by Halle's coolness. "Surprised is the wrong word, amazed is more appropriate. I'll have to think this over, something is going on!"

Halle seemed to have little difficulty settling into the day to day routine of the prison in Aylesbury, probably because there had been no detailed mention of the case in any of the national newspapers. She was able to get notes to her friend Molly, one of which congratulated her on the outcome of the case. But Molly added a cautionary note: "Knowing all, or at least, the important details helped me to take the same position as you. Those at home will not be so well disposed." This upset Halle more when she thought about all that she had come through, "Yes, Molly is right! People invariably put the worst possible interpretation on things." For once she agreed wholeheartedly with her alter ego.

The early months of 1944 seemed to be the slowest ones in her life. The war in Europe appeared to be totally reliant on the Russians, while the Western Allies did a lot of talking about their new Commander-in-Chief, General Eisenhower, setting up a 'second front' but there was no sign of it according to the Russians. The time ticked remorselessly on and the coldness of the winter took an age to relent.

On the 7th February the Warden sent for her and with much sympathy informed her of her mother's death. Apparently Mr Maxwell had been in direct touch with the AG's office asking for parole for Halle to attend the funeral and it had been granted. "Mother dead! Good God how could you deprive me of her when I'm only months away from release?" she cried and prayed repeatedly through the remainder of the day.

The next morning she travelled to Belfast with a woman guard who accompanied her every step of the way. The Requiem Mass in St Matthew's was one of the most moving experiences of her life. To sit in the front pew with her family and have friends and neighbours gathered about gave her strength. The Latin added a sense of piquancy and the final blessing had her in tears. Outside, the horse and the hearse in their total blackness, added to the gloom of a dank dismal day. Looking at the faces amassed in the cortège behind her she recognised many of her past friends but she came to a shuddering halt when she saw Ian standing, incognito, behind the large assembly. She put her hand to her mouth and her brother Brian thought that she was overcome and reached out to support her in case she fainted. Halle looked away but not before Ian indicated his sorrow for her predicament.

The walk behind the funeral along the lower Newtownards Road and over the Bridge End made Halle aware that she was now without maternal love and she quickly stepped up into the carriage when the cortège came to a halt on the Queen's Bridge.

Because of the distance to Milltown Cemetery, and the limited supply of carriages, it was mostly family members who were present at the graveside.

Before the priest spoke of "Ashes to ashes" her brother spoke about his mother in English and then led those present in a prayer in Irish. Halle's father, usually so detached, was unable to take part and spent most of the time in the cemetery sitting in the carriage. When the final spadeful of soil was deposited on the coffin Halle turned to see Ian but he was making his way back to the gates.

The return to prison was a much deeper wound than the original incarceration but with the onset of spring Halle looked forward to time passing more quickly. The war, according to the British press, was a slow haul up the length of Italy and a time, which many thought would see the invasion of Europe, passed with the general public only having a rapidly disappearing recollection of the Italian surrender in 1943. Then, after many false dawns, on the 6th June—D-Day—at last! Halle felt that she was turning British, or, more acceptably, American. To her the British reports on the progress seemed to suggest that only *they* were involved in the hand-to-hand battles in Normandy. She wondered how her friends in Poland were surviving the Russian onslaught on the Germans knowing the Soviet forces tendency was to wipe out everything in front of them.

Early on the morning of 21st July Halle was astonished to see Maxwell outside her cell along with the Warden. "Good news!"

"Good news? Don't use those words unless you mean what I want you to mean!" Maxwell laughed, "I wouldn't use them without good reason!"

Halle slumped into her bunk, "My God... how did you manage this?"

"The amazing thing is I didn't. The AG rang and said they were giving you early release because of your good behaviour."

"This really stinks! This puts the mark of Cain on me! Don't you see?" Maxwell looked baffled, "you'd better explain in words of one syllable."

"I was already under suspicion, as I told you, for not following normal practice about going to court. Then my light sentence and now this—the final blow, no one back home will believe anything I say. And it's much worse in another way because I can't go somewhere else and disappear. I'm being deported back to Belfast!"

"What do you want me to do? Apply to have the deportation section of the sentence rescinded?"

"How long will that take?" He shook his head and raised his shoulders, evidently he had little hope of success. Halle's face fell, "I'll just have to hold on to this runaway train until it comes to a halt."

"Your life's not in danger, is it?"

"No! But I'll be the leper in Republican circles when I get back."

"What will I do about Ian—do you want him informed as to what has happened?"

"If I've got to suffer rejection he may as well join me because it's bound to be coming his way as well!"

Once Ian reached the docks in Belfast he attempted to get down the gangway as quickly as he could to greet his parents and relatives but he was shoved into the first horse and cab available. He couldn't believe that these worn out old cabs had made a comeback to the streets of Belfast. He shouted to his father above the hubbub of relatives who had managed to scramble in beside him. "Where have all the taxis gone?"

"There is only a few left what with the petrol rationing and they run on gas." Ian laughed convinced he had misheard him, "Gas! That's a good one." His father didn't hear him but as chance would have it as they passed along Bridge End a car drove out from Graham's Place with a huge balloon wobbling about on its roof. Luckily Ian remembered he was home and he managed to modify his language, "My goodness, what is it?"

"It's one of those I was talking about—a 'Fast Taxi' going on gas!"

"'Fast Taxis'? I didn't think they would be as farsighted as that. I didn't see any of them about the last time I was over."

"No but you rarely went into town as you spent so much time visiting your friends and relatives—notice the order I put them in!"

Ian ignored the jibe and continued studying the populace as he was driven over the Queen's Bridge. He wondered how people who couldn't afford to pay the rentman when he left had suddenly become affluent. Passing St. Matthew's RC Church he heard his relatives muttering about the Free State's neutrality. "Funny," he recalled, "how many of the women folk thought the world of De Valera for standing up to Churchill when he tried to bring in conscription for Northern Ireland at the beginning of the war." His other voice took up the challenge immediately, "Back home and already that bitch has got you under her spell. This is all going to end in tears."

In an attempt to dispel the evil machinations of his own mind he was forced to look at the young women who seemed to be on the Newtownards Road in large numbers. "The probability is that they're Fenians too!" spoke his abrasive voice with a determination not to let him off the hook. "What is the Corporation going to do about these blitzed houses?" he asked his father. "They'll get no money from the Exchequer until the war is over. Most of us are too glad the air-raids are over to concern ourselves with rebuilding." Ian smiled; at last he had a way to deal with that unremitting

361

voice and he could look forward to meeting Halle with impunity.

Once he was back home it didn't take him long to get back into civvies and get "out for a breath of fresh air", as he told his mother. Passing Williamson's newsagents he thought it would be a true homecoming if he bought the *Northern Whig*. He had the money in his hand when he spotted a photograph on the front page of the *News Chronicle* and there and then he took it instead.

Halle had got into the habit of counting her toes and fingers while she was in prison; it was a way of reminding herself how fortunate she was to have escaped permanent injury at Plock. Now, at home, she did it for the umpteenth time that day. "Home in one piece," this to no one in particular. "It's an implausible story to tell without missing appendages."

Psychology was still regarded as a mythical science in Belfast and, for all Halle knew, everywhere in the world. As for herself, she didn't think much of it either; of course she had nightmares and bursts of crying but she didn't regard these as having anything to do with psychology. "I suffer from nerves," she told her father when he enquired about her health and how she was standing up to all the stresses and strains.

There were issues, which she was reluctant to address, not least, the problem of Ian and his visit later in the evening. She put that to one side, it would be dealt with face to face and nothing would be spared. At this point in time, however, she was looking back and had began to recognise her own shortcomings which surprisingly included the certainties that had sent her on this circuitous route back to her starting point. By far and away the big topic on her mind was how her former colleagues and friends would receive her. Her Mr Pessimism was back in vogue, "You'll never be accepted— unless you're prepared to stand on the Custom House steps and proclaim your innocence to the world, except for the two charges for which you were found guilty. Oh! Even then your Protestant 'friend' will desert you!" In the interim Mr Optimism had left the battlefield scurrying to get away from an unwinnable position. "I'm just going to have to leave, there's no alternative. Perhaps I'll talk to our Sofia the next time she's in town and see what she thinks."

She was jolted out of her reverie by the sudden recollection of Ian's visit. It took a moment for her to realise that he would be there within the hour. She wished she had more time to think matters over but she did know that her feelings for him had grown. "Why?" she asked herself, "Because he has been more forthcoming about his feelings for me." She rose and paced up and down the room cursing the shortage of time, "I need more time to address this more objectively." But even as she thought this she realised that the emotional sense to romance excluded the objective or, at the least, gave it second place to subjectivity. Nevertheless, she went through a list that came to her mind without undue mulling over it.

"Could I subjugate the hatred I had for him that once engulfed me, even though I echoed the Republican cry for the unity of the orange and green and the dissenter? Could I carry on with this strange affair in the repressive moral climate, which existed in the North and, in Ian's mind, in the South? More importantly how would Ian answer the same kind of questions about his position? Could he leave the Orange Order? Could he overcome his hatred for Fenians in spite of claiming 'Civil and Religious Liberty for all'?" In her mind he was bloody sure he could get away with an affair with a Catholic girl, but to marry her—which would be the expectation of her and her family—hardly likely.

Halle was anxious that as many of the issues as possible would be dealt with openly. She began talking through the agenda she had concocted in her head, "Thankfully Dad goes up to *The Farmers' Rest* on a Friday night and then heads down to see some of his mates. Brian and John make the rounds of the pubs until the early hours, even though they're supposed to close at 10 p.m. That means that we have at least four or five hours to thrash things out… The knock brought her to her feet and with a quick glance in the mirror and the automatic hand to the hair she was ready to open the door. She knew it would be Ian, 'Mister Punctuality', and no matter how well she was aware of it, it still was an unnerving experience for a casual timekeeper like herself. He kissed her more on the cheek than she would have wished. "Perhaps," she thought, "he has dealt with all the remaining questions while he was being retrained in Lancashire.

He walked, briskly enough, to the armchair by the fire. Halle thought, "I must put coal on that before it goes out," but Ian appeared to ignore the lack of heat and looked up at her. Halle anxiously looking for any sign of what was coming wondered if the fire, somehow, was an indicator of the situation in Ian's mind. "Just a minute, I was about to put more coal on it when you came in." She turned away but not before she noted a glow in Ian's eyes and went out the back for a shovel of coal. The look in his eyes had changed and she rushed to deal with the fire hoping that it was its lack of brightness was the cause.

"I have some really bad news, particularly for you."

"What?" Ian tossed a copy of the *News Chronicle* on the table. "Look at the photo on the front page—do you recognise anyone?" Halle stared open mouthed at a picture of a soldier and a young woman. "My God! It's us! Where did that come from?"

"It must have been taken when the court case was going on, that's the only time we were together in public while in England."

"But that was months ago!"

"Probably they dug out the picture from their library when they heard of your release—after all who would know where and when it was taken?"

"But my God, the damage it will do!"

"To both of us," exclaimed Ian.

"Sorry, but all I can think of is how will this be interpreted by my friends. This is all they need to be convinced that I'm a traitor, especially with me being released earlier than the due date."

"For my part, I can kiss good-bye to the Orange Order for definite! It was difficult enough when I was seen at your mother's funeral but now they'll be convinced I helped you to get out of prison!"

"I didn't know you had been spotted at Milltown!"

"Not there, I was seen coming out the front gate of the chapel on the Newtownards Road."

"I don't like you saying you did nothing for me, because you did; if I hadn't had you on the outside doing all the work I would still be inside. Look Ian, every minute could be important—you'd better go now. If any of the hotheads saw you coming up the street they're liable to be waiting on you and give you a beating."

Ian looked pensively at her for a moment; "All my hopes are going up in smoke; the prospects of us being together grow less and less."

"It's what I feared all along, as you know. But go now and I'll try to get in touch with you in a few days when this has died down a bit."

As the days passed Ian realised that the prospects of hearing from Halle were negligible.

EPILOGUE
(October 1946-April 1947)

WOLLONGONG LOOKED DISTINCTLY hazy in the evening light of an autumn day. Halle and Manya looked out at their new home with eyes that sparkled with a new dimension of hope. "Was that a lake we passed, Halle?"

"Just a minute, I have to practice my Aussie accent. 'It sure was!' Is that any good?"

"Not bad for an American accent but you're going to have to spend the rest of your life practising an Aussie one because that was just plain awful."

"Are you glad we've left the hostel?"

"Betwixt and between."

"Where do you get these expressions?"

"Mostly from you and your Irish neighbours."

Ian was meandering along the main street, merely getting used to his bearings. The first thing he noticed was the name of the street—Crown Street. Immediately he felt comfortable, "This is the place to be, somewhere totally British without the festering sore of religion to bother me." He no sooner had established this thought than he was distracted by seeing a little girl running down the hill towards him but clearly had her eyes on someone that he took to be her mother. She didn't look like the average Australian child; she was wan and thin, "Probably another émigré like myself. But there's a brittleness about her that I don't possess—at least I hope to God I don't. She must have come through some kind of hell." As he walked on he concluded that that must be the average condition of children old enough to remember the past yet strong enough to discard those parts which tended to hurt.

"You're at it again—judgement is a big thing with you, isn't it? Why couldn't she be an Australian who has been ill?" His alter ego made no attempt to answer; those obsequious nods he had made to it in the past were over, as to what his mind wanted or even hinted at he was determined to put aside. He turned back in the direction from where he came but stopped when he heard a voice calling, "Be careful Manya! Take it easy, you could fall."

His heart leapt, he knew that voice, and his own voice warned, "Well it sounds so familiar but don't get yourself built up." He quickened his pace to gain a better view of the two, "Yes, she's tall and willowy, as I recall and that's her voice, definitely!" He was gaining on the pair in front but his anxiety lest they turn off one of the side streets made him call out, "Halle! Halle!" and he broke into a run.

The woman had stopped to speak to the child and looked up to see who the caller was, instantly her face lit up and she clutched her breast as if taken aback. She bent once more and spoke quietly to the child who turned round and looked at Ian and started running wildly towards him and finally flung herself at him almost knocking him to the ground. "Ian! Ian! You came back for Halle!" He swung the child up without being completely sure who she was, then it came to him: "It's Manya!" He hugged her with a warmth he never imagined he possessed and only put her down to engulf Halle in his arms. They hugged for some moments and then the questions poured forth.

"Why do you want me to meet the boat from New Zealand right now?"

"Well I have to take Manya to see a friend of her mother's who is coming to see both of us."

"Do I know her?"

"Him. Yes, rather well."

"Now whatever you do don't tell who!"

"A bit of suspense in your life would do you good!"

"You've got to be joking! Since the day and hour I first came across you all I've had was suspense! Come on, out with it, who is it you're expecting?"

"Aleksander..."

"Aleksander Kosciuszko?"

"Who else could it have been? ... don't start thinking about it now."

"What is he doing in New Zealand? And I don't mean is he farming?"

"When the communists set up the new Polish State at the end of the war he knew he was in trouble because he had represented the AK in talks before the German surrender and he knew he had to get out."

At the quayside, looking up the gangway at the descending passengers, Halle and Ian failed to see Aleksander. Consequently they were taken aback when they heard a voice call their names. They stared in amazement at the skeleton that Aleksander had become but they put the thought behind them as they rushed to welcome him. "Where did you find him?" called the voice of Aleksander as the skin and bones of the man tried to disengage himself from Manya's bear hug. "We'll talk about us later, if you don't mind. More important, how are you?" He managed to mutter he was fine, while all the time being molested by the little Polish girl, as the group made their way to the taxi Halle had hired.

Later, once they had settled Aleksander in his room, Halle spoke to him about his health, telling him he had deteriorated since she saw him eighteen months ago. He admitted losing weight but put it down to the change of climate and diet. Halle immediately changed the subject realising that she had made a *faux pas* in raising the issue in such a way.

"Now that the both of us have got you here we're hoping you can enlighten us on a number of things that happened in Poland. I know it's some time ago but, I can't speak for Ian, I'm desperate to know the whole truth about those times." Aleksander smiled, "For once in my life I am the centre of attention," he then paused for a breath; "I have to go back to 1938; according to what I heard from the General. Apparently the High Command of the German Army had been divided about the war before it begun. No one was supposed to know that some of them had contacted the British before the occupation of Czechoslovakia in March 1939. Chamberlain either pretended it hadn't happened or really, I suppose, he did not want to know."

"Is it possible that Chamberlain was confident that he had an agreement that would bind Hitler to peace?" asked Halle.

"I would say that was probably the case," answered Aleksander, "but please do not interrupt, I have difficulty concentrating and remembering.

"Well the way the General related it to me General Halder had talks with various members of the British government, and many military figures, asking for help to overthrow Hitler."

"Excuse me. You mean that the authorities at the time just let an opportunity like that pass them by?"

"Oh no! The British had been around diplomatic circles too long to let the prospects of a points win disappear while others searched for a knockout! Sorry, did I sound like a politician? No, I was informed that they approached the Canadian Government who sent agents into France in 1940. They were to make contact with those Generals whose names had been given them by the British. By this time most of the conspirators headed regiments in France. It took some time before these agents spotted that those they where watching were under constant surveillance by the Gestapo. Indeed it was only when one of the Canadians was caught and apparently confessed under torture that he was spying on some members of the General Staff that the rôle which the Gestapo was playing came to light."

"What rôle was that?" asked Halle reluctantly, being conscious that she didn't want to put Aleksander under pressure.

"I'm sorry, I think I've got ahead of myself," and he composed himself again, explaining that the remaining Canadian agents only realised that the Gestapo knew precisely what had been going on and had been aware of the situation for some time. "Well, maybe not all but at least some of them at the top, or near the top. As you know Halle, one of them was a man called Hengist, I'll come back to him shortly."

There was a certain amount of backtracking to be done by Aleksander as he tended to lose the thread of what he had been saying. "Our intelligence people thought that the captured Canadian unwittingly made the undercover men from Hengist believe that Hitler was about to be assassinated but we can't be too sure about this. Actually that was not the intention at all, at that point in time, they were merely trying to stage a *coup d'état*. I think 'merely' is the wrong word. Is it fine?"

"Of course," encouraged Ian.

"Anyhow the General told me it was later that the issue of assassination was considered." Aleksander looked round to see if there were to be further interruptions, "I think I had mentioned General Beck and his involvement?" The other two shook their heads. "In any event it changed direction from an attempt to overthrow Hitler to doing away with him sometime at the beginning of 1943. The Gestapo was somewhat premature in their assessment of an alleged putsch being turned into an assassination attempt but some of their officers were honoured."

"By whom?"

"By Hitler. The man I spoke of earlier, Hengist, was honoured with a special medal from Hitler marking his work in preventing his assassination. Of course it did not mention this in the citation but that was what it was supposed to be about."

Halle put up her hand to stop Aleksander, "I'm sorry, I'm totally lost. Are you saying that he had some other motive for spreading the idea that there was to be an assassination attempt? And for that matter, what about the Canadian you spoke of earlier, is this all guesswork?"

"You must have heard about the V1 and V2 flying bombs?"

"Of course, but what have they got to do with this?"

"Well it was our intelligence team which warned London about the Germans building them in Peenemünde in Holland. In fact the message was sent from Warsaw to London. Does that give you an idea of how successful they were?" Halle nodded and Ian remarked, somewhat ironically, "Let's face it, from where we sat in Plock and elsewhere in Poland the AK knew everything that was going on, including our disagreements!"

Halle and Aleksander laughed before the latter started again, "Maybe my next revelation will make things clearer. The apple cart was overturned by someone in British Intelligence who, according to Polish intelligence, was the originator of the so-called 'assassination plot', who passed the news of what he *thought* was happening to the Gestapo. This is where Hengist appeared on the scene. Hitler wanted him to investigate the truth of these two assertions from the Gestapo—one, that there was to be a *coup d'état* and the other was that there would be an attempt to assassinate the Fuhrer. Of course, Hengist began a whole complex web of spying on their own generals and *aide de camps*." Aleksander shuffled his feet and stood up to relieve the cramp in his body. Ian asked was there something he was worried about, "Not worried as such but it's a bit difficult to follow the various patterns the story now takes. Perhaps Halle could relate how she arrived in the midst of this."

Halle cleared her throat, "Machiavelli was an amateur compared to the British! I must say immediately that I had no knowledge of any of this. I arrived on the scene at Irland-Rekation, the radio station in Berlin, and there unwittingly became friends with an English girl who had Canadian citizenship as well. From what Alek has said and from the information that Ian got from Sheila in England it now appears certain that she was one of that team of undercover agents." Halle saw that Aleksander was in some difficulty, "Perhaps we should leave it until tomorrow. Alek you look beat out—sorry, I'm back into Belfast colloquial—far from well." Ian was quick to agree and it wasn't long before Aleksander left to return to his lodgings.

Next morning, when he arrived, it was clear that neither he nor Halle were keen to put Aleksander under the microscope, yet their anxiety to hear what went on back in those war years was high. They needn't have feared, Aleksander wanted to finish what he had started, although he had to be reminded just where they were when they finished for the night. "Halle was describing the situation she found in the Radio Station not long after she arrived to work there," supplied Ian.

"I had just began talking about Sheila and her Canadian connection… anyhow, I was in a position to hear the rumours circling the building and warned her that she had been spotted as a likely spy or double agent."

"Could you explain just how you got the information?" asked Ian.

"You will not understand… well… a former colleague of mine had worked there and was privy to information from the top and he warned me, thinking the description fitted me. All right?"

"I suppose so but I wish you would be more honest and straightforward, all these things are behind us, there's no need to be secretive now."

"His name was O'Driscoll and he was a spy for the Germans in England. Originally he had been a liaison officer for the IRA and the Nazis. I hope you are content now! Anyway, my boss told me—I think it was my boss— 'Your friend has died suddenly'. You can imagine my surprise when I learnt that that was not the case when I was imprisoned in London. Apparently someone had spirited her away knowing that the German authorities would do a cover-up in order not to frighten the staff at the radio station. In the days and weeks, which followed I was determined to get out of Germany as I was convinced they had murdered her. I had only a limited knowledge of German and had no friends in the country, it was then that I thought up the idea of recruiting for the German Army as a way out."

"Whatever gave you that idea?" asked Aleksander.

"Curiously I had been working on an item about British propaganda in their so-called colonies and I wrote about *Sir* Roger Casement for a radio piece, so I suppose that is where I got the idea."

"Why the emphasis on the 'Sir'?" somewhat petulantly asked Ian.

"Because I recollect you having a go at me for not giving him his title or was it me?" smiled Halle. "But to continue, I was somewhat surprised to be offered the job so readily but was shocked at being given the title of colonel because as the general put it, 'you'll be able to deal more readily with the camp commandants'. I soon discovered that the title gave me access to officers' messes and only occasionally to overnight accommodation.

"But the next move caused me a great deal of anxiety. I was directed to various POW camps in Germany but in such a way that I frequently bypassed those which were more important."

"Sorry to interrupt I just don't follow the point of that," remarked Ian. "I never figured the reason out," said Halle, "hopefully Aleksander will fill in the missing information. Another strange fact, my friend Sheila pointed out to Ian, was that the generals suspected of involvement in the overthrow of Hitler had their headquarters in none of these regions but I often spent the night in these places."

"From what I understand," began Aleksander, "you have touched on the salient point in all of this. Some of the upper echelons in the Gestapo were calling the tune—I think that is one of those sayings of Ian's—by deliberately diverting attention from those involved in the assassination attempt. It appears that this man Hengist was deliberately tying her to generals who were not involved."

"I think I can follow the points you are making but what I find difficult is how some people, like Hengist, an avowed Nazi could swap sides without too much effort…"

"Just a minute Alek," said Halle and then turning faced Ian, "You know what happened? How?"

"I'm just adding two and two. Stop me if I've got some of this wrong Aleksander. Hengist and some of his cohorts in the Gestapo cooked up this plot to mislead Hitler and Goebbels into thinking there was an assassination attempt about to happen. Isn't that true so far?"

"Yes, so far so good—another one of Ian's expressions," said a smiling Aleksander, "but what was the advantage of that?" and turning to Halle, "That's the real test question!"

"I think that Hengist was attempting to mislead the main body of the Gestapo and the Nazis into thinking that these Generals who appeared to be on Halle's itinerary were those really involved. Halle was easily portrayed as a Canadian spy, that Belfast accent of hers could easily pass as typical of a Canadian and then her tie up to the woman who got away. Was it Hengist who helped her escape?"

Halle still shook her head, "Hold on a minute, you still haven't explained what was the advantage—you've been too well taught by your Unionist parents and others to avoid answering the question." Ian laughed, "It's not like you to be so slow but I was giving you a chance to work it out."

"You're sliding away from answering!"

"Please, please do not indulge in these diversions, you always end up fighting. Come on Ian, it's obvious that you have worked it out." Aleksander's anxiety to avoid a scene brought Ian back to the point. "The way I see it was that they wanted a diversion so that the German police and others were chasing shadows, allowing the assassins time to work out how they could kill Hitler."

"You've hit all the nails on the head, Ian—you must be sick of me using your phrases—and although you haven't mentioned it outright, I mean the one regarding Hengist's treachery, it's clear that you caught on to his deviousness. I was at the meeting between Halle and General Tadeusz Bór-Komorowski…"

"Ah! That explains something else," interrupted Halle. This time it was Ian's turn to be perplexed, "What was that?"

"Do you not remember that list of oddities that I wrote out?"

"Yes but what one have I forgotten?"

"I think it was the last one, the one where I quoted Hengist's remark on board the ship going to Sweden 'I need to keep you alive and out of Britain for a few months'.

"Excuse me this time," said Ian, "What was the point of Hengist holding you prisoner?"

"You've forgotten the most important phrase, 'until I get instructions?'" remarked Halle, suddenly aware that both of them were looking directly at Aleksander who seemed to be far away. Ian was the first to react, "Could you explain Aleksander, what had been going on then?" The Pole's far-away look disappeared and the old sharpness reappeared, "'Until I get instructions'? You'll have to explain to me in what regard these words were used."

Halle went to great lengths to tell the story of the incident involving Hengist. "Ah, yes, I recall hearing of that when I discussed the position with the General when he received the message from British Intelligence."

"So the British did contact you—well not you directly—the General?"

"Indeed they did. They wished to know if there was any truth in the statement that you made about being thanked by General Bór-Komorowski for your help in Poland. The General replied after he spoke to me."

"Do you know what he said?" asked Halle.

"I have a good idea but I didn't see the actual words."

"Did he agree with what I had said to the British Attorney General?"

"No!"

Halle was totally aghast, then calmed down thinking that Aleksander was in no fit state to address questions relating to the period before he had gone through so much suffering. However, Ian wasn't prepared to let sleeping dogs lie, "What do you mean—no?"

"Well… What's the word for a mystery that has been solved?" Ian and Halle fished around with a variety of suggestions before Aleksander accepted the word, 'denouement'. "You see the General could not divulge exactly what was going on, but he knew that the British were aware of the attempt to assassinate Hitler because it was they who had employed Hengist to mislead the Nazi authorities in the matter. We knew we could not adequately explain in a coded message what we wanted, so the General must have decided to repudiate your statement and at the same time requested that charges relating to your time in Germany and Poland be dropped."

"And that means what I thought was a coincidence wasn't!"

"Are we off on another tack again?" queried Ian raising both hands in the air.

"Maybe you don't recall but I was released on the 21ˢᵗ July 1944. Has that any significance, up to now I thought it was merely by chance it had happened?" Aleksander launched into a series of coughs and Ian patted him on the back, "I was attempting to answer your question; that was the day after the attempt on Hitler's life."

"Thank you for that—other people are not as perceptive as you!" she remarked glancing at Ian. "But does any of this answer my question about Hengist?" Ian was determined to come up with some explanation, "From all that Aleksander has said about him working for the British he was taking instructions from them about his use of you. They must have been fearful that you, being picked up by the British Army Medical Corp, would have revealed what was going on so they wanted Hengist to keep you prisoner until the attempt had been made."

Halle was still in difficulty, "OK but what about my escape from hospital in Warsaw, what was that about?" Aleksander smiled, "Now that is an easy question," and he looked at the stunned looks of the other two. Ian was first to reply, "No, how you can make out that this is an easy question is beyond me. Why would the Nazis want Halle to escape?"

"Drop the word 'Nazis' and ask who would want her to get free."

"I suppose the only other person there was Hengist. But why would he want her free?" pursued Ian.

"I'm a little anxious that neither of you have even made a wild guess," responded Aleksander. Halle was fretting, "Ah, come on—do you have knowledge or is this just another educated guess?"

"I assumed that anyone would arrive at it. Well, the way I see it is this: Hengist was still working to ensure that his superiors saw Halle as the courier between those involved in launching an attack on Hitler and the generals. He could not protect her in the hospital from those in the Gestapo who wanted to have her arrested and tortured to reveal the names of those involved. He obviously knew we, the AK, were watching the whole game and were actively involved in some way; clearly the British would have kept him aware of our interest. I think it is clear that he wanted rid of Halle, as she was becoming too hot for him to handle, sorry for the phrase Ian. He probably concluded that we would hold on to her until the assassination attempt was made. But at that juncture we were under real stress from the Nazis and also the communists were making our position awkward. In addition we had the both of you to contend with and your desire to be on your way. The General, without letting me, or perhaps anyone into the secret, decided that by the time you escaped and made your way to England the matter would be over. Of course that is where he miscalculated."

"So it was the General who dreamt up the escape in the first place?" queried Ian.

"I suppose so—with the help of his intelligence team," thoughtfully responded Aleksander. Halle burst out, "How, in the name of all that's holy, did he talk to us in that church and not give us the information?"

Ian however had other fish to fry, "Just a minute, before we leave the subject. The person who intrigues me the most is Hengist. A real reprobate."

"Well," began Halle when she managed to hold back on a question about the General, "Indeed I wonder at what possessed the man. Clearly he was devilish clever, wanting the Gestapo regulars to see me going to the officers' mess in these camps and encouraging them to add two and two to make twenty-two."

"Oh, you see now what they wanted? You, in your ignorance, would look as if you were giving these officers information, from one camp to another, across both Germany and Poland. That *was* devious," commented Aleksander.

"Still, as the General said, you led them a merry dance round Germany and Poland and even *if* nothing was achieved by it you gave the men involved an opportunity to oust the Nazis. Besides the AK in Poland thought it was all worthwhile but the General wanted to warn us about Hengist's agents but clearly he knew more than he would ever say," responded Ian.

"I was taken aback by that, surely he could have warned us and we would have been under less pressure knowing that I wasn't his target." Ian smiled a knowing smile; "Two very good reasons why he didn't say. The first was *you* yourself; and second was even if he had had absolute faith in your integrity the moment he told you, you would have behaved differently and that was the last thing he wanted."

"Sure I wouldn't have revealed anything—besides who did I know who could have passed the information on?"

"That's not the point, you put your finger on it a few moments ago."

"What did I say?" queried Halle her forehead furrowed with wrinkles. Ian deliberately was slow in responding, "'The Germans saw me as their ally against the British' is what you said. And if you remember the General had grave doubts about your reliability at first and although Alek came round there was no way the General would take a chance by telling you that Hengist was a British agent."

Halle merely nodded, she was thinking that she was the person who had suffered most, mentally and physically, from the tactics of Hengist and his ilk but she still could not understand how the man could go from total support for Hitler's national socialism to outright opposition. "The British must have promised him more than money for him to turn his coat," muttered Halle, her old republican scepticism coming to the fore.

Ian was the first to speak, "I still do not grasp how our government could use such a person—he seems to have been involved in the deaths of many people, I suspect as many before the war as he had up to his death."

"I have been the person with all the answers up to now. But perhaps one of you could work out something which has just struck me," asked Aleksander.

"Hold on! Hold on a minute, I know what you're going to say," shouted Ian.

"For God's sake do it a bit quieter!" complained Halle. "Yes, tell us now or forever told your tongue!" Aleksander burst out laughing, "Hold your tongue?" Halle and Ian smiled and attempted to talk over the other in an effort to explain. Aleksander held up his hands, "Tell me later, I'm anxious to hear this bit of mind-reading from Ian."

"You see I thought of this point but I didn't want to look foolish by asking as I assumed that both of you knew the reason."

"OK, you've explained your stupidity. What was it that Alek couldn't make sense of?" asked Halle in a more studied way.

"I hope I'm right—actually I think there's more than one question needs answering."

"Get on with it!"

"Well, why did Hengist report us to Captain Borg if he wasn't prepared to let the Swedes intern us?"

"That's exactly the point I was about to raise when I was interrupted so rudely," smiled Aleksander. "Any answers?"

Halle cleared her throat, which Ian recognised as her way of preparing an answer off the cuff, "Go ahead, we know you'll make up some answer."

"No—I was thinking, what was the point of him reporting us to the captain if he was determined to kidnap me?"

"This reminds me of that radio programme which asks you to write answers on a post-card," remarked Ian. Halle ignored him and suggested that Hengist had acted that way in order to give himself some cover in the event of the kidnapping not working. "You mean he had thought of the possibility of failure?" asked Alexsander.

"Knowing the man I suspect that he always kept a second plan ready in the event of a foul-up. For example what do you think he was telling his superiors about my disappearance? I'll bet he was blaming the AK which would have implicated them in the attempt on Hitler's life."

"One other thing, how did he have all those resources of men available to him in Gothenburg?"

Aleksander in a tired voice suggested that the agents were already working in Sweden spying and, in particular, keeping an eye on Allied prisoners and their escape routes. Halle saw the tiredness etched on Aleksander's face and stood up bringing the subject to a close. "You have had to earn your holiday with us, Alek. It's wonderful that you are here. Each of us has benefited. I have loved listening to you and Manya speaking in your native language. It has made me more aware of her need to be in contact with Polish people culturally and I'll make sure that happens. But now it's time for you to get your rest and for Ian and I to sort out our problems, which somehow seem bigger than those we had in the war."

When they were alone Ian referred to the blunder Halle had made at the outset, "You made a real 'fox's paw' of that, didn't you?" and Halle recognising the old Belfast saying smiled and acknowledged her mistake.

The problems, to which Halle referred, had been put on the long finger from that meeting in Crown Street. Both realised that there were issues to be addressed once more and both were reluctant to open old wounds but knew that the longer they put the matter off the harder it would be to reach a satisfactory conclusion. They were keen to talk but not at all sure how to engage in the *right* kind of talk. Their opening chat was not unlike the first moves in a game of chess; 'Have you heard from your family?'; 'What's the latest from home?'; 'How have you been keeping since…'. Tension accompanied their every change of topic, and as the choice of subject areas diminished their language became more and more stilted. Finally, when they both began to dry up, Ian asked what, when and why she had come to Australia. There was an unnaturally long pause before Halle recited her obviously prepared story. "I never settled back home when I was freed, that photograph in the *News Chronicle* was a blow, I think my Republican friends didn't know what to make of me and to be honest I had seen enough violence to last me the rest of my life."

"How did you find Aleksander?"

"You have knocked me off my stride… well he wrote to the Attorney General in London about how the case had gone after he was released."

"He was captured?"

"Yes, at the end of 1943 and spent some time in Auschwitz and then in Treblinka. He was moved around and constantly tortured in various camps. Whoever had fingered him knew that he had been liasing with the communists; the Nazis wanted information from him that he didn't have."

"Was he a Jew—I thought there were only Jews in those camps?" asked Ian and proceeded to answer his own question, "No, of course he wasn't!"

"How are you so sure? That could well have been the trumped up charge or maybe it was a genuine one? So what? Anyhow when he was released someone put him in touch with Wislawa Holender, Teodor's daughter and Manya. They looked after him for a time, as he couldn't find his family. But with the amount of forced movement from the Nazis and then the shear fear of the Russians, naturally induced by stories emanating from northern Poland and the recollections of the time when the country had been divided by the Russians and Germans, many thousands took to the roads. Eventually, however, his family caught up with him and they all returned to the remains of their old home, which was merely a hulk."

"How did you have Manya to stay with you? Is it permanent?"

"Yes to your second question. Aleksander knew it wouldn't be long before the Russians came looking for him so he got a friend to take his family out of the country while he made arrangements for others. Then Wislawa was arrested because she was a landowner and sent to Siberia. Before the authorities took her away she contacted Aleksander and asked him to get the child to me. What could he do?"

"But how did he find you again?"

"Well he still had my old Belfast address from then. Of course my father sent the post to me here and I immediately agreed to take Manya. One of the best decisions I ever made. *Now* can I get back to the story I had prepared for you!"

"By all means—when did I ever stand in your way when you wanted to do something?"

Halle ignored the humorous intent, "Shortly after you left that night in '44, I went to see my sister Sofia to seek her advice. We eventually agreed that it would be better for me if I left the country, seeing as the difficulties I was in, in Belfast, would be similar in Dublin. But with my record I couldn't get into any country I wanted. Sofia simply gave me her name as she had no intention of going anywhere. So I applied for a passport and everything went fine from there."

"Maybe now we can discuss *us*." asserted Ian, "Just *where* do we stand?"

Halle took a deep breath, "I just don't know. I had thought that seeing you again would never happen and even if it did I didn't expect to be affected the way I've been."

"That's precisely how it struck me, I mean I saw by your actions and looks that you were taken aback on seeing me and when you sent Manya to greet me I knew you still loved me as much as I loved you. But before we go into an ecstasy of enjoying this moment, do you feel there is a chance we can be together?"

Halle put her face into her hands and she cried with a mixture of happiness and fear, "I want us to be together and this time, in this place, I feel confident that we will be, if it's God's will."

"Tell me Ian what brought *you* to Australia and of all places Wollongong?"

"I found myself in a situation not altogether different from you. You were right! The photograph in the newspaper was the last straw. Being seen at your mother's funeral had been bad enough. I applied to come here and I intended to get off at Perth but somehow I ended up in Sydney and they got me a job in the steel mill here and that's it!"

Halle stood in wonderment, "If ever there was a sign of the Almighty's Will this must be it!" and Ian flung his arms around her. Inevitably they wound up spending the night in her bedroom whispering of their love and admiration for the other but promising never to let Ireland, North or South, or even united, affect their relationship again. Talking things over the next morning Halle spoke of her father and his fondness for the work of Swinburne, "You know he would often quote the line, 'one tires of scented time'. But for us I can't see us tiring of the good times that we hope are coming."

Post for Manya or Halle was a rare commodity and next morning Halle was very pleased to see an envelope lying on the floor when she came downstairs. The English address meant nothing to her and when Manya asked, "From whom was it from?" they began a whole guessing game. Eventually Ian arrived on the scene and put in his sixpence worth. Inevitably they had to open it to resolve the question. "It's from Sheila!" exclaimed Halle. Of course that meant she had to explain who precisely was Sheila. The letter read:

Dear Halle,

Recently a friend of mine, here in England, found herself in some legal tangle and she asked me about a solicitor and of course the only one I knew of was your friend Maxwell. I took her to his office and when she had finished I introduced myself to him. To say he was delighted is putting the matter mildly, he wondered if I had been in touch with you and when I told him I hadn't your address he immediately told Kathleen, his secretary, to get it.

Inevitably we chatted about your difficulties back then and he said something about you being convinced that whoever had been behind the employment of Hengist had something to do with your being 'set-up', as he so aptly described it.

When I got home I began to remember little encounters I had with some members of British Intelligence while I was being trained for the business in Berlin. Most of those I met had been involved in Irish affairs for years, indeed some had colleagues killed back in the twenties. But there was one who told me his father had been a policeman and had been murdered in some town near Belfast. Curiously his name came to light quite recently in an internal investigation on the issue of recruitment. Of course the matter of taking on well known Nazis was high on the list of things being looked at—whether any or all of this adds up I don't know but he was implicated in the recruitment of Hengist. Perhaps this will set your mind at rest, and more importantly, convince you that not *all* the English are like him. I will be returning to Canada next month and when I get settled I will write and let you have my new address.

Love and regards,
Sheila

"Alek, come down this instant!" A weary looking, tired man finally appeared. "This better be good Halle. You know I have recollections of you and Ian at war—in more senses than one and I trust it's nothing to do with either one of them!"

"You recollect that Canadian spy that began all these problems? Of course I'm only joking. Well she has written to me and, more or less, confirmed that there was someone in British Intelligence determined to get me into further trouble, so that is the last mystery now unravelled."

"It's not the last mystery—just where did Ian spend the night? Don't answer that! Your face is a give-away."

At the end of Aleksander's short stay the three of them escorted him to the ship Ian and Halle wore the only reasonable clothes they had, although they knew they were woefully out of fashion. Manya running to keep up, shouted, "You look like the relics of old decency!"

"Manya where do you hear such expressions?" asked Ian.

"From you and Halle and all the Irish gang that live in this district."

With some difficulty Aleksander made it up the gangway to the deck. The ship was crowded with people going on holiday to New Zealand or holidaymakers returning home. Ian and Halle stood on each side of Manya holding her hands and occasionally dropping them in order to wave both hands to Aleksander, who smilingly reciprocated. The Tannoy system, with much crackling and interference, warned prospective passengers to board, as this was to be the last call. The announcer's voice was replaced with a band recording of an old hymn; *There is a Happy Land*. Halle recollected, with a great deal of nostalgia, her father's rendition of it. The words, almost in time with the crackling music, she heard again: *There is a Happy Land/ Far, far away. /Where Saints in glory stand, /Bright, bright as day.* Suddenly she found herself singing in a welter of tears and turning she saw and heard Ian singing and laughing at his Boys' Brigade version: *There is a Happy Land/Far, far away. /Where we get bread and jam/Three times a day.* Halle turned to reproach him but he continued: *Ham and eggs we never see/Yet we're always full of glee/There is a Happy Land/Far, far away.*